BELONGING
Hope, Truth and Malice

Beauty of Life
Book Three

Laura Acton

ISBN: 9781520897509 (paperback)

By Laura Acton

Beauty of Life series

FORSAKEN: On the Edge of Oblivion
SOLACE: Behind the Shield
BELONGING: Hope, Truth and Malice
OUTLIER: Blood, Brotherhood, and Beauty
PURGATORY: Bonds Forged in Hellfire
SERENITY: A Path Home
GUARDIANS: Mission to Rescue Innocence
SECRETS: Passion, Deceit, and Revenge
OUTCAST: Trust, Friendship, and Injustice
WHITEOUT: Above and Beyond
BREAKPOINTS: Slow Spiral Down *(Coming soon)*

Strike Force Zulu series

ZULU SIX
BLOOD BONDS

Acknowledgements

Kate, Lisa, Venetia, Julianne, and Martha
you are my very own cheer squad.
I couldn't do it without you four ladies.
Thank you for all your awesome input and support!

Contents

BELONGING
Hope, Truth and Malice

Breathe, Just Breathe

 *1*

July 16
Outside TRF HQ – 5:25 a.m.

Daniel Broderick felt so drained. He managed to open the door of the patrol car without hissing in pain as he moved his right arm. Painstakingly slow, he exited as he mumbled, "Thanks for the ride." Dan used his hip to shut the car door before glancing up at the multi-story Toronto Police Tactical Response Force Headquarters.

Through the open car window, Constable Marc Fargusson replied, "Just doing my job." As the seasoned patrol officer drove away, he only shook his head slowly. *I have been on the job for a long time, too long. I have seen too much over the decades, but never something like this. How do TRF constables cope with the stress? Day in and day out, they deal with stuff like this. It would take a resilient person to handle the burdens of this job.*

Marc doubted he could ever do their job. He chided himself for not saying something different, something helpful, or comforting. *The young man is in so much pain—physically and emotionally. It is etched into the officer's face, and all I offered him is a platitude with no solace or help. How pathetic can I be?*

Usually better with words, Marc learned the value of them long ago. Words could and had saved lives. He wished to turn around and convey a more meaningful message to the weary constable, but he sighed and continued to drive back to the station because his shift officially ended hours ago, and he too was thoroughly exhausted.

Dan stood in the TRF lot—for how long he didn't know—as the patrol officer's words 'rolled in his head. *That is my mantra,* Dan dully thought.

His head hung, not moving, stone-cold still, not breathing. He succumbed to the burning need for air and took a painful breath in, followed by a slow, painful exhale. *Cracked ribs suck.*

So tired and hurting, Dan's heart, soul, and mind had been torn to bloody shreds today, leaving him extremely conflicted. His physical body wasn't in much better shape, but at least he was not bleeding out uncontrollably like his heart and soul.

Can I walk in? Should I leave? Dan lifted his head sluggishly and peered at the building. Here is where family, his new beginning, and a sense of belonging resided. Things he treasured and lost twice before joining Alpha Team.

But after yesterday? Was it only twenty-four hours ago when I arrived here so happy? Yeah, one day. So much happened in such a short period. Do I belong anymore? Do they still want me? Would they care if I left? Did I blow it again? Will I be forsaken a third time?

He let his head drop again as he thought about the first time he had been forsaken. At nine-years-old, his parents disowned, abandoned, and rejected him after he failed to save his sister. After she died, he only received censure from the general—never meeting expectations. Repeatedly told he was not worthy, he didn't belong because he did not protect his little sister, and he should've died instead of Sara.

After Sara's death, he was banished to the Arctic Special Forces base in the northern Yukon Territory. He grew up in isolation, in his very own ice prison, cut off from everyone he ever cared about. The general showed him no acceptance, no tolerance, and no compassion.

My father didn't want me but nonetheless demanded perfection. I never measured up, no matter how hard I tried. I only succeeded in demonstrating I would never be the perfect son he required. No, not a son. That is wrong. The general didn't want a son, all he wanted is a soldier. A perfect soldier! But I never met those expectations, either. I almost died trying to be what he desired. Why did I strive for so long to be what the bastard wanted?

Dan corrected himself. *No, I didn't do this for him, I did my best because Brody dreamed of being in Special Forces.*

He joined for his best friend and brother, Brody Hunter, but after he killed Brody in a friendly fire incident, staying became utterly impossible. Dan flipped off General 'Badass' Broderick, literally and figuratively. He broke with generations-old family tradition and exited military service while still young, able-bodied, and alive.

He lost his second family—his unit brothers—the day he blew Brody away. They had forsaken him because he committed the most heinous sin. He killed one of their own. He destroyed their brother.

Pain so deep … *Breathe, remember to breathe.*

Does my new chosen family want someone like me around? Can they still accept me after what had occurred yesterday? Only a day ago, all the pieces clicked together, and I finally recognized I belonged.

Joining them was no walk in the park. Not one of them wanted me on their team. They made it abundantly clear for months, but then something changed, and things improved. They embraced me … but will they, can they, after yesterday? Dan didn't know.

Will I find solace or condemnation with them now?

Dan forced himself to take a measured breath in. *Words and deeds wound deeply, slashing, and shredding until nothing is left.*

"I'm a killer. My father trained me to be one since I was old enough to hold a gun. No emotions, breathe in, hold, aim, squeeze softly like a caress between heartbeats, and snuff out a life," Dan whispered to no one.

Is NRB Agent Dick Donner right? Am I unfit? Was I too quick on the trigger? Am I an actual murderer and a liability to my team?

Dan blanched as he recalled Agent Donner's accusations. "Six! Six, Broderick! Do you hear me? Six people, you killed today! Without a second thought. In cold blood. You snuffed six innocent lives! You're so sure of yourself, so cocky, always too fast to pull a trigger.

"You're a murderer. Your badge isn't a license to kill. You murdered Aaron as sure as if you had fired the bullet. How can you believe you're fit to be a TRF officer? You put your team at risk every time. With every person you slay, you smear blood all over their hands, too!"

A deep sigh escaped, followed by a shaky, shallow intake of air. His body ached too much to take anything other than insubstantial breaths. Dan started to move listlessly towards the entrance.

Time to face whatever is coming. I am many things, but a coward isn't one of them. Even if this rips the last vestige of my soul from me, I will face the team. This is all my fault. Isn't it? So much blood on my hands, I'm the one who pulled the trigger six times. No, wait … only five times. But six deaths belong to me because I failed to be quick enough on the fourth shot.

"Crap, I'm so confused. Death comes if I'm too fast or too slow." He kept moving. Only a few more steps and he would be at the door.

Dan would endure whatever they threw his way … always did. Allow them to vent every hateful emotion and thought they held for him and pin the blame for all this blood where it squarely fit—on him.

He would take it in, push it down, seal it in the dark, thick-walled place he contained all his hurt, shame, guilt, inadequacy, and failures. Never would he allow his weakness and pain to show. His mask, his shields, and his walls were well-built after years of construction.

His hand on the handle, Dan reminded himself, *Breathe, just breathe …*

Your Place or Mine

Rollback Two Days
July 14
Fire Stick Grill – 10:00 p.m.

Lexa McKenna laughed as she set her beer down. Dan was in rare form tonight. She enjoyed having dinner with him—so much so, they lost track of time. From the secluded table, Jarmal nearly always had available for them, Lexa glanced around the restaurant and noticed only a handful of people left, mostly staff doing clean up.

She smiled at Dan. "We need to be going. Appears to be closing time."

Dan scanned the area and noting only two other occupied tables with patrons in the process of paying their bills. He refocused on Lexa. Tonight had been a fun night, and he didn't want it to end yet. "How about we head over to Timmy's and hang out in the back of your Jeep for a while?"

"We've got shift in …" Lexa checked her watch, "… seven hours. We ate dinner and should be in bed by now."

Dan leaned back and grinned. He let her words sink in as his eyes twinkled with a fond memory and the light of the candle between them. His mind rolled back to last July fourteenth. *Dinner, yeah, dinner.*

Lexa bit her lower lip as Dan's velvety sapphire eyes lit with the spark of heat. Another Freudian slip. Those occurred far too often in the last few weeks, ever since she almost kissed him in the locker room. She huffed out, "You *know* what I mean."

"Do I?" Dan drawled lazily with a suggestive wink, followed by an innocent lopsided grin.

"Ooooh, Broderick. I swear, I'm gonna have to stop having dinner with you." Lexa dug in her purse to find her credit card, trying desperately to suppress the pangs of craving building in her.

Dan chuckled. 'Having dinner' had a very different connotation one year ago. He would love to have dinner with her like that again. *But Lexa is never going to let that happen. She told me it would never be repeated. In fact, in her mind, our one night of sizzling, hot sex at the Grand Citadel Hotel never happened.* A different story played in his mind, a night he wouldn't ever forget, and something he desired to repeat, despite the risks.

He reached for his billfold. "I got tonight. I still owe you for two days ago when I forgot my wallet." Dan pulled out cash and put it on the table before standing. "Ready?"

Lexa nodded and put her credit card away. She picked up the bag of double chocolate chunk cookies Jarmal always gave her and motioned to Dan not to forget his bag of oatmeal raisin walnut cookies. The two strolled out of the restaurant after waving goodnight to Jarmal and D'Ante Tate.

Jarmal watched Dan go and smiled, happy for him as his friend appeared contented. He worried about him for a long time and never thought his boisterous spirit would return. Jarmal's heart warmed, witnessing Dan move forward with his life. Turning to D'Ante, he asked, "How much you wanna bet she is the one who will hook him?"

D'Ante laughed. "Another bachelor bites the dust. Speaking of which, how are things going with Tia Walsh, your cute TRF dispatcher?"

Jarmal's grin faded. "Sadly, our schedules don't mesh. She is sweet as pie, but it isn't gonna go anywhere romantic with her. We'll be friends, and I hope one day she finds her perfect main dish."

Shaking his head, D'Ante said, "Everything's food with you. Time to expand your vocabulary, brother."

Shrugging, Jarmal replied, "I'll find my creampuff one day, and she'll appreciate my way of speaking. Come on. Help me finish up with the books so you can go home to your cupcake."

As they ambled towards the office, Jarmal's phone rang. Checking his caller ID, he smiled and answered with a happy tone. "Hey, Squid. How's the Navy treating you, little bro?"

D'Ante shouted towards the cell, "Marquise, if you phoned me, you'd be called by your real name."

Jarmal shoved his older brother playfully. "Hush, Squid called me. You wait your turn." Then back to his youngest brother, Jarmal said, "So, how's everything?"

As they arrived at the office, Jarmal put the phone on speaker. Three of the four Tate brothers enjoyed catching up with each other's lives because they had not seen Marquise since their Christmas ski trip. With months of tidbits to share, it would be quite late by the time they finished.

Outside Fire Stick Grill – 10:05 p.m.

After putting his sack of cookies in his bag and zipping up, Dan reached in Lexa's Jeep for his helmet. She stood at the rear of the Jeep, flicking her keyring around her finger as he retrieved his stuff from the rear passenger seat. Dan slung his go-bag over his shoulder before moving to the back of the vehicle after shutting the door.

"An enjoyable night," Lexa said as the keys continued to circle her index finger.

Dan stopped closer to Lexa than he should, invading her personal space. Resisting the pull to be close to her and kiss her, became harder with each passing day. "Yeah."

Lexa's feet wouldn't listen to her rational mind. Common sense told her to leave, to vacate now, but her feet remained solidly in place, defying sensible behavior. The desire to kiss Dan burned a hole in her. She wanted to taste his lips again. Being so close to him, she needed to remind herself to breathe. When she inhaled, his woodsy, musky scent came with the oxygen and nearly undid her.

A year ago, today, she shared a one-night-stand with Dan and Lexa couldn't block the images of the delicious night from her head. She dated a few guys in the past year, but she kept measuring them against Dan, and they always fell short in some manner.

Lexa stared at his lips, and the electrical current which crackled between them came to life. She wanted him ... badly, really, really badly.

Dan gazed at Lexa's eyes, which focused on his mouth. *Yeah, kissing her again is what I desire, too.* His mind conjured up memories of the fateful night she sauntered into the Grand Citadel bar. Her hair now flowed around her face as it did that night. Dan ached to run his fingers through her rich, dark auburn locks again. He craved ...

Lexa's keys fell to the ground, and she ignored them as she leaned in, unable to resist his oh-so-kissable lips any longer.

Dan started to bend down to retrieve them for Lexa but found himself face to face with her, a fraction of an inch separating their lips. Dan's heart skipped a beat as he forgot to breathe. His helmet slipped from his grasp and clattered to the ground—forgotten.

Lips came together softly at first as Dan's hands reached around Lexa and drew her close. He pulled back slightly, and their eyes met. Passion flared in hazel and blue eyes. Lips crashed together with long-suppressed need. Lexa's body molded to Dan's. Resistance became futile—primal attraction won the battle with restraint.

Breathing heavily, Dan asked, "Your place or mine?"

"Mine's closer," Lexa murmured into his mouth, not willing to break the liplock. After several more minutes of heated kissing, she reluctantly drew back. Lexa noted Dan's glazed over eyes, and blew out a shaky breath. "You okay to ride?"

Dan grinned. "Yeah. You okay to drive?"

"Yeah." She leaned down to pick up her keys and Dan's helmet.

Ogling Lexa's bottom as she bent over, a surge of lust-filled Dan. *I'm going to do this. I'm going to defy logic and risk everything to be with Sexy Lexie. Jon might call this an unacceptable risk, but as far as I'm concerned, this is calculated.* The indescribable pull of his soul towards Lexa bordered on the extreme. He must take the risk. Dan could no longer deny his heart's desire.

Lexa handed Dan his helmet. She couldn't believe she would jeopardize her career, all she worked for, everything which defined her and gave her life purpose for a mere man. The concept remained beyond her comprehension, yet she didn't have a choice. This inexplicable attraction to him became overwhelming and too difficult to fight.

Dan wanted to kiss her again. Instead, he took his helmet and put it on. If he didn't, a high probably existed, he would be pushing Lexa up against the wall and having a quickie in the parking lot of Jarmal's restaurant. Lexa deserved to be treated much better, so he quelled his raging desire.

Clenching her fob tightly, Lexa said, "You'll need to park in my garage when we arrive at my place. Can't leave your bike visible on the street—too recognizable."

Dan tightened the helmet strap on his and reached into his pocket for his key. "Why? Not like anyone from TRF will see." Glimpsing her stern expression, he conceded, "Okay, okay, in the garage. I'll follow you."

Nodding, Lexa headed for the driver's side and hopped in. As she turned over her vehicle's ignition, Dan's Ducati roared to life. *This is madness, sheer utter madness. If we are caught, we'll be kicked off the team for sure and possibly fired.* Lexa tried to push her worry away as the heat at her core increased. She settled her rational mind by saying, "Just tonight, only tonight. We aren't dating. One night is all I need to rid this bizarre craving from my system."

The devil on her shoulder smugly smiled. *"We'll see about that."*

Lexa's Home — 10:30 p.m.

Arriving a few moments before Dan due to traffic, Lexa hopped out and waited for him to pull into the garage before pressing the button to shut the garage. After Dan switched off his motorcycle, the only sound came from the rumble and whir of a double-wide door rolling into place, sealing out the outside world. Once closed, Dan and Lexa existed in a world of their own.

Lexa gazed at Dan as dismounted with cat-like grace after removing the bright red helmet, which matched the color of his sleek Ducati. Dan's fluid motions always attracted her attention. *How does this muscular man move so gracefully and silently?*

The image of a panther popped into her mind as she stared at the man whose all-black clothing and body movements mirrored those of the agile and powerful cat. She scanned Dan from head-to-toe, well actually more like boots to mane.

Starting with his feet, she noted the soft, black chukka boots. He almost always wore boots of one sort or another. She remembered him saying once he preferred to run in boots. He only wore cross-trainers for workout.

Her eyes advancing upward over his legs clad in a pair of tight-fitting black jeans, they showed his defined thighs much better than the looser fitting gray cargo pants of their uniform. At his waist, a black belt with an unusual brushed nickel buckle ... not for need, but more a fashion statement, or so she initially believed. During a dinner four weeks ago, she inquired about the interesting shape and learned the buckle contained a small knife. Dan confessed he hated being unarmed. So function, not fashion, to facilitate a practice Lexa assumed born of need and a holdover from his days as a soldier.

Lexa continued her perusal in the dim lighting. He wore a black long-sleeved button-down shirt over a black undershirt, reminiscent of their black uniform shirts—minus the patches identifying them, their rank as constables, and their sniper qualifications. The final article, a black leather jacket worn over the shirt, completed her picture.

However, Dan's coloring more resembled a majestic lion. His slightly mussed, golden blond hair a crowning glory, attracting the notice of many ladies. His jawline showed a hint of golden stubble since Dan had not shaved since before coming in for today's five a.m. workout. She liked both the clean-shaven and the more rustic two-day stubble looks Dan sometimes sported.

Their eyes met, and Lexa became lost to a surging lust. *No turning back now. The sexy panther will be devouring me tonight, and I'll willingly offer my body to satisfy his hunger ... truthfully ... my craving.*

Dan slid off his bike and set his helmet on the seat. He shoved keys in his pocket before peering over at Lexa as she waited for him by her door. He paused as her eyes raked up his body and met his eyes. The heat wafting off her almost reached him all the way across her garage. Shifting his go bag on his shoulder, he started forward, still trying to wrap his mind around the fact she invited him to her place.

They met at her door and stood inches apart. Both inhaled deeply as Lexa's hand turned the knob on her kitchen door and pushed it wide open. Dan preceded Lexa into the house then turned towards her as she entered.

Unable to resist any longer, as the door swung closed, two bodies melded into one. Fire hotly burned, scorching roving hands as lips urgently crushed together. Bags and keys dropped, discarded and forgotten in the heat consuming both.

Dan moved Lexa backward towards her island counter. His vision sharp in the darkened room, his sense honed after years of functioning in an environment devoid of light. He lifted her and set her on the countertop as his tongue delved in to savor her sweetness. He inhaled the fragrance of jasmine as his fingers carded through her soft, natural waves. He liked her hair down, the way she wore it off shift. The auburn tresses framed the ivory skin of her face beautifully.

Lexa kicked off her slip-on sandals as he positioned her onto the island. Kissing became fierce and needy as her hands moved of their own accord from the back of Dan's neck to the buttons of his shirt. The desire to touch his skin overwhelmed her.

So lost in the moment all his nerves firing, Dan didn't realize she unbuttoned his shirt until Lexa broke their kiss, pushed his arms down, and yanked off his button-down shirt and jacket in one movement. His still tucked in Oxford hung behind him from his jeans. Dan pulled the fabric from his pants and let it fall as Lexa's fingertips brushed over his abs still covered his tight-fitting t-shirt on her way to his buckle. When the fastener caused her difficulty, Dan undid it himself.

As Dan worked the tricky belt latch apart himself, Lexa took the opportunity to pull her tank top up and off, not caring where she dropped her clothing. Her hands worked his jeans button as he undid hers. Dan lifted her slightly, she shifted her hips to shimmy out of her pants, and he finished removing them, depositing them on the floor with the other articles. She now sat on the counter in only her plain, black bra and black panties … the serviceable, bland ones she wore at work.

Dan sucked in a breath as he touched Lexa's bare shoulders and lightly caressed down her arms as he gazed at her covered breasts. He fantasized about this moment ever since he cleaned her kitchen. As he wiped down her counter on February fourteenth, he imagined what it would be like to sit her here and caress her. *Reality is so much better.*

Lexa tingled where his light stroke traveled. Electricity shot through her body, causing her to shiver with anticipation. She reached out for his cheek, wanting him to lean into her touch like he did in the hotel room a year ago. He didn't disappoint. His head tilted into her palm. Lexa wished for more illumination, barely able to discern his features in the dark kitchen. She pulled him closer and seductively said, "We've eaten dinner. Time for dessert. Perhaps we should take this upstairs …"

That was all the invitation Dan required. He leaned down and captured her mouth again as he lifted her. Lexa's legs wrapped around his waist as Dan continued to kiss her, and he made his way through her house and to the stairs. He knew his path thanks to his recon the night he brought her home and carried her upstairs after she sprained her ankle.

Fully engaged in kissing him, wanting all of him, Lexa scarcely registered Dan carrying her up the steps to her bedroom. Her world refocused when he laid her on her smooth, cool comforter. She pouted, lips cold and bereft when he pulled back and straightened up.

With her blackout window shade lowered, a necessity for sleeping during days when they had the night shift, her eyes sought him out in the inky room. She wished for sufficient light to view his perfect abs, but focused on Dan's silhouette instead. Created by the dim hallway light behind him, she smiled as the apparition's arms grasped the hem of the t-shirt, pulling it over his head, ruffling his hair in the process. When a hand moved towards his back, she wondered why until a shadow of a square materialized and realized he withdrew his wallet.

Dan grinned as he pulled out protection. "I'm prepared this time." He shoved his billfold back into his pocket and proceeded to strip off the rest of his clothing. He gave nary a thought to his scars in the pitch-black room. Lexa would need the vision of a cat, to glimpse them.

As he crawled on the bed, hovering over her, allowing their bodies to touch, Lexa's core melted, and lava flowed through her veins. She roved over Dan's muscular shoulders and down his taut biceps exploring her panther man. Their lips connected again, and fiery sparks cascaded behind her eyes.

Lexa was not cognizant of when he removed the remainder of her clothing, but the warmth of his palm closing over her naked breast hitched her breath and caused her to moan and arch up. Dan skillfully and artfully teased and pleasured her, driving her to the edge and to the point she needed all of him.

Never breaking the connection, Lexa managed to maneuver herself on top. She located the foil package, opened it, and deftly applied the condom to Dan's erection. Lexa closed her eyes and sighed as she took him in. She rocked slowly at first, adjusting as his ample size filled her completely. She set an increasing rhythm increased, and he followed.

Dan groaned in ecstasy as their tempo increased. He caressed every inch of her smooth, soft, quivering skin. Need rising, compelled to thrust deeper and faster, he gripped her hips, urging her motions to match his.

Close, so very close, Lexa moved at a frenzied cadence. Needing a purchase to keep from rocketing skyward, she grasped his shoulders, and her short, manicured nails dug into his skin. She screamed, "Daaaaaan," as she exploded in pure white heat, separating from this world and reaching the stars.

Dan held Lexa's hips and plunged into heaven several more times as Lexa's body pulsated around him. His climax shot him into space, as he moaned out in a deep, guttural tone, "Lexaaaaaaa."

Lexa collapsed onto Dan's chest, her breathing coming in short pants as she floated downward. Her ear rested over Dan's heart, and his rapid beats matched hers as did his ragged breaths. The air in and out of their lungs the only sound in their private world as Dan's arms wrapped around her securing her to him.

Most conscious thought exceeded Dan's abilities at this point, the only thing he knew for certain was he could describe his feelings now. Lexa in his arms … absolute perfection. Though TRF protocol deemed fraternization inappropriate, something so right couldn't be wrong. He would gladly risk all and break the rule until the end of time to be with Lexa.

As the fires of lust banked, Lexa's mind whirled, contemplating the ramifications of what she did. She gave in to temptation, and it might ruin her. *Did I really just do this? Is this only another one-night stand to quell the hunger which gnaws at me when I'm close to Dan? Will this single night sate my craving? Or am I doomed to fall for a man, who once he gets what he wants, will discard me like my father and brothers?*

Exhausted from their long day, Lexa slipped off into an uneasy sleep as her mind tried to resolve her internal conflict. No resolution came before the Sandman claimed her.

Dan continued to caress Lexa's back as her soft, regular pattern of breathing indicated Lexa had fallen asleep. They had not shared a word afterward. Each lost in their thoughts. He understood his part in this but now wondered why Lexa took the perilous journey into uncharted territory with him. He pondered for a long time as he lightly ran fingers over her soft, smooth body and drifted off without finding an answer.

A Unique Situation

 *3*

July 15
Dan's Apartment — 4:55 a.m.

Dan had woken with a start, glanced at Lexa's clock, and promptly panicked. He slept straight through without a single nightmare waking him, like the previous time he slept with Lexa. But one glimpse of her clock caused him to leap out of bed, pull on his t-shirt and pants, and call out to Lexa they had overslept. The surprise in Lexa's eyes when they opened … priceless. Dan couldn't remember a single time Lexa arrived late to work in the past year. She roused as fast as him and pulled on undergarments.

He gave her one quick kiss on the cheek and flashed a lopsided grin before dashing downstairs. After cramming his feet into his boots, sans socks, and shoving his socks and button-down shirt into his go bag, he shrugged into his jacket as Lexa called down to him, he better not be late or Jon would read him the riot act.

As he raced for TRF headquarters, wondering if Lexa would make it in on time, Dan realized he needed a clean uniform, so diverted to his place. No two ways about it now … he was gonna be late. After rushing into his apartment, shoving his clothes into his bag and changing his shirt, he figured he would catch hell from Jon anyway, so he decided to brush his teeth.

His phone ringing interrupted his thoughts. Leaving the toothbrush hanging, he reached into his pocket to grab his cell. With a mouth full of brush and paste mixed with saliva, Dan answered with a muddled, "Broderick."

Her eyes scanned the kitchen floor for the fifth time as the call connected, and Lexa blurted out, "Do you have my keys?"

Spitting out toothpaste, Dan replied, "Keys?"

"I can't find them anywhere. I had them when we entered my kitchen. I searched the floor and my bag. Did they fall into yours?"

Dan scooped a handful of water into his mouth and swished. *A quick brushing is better than none.* He spat out the water. "I don't think so. It stayed zipped last night. Let me check."

Lexa paced, trying to remember where she put her second set of keys. She moved everything around while remodeling. Her mind also whirred on how to explain both she and Dan arriving late on the same day. *Will anything show in our demeanor? Will yesterday be the last day of my career with TRF?*

Dan rummaged through his bag, and his hand landed on a set of keys. He groaned. "Sorry, Lexa. I must've picked them up by accident when I threw my shirt and socks in."

Lexa echoed his groan. "Are you going to be on time?"

"No. Needed to stop at my place for a uniform." Dan gripped Lexa's keys. *Bad, for both of use to be late.* His mind sought a semi-truthful deflection. "We can tell the Boss your Jeep wouldn't start and called me to pick you up."

Fearing something might give them away if they arrived together, Lexa responded, "Coming in together would be bad, really bad. No. No, that won't work. Boss perceives things and may figure out what we don't want anyone to know. I'm not about to commit career suicide today. I'll find my other set then head in."

Dan nodded though Lexa couldn't see him. She had a point. Boss did detect things no one else did. Now that he opened up a bit to the team and allowed them to peek behind his shields, Dan found it harder to hide certain things. "Okay, sooooo … I'll give them to you sometime today?" He grinned. "Perhaps we can enjoy dinner after shift again?"

Lexa growled. "I'm not sure. We'll see. I'm uncertain we … this … I don't know if I can do … we're friends, colleagues … I shouldn't … we—"

As Lexa struggle to complete a sentence, Dan recognized this rattled her and interrupted, "Hey, it's only dinner. A burger and a beer. We have to eat. We can talk … just friends talking. Perhaps friends with benefits. Not that anyone else needs to be aware of the extras."

Lexa grinned despite her conflict. *Friends with benefits. Is this possible?* "I'll see you at workout. Come up with a decent excuse for being late or Jon will work your ass off and probably make you count ammo for the next three months." She hung up and began to search in earnest for her backup keys as her mind twirled on the extra benefits of being friends with Dan.

Dan laughed as he disconnected, shoved the keychain into the bag's outer pocket, zipped up, and slung it over his shoulder, before rushing out the door. He detested lying, not that he didn't possess the ability, his black op missions sometimes required misdirection, but in his personal life, he preferred the truth. Lies destroyed relationships, and he had no desire to lose his chosen family by being outright deceitful with them. He needed a partially true excuse.

TRF HQ – Gym – 5:20 a.m.

"Hey, Dano, you're late," Jonathan Hardy, Alpha Team tactical lead, called out as Dan strode into the gym. Jon wiped the sweat from his bald head as he tracked the rookie. Something appeared different with the rookie this morning. He narrowed his gray eyes as he assessed Dan.

"Morning, Jon, Bram, Boss," Dan replied with a solid smile as he walked to the heavy bag while taping up his hands. "Sorry, Boss, won't happen again. I fell asleep without setting the alarm and overslept." He found an honest response though lacking in finer details of why he forgot and whose bed he slept in. Omissions, he did not need to reveal to them.

Jon, Bram, and Nick all shared a glance. Albeit wholly out-of-character, their rookie arrived late and with a real smile gracing his face. Dan appeared relaxed, well-rested, and comfortable. Until today, Dan always projected a defensive edge. Each man wondered what caused these positive changes. Contented with the occurrence, they decided not to pry and grinned as they returned to exercising.

As he started his bag workout, Dan silently reflected. He slept so soundly with Lexa in his arms. No nightmares intruded his dreams to wake him in the wee hours of the morning. He remained unsure if her presence in his life would be only another one-night-stand. Secretly, he hoped Lexa would be willing to take the risk and find out where things might go. Friends with benefits would be a safe place to start.

His attraction to her was undeniable, and his realization last night that it felt so right with her—something he never felt with another woman—staggered him. Could Lexa be his one? Dan knew Broderick males only married once. They waited until they found the one who completed them—their soulmate, some would say. Something Dan comprehended despite his estrangement from the family.

Is Lexa my one? The scary thought would mean choosing between her and the team. Dan was unsure he could make that decision. He only reached the point of feeling he belonged here, and they accepted him ... his third chance at having a family.

He glanced at Bram. *Family. If only I didn't keep losing family. My attraction to Lexa is so strong, and it can't be wrong. Take it slow, there is no need to rush things. Lexa is clearly confused. Never seen her so unsure with words before. Yeah, no rush. Stick with friends with benefits and find out where it leads.*

Dan smiled. *Sticking with TRF is the right decision. I'm home here ... this place, these people, I belong here.* His phone lying on the bench started to vibrate. He stopped punching and went to grab it, wondering if it was Lexa. *Maybe she couldn't find keys and needs me to pick her up after all.*

Dan's face darkened a moment as he hit ignore. No way in hell he would take a call from the general. He allowed the general to interfere in his life for far too long.

Resuming his workout on the punching bag, his hits harder as his mind drifted back to the call from his father which ended up with a busted phone in the Pond when he threw it in anger. Dan still couldn't figure out why the man would withhold his mail. *Why would he do that? And why didn't anyone from the family ever contacted me if my cousins never received my letters?*

The answers to these questions might be revealed if he ever accepted any of the repeated calls from General-Wants-To-Control-My-Life, but let every single one go to voicemail and deleted the messages without listening to them. *I'm sick of giving him any power over my life. It is time to move forward and make a new life for myself outside the general's reach.*

For now, that meant he must keep his distance from his extended family. He couldn't stand it if his cousins or uncles tried to talk him into returning to the military. The way of life for Broderick males—was not his now. *I need to be a different man, I desire to save lives instead of taking them. I'm tired of being a point-and-shoot soldier. I must rebuild my life.*

He grinned as he punched the heavy bag. *I'm building a life here—the pieces are falling into place. Amazing what changes can happen in a dozen months. Last year I walked into this building a broken man, hanging on by a gossamer thread, met with disdain and rejection … an unwanted seventh member forced onto Alpha Team. But everything changed.*

They reached out, provided me solace, and kept me from falling off the edge into oblivion. Bram, Lexa, Loki, Ray, Nick, and Jon are the reasons I am alive today, Jon especially. When Jon appropriated my pistol on May twenty-sixth, he prevented me from ending my life. These six people are now my chosen family, and I will safeguard them with my very life if necessary. The beauty of life, the ephemeral thing Brody said existed, might be within my reach.

Dan stopped his musings, realizing in addition to Lexa being absent, Loki and Ray also not in the gym. He halted his workout and looked at Boss. "So, I'm not the only one late today. Where are the others?" Dan asked, even though he knew where Lexa was. He hoped she found her second set of keys and didn't need to take a cab. Although doing so might help strengthen her excuse for being late.

Sergeant Nicholas Pastore averted his gaze in time so the rookie wouldn't realize he had been studying him. Nick spotted the flash of anger cross Dan's features when he checked his phone, and how hard Dan hit the bag afterward. Glad the smile returned to Dan's face, Nick slowed the treadmill. "Lexa called to say she'll be late, something about a problem starting her Jeep. Loki and Ray, well, it's their day for a coffee run. They must be stuck there."

Dan grinned. *She used the excuse I suggested. Good, it is the truth, you can't start a Jeep without keys.*

Abraham De Haven, Bram to his friends, piped up from his treadmill, "So, Danny boy, you're the only one without a decent excuse." Turning to Jon, he jokingly asked, "Does that mean Danny gets extra cleaning duty? Perhaps counting ammo for the next month?"

Jon smiled and cocked his head as he continued to lift weights. "Depends."

Dan shook his head. *I'd count ammo from here to eternity if I can spend my nights with Lexa.* He pushed the idea down. He couldn't risk Boss glimpsing those thoughts at work, or he would lose everything.

At that moment, Loki, Ray, and Lexa all rounded the corner into the gym. Alexandra McKenna, team profiler and sniper, noticed Dan's thousand-watt smile. His smile lit up his whole face. *He is devastatingly handsome when he smiles. Never seen one quite like that on him before—it is a beautiful sight.*

Something inside Lexa wanted to believe she played a part in creating the smile. *Perhaps I did.* Last night replayed in her mind. The pull was strong. Maybe … just maybe … she might risk it all to be with him. But it must remain a secret because there was no way she would give up Alpha Team.

They were her family, and she adamantly refused to lose a second one. Being abandoned by her natural family nearly broke her, and she didn't think she would survive without her chosen one.

So if, and she meant a BIG if, she decided to continue a forbidden friends-with-benefits relationship with Dan Broderick, it would have to be a well-kept secret. The team could never know.

Striving for normalcy, Lexa asked, "What depends on what?" as she smiled at them and moved to a treadmill.

"Well, you see …" Jon allowed his gaze to roam from Dan to Loki to Ray, and lastly to Lexa. "All you young pups are late on the same day. None of you got your butts in here on time. No one respecting my authority as tactical lead. So, I must decide what punishment to dole out," Jon sternly said.

Nick's and Bram's amused smirks ruined the effect of Jon's stern voice and steely gaze entirely. "Aw guys, you two are worthless, thought you had my back on this." Jon chuckled.

Bram chuckled and grinned.

Nick laughed as he ran a towel over his forehead to sop up the sweat dripping down in steady rivulets. "This is certainly a unique situation. Don't believe this ever occurred before. An extremely rare event when anyone is late, and much less more than two late on the same day. As far as memory serves, we've never had over half the team tardy. Jon, we might be slipping. Perhaps it is time to instill a little more discipline, everyone who arrived after five scrubs the floors. What'd ya think?"

Before Jon could reply, Dante Baldovino's excited voice cut in, "This is an omen today will be totally awesome and unique. Could be something so profoundly different and life-altering than we've ever experienced? How cool would that be?"

Raymundo Palomo shook his head at his best friend's animated antics. Loki resembled a little boy sometimes—an endearing quality Ray appreciated and enjoyed about the geeky techie. Ray asked, "Who wants their coffee?" Then he handed out the beverages to everyone, and a collective sigh materialized as they all took their first drink.

The team happily bantered with one another as they continued their workout. The ensuing conversation remained light and fun as everyone offered up suggestions on how a day could be unique for a TRF team. Loki was currently on a rant about maybe aliens would pop up, and his bomb-sniffing robot, Lucille, would save the day.

Dan grinned. For him, something profound already occurred today. For the first time, in so long, he felt truly happy. These five men and one woman became his chosen family. They accepted and cared about him ... he belonged again. He would protect them, and they would cover his six too, or as Boss liked to say, 'my hand is on your back.'

His smile grew as he transitioned to the treadmill. *I have family again.* He risked opening up and exposing his soul after losing a family twice before. When he arrived a year ago, the sense of abandonment and loss pervaded his being, isolating him, leaving him so lonely it physically hurt. Both times Dan lost his family, he recognized he was responsible for the death, which resulted in his denunciation.

Cheerful for the first time in a very long time, Dan hoped fate would be kind to him as he glanced around, stopping briefly on each member of Alpha Team. *Sergeant Nick Pastore, a wise and fair man. Tactical Lead and fellow sniper Jon, an enigma but exceptional leader. Entry specialist Bram, kind and approachable regardless of his size. Information officer Ray, calm and steady. Technical and explosives expert Loki, a jokester with combat skills. Profiler and sniper Sexy Lexie, your heart saved many ... me included.*

Here, this place, with you six, is where I make a real difference. I will not fail again. I vow always to watch your backs and to give my life to protect yours ... I will not lose a third family.

Nick, Jon, and Bram shared a knowing glance with each other. Their unvoiced conversation conveyed, *'Today is a unique day—a good day.'* They all recognized something changed in their stoic rookie's demeanor. An actual light shone brightly in his sapphire blue eyes this morning, the ever-present dark smudges under his eyes appeared to be gone, and he wore a genuine smile on his face.

They each perceived a subtle shift in their team, too. Their family had grown, and everyone fully accepted a talented young man into its fold. Dan would now and forevermore be a valued and loved member of this family.

Fortunately, it had finally happened. Unfortunately, it took a lot longer than it should've … the fault they accepted as leaders and senior members of this team, they shouldered the responsibility.

Nick cut his workout short to review paperwork in preparation for Dan's annual assessment. With today being the rookie's first anniversary, Nick needed to have a conversation with Dan. A year gave a rookie a practical understanding of what it took to do this job. TRF didn't fit every constable … sometimes they didn't possess the necessary abilities, but most often, officers decided the demands were too much, so they chose to leave. Although Dan possessed the aptitude to succeed here, he must ensure Dan wanted to stay.

As he headed out of the gym, Nick nodded to Jon and received a grin in return. They spoke last night, to gather Jon's inputs on Dan's performance—all positive with the exception Jon still thought the rookie took too many unacceptable risks. A bone of contention between two alpha males, which Nick believed would eventually be resolved.

You Know My Cousin

4

Master Seaman Marquise Tate entered Lieutenant Scott Broderick's office. Struck yet again with how much Lieutenant Broderick resembled Dan. They could definitely pass for twins. The only differences he noted up close ... the lieutenant appeared a bit older and the picture of health, unlike Dan, when he last saw him.

When he met Dan in October, he looked like shit ... way too thin, pale, with dark circles under haunted eyes. The guy needed rest, and Marquise supported Jarmal's decision to slip sleeping pills into Dan's meals. It pleased him to find out from Jarmal last night Dan appeared to be doing better.

Marquise came to attention and waited to be acknowledged.

Scott glanced up. "At ease. Do you have the file I requested?"

Relaxing and holding out his report, Marquise responded, "Yes, sir. I also pulled details on the surrounding area and included it in my analysis."

Taking the folder and opening it, Scott perused the details. "Excellent work. This will speed things along."

He peered up at the master seaman. Scott noted his professional bearing and aptitude a few times since he took over. His predecessor spoke well of the young seaman indicating Tate to be intelligent, insightful, and willing to go the extra mile. Scott believed this man had a solid career ahead of him.

Scott asked, "What's your take on this issue?"

Wow! Surprised the lieutenant requested his opinion. "Appearances are deceiving. Gives the impression of a valid threat on the surface, but I don't buy it. This has earmarks of being a prank."

"How so?" Scott queried, intrigued. He held the same viewpoint but needed facts to support his theory.

Marquise launched into his reasoning, and the two discussed all aspects of the supposed threat to the Halifax Naval Base in Nova Scotia. After forty minutes, the exchange concluded, and Scott now possessed solid facts required to make recommendations to his commander.

Scott stood and held out his hand to the young seaman. "I appreciate your insight. There is a bright future for you. There's an opening coming up shortly in my team. Are you interested in a transfer?"

Marquise beamed, he couldn't help the vast smile which spread across his face. "Yes, sir. Absolutely! Boy, you're as good a man as your cousin Dan. I swear Brodericks are lucky charms for Tates."

A stab of pain coursed through Scott at hearing Dan's name, but curiosity intruded. "You know my cousin?"

"Sure do. Through my brothers, D'Ante and Jarmal. Mostly Jarmal. I bet you're happy Dan's doing better lately. Man, he was in such a bad headspace when I met him in October. He looked like he had been keelhauled, but Jarmal said he's doing much better."

Scott whirled inside. He searched for Dan all year, ever since Uncle Will indicated Dan left the military after killing his best friend Brody Hunter in a friendly fire incident. Uncle Will remained tight-lipped on the details. Scott understood security must be maintained, but the total blackout on Dan afterward infuriated him.

He highly suspected, but couldn't confirm Uncle Will invoked a blackout protocol on Danny. His uncle would be a complete idiot not to grasp Dan's need for family support after killing Brody. This felt like Sara's death all over again when Uncle Will whisked Danny off to the Yukon base.

Sure, the psychologist recommended Dan be away from where Sara died, but the move to a frozen wasteland cut Danny off from the rest of them. Scott always disagreed with the decision, but failed to speak his mind … at seventeen, none of the adults would've listened to him anyway.

Scott kept his emotions in control. "Where did you meet him?"

Marquise smiled. "In Toronto. My brothers still live there. Jarmal opened a restaurant. He saw Dan after a police situation. Said Dan looked like shit on a shingle. That's when Jarmal found out Dan lost his best friend. Dan's sergeant asked Jarmal to watch out for Dan for a few days."

Sergeant? Is Dan still in the military? Is it a ruse Dan took early release? CFB Borden is outside of Toronto. Is Dan in a safe house there? So many questions ran through Scott's mind. "Do you know the sergeant's name?"

Scrunching up his face, trying to recall, Marquise took a few moments to answer. He grinned when it popped into his head. "Yeah, I'm pretty sure it is Sergeant Pastore. Yeah. Friendly guy who seemed real concerned about Dan's health, Jarmal said."

The name Pastore set off all kinds of bells in Scott's brain. *Dr. Jasper Pastore is Uncle Will's friend from the time they served together in the same Special Forces unit years ago. But Pastore isn't a sergeant; his rank is a major.* Scott recalled the doctor had a couple of kids, one son, but nothing more about the family. *Could this sergeant be related to Dr. Pastore ... perhaps his son?*

Scott thought it would be strange for the sergeant to ask for outside help with an active blackout protocol. He probed a little further, "Why did Sergeant Pastore request your brother's help with Dan?"

Marquise sighed. "Jarmal shared with me Dan had a rough time integrating with his police TRF team. The tough call they handled that day affected Dan somehow, and he took off running after punching the shit out of the brick wall. His sergeant sent two constables on his team to find him after the tactical leader was put in a car and taken off to be interviewed. I guess the constable made a lethal shot.

"Jarmal cared for Dan for five days. Slipped him sleeping pills to quiet the nightmares to help him sleep through the night. Made sure he ate too—he was so gaunt and pale. Jarmal revealed to us Dan appeared in worse condition than when he first met him years ago while Dan recovered from some significant injuries in Kandahar."

He stopped his rambling. *Surely, I'm not telling him anything he doesn't already know.* With that thought in his mind, the lieutenant's black expression surprised Marquise. Blue eyes darkened and narrowed as a cold fury built in the man before him. Marquise would swear the ambient temperature in the room dropped by at least twenty degrees.

Marquise sucked in a breath and unconsciously took four steps backward as the smile on his face disappeared. He didn't understand what pissed off Lieutenant Broderick, but no way in hell he wanted to be in the path of the lieutenant when he let loose his fury. Swallowing the lump of fear forming in his throat, Marquise tried to figure out what he might've said to produce this reaction.

Scott clenched his fists as rage built. *Toronto! Dan's been in Toronto all this time? Only four hours away. Uncle Will is going to pay for this. This is beyond comprehension.*

He knew about the TRF. Walter Gambrill, Uncle Will's oldest friend, and Dan's godfather, commanded the Toronto Tactical Response Force. *Uncle Will is hiding Dan in plain sight. Hell's bells, damn him! How could he do this to us? To Danny?*

Reining in his fury when the master seaman stepped back, Scott said, "That'll be all for now. Thank you for the information on my cousin." A rational thought entered. *Uncle Will loves Dan. He wouldn't deny Danny his family unless there is a valid reason to put him on blackout protocol.*

There must be a good reason to keep our family in the dark. Perhaps this is related to Pletcher. The man tried to kill Becca and is still on the loose. Aunt Yvonne and Becca are currently in an unknown safe location. My mom is beside herself with worry for her identical twin sister and her niece. Perhaps my uncle is protecting Dan, too.

With that thought, Scott added, "Please, do me a favor and keep anything you know regarding my cousin to yourself. It could be a matter of his safety."

Viewing the ice storm dissipate, Marquise relaxed a little, but not entirely. "Sure, no problem."

Not missing the wariness in Tate's voice, Scott got ahold of his emotions and shoved them down. "Sorry for my unprofessional display of anger." He deflected with humor as he chuckled. "Little cousins don't always share things they should."

Marquise smiled. "Family. Hard to live with them—impossible to live without them. I've been known to keep things from my elder brothers. They can be a pain in the ass when they go all protective."

Scott smiled. "Yeah, I hear you. My little brother Kyle and younger cousins can be trying. Very trying. Being an elder comes with certain responsibilities, ones the youngers don't always understand."

"True." Marquise understood well what Scott was saying. He relaxed entirely as he shared, "But we youngers are more capable than we're given credit for. And we appreciate our elders—just not so much the lectures when we've done something stupid, especially when we already know it was imprudent."

That made Scott chuckle. "Thanks again for your information on the issue, and on my cousin. If you're not put off by my show of temper, I'll initiate the paperwork for your transfer." Scott rounded his desk and approached Marquise.

A genuine smile came to Marquise's face as he stuck out his hand to shake Broderick's outstretched hand. "I look forward to it, sir."

After they shook hands and Tate left, Scott pulled out his phone. High time to contact his dad. Now knowing Dan's location, he would demand answers from Uncle Will. No longer a seventeen-year-old kid, Scott would insist his opinion be heard, but he understood working through his father, and other two uncles would be the best course of action.

They were the only ones who Uncle Will would listen to. And if he remained reticent to provide details, Scott had no doubt Dad, Uncle Mark, and Uncle Ryan would find a way to pull the particulars from him, even if they must fly to Afghanistan and beat them out of their oldest brother.

Ottawa – Captain Erik Broderick's Home – 0625 Hours

Erik Broderick disconnected the call after speaking with his eldest son. He began pacing when Scott told him what he learned about Dan. Erik fought to remain calm and not give in to the building rage. Thoroughly pissed off at his eldest brother. *William can be so misguided when dealing with Dan. His heart is in the right place, but his execution is severely lacking and ends with disastrous results most often.*

He agreed with Scott there might be a reason for William to place Dan on blackout protocol … but if Dan were in Toronto and on the police force, he would be wide open. *What is William thinking?*

Ann Broderick poked her head into her husband's study. "Everything alright?"

Blowing out a frustrated breath, Erik opened his arms in invitation. Ann moved forward, clasped her arms around his waist, and held tight. Erik embraced Ann, pulling her close. *What can I tell her?*

"That bad, huh?" Ann tilted her head up.

Erik snorted. "Never can put anything past you. It isn't good. I must call Will."

Ann tensed, concern for her twin and niece increased. "Are Yvonne and Becca okay?"

Peering into the green of his beautiful wife's eyes, Erik perceived her worry. He kissed her forehead. "Our girls are alright. This is about Danny."

"Danny? Wha … what is it? Is he okay? Please, tell me he's not injured again." Ann's eyes shone with trepidation.

"Yes, I believe he's fine."

"What do you mean you believe?"

Erik pulled Ann close again and stared at the wall of books across the room. Ann's fear tugged at his heartstrings. "Just that. Scott may have found out where he is. My brother has a lot to explain if Danny is where I think he is at."

Ann sighed into Erik's chest. "Don't tell me, William messed up again."

"Quite likely." Erik drew in a deep breath and blew it out slowly. "I should've decked Will after the Tarzan incident when Danny was seven. Perhaps he would've learned. Things might've been different."

Reaching up to caress Erik's cheek, Ann said softly, "His heart is in the right place. He loves his boy more than his own life. He would take a bullet for him without blinking. Try to keep that in mind when you speak to him."

Erik glanced down. "I'll try. But Will's made one disastrous decision after another. He doesn't recognize Danny isn't him. Danny possesses more of Yvonne's spirit though he looks so much like William. My brother thinks he knows best, but he botches things so badly when dealing with Danny."

Ann sensed Erik trying to contain his temper over his concern for Dan. Erik had a tell—he tended to refer to Dan as Danny when disturbed. Ann kept the knowledge to herself. Erik could be a hard man to read, like all Broderick men, he hid his softer side from the world, and sometimes that spilled over into family time, too.

Although the hardest Broderick male to interpret was General William Arthur Broderick. Her twin sister's husband could clamp down and hide all emotion. If she didn't know him as well as she did, she would think he hated Dan.

The actions he took in the name of love and protection backfired so often it was not funny. Her sister Yvonne tried so hard to change William's mindset concerning young Danny. But she had not been successful, and more pain ensued for Yvonne, William, Dan, and to some extent, Becca. Dan suffered the most though. Her nephew needed familial support in the worst way. His estrangement from the entire family caused pain for everyone, especially her son Scott. Before the death of Sara, Scott shared an extremely close relationship with Danny despite being eight years older.

Pulling back slightly, Ann said, "I'll go make you some coffee while you contact Will. It's what, about three o'clock in the afternoon in Afghanistan now?"

Erik nodded. "Yes, about that time."

Ann strolled to the door to give Erik privacy. The brothers were close-knit, and when their careers prevented them from communicating pertinent details about family, it stressed them all. The years Dan served in Special Forces had been the most nerve-wracking. They had so little information on Dan over the years and then nothing for the past four. Not one card, one letter, phone call, email, or visit … like Danny dropped off the face of the earth. Perhaps things would change now.

Protecting Family

5

July 15
Afghanistan – Outside General Broderick's Office – 1510 Hours

Corporal Cody Merrill exited the general's office. He needed to inform Major Plouffe the general began to make inquiries. Questions which if he uncovered the truth would spell disaster for both of them. Though fairly certain no answers would ever be found, Merrill still worried.

Over the years he meticulously applied extreme care in covering their tracks. And this past year came with complete relief. With Dan out of the service, Plouffe didn't request him to cover up or supplant false intel to keep General Broderick from discovering Plouffe's activities, or to take advantage of his hobby to ensure things remained buried. Though, the major did require him to collect a bobblehead in January while in Vancouver with the general.

Cody smiled. *Well, it isn't all bad. I demanded and received a handsome fee to acquire that particular bobblehead ... an easy shot which didn't require my expert skills.* He glanced at the phone, wishing Plouffe was still in Kandahar so he could stroll over to his office to inform him, but Plouffe traveled to Ottawa recently, so he must wait until the office cleared out before it would be safe to contact him.

Afghanistan – General Broderick's Office – 1510 Hours

After Merrill closed his door, General William Broderick leaned back in his chair. This whole business with Pletcher weighed heavily on him. The man almost killed Becca. Only Becca's quick thinking and the fact Drake and Jack tailed her saved her life in France. Though upset Pletcher managed to escape, he believed Jack and Drake did the right thing. Becca's safety would always be more important than catching Pletcher.

When Mike reported to him, Becca jumped from the vehicle and rolled, nearly going over a cliff, his heart stopped for several beats. The description of events not only conjured images of his daughter's near-death but also brought forth twenty-seven-year-old memories of the same stretch of road.

Becca leapt out in the precise location Colonel Grasett and Lieutenant Colonel Elkins were killed and he almost died. Luckily, Becca only ended up with a broken wrist, some cuts, and a whole lot of bruises. He came close to crying in front of the men when he reached her hospital room.

His beautiful daughter looked so much like her mother, except her eye color. Becca's eyes were Broderick sapphire blue instead of Loving emerald green. It took all the control he possessed to stop the tears from entering his eyes when he viewed her battered body. He gruffly ordered the men out before gently embracing his girl as she sobbed.

Becca cried herself to sleep that day. William couldn't bring himself to let her go for hours. He cradled his little girl—who was not so little now—in his arms. It brought back so many painful memories. He already bore a pain no parent should ... he lost precious Sara ... his first daughter.

He also lost his son the day the car hit Sara. Her death took all the light from Daniel, and nothing William or the rest of the family tried over the years ever brought it back. It took an outsider to bring back the light to his son— Brody Hunter. But now with Brody gone, all brightness faded from Daniel again. William still feared he might lose Daniel entirely.

Raking his fingers roughly through his military-cropped, blond hair, William growled in frustration. He wanted Pletcher found and dealt with so his wife and daughter could come out of hiding. He worried the situation put undue strain on Yvonne's health because of her Chronic Fatigue Syndrome. CFS tended to be an exasperating, debilitating, and difficult disease.

It took years to diagnose, and they dealt with several doctors—assholes— who suggested all her problems existed in Yvonne's head. Finally, they found Dr. Wentzel, who recognized Yvonne's symptoms and understood CFS was real a physical condition, not a mental one and devised a treatment program.

Sometimes William wondered why Yvonne developed CFS and her identical twin Ann didn't. Not that he wanted Ann to suffer. Over the years Ann had been an invaluable help to Yvonne. Dr. Wentzel explained, although identical at birth, each lived different lives. They traveled to different countries, locales, were exposed to different experiences, stressors, etc. He said many things might've triggered a cellular difference resulting in one suffering from CFS while the other did not.

William wanted Yvonne free of the safe house to help with Daniel. Their son refused to answer his calls. He left a few disjointed voicemails, but his delivery lacked sincerity, and he never got the words he needed out.

The day he called Daniel to tell him about the stolen mail, he screwed up again. He should've started with 'Someone stole your letters, and I started an investigation.' If he began with those words, Daniel likely wouldn't have jumped to the wrong conclusion.

Though he possessed the best of intentions, somehow, he always said the wrong thing. It boggled his mind how he could be so eloquent, clear, and persuasive in all his military dealings, yet became a blithering idiot when he spoke to his son. Guilt for all the poor choices he made regarding Daniel weighed on his shoulders and in his heart.

William wanted to wrap Daniel in his arms, take the pain away, and tell him he loved him and always would. But Daniel wouldn't accept anything of the sort from him. His every overture of affection rebuffed and met with trepidation—an excruciatingly painful experience when Daniel was a child. His boy refused to allow him to hold and comfort him when hurt or sad.

He comprehended all too well he messed up so often over the last nineteen years. Many people tried to tell him, but he remained too stubborn to listen before he ruined the father-son relationship. Now only a general-soldier association remained. With every fiber of his being, William regretted his previous decisions.

Lifting his head, William gazed, at the only photo he kept on his desk. Christmas twenty-two years ago, memories of which he cherished. He held baby Becca in his arms while four-year-old Sara sat on Yvonne's lap, and sitting between him and Yvonne, six-year-old Daniel ... all beaming bright smiles. His young family ... all happy and the last Christmas Daniel ever called him Dad. William deeply regretted using his own upbringing, one regimented and lacking demonstrable emotions, as a model for raising Daniel.

But how this led to Daniel believing he would wish him dead instead of Sara and blame him for Sara's death, still mystified William. Though keenly aware of his part in this problem, pieces neatly assembled, the critical piece of this complex puzzle eluded him. He and Yvonne hoped to one day to find the missing piece and unlock the mystery of Daniel's misconceptions.

He wanted his son back, even though William didn't think he deserved Daniel. William conceded his harsh and distant behavior factored into this quandary, yet still believed he did right by preparing his boy for military life and protecting Daniel after he joined the service. His phone ringing brought him out of his ruminations. Noting the caller ID, he said, "Hello, Erik."

"WILLIAM BRODERICK, YOU BETTER HAVE A DAMNED GOOD REASON WHY YOU PUT DANNY ON BLACKOUT PROTOCOL BUT DIDN'T ASSIGN ANYONE TO COVER HIS SIX. IF MY NEPHEW DIES, IT'LL BE ON YOUR HEAD!" Erik exploded. He didn't mean to, but all the anger below the surface boiled up and he couldn't suppress it from spewing forth.

William surged to his feet concern ripped through him. *Daniel ... die?* He shouted back at his brother, "WHAT THE HELL DO YOU MEAN? IS DANIEL IN DANGER? WHERE DID YOU GET YOUR INFORMATION? WHAT IS THE THREAT? DO YOU KNOW SOMETHING ABOUT PLETCHER?"

Taken aback by Will's reaction, Erik lowered his voice. "William, I don't have a specific threat to Danny. Calm down."

His heart erratically beat at his brother's words, causing William to take a calming breath and lower his volume, too. "Start at the beginning, Erik, and make yourself clear."

"Okay, first. Why did you place Danny on blackout protocol?" Erik asked, trying to control his emotions.

"I didn't. Why do you think he is?" William inquired, bewildered.

Erik paced his study. "Because no one in the family knows where the hell Danny is. You never told us anything. Not a damned word."

William slumped into his chair. "I believe Daniel needed time to sort things out on his own. I didn't want the family—"

Interrupting his brother, Erik shouted, "YOU DIDN'T WANT OUR FAMILY TO WHAT ... COMFORT HIM IN HIS TIME OF NEED? OFFER HIM THE SUPPORT AND PROTECTION HE WOULD DESPERATELY NEED AFTER LOSING BRODY IN SUCH A HORRIFIC WAY?

"WHAT? WHAT DIDN'T YOU WANT US TO DO? TELL ME NOW, AND IT BETTER BE A REASONABLE EXPLANATION. IF IT ISN'T, I SWEAR I'M GONNA BEAT THE SHIT OUT OF YOU THIS TIME!"

The venom in his younger brother's voice burned. William recognized he blundered again. He thought he did right by Daniel. He wouldn't want to be smothered by family if it were him. He would want time alone to come to terms with the loss and put his head back on straight. He sighed dejectedly. "God forgive me, I bungled things again. I'll never make the right choice when it comes to my son. Dammit, Daniel deserves better than me for a father."

Erik sagged into his chair at the dejection in his brother's voice. "Talk to me, Will. Tell me what's going on. I'm aware Danny's in Toronto. Scott found out this morning from a master seaman in his office—totally by accident. Time to clue us all into what is going on."

William blew out a breath. Without Yvonne to confide in the past few months, his mooring lines cut ... he drifted. She steadied him and helped him navigate rough waters with Daniel.

"I never put Daniel on blackout protocol. I only thought he needed time to sort out his emotions without being hounded. Regrettably, his unit, the men Daniel relied on for years all turned their backs on him. I can tell you I wanted to knock some heads when they walked away from him. I never dreamed they would blame him for Hunter's death, but they did.

"None of them would talk to him or even look him in the eye in the hospital and never visited him while he was on suicide watch. I checked the logs and they never once signed in. How could they do that to him? They pissed me off. I wanted to beat some sense into them—but I couldn't. Tom helped me realize they're likely as devastated as Daniel and only need time to cope … but they treated him so poorly and left him alone.

"Things ended badly here for him. The guards I assigned to safeguard Daniel attacked him instead. The bastards tasered him into unconsciousness. And the day Daniel left, I found out several soldiers under my command assaulted him while he packed. Daniel refused to press charges, and the MP in charge of taking the report said Daniel's statement gave the impression he believed he deserved the beating, which emphatically my son did not.

"Several weeks later, a massive brawl in the mess tent occurred, started by Sergeant Srònaich O'Naoimhín, resulted in twenty of my men in the brig and another five in the hospital for several weeks. I was unable to determine the reason for the fight when every single soldier clammed up. Even threatened a few with a dishonorable discharge and it didn't open their mouths.

"There were rumors, but only whispers, this was a case of unit justice—a court-martial offense if true. I didn't press further. I wanted to determine the truth but feared if I pursued the matter, I would lose most of my elite units. I think they sought justice for Daniel's beating.

"But given the sheer number involved in the fracas, I'm not sure who is friend or foe to Daniel. Which is why I refrained from telling anyone where Daniel went … I didn't want him to deal with any unwanted visitors." William took a breath and headed for his coffee pot.

As he poured a cup, he marveled at Erik's control. He hadn't interrupted him once so far. "By chance, back in January, I discovered Daniel's mail had been intercepted for many years. A sniper murdered a former soldier in Vancouver as he composed a letter addressed to me. The man formerly worked in the mailroom in Ottawa and Kandahar.

"I won't go into all the details, but suffice to say, someone coerced him into stealing all of Daniel's correspondence and forwarding it to the blackmailer. He was in the middle of writing the blackguard's name when he was shot. All I have to go on is the first two letters of the name, Pl."

Erik listened, dumbfounded by the news. He didn't agree with William's methods or decisions, but familiar with how his older brother's mind worked, especially when family was threatened, his actions made a weird kind of sense. Will would always protect Dan, but as usual, did an astonishingly inept job.

But this new information about the letters stunned him. Erik interrupted his brother, "Will, someone stole Danny's letters? All of them? How long? For what purpose?"

William sat again and took a long sip of his coffee. "Not everything. At least not at first. Sadly, this occurred the entire time he was deployed. The confession said after three years, the blackmailer told him to burn all correspondence to and from Daniel."

Erik attempted to wrap his head around this development. "Did you tell Danny? Is he aware?"

"I tried to inform him in April, but I put my foot in my mouth. He thinks *I* stopped his mail, and ever since, he's ignored all my calls and voicemails." William leaned back, wearier than his fifty-seven years.

"Why didn't you call me, Mark, or Ryan? We would've visited Danny and explained." Erik stopped. Berating William wouldn't solve anything. Though often misguided, William loved his son.

The full weight of this revelation hit Erik hard. His heart ached for his nephew. "My God, William. Danny must believe we all abandoned him if he hasn't received any of our letters in years. Will, this is bad, very bad. I'm going to arrange for a Broderick invasion. Danny must be told the truth. We would never abandon him. Never."

William recognized and accepted he failed yet again. "Arrange it, and I'll be there, too. Let me know when everyone can swing leave. But …"

"But what?" Erik asked.

"I make a lot of errors with Daniel, but I think only the guys should come. If the whole family descends, it might be too overwhelming for Daniel." William toyed with his coffee mug, waiting for Erik's response.

Erik considered Will's words. "Alright. Just the boys for now. I'll call Mark and Ryan, and they can call their sons and set things in motion. What about the Pletcher threat? Do you think he's the blackmailer?"

"I'm not sure. His name does start with Pl, but there's someone else I'm looking into. I can't say anything over an unsecured line. If it pans out, Special Forces will be rocked to the core." William glanced at his door as a soft rap sounded. "Hang on a minute." To the door, he called out, "Enter."

Lieutenant Mike Galloway, the general's lead security man, entered. He spotted the general on the phone and quickly said, "Sir, I hate to intrude, but this is urgent."

"Erik, I'll call you back later." William hung up and turned his attention to Mike.

Closing the door, Mike strode to the desk. "Drake and Jack think they found a lead on Pletcher. They believe he's in Montreal. One of his aliases booked a flight to Toronto tomorrow, and another of his aliases purchased a ticket to Vancouver as well. With your permission, I'll fly out on the evening transport. Craig will stay here with you, sir."

William nodded. "Partially agreed. Take Craig with you."

"Sir, that leaves you here unprotected. Not happening," Mike protested.

William stood and used his command voice, "That's an order, Lieutenant." His voice dropped to above a whisper, "Mike, my family is more important than my life. Yvonne and Becca are in Vancouver and Daniel's in Toronto. If Pletcher is going after them, you need your whole team. Two can head to each destination if you don't catch him in Montreal."

Mike nodded. "Roger." He turned to leave but stopped and pivoted to face his mentor. "We'll capture Pletcher, sir. If you need to travel, take someone from Hammer's unit. I trust the men in his unit implicitly."

A small grin came to William's face. *Mike is a trusted and good friend.* "Wilco." After Mike left, William sank backward into his chair. It would be helpful to find out if Pletcher was the mail theft culprit. One thing would be resolved, but it wouldn't solve everything.

His gut twisted, concerned he had a major problem in Special Forces. More specifically a Major Plouffe problem. William opened his lower drawer and pulled out a file. He flipped it open and stared at the photo on top of a stack of pictures. This was the last one he received ... different from the other ones delivered to him through the years.

He couldn't stop the tears as they forced their way into his eyes. Daniel and Brody appeared so happy in this snapshot. But the writing across their chests turned his stomach and burned his heart. Written across Brody's ... 'All clear 184,' and across Daniel's ... 'Bite the bullet.'

His voice choked with emotion, William gazed at his son's smiling face. "I promise to get to the bottom of this. You will not bite the bullet. You hear me, Daniel? You will not take your own life ... you are not responsible for Brody's death."

Life is Good

 *6*

Walter Gambrill stopped outside the gym and listened to the banter of Alpha Team. Dan's laughter and a bright smile on his face made Walter grin and validated his belief this team would help Dan through his grief. At one time he feared never to witness his godson's light again. Walter lingered a moment longer, enjoying the sight and sound of Dan's happiness before heading to his office, not wanting to intrude.

As he walked, he sighed with relief. Though it took much longer than he expected, Alpha Team now appeared to be gelling like a fully integrated team. He bore some of the blame because of the way he placed Dan on Pastore's team. Typically, they didn't do tops-down assignments. Forcing Dan on them without their input created the initial hurdle.

Aaron's constant jibes about string-pulling and favoritism augmented the barricade erected between Dan and his team. So did circumstances Walter never considered. Hardy's biased history with Burl and Alejandro caused the entire team to overreact when Hardy unjustly painted Dan with the same brush as those two. As a result, they all became hyper-critical of Dan's every rookie mistake without trying to mentor him. The uncharacteristic behavior shocked Walter … none ever displayed such disrespect to any other rookie.

Walter hated to admit their comportment probably would've continued unchecked until Dan left, if not for his threat to disband their team if they didn't readjust attitudes. He still was not entirely sure what caused them to recognize the lost and grieving soul in their midst, but Walter acknowledged they came too damned close to tipping Dan over the edge with their callousness. Though once Pastore identified the error, how Nick went about rectifying the mistakes pleased Walter.

Well worth the five days off he orchestrated for Alpha Team. An unpleasant yet eye-opening experience for Nick, Jon, Bram, Ray, Lexa, and Loki when they realized the harm they caused Dan. It took a long time to fix because a broken trust had to be rebuilt.

Though grueling for each member at times, Walter remained happy they didn't give up ... because they became the team he initially expected. *Better late than never. And although the weekly meetings with Pastore to check on Dan's acceptance are no longer needed, I will continue to keep tabs from a distance. I won't hesitate to step in again if warranted.*

As he opened his office door, Walter smiled broadly, anticipating a glowing review of Dan in Nick's annual assessment. He would enjoy telling William about Dan's smile and laughter in his next update. *Today is a grand day.*

TRF HQ – Briefing Room – 6:55 a.m.

Nick finished reviewing the files and closed them. He swung the chair and stared out at the city, not focusing on anything in particular as he mulled over the past year with the rookie. Dan made decent progress in transitioning from elite soldier to urban constable.

Their world was not black and white—shoot the bad guy. No, they worked in a gray world where the subject was often a regular Joe experiencing the worst moments of his life and making poor choices. However, in their grayish world, they still must follow clear-cut rules of engagement and make split-second decisions. They were not judges and followed specific protocols, which sometimes required them to end a life. Dan took lethal action several times in those challenging situations.

The Playful Minds Daycare call came to mind—Dan's first lethal with the team. Nick perceived circumstances which required his rookie to take a fatal shot while in the presence of children, hit Dan the hardest. Nick understood incidents involving kids were tough on the entire team, especially when they ended in a death, but he noted Dan became very quiet after those calls.

One area I need to probe to make sure Dan isn't unduly affected by that type of call. He is still hard to read, but now Dan allows emotion to show sometimes, it is getting a bit easier. And the smile on his face this morning ... fantastic ... wonder if there is a specific reason or is it because he recognizes we want him on our team?

His reflections shifted, and he grinned thinking about what an asset Dan became to their team. Nick couldn't imagine a team without Dan now. A one-eighty shift from his and the whole team's attitudes, a year ago. The transition had not been easy ... more like walking through hell. Everyone made mistakes and took a long time to rectify their errors. Luckily, Bram and Lexa forged a path the rest of them followed.

Bram made the first connection with Dan. He recognized something the others failed to notice. Dan's emotions often played in his eyes, even when his expression remained unreadable. Bram's particular brand of fatherly gentleness, born from his nature and the fact he had four little girls helped Bram create a link to Dan none of them had been able to emulate … yet.

Lexa, the heart of their team, found an effective way to chip away at Dan's shield … much like one of her remodeling projects. She chiseled out a hole and installed a window so they could all view the man behind the shield. Ever the renovator, Lexa set about restoring the wounded soul in their midst, helping them all to build a stronger foundation.

Though it took longer than he anticipated to bring Dan into their fold, and it still burned knowing he caused Dan so much pain, he accepted what Bram pointed out to him over the past few months. Soul-deep agony surrounded by impenetrable walls were not the result of a few months of mistrust or callous words and actions. Those thick walls took years to craft and reinforce.

But today Dan came in wearing a genuine smile. And the rookie appeared more relaxed and rested than ever. *Did we finally breach Dan's walls? Does our rookie now accept he is a member of the family? Does Dan realize he belongs?* Nick sincerely hoped he did.

The team filtered into the room for the start of shift briefing bringing Nick out of his contemplations. With no warrant calls on today's docket, he decided to make it a patrol day to create an opportunity to talk privately with Dan. Nick noted the smile remained firmly affixed to Dan's face as he and Loki teased Lexa about her Jeep not starting.

For a moment, he thought Lexa might punch both of them, but then she laughed as she pestered Loki about his choice of car. She suggested he might do better with the ladies if he owned a motorcycle like Dan or a truck like Ray. Loki's retorted at least he didn't drive a minivan like Bram which pulled the father of four into the friendly banter.

Nick grinned as he surveyed his family. *Life is good—really good.* He glanced up at Jon, who settled in beside him. "One big happy family."

Jon nodded. "Yep, about time. It's been a quiet six-weeks. Not a single injury for Wile E. Coyote."

Nick chuckled. The nickname fit Dan well, but he still preferred Dantastic. The rookie was truly a fantastic person.

All thoughts and conversations stopped as the klaxon alarm sounded and Tia called over the loudspeaker, "Alpha Team, critical call, shots fired." The team rushed to gear up as Tia continued to provide details. "911 reports several gunshots at Bang Fitness on Bay View Ave. I'm sending the full address to your phones. There are at least two hostages according to the caller. The subject is an unknown male."

As Loki put on his headset, he quipped, "You gotta be kidding me. Shots fired at a place called Bang Fitness. Talk about irony."

Snickers could be heard from most of the team. Loki never failed to lighten the tense mood with some witty, or not so witty, remark.

Tia stifled her chuckle. She loved Loki's sense of humor. *He's so sweet, too bad I don't date cops.* "Units are on scene and establishing up a perimeter. Constable Landau said three witnesses are available for you to talk with when you arrive."

"Thanks, Tia." Nick then directed, "Lexa and Ray, find out what you can from the witnesses. Find out if they can identify the subject, hostages, and what prompted this. Loki—"

Loki preempted Boss. "Get blueprints and tap into the cameras if they exist. Got it."

Nick loved how well his team worked together.

Outside Bang Fitness — 7:15 a.m.

Arriving on scene, three black SUVs and a command truck came to a rapid halt. Lexa and Ray headed off to question the witnesses as Loki stepped into the back of the command truck. Nick engaged with Constable Landau to obtain an update on the current situation.

Jon rounded the back of an SUV to gear up as he handed out tactical assignments. "Bram, need you to determine the best entry point. Dan, you're Zulu One. Find a position then locate the subject after you've set up and determined the number of hostages."

A chorus of, "Copy," sounded through the headsets.

Dan rapidly assessed a myriad of conditions as he scanned the businesses across the street from the gym to determine which one would give him the best vantage. With the fitness center's floor to ceiling windows, visibility inside shouldn't be a problem from a second story, but the roofs were too high to give a proper view into the ground floor gym.

He picked a business with windows on the second floor, which opened. The position would give him decent visibility to the entire gym, and if he had to take a shot, he could do so without damaging the business' windows. Dan slung his Remi case over his shoulder and grabbed his kit from the back of the SUV before sprinting across the street.

Relax Now

As he strode in, the intriguing name, Relax Now, made sense to Dan ... a massage therapy spa. Dan noted several customers and realized patrol officers still needed to clear this business.

The looks the patrons gave him as he entered were priceless. Dan came to understand most people tended to be a little awed by a TRF officer in full tactical gear. The team liked to joke it was because they wore the 'cool pants.' Dan received a few smiles and come-hither expressions from the ladies in the reception area, not that he usually noticed because focused on his duty.

His short golden blond hair, intense sapphire blue eyes, and rugged features had that effect on women—even without the TRF uniform. And today, all that was enhanced by a beautiful smile plastered to his face. Dan remained mostly clueless to the effect his handsomeness had on women—devastating.

Dan calmly informed the manager of his need, and she immediately granted access. A constable arrived behind Dan to secure the building which gave Dan a sense of relief, having someone cover his six so he could concentrate fully on the situation.

So far, he had not run into anyone he knew from when he was in the Fourteenth Division. *Not sure what would happen if I do. Would they even remember me? Ten years is ancient history. An ugly time in my life—one I would rather not recall at all, but especially not today—I'm happy and don't want to spoil my mood.*

As he set up the rifle, Dan listened to the chatter of the team, keeping abreast of the developments, but he couldn't keep his mind from wandering a bit to how very happy he was today … doing something he loved, helping people, and he belonged to a family. Belonging felt wonderful.

It had been a long road to this point. He was not to the point that he truly trusted everyone, but they accepted him. They allowed him to remain aloof and didn't push him to open up, which boded well for him to share with them eventually. He connected with Bram, and talking to him was comfortable.

And Lexa, Sexy Lexie, yeah, exciting with potential. Though he still didn't know where things were headed—they needed to talk, but last night was more than he hoped for. To touch her, to kiss her, and hold her again … yeah, he was happy, really happy. Dan tuned back in as Loki spoke.

Outside Bang Fitness – Command Truck

"Sorry, Boss, no cameras in the building. The owner wants to make sure people don't feel uncomfortable when working out. Apparently, many people feel self-conscious about video cameras taping them while they sweat.

"Doubt our Lexa would mind. Neither would Dantastic. He would probably go shirtless to show off his six-pack abs and he-man biceps. A true camera hog," Loki joked.

Relax Now Across from Bang Fitness

Dan lightly laughed at Loki's comment. He liked the techie. Sometimes Loki could be over the top, but he made him laugh a lot lately. Laughing helped heal his soul. "Loki, you're just jealous I can bench more than you."

Nick smiled. "A little more focus now, boys."

Dan opened the window to scan the gym's interior with the high-powered scope. "Boss, Jon, found a spot with a decent view of the whole gym. No blind spots. Got a twenty on the subject. He's against the green wall, about mid-way between front and back, near the free weights. He is pointing a handgun at the head of the female hostage kneeling in front of him. A second hostage, male, also on knees, is facing the female hostage. No additional hostages inside."

As Dan lay down on his stomach on the massage table to line up the shot, Nick replied, "Good info, Dan. Let us know if anything changes."

"Copy. I've got the solution," Dan informed them as he settled in to watch and wait as his teammates—no, his family, worked their magic. His professional sniper mask slid into place, but there a faint hint of a smile appeared ... something which had never been there in all of his life when readying for a shot.

Bang Fitness

7

"Subject's name is Clive Parch, a personal trainer here until last week. According to the assistant manager, he fired and banned Clive from the gym because a woman accused him of unwanted sexual advances and inappropriate touching during training sessions," Lexa shared.

Loki couldn't help himself as he responded, "And more innuendos for Bang Fitness. I could sooooo have a field day with this."

As Soft snickers came from several teammates, Nick said, "Jon, let's slowly move inside and gain Clive's attention to start a dialog." Nick entered with Ray and Jon providing cover with the shields. Bram procured a position allowing him to cover the single rear exit as a precaution.

"Loki, join Bram in the back since there's no techy stuff for you to play with here," Jon directed.

As he entered the building, Nick quietly asked Lexa, "Did you identify the hostages yet?"

"Yes, the woman is Lori Plane. She's the one who lodged the complaint against Clive. The male hostage is Neal Johnson, Lori's boyfriend.

"One witness I spoke with is a former client of Clive's and indicated Clive exhibited violent mood swings recently. Last time he worked out with the trainer, about two weeks ago, Clive got mad at him for doing nine reps instead of ten and threw a free weight at his head. Missed him, but afterward, he refused to work with Parch again.

"The last witness said this is out of character for Clive. He believes Clive's been under stress while preparing for a weight lifting competition. Said the trainer's been bulking up fast, thinks the accusations are false, and Clive is upset at being banned from the center so close to the competition."

"Why does he believe they're false?" Nick asked.

"Says Clive doesn't swing that way, and Lori's been hitting on a lot of the guys here trying to make Neal jealous," Lexa expounded.

"The instant muscles might present a problem, Boss. Clive's as big as a freaking house, bigger than Bram, not normal. Wonder if he's taking steroids? Might explain the anger issues," Dan suggested.

Bram relayed, "If that is true, talking to him will be difficult. An officer in my Division years ago got into steroids—messed him up bad. His rage would go from zero to sixty in the blink of an eye. He went off the deep end one day because one of the guys borrowed a pen from his desk. Took four men to restrain him, and three ended up injured—one required a trip to the emergency room. Careful in there."

"Good to know," Nick said before starting negotiations with Clive.

Relax Now Across from Bang Fitness

As Dan observed through the scope, noting Clive gravitated all over the place emotionally. He had an inkling how this would end ... *badly*. Clive swung from red to yellow and back to red with amazing speed. Nothing Boss said seemed to be working.

The woman, Lori, appeared frightened. Tears ran down her cheeks as she gazed helplessly at her boyfriend in front of her. Dan couldn't view Neal's face but empathized with the emotions the guy might be experiencing.

Sometimes people end up in circumstances with no control and needed someone to help. That's why TRF exists. Dan smiled again, slipping slightly out of sniper mode. Not because of this situation, but because he was here with Alpha Team and they would do everything in their power to ensure Lori, Neal, and even Clive came out of this mess unharmed. He hoped Boss would be successful in talking Clive down.

Sadly, right after his thought, Clive escalated once again, hitting Lori on the head with the back of his hand and shoving her down while lunging forward and pointing the pistol straight at Boss' head.

"PapaGolf," Jon called.

With no hesitation, Dan took the shot. Delays could cost an innocent or teammate their life. Of all the snipers in TRF Dan's reaction, time was quickest. Hell, he had been the fastest shooter in all of Special Forces during his time with them. His father started his training at six-years-old.

At the age when most kids engaged in sports, played video games, watched TV, or rode bikes in the park, he spent hours upon hours at the rifle range with the general. By the time he reached eleven, if he didn't hit the targets where and when required, his strict father meted out brutal punishment.

Clive crashed to the ground, a direct hit, leaving no chance of a twitch of a finger on the gun. Dan rarely missed. In fact, he couldn't recall the last time he did. However, Dan remembered with clarity the day he wished with every fiber in his being he failed to hit his mark. All traces of levity vanished as memories of Brody's death flooded into his mind.

"Subject neutralized," Jon softly called into the headset.

Dan lay stock still, his breath held, as the pain of taking another life and remembrance of Brody washed over and through him, carving one more line in his wretched soul. He hated taking life but recognized the necessary outcome in certain conditions. But that didn't make it any easier. He ended the lives of so many. Death became all too familiar to him—but never easy.

The general was a cruel bastard who ordered him into nonstop missions. Other members in his unit got downtime, but not him. While they took a break from the horrors of fighting terrorism, he would be assigned to other active units ... always operations with a high death count. Sometimes Dan wondered how many lives he could end without completely losing his soul.

He kept tally of the exact number of people he killed, though he would never share the figure with anyone. Too painful to allow others a glimpse of how much blood stained his hands. It would color their perception of him and the person he desperately wanted to be.

Breathe, remember to breathe, Dan reminded himself. He sucked in a deep shuddering breath then harshly blew it out.

"You okay, Dan?" Jon quired, catching the ragged breaths. He understood the effect of taking lethal action. The first breath after always burned. Took time to clear his head too, even if he saved an innocent. Jon remained amazed, and frankly a little scared, at how rapidly Dan righted himself afterward.

"Be right out. I'm fine," Dan managed to reply smoothly. The last two words seemed to be his standard reply. It was true. Dan didn't like to lie. Fine was an absolutely true statement according to his definition. Instead of the simple word fine, his FINE meant Fucked up, Insecure, Neurotic, and Emotional. Who wouldn't be FINE after ending a life?

His post-shoot mask slipped firmly in place as Dan pushed the pain and the image of Clive's eyes down, down deep, into the dark place he built to keep those things locked away. He grabbed his kit and Remi before headed out to the Nonpartisan Review Board Agent who would be waiting for him. He hated the interviews with a passion. They required him to relive the event in excruciating detail.

Dan understood the legal and ethical necessity for NRB interviews. It kept the police force accountable and ferreted out inappropriate use of lethal force, but the process could be brutal, and sometimes it became difficult to hide his emotions behind his stoic mask.

Some NRB agents acted with sensitivity, at least others indicated they did. So far, Dan had not experienced understanding. Agent Thornbuckle and Agent Donner conducted all his interviews thus far. Thornbuckle tended to treat the inquiry as a formality to validate the auto-scripter account. He stuck to only facts with Thornbuckle, no emotions dredged up.

However, as in all professions, some people were assholes. Agent Richard Donner belonged to this category and relished making the interview as painful as possible. Unfortunately, Dan most often ended up with Donner. He didn't like the guy and truly believed Richard lived up to his name, a real Dick.

As Dan trotted down the stairs, he wondered if today would be a Dick day. Thoughts of his first lethal experience with TRF came to mind ... his first encounter with Agent Dick Donner. At the time, Jon still treated him like a pariah, and they butted heads often. Only on the job for three weeks, Jon had not explained nor did he ask Jon about the after-action procedures, so he possessed no guidance on what to expect.

Dan didn't realize he was allowed a lawyer. No one told him—certainly not Dick. Agent Dick told him to strip to his boxers and sneered at his shocked expression. He never anticipated the need to remove his uniform and was glad he had not gone commando that day. Now aware of the process, he always wore undergarments while at work.

After disrobing, he sat shivering in the ice-cold room, answering the same questions repeatedly for hours. Dan decided Dick got his jollies by listening to sickening details. He kept asking for more descriptive words to 'paint the picture.' Questions which couldn't possibly relate to determining justification for a legally sanctioned use of lethal force.

His lawyer, Dale Gibbson, stormed into the room three hours later and unleashed a tirade on Donner. Gibbson lodged a formal complaint against Dick when he found out Donner failed to follow basic protocol. Gibbson had been appalled Donner forced him to participate in the interview in only his underwear. The session ended swiftly after Gibbson arrived.

Dale's number resided in his phone contacts now, and Dan called him on the way to NRB. Though unsure how Dale managed to always arrive at NRB before him, Dan appreciated having the lawyer in his corner.

Outside Bang Fitness

As he exited Relax Now, Dan chuckled slightly as he recalled how Gibbson made it clear he thought Donner forcing him to be interviewed in only boxers equated to cruel and brutal behavior. What Dan never shared with Dale or anyone else for that matter, he wished all the *cruel or brutal* interrogations he endured had been as cozy.

The faded scars covering his torso were a visual testament to truly merciless interrogations. Dan sighed when he spotted Agent Donner waiting for him. *Shit, fate hates me, Dick again.*

As he headed for the NRB vehicle, Dan began to prepare himself mentally to deal with the prick. Most people would believe the worst scars were the visible ones inflicted by the terrorists, but his worst ones, the multitude of agonizing scars on his heart and soul remained invisible to human eyes.

"Aw crap, my head's all over the place today," Dan spoke his private thought aloud as he approached Donner to hand over his weapons.

"What's that, Dano?" Jon glanced over as Dan neared the agent, worried by Dan's comment. *Damn, he got Agent Donner again—Dan always seems to draw the damned prick.* Jon cringed as he recalled Dan's first interview. He failed to enlighten his rookie as to the administrative procedure, and as a result, the over-zealous agent got away with mistreating Dan.

Realizing he voiced his thought, to deflect, Dan flippantly said with a hint of sarcasm, "Said nothing, Jon. And hey, you're not supposed to talk to the subject officer."

"Okay, so you're following protocol today, Danny boy," Jon glibly retorted trying to lighten Dan's mood.

"Told you before not to call me Danny boy," Dan laughed.

"Oh, so boy is okay, but Danny boy isn't. I'll make note," Loki interjected.

"Lexa's the only one who's allowed to refer to him as Danny boy. Something about her Irish heritage," Bram joked.

Jon grinned. "Bram, don't you dare start warbling '*Oh, Danny Boy.*' Leave the singing to Lexa. At least she can carry a tune."

"Don't bring me into this, boys." Lexa put extra emphasis on boys. "I'm over here, minding my business. And I won't be singing for anyone of you." Lexa secretly admitted she would like to serenade him—someday.

"Easy children, settle down. Dan, we'll see you for debrief at HQ when you're done with NRB. You did good," Nick said as he took off his cap and rubbed his hand over his face … attempting to figure out how he lost Clive. Replacing his hat, Nick moved towards the command truck.

The good-natured banter brought the smile back to Dan's face, happy to belong somewhere again. About to respond, the retort stilled on his lips when Tia's voice came over the headset.

"Alpha Team, critical call, shots fired, alarms triggered, Central Bank in mid-town," Tia reported.

During the exchange, Jon strode over to where Dan stood with the NRB agent. They would need Dan for now. Jon adopted his sternest face and addressed Agent Donner. "My officer is needed in the field. Bag his gloves and rifle. When we're finished, you can have him back."

Although rare, an establish precedence existed for this course of action. Critical calls and team safety trumped NRB interviews. Donner's demeanor changed, appearing none too happy with the situation, but he acquiesced taking the Remi and gloves only, leaving Dan with his unused sidearm. Donner glared at Broderick's back as he and the rest of Alpha Team ran to the SUVs to head to the next call.

Central Bank

 *8*

Alpha Team sped toward Central Bank in mid-town. Cross-talk via the headsets remained minimal as everyone mentally stowed the last call to put full focus and energy into the current one. They did this often. Sometimes on a bad day, they responded to three or four critical incidents in a row.

Each used their own method to process and prepare, although some achieved mental readiness quicker than others. Lexa glanced at Dan in the passenger seat, wondering how he changed gears so fast. His process appeared as simple and quick as simultaneously closing one door and opening another.

She started covertly studying Dan shortly after the team's heart-to-heart discussion regarding Dan back in October. Lexa couldn't believe nine months passed since the painful meeting. Everyone except Dan showed up at Boss' home at eight a.m. as instructed. When asked about Dan's absence, Boss merely said he exempted the rookie. And to this day, none of them shared the details of their tête-à-tête about Dan with him.

Boss started the meeting by eyeing each of them then stated, *'We have a serious problem with team dynamics.'* After taking responsibility for the problem and for allowing it fester, Boss pointed to several boxes and said they would be going through transcripts. He wanted them to pinpoint their mistakes interacting with Dan and make a plan to resolve the issues.

That launched what became a distressing yet illuminating examination of how dreadfully they dealt with their rookie ever since Gambrill inserted him on their team. The complex assignment took five days to analyze what they did wrong, process wide-ranging emotions, and devise a strategy to fix their relationships with Dan. Loki, with his twisted sense of humor, dubbed the session *'The Proper Care and Feeding of Dantastic'* discussion.

Lexa still recalled Boss' words, *'Listen closely. We are human, and we make mistakes, but we help strangers every single day. Let's do what we do best and save one of our own. We can salvage this. It won't be quick, and it won't be easy, but I believe in all of you. We are more than a team … we are family. Our family needs to support our newest member through his time of grief and help him realize he belongs. Because if we don't, we will lose an amazing person.'*

Boss is right. Dan is amazing. He is also prophetic. Resolving the issue took nine months … neither easy nor quick. Though Dan's smile in the gym this morning indicates something changed with Dan.

I hope his cheerfulness isn't only due to the mind-blowing sex we shared last night—although to be honest, it probably played a role. She remained uncertain whether their encounter should be limited to a one-time event or should she allow herself to find out where this might lead, but her little devil corrected her, *"A two-time occurrence. Go for it. What do you have to lose?"*

Lexa breathed out, "Everything."

Dan glanced over at Lexa. "What did you say?"

"Nothing. You ready for this so soon after a lethal?" Lexa deftly changed the topic.

"Yeah, nothing I haven't done before."

Lexa furrowed her brows. "What?"

Dan rolled his eyes up to the SUV's ceiling. *Can't believe I allowed that little nugget to slip out.* His gaze shifted back to Lexa. "I only meant I have experience going from one mission to another with no break. I'm fine to take another shot if necessary."

Flicking her eyes to Dan then back to the road, Lexa began to wonder about his time in the military. *Yeah, I guess with his time in Special Forces, taking more than one lethal shot in a day would be routine. What were his days like?*

She wanted to know more about him. Sure, she learned tidbits about him from their dinners, but Dan divulged little, if anything, from his past. They mostly chatted about current events and the other members of the team.

Her mind wandered to their romp in the dark. A warm flush crept into her cheeks as she recalled the magic of his hands. She wished there had been more light in her room. She wanted to view his whole body and drink in his sexy masculinity. Lexa blew out a breath and stopped her inappropriate thoughts. *I'm on the job … now is not the time to be thinking about Dan's hot body.*

Lexa came back to the present, catching only the final piece Tia shared about the current situation, "… and the people who got out said they appeared to be military types."

Chiding herself for being so distracted she missed Tia's details, Lexa muted her headset, bit her lower lip, and gave Dan a pleading expression. "I didn't catch everything. Recap for me, please." Then unmuted her headset.

Dan flashed her a lopsided grin and winked. "So Boss, if I got everything, there are three subjects, possibly military trained, armed with automatic weapons, four hostages, one is a baby, so no CS gas, only one way in and out of the bank, five people exited before the subjects herded the hostages to the back, and no one harmed so far. Did I miss anything?" he finished as they pulled to a stop.

Lexa smiled and mouthed a silent 'thank you,' then cringed as Jon said, "No, Dano, didn't miss a thing. Concise recap though for anyone not paying close attention."

Dan winked at Lexa once more as they both exited the SUV. Lexa wanted to growl at him. It was as if Dan perused her mind, and her thoughts betrayed her. *Argh! Dan gets under my skin like no other man ever. This doesn't bode well for me at all.* Lexa headed straight to where patrol officers gathered the five witnesses, stuffed her personal mindset down, and refocused on her job.

Outside Central Bank — Command Truck — 9:40 a.m.

"You know what I need," Nick stated as he entered the command truck.

Loki grinned. "Eyes inside in two minutes, Boss. Hopefully with sound. Just gotta hack their security password unless there's a manager who can provide it to me quicker." Loki started to make the connections to the feeds.

"Sorry, Loki. I checked with the five who got out, no managers, only customers," Lexa informed him.

Stepping halfway into the truck, Jon said, "Nick, I want Dan covering you if you go in. If these guys are military, he might be the best one to connect. Give him a chance for field training with you right there to guide him."

Jon suggested it partly for the stated reason and partially because Dan took a lethal shot in the previous call. And no matter how swiftly Dan appeared to process the associated emotions, Dan's comment about his mind being all over the place rang in Jon's head.

Though unlikely Nick would hand off negotiations to Dan, it would be a safer place for him now, especially if the subjects wore tan fatigues and or possessed green eyes. If Jon could prevent it, he would never again put Dan in the position which arose last October when Dan froze taking the shot during the Mulberry Apartments call.

Ray perceived Jon's suggestion made Loki nervous before glancing over at Jon and Boss, waiting for Boss' answer. Ray didn't think negotiating would be the best idea for Dan ... the rookie required more training. When Boss didn't answer right away, Ray chuckled, hiding his uneasiness. "Jon, you do recall, Dan called me an asshat and failed to listen to my demands in our last negotiating drill."

Nick narrowed his gaze on Ray, miffed he would bring up the faux pas, afraid it might shake Dan's confidence. Nick decided he needed to show Dan he believed in his ability. "Sounds, like an excelled plan. Dan understands military jargon. I might need some help."

Damn! Once the words left his mouth, Ray realized how his disparagement might undermine Dan's budding skills, though Ray genuinely worried about throwing the rookie to the wolves before he gained enough competency. Doing so might destroy Dan should he fail. Ray hoped Boss would be able to negotiate. Still reproving himself, Ray directed his attention to the monitors, captured an image of each subject, and began a facial recognition search.

Outside Central Bank

Dan blushed at Ray's words as he and Bram grabbed shields and trotted over to a position near the entrance. He sucked at negotiating, and he feared he would botch things the day he must do it in the field, but if Boss told him to take over, he would do his best. Dan only hoped his effort would be sufficient and didn't result in any deaths. The one factor shoring his confidence in attempting mediation is Boss would be with him and assist if he faltered.

Bram patted Dan on the shoulder. "Don't listen to Ray. He's only joking. Relax, you'll do fine if need be."

As Jon exited the command truck, he scanned the area for Zulu positions. "Ray, Loki can run facial rec. I need you to take over gathering information from the witnesses. Lexa, grab your Remi. With Dan inside I need you for Zulu Two. We've got a baby inside, so we need someone covering each subject."

Ray and Lexa responded, "Copy," and executed Jon's commands.

Inside Central Bank

Three men anxiously paced, randomly pointing weapons at the hostages. One stopped and peered at their leader. Due to his damaged larynx, his voice came out in an eerie, wraithlike whisper, "This will work, right?"

"Yes, Marty," Jason reassured.

The third man's hands tremored nearly uncontrollably. Garth's voice quavered as his hands shook. "This better work. I'll make it work. I can't take anymore." He headed for the mother with a babe in her arms.

A young mother cradled her infant closer, trying desperately to protect her child from the terror of this situation as the trembling felon approached. She only came in to deposit a gift from her mother. The tidy sum would add to her daughter's college fund. Tears flowed as she wondered if her baby would have a future, or would this be their last day on this earth. She assumed the jumpy men came to steal money for drugs.

The bank manager, a slightly portly man with a receding hairline, four kids, and a loving wife, put himself between the mother with the baby and the shaking gunman. "Please, don't hurt us."

Jason turned and shouted, "BE QUIET!" He waved his gun at his hostages. "No speaking, be silent, and this will be over soon." A twinge of regret crossed his mind at the fear on their faces, but they really didn't know fear ... certainly not like he did. *I must do this ... no other options exist.*

Marty's quaked as he reached for a woman who reminded him of his mother. He almost apologized to her, but his resolve strengthened. *This will be over soon.* "Over here. On your knees," he rasped out. Speaking still hurt, every word an effort. Marty rubbed his throat. His voice would never be the same, but that wouldn't matter before long.

Garth left the woman and baby where they were and took a position behind them. His eyes darted in every direction as he wiped beads of sweat off his forehead. *Nowhere is safe. They can be anywhere—anywhere. They'll come for me again. I won't survive. This is my only alternative. At least this way nothing is unknown.* He breathed out an unsteady breath. *So tired—so very tired, but everything will be over soon ... no other way out of this hellish life.*

Jason studied the bank's manager. *What a comfortable life he lives. Fat and happy, while I ... we ... paid the price for their easy lives.* The ever-present anger surged in him as the ringing phone announced TRF's presence. *Time to make this happen.*

Outside Central Bank

Nick engaged with the subjects. The list of their demands sounded like something out of a B movie. Unrealistic and if the circumstances were different, they would've been considered comical. But Nick wasn't laughing. He found no humor in the present situation.

When no additional details could be gleaned from the witnesses outside, Ray rejoined Loki in the command truck. They identified the subjects as Corporal Jason York, Private Garth Summers, and Private Marty Green. Jason, the one speaking with Nick, appeared to be the leader of the trio.

Dan, Bram, and Nick cautiously moved towards the doors of the bank when Jason agreed to allow them in. Nick's mind worked a mile a minute. Something didn't seem right about the picture, so he waited for more information from Ray and Loki before he went in with Bram and Dan.

"They all came home from Afghanistan within the past three weeks, but no additional data on their service records are immediately available. We need proper authorization to access their files," Ray stated before requesting, "Tia, can you work on that please?"

"Will do, but it might take some time," Tia responded.

"Tia, forward the info to Loki when it comes. Ray, I need you to grab another shield, make your way into the bank, and stay closer to the hostages if possible. Be ready to cover them if necessary." Jon continued to give orders, "Dan and Bram, your primary subject will be Jason. Mine is Marty. Lexa, you focus on Garth. Bram, if Nick turns negotiations over to Dan, I want you concentrated on Jason."

"Copy," each replied. Ray rushed out of the truck, obtained a shield before joining Boss, Bram, and Dan at the entrance. The quartet made their way into the bank.

Worse Than Bombs or Death

9

Nick continued to talk to Jason, trying many angles to connect with the angry man haphazardly waving the gun. He noted the other two shook and appeared nervous. Something didn't add up, and Nick wondered for a moment if someone forced these men to rob the bank.

But Jason escalated and waved his gun again as he yelled, "YOU DON'T GET IT. YOU'VE NEVER BEEN TO HELL ON EARTH. THE THINGS THEY DO TO YOU … YOU'LL NEVER UNDERSTAND."

It clicked in his head. *I'm dealing with something else—PTSD. These soldiers only arrived home three weeks ago.* Nick pitched his voice soft and calm, "You are right. I have never been in the army. If you lower your weapons, I can find someone you can talk to who understands what you went through. Can you put the gun down, Jason?"

Desperate, Jason's voice vacillated between shouting and a normal level. "NO, NO, I CAN'T, NICK. YOU DON'T UNDERSTAND. YOU CAN'T. YOU WEREN'T IN THE MILITARY. You don't got any concept of what we endured. You sit in your cushy homes and leave us to deal with all the shit on our own. YOU WILL NEVER COMPREHEND!"

Jason discerned they didn't understand. *All they want to do is talk, and I need them to take action. Why aren't they shooting? What can I do to get them to end our suffering?*

Nick glanced at Dan, and with a tilt of his head, he asked, "Do you think you might be able to connect?"

Shit, I don't want to do this. Dan ignored his thought, and with a slight nod, he answered in the affirmative. He drew a deep, steadying breath, gradually exhaling to settle his nerves and slow his racing heart.

Nick inched over to Dan, and they switched positions with Nick taking the shield and raising his weapon while Dan lowered his. Bram took over, aiming at Jason completing a seamless transition of roles.

His anxiety increasing, Jason tapped his fingers on his thigh. *How do I make them shoot?* When Jason returned his gaze to the cops, he recognized the older man now stood behind the shield pointing a gun at him, and a young blond cop now inched his way out from the protective barrier holding his empty hands palms outward. *Why did they switch up? What's going on. Shit! Marty and Garth are counting on me to make this happen.* He started to raise his gun.

"Jason, my name is Dan Broderick, I'm also with the TRF. I would like to talk with you and try to resolve this, so no one is harmed." Dan took a slow breath in and out to calm the adrenaline coursing through him and glanced to Boss who gave him an encouraging smile. "Can you tell me what you need?"

"Like I told the other guy, you can't understand. You don't get what it's like over there. YOU'LL NEVER UNDERSTAND!" Jason repeated.

Garth's eyes darted to Jason. *He is not making this happen.* He swallowed his fear. *I'm going to have to do this. I have no other choice.*

Marty painfully whispered, "Jason, do it."

Jason began shaking as his memories overwhelmed him. This was too much, too much. His voice shook with raw anguish, and a good deal of anger as he blurted out, "Terrorists captured us … they did things inhuman things. You think the only issues we need to deal with are dying buddies, being blown up, or shot. But there are things much worse … you don't know … so you can't help. No one can."

Dan listened and comprehended. *But how to help them? Jason isn't thinking. Clearly, none of the three are.* They all possessed desperate, haunted eyes Dan knew all too well. Those same eyes stared back at him from a mirror for months. Dan suspected they wanted to die, to force the team to shoot them— to commit suicide by cop. *How can I stop this from happening?*

He realized he was the only one on the team who had even a snowball's chance in hell of honestly connecting with these guys. *Crap, I don't want to do what I must do. Isn't gonna be pretty and I'm gonna pay for this for a while.* Dan hesitated, hoping to come up with another solution but found none. Baring his soul would be the only possible way to save them.

"You're wrong. I do understand." Dan fortified himself to continue.

Nick hissed. "Dan, the first rule, don't lie."

Dan shook his head slightly in answer to Nick, but spoke to Jason, "I work for TRF now, but before, I was Master Corporal Daniel Broderick, with Special Forces. Spent six years in Kandahar. I am well aware there are things worse than bombs and death. Talk to me, buddy, I want to help. What you're doing isn't your only option."

Jason remained silent for a moment then turned and stared at Dan trying to judge the veracity of his statement. "You were over there? Really? You are too damned young and innocent to have served, but even if you did, you never endured what we did."

His hands shook violently as the memories of what the terrorists did to him flooded his mind. Jason motioned to Marty and Garth. "We came from different units, but all ended up in the same hellhole. They slaughtered my unit in front of me then the bastards decided to keep me alive and torture me. Fed me only a handful of maggoty gruel and two glasses of water each day. They beat the shit out of me daily. Punches and kicks—so many, no place on my body left unbruised."

He shifted his gun then continued, "Then Marty showed up and three days later Garth. The bastards are vicious and inhumane. They didn't believe us when we said we had no useful information. We didn't. We're just grunts. They didn't care, they only laughed, then beat the crap out of us. After four weeks, we were rescued."

Pain and anger flared in Jason's face as he sneered, "Ha, rescued. That's a screwed-up word. I wasn't rescued—part of me is still there. I can't sleep. I keep remembering every hit, every debasing thing they did to me. You can't understand what it's like to live wondering if today is the day they will finally kill you and praying they would, just to end the pain."

Jason paced back and forth three steps, agitated again. Stopped, peered at Dan as he yelled, "YOU CAN'T UNDERSTAND!"

"Yes, yes, I can," Dan said, almost too softly.

Still staring directly at the constable, Jason raged, yelling at the top of his lungs, "HOW? HOW CAN YOU? YOU NEVER HAD TO DEAL WITH THAT." Gesturing at Dan with his free hand, Jason's voice fluctuated high and low, "Look at your untouched face—NOT A MARK ON IT!" His hand went to his scared face. "See mine? I BEAR THE MARKS. THEY CUT ME FOR FUN AND LAUGHED AT MY SCREAMS."

Jason's hand wildly swung toward Marty, "And Marty … they choked him so hard they crushed his larynx. And the things they did to Garth … I can't even begin to describe the inhumanity of what the sick bastard did to him with needles. THERE'S TOO MUCH LIGHT IN YOUR EYES FOR YOU TO HAVE EXPERIENCED ANYTHING LIKE WHAT WE WENT THROUGH. HOW DARE YOU SAY YOU UNDERSTAND!"

Dan's eyes shifted to Garth for a brief second as the visage of THE ONE'S face … the bastard who plunged red-hot needles into his stomach assaulted him. The sadistic bastard laughed as he screamed bloody murder. *I understand more than you can imagine.* He understood the animalistic fear in Garth's eyes— so like him for months.

Struggling to calm himself and push thoughts of his torture away, Dan turned his gaze back to Jason. Again, sympathetically and quietly, but now with a slight tremble, Dan replied, "I do understand."

Dan allowed his mask to fall completely away. The intense pain he kept deeply buried rose to the surface and resonated in his eyes as he ripped off the scabs covering his psychological wounds … hoping Jason would recognize he truly understood and allow him to help them. Dan peered straight into Jason's eyes and waited until they locked onto his.

Jason's gaze held tight to the young officer only a few feet in front of him. The bleak truth and brutal pain reflected in those blue orbs could never be feigned. The pain authentic and so intense the heat of it burned Jason's soul. For a second, Jason's breath caught in his throat. All his bodily movements ceased as he concentrated on the calm, clear voice.

Imbuing calmness he didn't feel, Dan began, "I understand precisely how you feel. I can't give many details because most are classified. A year and a half into my six years in Kandahar, a terrorist cell captured and tortured me for three months. No one ever figured out how they knew of my affiliation to Special Forces, but they possessed the information."

Jason's mind registered the ever-so-slight slump of the rigidly straight, broad shoulders as if they bent under the weight of the world. Most wouldn't have noticed, but he was so close and paid rapt attention to the figure in front of him.

"I suffered starvation, like you. They only fed me every few days … barely enough to keep me alive. Only enough so they could continue to torture me. The only water I got was what I could suck up off the ground when they hosed down the bloody floor or from routine waterboarding sessions."

Dan subtly shook his head back and forth, slowly inhaled and exhaled, as he thought but didn't share, *still can't stand water hitting my face.*

Jason noted an audible slow breath in and out, and then the officer's voice resumed with a soft growling inflection which communicated tightly controlled anger. "Their favorite methods of interrogation involved long, thin whips, needles, and steel-toed boots. They subjected me to many forms of torture, but I won't go into those. You are absolutely right when you said some people are depraved, inhumane, and evil."

In the command truck, Loki's eyes riveted to the video feed from the cameras. He zoomed in on Dan with one camera as he started to speak. Loki was the only one of the team who viewed Dan's face as he spoke.

Broken despair and suffering etched Dan's face, and made Loki gasp. Truth, agony, and raw torment blazed in his teammate's eyes. The techie suddenly found it impossible to breathe—an invisible vice squeezed his chest as his lungs screamed for air.

How can someone endure that and still be the strong, gentle, funny man I've come to call a friend in the past few months? He thought Dan's experience in the cornfield had been horrifying, but this ... magnitudes worse. Loki didn't realize silent tears slipped out until they splashed onto the keyboard.

Those in the bank became silent as Dan continued, "I was more dead than alive when my unit rescued me. There were days, in the months after I wished I was ... that I had ..." Dan sucked in a shuddering breath and exhaled to regain his composure.

"But eventually things got better. My buddies helped a lot, especially Brody. Having one person is all you need ... one person who always covers your six. For me, that was Brody. He held tight, never let go, and wouldn't let me succumb to my darkest thoughts. Just one person is all it takes to pull you back to the beauty of life—to help you remember most people are good and kind.

"I understand it is hard, so very hard, but you can tuck your experience away. The memories will always be with you, but you don't have to allow them to control how you live your life. You can acknowledge they exist then store them away in a safe place."

The whole team reeled from everything Dan shared. They had no idea he had been tortured. Sure, the guys had seen his torso when changing, but the thin lines—all those faded lines crisscrossing his chest and back—they never imagined Dan suffered through hell. They recognized it took unfathomable courage to lay himself open like this for all to witness.

Lexa, having never seen him shirtless, had no visual reference for the torture Dan described, but it was the words he almost said which impacted her the most. *He was tortured so badly he wished he died.*

She prided herself on being a consummate professional, but this ... this pierced straight to her heart. Totally beyond her capability in the moment to stop her body's reaction to this revelation ... Lexa's hazel eyes welled with unshed tears, and a small sob escaped her constricted throat as grief for what Dan endured overwhelmed her.

Nick never imagined this call would cause such pain for his rookie. *Dan connected with the subject, but at what cost to his well-being? Can Dan bring something like this to the forefront and tuck it away in his safe place again like he told Jason? I'm not so sure.* The call at Playful Minds nearly sent Nick back to the bottle when it dredged up memories of his little boy lying dead outside his daycare. That call had been rough on him, but it was nowhere near what Dan was doing to connect with these men.

Other horrible thoughts crowded into Nick's mind. *Will Dan be able to maintain objectivity? Where is Dan going with this? Can Dan turn this into a good conclusion?* Nick recognized the signs of a desire for suicide by cop. *What will it do to Dan emotionally if these men die?*

As Nick attempted to figure out how to guide and protect Dan so this call ended in a good way for all, Dan's quiet and firm voice said, "So, Jason, now that you know I understand. What do you need? How can we end this with no one getting hurt? We've all suffered enough pain for several lifetimes. Can you help me, help you by putting the guns down?"

Bram kept close tabs on his assigned subject, searching for any signs of threat towards Dan or the hostages. What witnessed in the man's eyes was pain or the reflection of another's pain, and then decision. Bram tensed, not sure what choice the man-made. He waited—ready to fire if need be.

Dan took a small step toward Jason and reached out his right hand, palm up. Jason remained still. Dan took another step forward. "Will you hand me your gun, please?"

Jason still didn't move.

Another step closer. One more step and Dan would be able to touch the weapon. Dan stopped and gently pleaded, "Jason, please ... choose the beauty of life ... please."

Everyone's eyes except Jon's and Lexa's remained riveted on Dan and Jason. Waiting.

It all happened in the space of three heartbeats, but it played out in a sickening slow motion for Alpha Team.

Heartbeat One:

Jason lowered his gun, ready to hand it to Dan.

Dan smiled and reached for the pistol.

Marty lowered his weapon ready to surrender choosing life.

Lexa blinked unshed tears from her eyes to clear her vision.

Garth raised his hand and fired a short burst from his Glock.

Heartbeat Two:

Lexa fired.

Dan crashed to the ground.

Heartbeat Three:

Garth went down.

Nick, Jon, Loki, Ray, and Bram all yelled, "OFFICER DOWN!"

Lexa sadly said, "Subject three, neutralized."

Jason dropped to his knees, his face contorted in agony as he stared at Dan's unmoving body and screamed, "NOOOOO!"

Napping on the Bank Floor

 10

July 15
Inside Central Bank

Time sped up to normal and controlled chaos reigned. Lexa and Jon sprinted to the bank from their Zulu positions. Lexa paused only long enough to shove her Remi into the hands of the NRB Agent who stood nearby waiting for her. She didn't give a flying fig about breaking protocol. She was the reason Dan now lay on the ground and still. She must reach him to find out if he lived or she caused his death.

Jon called for Tia to send EMS to the scene as he ran to check on Dan. *Dammit, this isn't how I wanted this call to end. Dan bared his soul, trying to connect, and now he is lying motionless on the floor. Shit!*

Loki raced flat-out from the command truck directly to Dan. He witnessed a myriad of emotions on their normally stoic rookie. Pain and torment as he shared and connected, a gentle smile when Dan recognized Jason would hand over the weapon and choose life and shock as Dan jerked when bullets hit him. All this ran through Loki's mind in a frantic loop. As Loki ran, he prayed Dan still lived.

Having taken a fair number of slugs in the vest, Bram understood close range shots hurt like the devil and could crack ribs. He wanted to examine Dan but focused on his job to disarm and cuff the subject. He took the gun from Jason's limp hand, handcuffed the sobbing man, then helped him stand, and escorted him toward the exit. When an officer appeared, Bram gratefully handed off Jason. He pivoted, hoping Dan's body armor stopped the bullets.

Ray rushed forward to restrain Marty. The man shook like a leaf, and his breathing became ragged. His subject required EMS assessment, plainly overwrought, and on the verge of collapse. He secured Marty and started to lead him out as he glanced over at Dan. *Damn, he still isn't moving.*

This isn't the outcome I wanted for Dan. Negotiation is not Dan's strong suit, and he did so well ... he connected. Ray's stomach turned as thought about why Dan was able to connect. *All the scars on his torso ... tortured for three months by terrorists ... ungodly horrific.*

Though he too desired to go to his rookie, Nick followed protocol and went to Garth ensuring the safety of the hostages by securing the weapon of the dead subject first. Nick glanced down at the tortured soul who found no other way to cope with the horrendous abuse he suffered. The troubled man made up his mind to die today, and nothing anyone could've said would've changed his mind. *So very sad.* Nick shifted his gaze to his team, converging on Dan's location. *Dan did well, but at what cost to him personally.*

Three hostages stood rooted in place, frozen in utter shock by what occurred. Tears filled their eyes after listening to the dialog between the gunman and constable. A young mother cradled her daughter close, shielding her from the view. The middle-aged woman sobbed as her body shook uncontrollably, and her knees wobbled, and she sank to the ground. The bank manager's mouth hung open and slack as he stared at the brave, young officer lying motionless on the marble floor as he thought life could be so cruel.

Loki reached Dan a split second before Lexa and Jon. Each one dropped to their knees to assess him. Loki breathed heavily, due to the speed of his run and the emotional scene recently played out before him on the monitor. He couldn't speak as his hands roamed over Dan's body searching for damage.

Lexa tapped Dan's cheeks, hoping to invoke a response from him as she urgently called, "Dan. Dan, wake up. Dammit, Dan, don't do this to me. Don't let your death be on my hands. DAN!"

Jon didn't spy blood as he scanned where Dan lay. He visually inspected Dan, locating two slugs lodged in the rookie's Kevlar vest. One in the upper left over the collarbone. If the bullet struck an inch or so to the right, it would've pierced his neck. The other mangled slug caused Jon to shudder as he found it embedded over Dan's heart. *Without a vest, he'd be dead.*

"They're in the vest," Jon called out, to the relief of the entire team.

A fraction of a second later Dan forcefully coughed and frantically gulped like a fish out of water attempting to pull air into his lungs. Dan didn't comprehend anything other than pain radiating across his chest and left shoulder, and the need for air. He thrashed, trying to sit up, as he attempted to suck air in.

An annoying buzzing started in Dan's ears, and something forced him down when he needed to rise. He couldn't draw in enough air and began to panic. *Air, I need air* ... cough, *hurts* ... cough, *ow shit this hurts.* Dan tried to concentrate the droning to make sense of the sound instead of focusing on his pain and the dire need for more oxygen.

A commanding voice broke through his swirling confusion as Dan fought to rise again, needing to inhale, believing lying down restricted his ability. Words with resounding clarity and authority ordered him. "LAY STILL. DO YOU HEAR ME? STAY STILL. STAND DOWN, BRODERICK."

Dan's mind registered the command. Compliance to orders so ingrained in him he instantaneously stopped fighting whatever held him down.

Once Dan quit thrashing, Jon elevated Dan's torso a little to make it easier for him to breathe. Lexa moved and positioned herself to cradle Dan's head on her thighs as she knelt.

"EMS is on the way. Easy now, control your breathing. Relax. Sniper breathing," Jon coached as he made headway against Dan's fight reflex.

Dan struggled to comply with the command, but his breaths came in a jagged cadence.

"IN—HOLD—TWO, THREE, FOUR—RELEASE. That's it. IN—HOLD— TWO, THREE, FOUR—RELEASE. You're gonna be okay, in the vest. Relax," Jon continued to speak in a demanding tone since the rookie responded well to authority.

Dan listened to the words and followed orders. *Thank goodness for guidance, my body forgot how to suck air in.*

"Alright, Dano, open up, look at me. In—hold—two, three, four—release. Let me see those blues. In—hold—two, three, four—release. Come on. You can do it. In—hold—two, three, four—release. OPEN YOUR EYES NOW!"

Dan's lashes fluttered up at the shouted command; obedience overrode his desire to keep them shut.

"There you are. Okay, okay. In—hold—release. You scared the shit out of us. Stay still and keep those eyes open. That's good. Steady breaths. In—hold— release." Jon sighed with relief.

Damn, the kid responded too well to my commanding tone. Jon hated to yell at him while in this state, and he didn't miss the reproachful glares from several people around them, but Jon understood he did the right thing to help his teammate. The tone and volume cut through confusion and pain in a way nothing else could and allowed Dan to respond instinctively.

"Get ... it ... off ..." cough, "off ... please," hiss, cough.

Jon lifted Dan and continued to count breaths for him as Loki attacked the straps with speed to remove Dan's vest. Once off, Jon carefully resettled Dan on the ground with his head in Lexa's lap.

"Better?" Loki asked and received a slight nod of affirmation.

Dan began to register his surroundings. Jon knelt to the right of him with his face close as he instructed him how to breathe. Dan read two emotions in Jon's features. The hard-set of Jon's jaw indicated anger, but his gunmetal gray eyes reflected concern and relief.

Shifting his eyes to the left, he spotted Loki kneeling and holding his vest. Loki's face showed a kaleidoscope of emotions, mostly fluctuating between sadness, fear, and relief with drying tear streaks down both cheeks.

Dan's eyes flicked upwards—above him, Lexa stared down at him. His head rested in her lap, and her hand gently stroked through his hair. *Feels so nice.* Her features solidly displayed anger, but her tear-filled eyes flashed with both distress and fury.

Nick, Bram, and Ray stood near him, their expressions showing varying degrees of worry. *What the hell happened? Why am I on the floor? I almost had Jason's gun.* He shifted, attempting to rise but halted as intense pain engulfed his chest. His eyelids lowered of their own accord as he slumped down. *Crap, how did I screw up this time?*

His ears were assaulted with a chorus of raised voices, one on top of another.

"Keep your eyes open."

"Come on, buddy, stay with us."

"Even out your breathing."

"Relax. Steady. Help is coming."

"You're alright. We've got you."

"Dantastic, hold tight, I'm never letting go."

Through the blur of pain, Dan couldn't distinguish who said what. Well, maybe one, only one person routinely called him Dantastic. Dan slowly forced his eyes to open and locked them onto Loki's eyes, concentrating solely on Loki as he rode out the wave of pain.

Loki dropped the vest and clasped Dan's hand again, giving his teammate a reassuring squeeze. "I'm holding tight. Never gonna let go."

Understanding dawned. The words ... Loki spoke his words to him. Loki wouldn't let him drown in the sea of pain and darkness. Loki believed in the beauty of life. Dan gave a slight return squeeze before concentrating on relaxing his muscles to help him breathe.

"EMS will be there as soon as possible. They're backed up with multiple calls in the area due to a fire at a nursing home," Tia informed the team.

As pain in his upper body began to recede and breathing eased, Dan discerned Tia's news aggravated his entire team, except himself. Dan would be happy if EMS never showed up. He also realized the team needed to focus on the job—not stare at him until EMS arrived. And he could use a few minutes alone to start to push agonizing memories back into the dark, thick-walled place where he contained all his hurt.

Excelling at using deflection, a skill developed and honed over the years, Dan took a tentative, deeper breath, and flashed them all a lopsided grin. With mock exasperation, he said, "What, I can't nap here, either?"

His wild, left-field comment garnered the desired response from most of his team … several relieved laughs and smiles.

Jon released a gut-deep laugh and in a mock stern tone said, "No, Broderick, the floor of the bank is definitely on the unacceptable nap locations list."

Dan's ability to sleep anywhere had been a running joke with them ever since Loki posted the list on Dan's locker back in May after Dan fell asleep in the back of the SUV. Jon found Dan asleep in some strange places during their break times. He always joked about the places and told Dan he couldn't nap there. The unacceptable nap location list grew yet again with the addition of the bank's floor.

As Jon stood, he shared a look with Nick, which communicated, *'He'll be okay.'* Each of them, at one point or another, had taken a hit in the vest. It hurt like hell and stayed tender for several days, but they were typically fine if no ribs broke.

Nick scanned his teammates and did a quick assessment of each member. Everyone except Loki appeared re-centered and back to normal. Loki, however, appeared shaken. Nick decided to speak with Loki later to understand the cause of his heightened emotional state, but for now, it would be best for most everybody to focus on their usual tasks, though he would give Loki a special one. Nick removed his hat and rubbed his face briskly. "Alright team, back at it. Wrap up the scene. Loki, stay with Dan until the medics check him out."

Loki nodded, and the rest of them dispersed to take care of business.

Nick and Loki helped Dan to a seated position. Nick crouched close to Dan and said, "Excellent work. I'm proud of you and glad you're a member of our team. You connected in a way none of us could've. Thank you. I understand that must've been hard. If you ever want or need to discuss what you shared today, I'm here … we're all here for you." He rose and stepped away to give Dan space to regroup and to hand the scene off to the inspector.

Dan appreciated the offer, but he would never willingly talk about those things with anybody again—once had been enough. *It is too agonizing to let them escape. Those feelings must stay locked tight in the dark prison.*

Crap! Let them escape and dark prison? I never used terminology like that before. Is it a prison? Did those emotions want to escape? Control yourself now, Broderick! Now isn't the time to try and sort this out. You are on the job.

For now, it is sufficient to think I pulled them out because using them was the only way to connect and save those guys. How I put them back before they kill me will have to wait. What? Before they kill me? Aw man, this is gonna be harder than usual to shove back down. Dan had never thought in these terms before—harm, yes, but not kill. He winced as another realization hit him almost taking his breath away as the bullets to the vest.

I did it again. Crap! Jon will be pissed if he finds out. I took what Jon refers to as 'unacceptable risk' again to save someone else. Dan sighed, relieved Jon wouldn't lay into him over this since he wouldn't ever be aware … because this 'unacceptable risk' was one, nobody else could see.

Loki fumed. *Dammit, dammit, and triple dammit! The rookie risked himself again.* He didn't think anyone grasped what Dan did. Boss was quite intuitive but only suspected based on what he said to Dan. Nick held out a hand, but Dan would be allowed to choose to accept the offer of assistance at this point because Boss wouldn't force him without proof.

Jon certainly didn't realize, or else our tactical lead would've laid into Dan already, injured or not. Loki reasoned he was the only one who knew without a doubt because he was the only one viewing Dan's face as he spoke with Jason. *Why does Dan always risk himself for others?*

During this call, Loki occupied a front-row seat and bore witness to Dan's profoundly wounded soul. Although Dan took two slugs, Loki understood the threat to him was not only physical. His history dealing with an abusive stepfather made him realize memories could be as lethal, if not more.

At the moment, Loki had no idea how to help Dan. But for now, he would keep an eye on him, and wait to be a lifeline if Dan fell. Loki had been, and still was, utterly serious when he told Dan he would hold tight and never let go.

Loki took a deep cleansing breath and plopped down on the floor beside Dan—thoroughly spent emotionally. "What's the prognosis, Dr. Broderick?" he quipped, trying to lighten the mood.

Deeply engrossed in his musings, Dan wasn't sure what Loki meant and stared blankly at him.

"Your injuries, ribs, shoulder?" Loki clarified.

Oh, right? The lightbulb went on in Dan's head.

Loki studied Dan as he began to probe his ribs and shoulder to determine the extent of his injury. He recalled Dan possessed at least some training in medical self-assessment and treatment thanks to the Special Forces. It was one of the few personal things he learned about the man. Other than what he—they—all found out. *Tortured for three months?* Loki swallowed as a lump formed in his throat. *No one should ever experience something so depraved.*

Aware of his body's reactions to injuries, possessing a mental catalog of every wound he sustained and how long it took to heal, Dan took stock of his condition. *Bruising will be vivid. Always is, even with a minor injury.*

The way he bruised garnered horrified gasps from those who spied them because they appeared worse than they were. He healed faster than average, except for bruising, and had a high pain threshold, which he appreciated since he hated taking pain medication of any type. He would rather deal with the pain then the loopy, out-of-control sensations painkiller usually caused.

"Well, the patient is bruised, but no real damage. He'll be sporting awesome shades of red, blue, black, purple, green, and yellow over the next few weeks. He might be a little sore and stiff, but no need for meds. Patient is released for active duty, effective immediately," Dan replied as he peered at Loki with an assessing gaze.

Loki snorted and laughed. "Can't wait to see the awesome colors. Your bruises are always spectacular."

Good, I've got him laughing. Dan's appraisal told him something bothered Loki. The techie's emotion always showed easily—so unlike his controlled mask. Obviously, something troubled his teammate, and Dan decided Loki needed something else to focus on.

"What do ya say we head to the command truck? I need a change of scenery," Dan suggested. "I can wait for the medics outside. I recognized Boss won't let me get away without them examining me, but at least we can get outta here."

Loki hopped up and offered a hand to Dan.

Dan grasped Loki's hand and allowed him to help pull him to his feet. A little shaky at first, he took a step and faltered.

Instantly Loki was at Dan's side, providing stabilizing support.

"Thanks," Dan said quietly when Loki steadied him.

"Anytime." Loki maintained his hold, following through on his word not to let Dan fall.

Laughter Heals the Soul

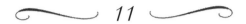 *11*

Loki and Dan made their way outside and arrived as an EMS rig parked next to the command truck. *Wonderful timing.* Dan allowed the emergency medical technician to help him up into the back of the ambulance and sat on the gurney while being poked and prodded.

Senior paramedic, Dave Kneller, grudgingly gave Dan an all-clear. Although his cursory exam found no damage other than the obvious bruising, Dave wanted the constable to be x-rayed to rule out fractures. Dan's insistence he was okay and the mention of his Special Forces field training persuaded him to back off and agree to clear the officer for duty.

Reaching to the side to retrieve his undershirt, Dan bunched it up, ready to put it back on as Lexa walked up.

Lexa began to ask about Dan, and got out, "How's our guy, is he—" when her gaze landed on his chest. Whatever she intended to say after, never left her lips. Eyes widened in shock as her hand flew to cover her gaping mouth. Tears started to well again.

Dan understood Lexa's reaction. Although faded now, his visible scars disconcerted most people when they first laid eyes on them. Dammit, drawing attention to them in public, screamed Julie all over again—well, not quite. Instead of horror and disgust as Julie exhibited, only distress and sadness emanated from his teammate.

He hurriedly pulled his t-shirt over his head and down. In the two times, they slept together, Lexa never viewed his scars. Though he realized if they continued their nighttime liaisons, she would've eventually seen them, but he hated to shock her in such a public forum ... she wouldn't appreciate it one damned bit.

Desperately wanting to redirect her thoughts, Dan plastered a cheesy, seductive expression and said in his best cocky voice, "Well, well, … Sexy Lexie finally gets to ogle my awesome, muscular body, Loki. Ya think she likes what she sees?"

Loki realized what Dan was trying to do—Lexa's reaction similar to his own when he beheld the terrible scars for the first time. Playing along, he chimed in with a nerdy-boy, falsetto tone, "Nah, you macho, all brawn and no brain, he-man types don't interest our sexy sniper chick. She would rather ogle this sleek, finely tuned, and intelligent Italian stallion."

Christ! Did they say that over comms? Lexa swiveled her head back and forth between the two of them with an incredulous expression. She pinned them each with a *'you're dead'* glare before she spun on her heel and stormed away, her ponytail bouncing and swaying with each step.

Dan and Loki gaped at each other with mock horror and fear and said simultaneously, "You're in trouble now, dude. Me? Yeah, you."

Then both broke down in a fit of laughter until Dan clutched at the pain in his chest and started to cough. Loki calmed and patted his teammate's back. As Dan's coughing eased and his pain receded, they stared at one another astonished they said the same words in chorus. The two men dissolved into gut-busting laughter once again.

Loki sucked in a breath as he grinned. *This is good. Laughter heals the soul.*

Lexa understood what those two did for her and loved them both for it. They gave her a reason to exit in a huff instead of standing there fumbling with other emotions brought on by beholding the tangible evidence of the torture Dan endured, especially since the raw anguish of what Dan shared still hung heavy around them all.

My God, the horror Dan suffered. No wonder he made love in the dark. He is probably afraid of being rejected because of the scaring. She mentally braced herself. *Now isn't the time to dwell on those thoughts.* Lexa responded angrily, "You two are in so much trouble. You better watch your backs."

Having overheard the whole exchange, Bram, Ray, and Jon emitted soft chuckles.

Lexa concentrated on deep breaths in and out. She slowed her pace to a walk and headed towards Boss, knowing she must go with an NRB agent, who likely would complain about her post-shoot behavior.

Nick piped in, "Behave, children. You do realize you're all still on the auto-scripter, right? Human Resources might be stopping by to conduct sexual harassment and sensitivity training if you're not careful."

Laughter exploded again, this time from every single member of the team drawing curious gazes from those around them not privy to the entire conversation.

When the chortling died down, Dan's mind wandered back to the workout this morning when he realized how truly and deeply happy being part of this family made him. His teammate's actions and reactions during this call tangible proof which affirmed his belief they counted him as family too.

A quirky smile flittered onto Dan's face as he finished buttoning up his uniform shirt and walked toward Boss. He must still deal with NRB from the previous call … Dick would not be happy about the delay.

Kendall Stevens, a seasoned NRB agent, recently transfer from Winnipeg, learned from several of her colleagues Alpha Team was considered the best. This was her first time on a call with them, and from her observations, her coworkers were right. This team handled the situation well.

Courtesy of an earwig which allowed her to listen in, she followed the dialog of the call and this latest byplay. A smile appeared as her delicate lips turned upward. Her first impression … *this TRF team demonstrates a rare trifecta. They genuinely care about the hostages, the subjects, and each other.*

Happy to be the agent of record for this call, Kendall would allow a certain amount of leeway today which other agents would not. Innately kind, she handled subject officers humanely when investigating them. She tried to be fair and balanced and bristled when procedures treated constables worse than criminals. Those procedures ticked her off, and she gladly ignored them when deemed necessary.

She arrived on the scene as they entered the bank. She watched in awe as they seamlessly worked and sadly listened to everything Broderick shared. So today, when McKenna threw the Remi at her in a desperate run towards a fallen teammate, Kendall backed off and ignored the 'take them before they talk to anyone' procedure.

The auto-scripter recorded the incident, and all the pertinent dialog would be captured for review, so Kendall chose to simply observe from a respectful distance and give Alpha Team the space needed to take care of one of their own after such an emotionally fraught call.

She believed officers to be humans with hearts who put their lives on the line every day to save strangers. Observing McKenna cradle Broderick's head and stroke his hair as they determined if he lived, touched Kendall. The way the entire team acted impressed her. They cared for and appeared to be fiercely protective—a factor evident in their actions today. Kendall breathed out her relief when she found out the young constable had not died.

Kendall arrived at the sergeant's location at the same time as Lexa and Dan. "Sergeant Pastore, my name is Kendall Stevens, I'm with the NRB. I must interview Constable McKenna. I can also take Constable Broderick with me if he is cleared for duty by the medic. I understand an interview is pending from a prior call."

"Dan, what's the word?" Nick queried.

"All clear, only bruising and little soreness to be expected." Dan scanned Stevens, wondering if he might be lucky at some point to draw her, she appeared empathetic for their plight unlike 'the Dick.'

Nick cast an eye over Lexa before thoroughly scrutinizing Dan, assessing their status. "We're all done here, and the units have taken over. So okay, you two go with Agent Stevens, and we'll debrief once you both return to headquarters."

Dan and Lexa nodded in acknowledgment, and the three turned to head towards the agent's car when Tia's voice called out, "Alpha Team. Critical call, armed robbery in progress at Bennie's Gas Station." She proceeded to relay the address.

Nick blew out a harsh breath. "Copy, Tia. At this rate, today's gonna be a long one." He fixed his gaze on Stevens. "Sorry, interviews must wait. I need them as of now." Nick waited for Kendall's nod of acknowledgment before hurrying away as he said, "Tia, details please."

Lexa shared a glance with Dan which conveyed, *'Saved by the bell.'* Both gave a quick nod to the NRB agent before jogging to their SUV.

"Jon, with me," called Nick as he approached the SUV. Nick needed a moment to talk with his second in command privately before they arrived at the next call.

"On my way." Jon sprinted to Nick's location. The team paired off and ran to the remaining vehicles. Lexa jumped into the driver's side and Dan in the passenger seat of one. Bram and Ray took the last SUV and Loki headed over to the command truck.

"Tia, a gas station robbery is typically a unit call, not TRF territory. What makes this one ours?" Jon asked as he turned over the ignition. He understood calls were not routed to TRF unless they met certain criteria, but this one sounded ordinary and he wanted full details.

Understanding the call might be tough on Nick, heck all of them, Tia replied, "Usually, but six young children are being held in the store. According to the officer on-scene, a daycare van stopped to fuel up on its way to a zoo trip. The children were inside when the subjects entered demanding cash, and the cashier hit the silent alarm.

"When a patrol unit arrived, things went downhill fast. One subject yelled he would start shooting kids if the police didn't leave. There are two subjects and eight hostages, unknown if anyone is injured."

After typing the address into GPS and noting the distance from their current location, Jon calculated how long it would take them to arrive. "Thanks, Tia. Inform the on-scene units our ETA is about ten minutes." Jon pulled away from the curb as Nick turned on the lights and siren.

A second EMS rig rolled to a halt next to the first one as three TRF SUVs, and a command truck pulled away from the bank. Jim Shea stared at the leaving vehicles when a flash of golden hair in the passenger side of one of them gave him a moment's pause. Something seemed familiar.

Whether driven by a sixth sense, wishful thinking, or haunted by guilt, Jim did a double-take whenever he glimpsed blond men lately. Though highly unlikely he would find him here, something spurred Jim to keep searching for his lost brother.

Putting the vehicle in park, Trey noted his partner zoned out again. It didn't occur often, but enough Trey grasped some severe shit must've happened to Jim while he served in Special Forces. Jim never spoke about what made him leave the military, and though curious, Trey never pried, because frankly, it was none of his business. Trey tapped Jim's shoulder to bring him back to the present. "Hey, bud, we gotta go."

Jim shook off the sensation as they both hopped out, grabbed their gear, and rushed towards the squad car. The medics on scene were busy with one of the former hostages because the middle-aged woman experienced a delayed stress reaction. When one of the men in custody started having difficulty breathing, dispatch sent Jim and Trey to treat him.

Arriving at their patient, they set to work assessing Private Marty Green. Corporal Jason York told them Marty had a damaged windpipe and asthma. The stress of the situation brought on an asthma attack and impeded his breathing ability. They positioned Marty on the gurney, strapped him in, and began oxygen before hustling him back to their rig. As they prepared to load Marty in the back, Jim overheard Brad and Dave talking as they packed up after the woman refused to be transported to the hospital and left with her husband.

Dave shook his head. "I can't believe they said that."

Brad chuckled. "I'm surprised they're still alive after they called her Sexy Lexie and a sexy sniper chick. Thought we might be treating two GSWs."

Now chuckling too, Dave nodded. "Yeah, me too. Lexa is Xena Warrior Princess of TRF. She's not someone you want to piss off."

"Damn, that's a good one, fits her well. She's tiny but fierce." Brad laughed. "Don't ever let her hear you call her that, 'cause, I'm not too keen on breaking in a new partner."

"I'll keep that in mind." Shifting his thoughts to the impetus of the comedy the witnessed, Dave's tone became serious. "But, man those scars ... those were terrible. His back appeared to be scored worse than his chest. I'm glad they did something to distract her. The shock and despair in her eyes when she glimpsed those marks. And when tears welled in them too ... the Warrior Princess doesn't show emotion. Hell, I treated her when she got hit by a crowbar. She was in so much pain but not one tear—not a single one."

Pushing the empty gurney into their rig, Brad mused aloud, "I wonder how he got all those long thin scars. Looks like it happened years ago with how faded they are. Perhaps I'll ask him the next time we check him out. If his track record keeps up at the same pace, he'll soon surpass Bram's record for bullets in the vest."

Marty listened as the medics prepared to put him into the ambulance. He lifted his oxygen mask, and his wraith-like voice rasped out, "He was tortured, just like me ... but he chose the beauty of life, not suicide." Marty coughed and struggled to inhale as the sensation of suffocating overwhelmed him.

As Jim put the mask back on his patient, his mind reeled. Scars on chest and back, torture, the glimpse of blond hair. But what affected him most was the phrase 'beauty of life.' Jim's hand went to his lower pants pocket and absently patted. *Still there, still charged, still ready at a moment's notice.*

Trey noted the color drain from Jim's face. "Hey, bud, you're as white as a ghost. You okay?"

Jim absently answered, "Yeah," as he turned to ask the other medics who they were talking about, but the patient began to crash and his whole attention refocused on saving the man's life.

More Important Than Food

 *12*

July 15
En Route to Bennie's Gas Station — Jon and Nick — 12:00 p.m.

Glancing over at Nick, Jon noted Boss motioned for him to mute his headset as he flicked his to silent, and waited.

"We've experienced two intense calls. Need your assessment of the team's readiness before we arrive at the next one," Nick said.

Jon thought for a moment. "Well ... you, me, Bram, and Ray appear fit and good to go. Loki's a little shaken. Based on his reaction to Dan getting hit, I think the camera showed him something the rest of us couldn't see. He is fine, but you should talk to him later."

After pausing to focus on shifting lanes to go around heavy traffic, Jon continued, "Lexa, well, she is angry with herself for allowing Garth to fire his weapon. And she set eyes on Dan's scars for the first time. That must've been upsetting. Still remember when we all viewed them." Jon shuddered. "But she pulled it together and is back in professional mode."

He took a minute to consider Dan's fitness status. "Dan, wow what a morning for our rookie. Neutralized a subject, shared some private and horrifying memories to help someone, and shot for his trouble. All that and he maintains the presence of mind to tease Lexa, helping her through a bad moment and enjoyed a laugh with Loki. I'm impressed with Dan's resilience. I would be inclined to say he is fit for duty ..."

When Jon hesitated, Nick stated, "I hear a *but* there. And I concur with all you said. Though I often worry ... strong, resilient ones such as you and Dan can take only so much. I understand where your reluctance is coming from. We need to go cautiously. Dan's a protector at his core." Nick paused to check his vibrating phone ... Tia provided him the name of the senior officer on scene.

"True. Something we've discussed before." Jon agreed.

Nick finished the text, blew out a breath, and reengaged in the conversation. "I believe he copes best when active. When we force downtime on him, he tends to become restless. I'm not certain, but I believe that is when he is most vulnerable. Working helps Dan process emotions and put them in the proper places."

Both contemplated what the other said, then Jon suggested, "For this call, we put him in the truck with Loki. Have him focus on tactical analysis away from the potential for lethal action and negotiating. Dan may want to protect others, but he needs safeguarding too. Give him an important task, but also a little space to breathe before throwing him back into the action full-force."

Nick approved of the idea. The two usually held much the same perspective on each member, and he liked when his tactical lead's assessments aligned with his. He and Jon worked well together, effortlessly filling in each other's shortcoming, thus making a stronger leadership team.

Jon asked quietly, "What about you, Nick?"

Nick drew in another breath. Calls involving young children always affected him. Regardless of the outcome, for many nights afterward, he experienced nightmarish dreams of finding Martin dead. "I'm fine."

"You sure?" Jon asked again.

"Yeah, thanks for asking though."

Jon glanced at Nick and nodded. "Okay, then."

En Route to Bennie's Gas Station – Bram and Ray

Ray and Bram started a similar conversation, but they veered off track. After motioning to Bram to mute his headset, Ray pressed the mute button on his said, "So, you think Dan is alright?"

Bram needed no time to respond as he had been thinking about Dan's state ever since viewing the mirrored emotion in Jason's face as Dan talked in the bank. "He's wounded beyond what any of us can even imagine."

That drew a quick look from Ray, but he misinterpreted Bram's meaning. "But the medic cleared him. They wouldn't do so if he is injured. Sure, he'll be bruised. Man, he bruises so intensely … a bit scary. I can't forget the first bruising I glimpsed. Scared the shit out of me. You remember? It was the day after we did all the hand-to-hand takedown drills. You had him act as the target for us, and we all threw him to the mat for hours."

Bram laughed and let his true meaning pass as he followed Ray's track. "Yeah. I recall. Made him be the subject because he got out of every maneuver I presented him with. We learned a lot from him. Dan barely flinched when he landed from all the throws or when we practiced using pressure points. I think we got schooled in only a portion of the techniques he knows."

Ray nodded. "Yeah, he taught us a bunch, but remember all the razzing we gave him the next morning when he joined workout wearing a long-sleeved shirt and sweat pants instead of the A-shirt and shorts he usually wears? Dan insisted he was cold, but he sweated like a pig. We all gave him more shit when he came out of the shower area, fully dressed and ready."

Bram chuckled recalling the day. "We went on the call where you and Dan climbed into the huge garbage container to pull out a kid. You two stank and Boss ordered you back to shower and change. None of us wanted to ride in a truck with either of you."

Ray grimaced at the memory. "A truly ungodly, awful smell. Something like skunk meets rotting fish with a side of vomit. Ugh. I was at my locker already half-dressed as Dan rounded the corner with only a towel around his waist using a small washcloth to towel dry his hair."

As the image came to mind, Ray grinned. "I scared the crap out of him when I suddenly yelled, 'HOLY SHIT! WHAT THE HELL HAPPENED TO YOU?' Dan jumped back about three feet and slammed into the locker behind him. His head whipped around, searching for who I yelled at and landed on me, confused when he didn't find anyone else in the room.

"I stared at him with my mouth hanging open. His body looked like it had been used as a paintball gun target. Almost every inch covered in bright red, blue, and purple hues. Dan registered me gaping at him and said, 'Oh, this, it's nothing, only a little bruising from yesterday's training,' and moved to his locker to dress."

Bram laughed at the recollection. "Boss, Loki, Jon, and I overheard your yell and raced into the lockers. The four of us stopped dead in our tracks when we saw him. Remember Jon's reaction? He went ballistic. Didn't believe in the slightest when Dan said it was nothing and he was uninjured.

"Jon threatened to relegate him to the truck for a week if he didn't let EMS check him out. I thought Dan would blow a gasket when he shouted, 'Dammit, Jon, I only bruise vividly, this nothing. Looks awful, but nothing hurts. I'm okay. If I beat you in the tactical course will you believe me and drop it?'

"I think Jon regrets agreeing to Dan's challenge. He was hard to live with for a while after Dan bested him in the course by fifteen seconds and broke his long-standing record by five seconds."

Agreeing, Ray nodded and smiled. "Jon's competitive … he was a bear for several weeks. But I think Dan is good for Jon … even though their dynamic can be difficult at times."

As they approached Bennie's both men quieted, unmuted their headsets, and mentally switched gears back to job mode.

En Route to Bennie's Gas Station — Dan and Lexa

Over in the SUV Lexa and Dan shared, the headsets were not muted. As they neared their destination, Dan continued to beg Lexa for a power bar. She enjoyed teasing him, payback for the comment earlier. Loki grinned as he listened to their repartee and drove the command truck.

Their banter began shortly after hopping into the vehicle. Dan appeared to be quiet and somewhat meditative if Lexa had to assign emotion to his demeanor. Then out of nowhere, a loud growling sound interrupted the silence.

Lexa snapped her head towards Dan. "What the hell is that for, Broderick?"

"Just my stomach," snorted Dan. "I overslept and didn't eat breakfast today. Only had the coffee the guys brought us this morning." He winked at her knowingly.

Trying not to recall last night while on duty, Lexa replied, "It sounds angry, better feed it." Then to cover her worries someone might guess they slept together, she asked, "Why did you wake up late?"

"Would if I could, because I was sleeping," replied Dan with a smirk. *Does Lexa really want to have this conversation now?*

"Don't you pack power bars? And that's a stupid answer, I asked why you were late not what you were doing," Lexa countered and flashed Dan a grin.

In the past six weeks, they started to communicate like this. Anyone listening to them might become lost with the multiple threads within the same conversation, but they never did. They viewed this as a small mental sparring session, something they both enjoyed.

When they initiated their unique type of dialog months ago, each possessed an ulterior motive. For Lexa, she wanted to learn how this man ticked. He was so different from any guy she had known, which made him intriguing. For Dan, he liked saying things which raised her hackles. The fire in her hazel eyes and a flush to her cheeks when slightly pissed made her so sexy and desirable he couldn't stop himself from doing it.

However, today, there appeared to be a new undertone born from giving in to the attraction both had denied for so long. Neither possessed a clue how to proceed—a private discussion for later each decided, but the nuance in their typical banter helped both settle after the emotionally charged bank call.

"Took care of the most important thing only before I left, and no it isn't a dumb answer it was because I slept," Dan retorted. And boy did he enjoy his slumber. Lexa's sated, soft yet firm body held close to him after a mutual release hands-down more effective than any sleeping pill.

"So what's more important than food? And yes, it is a ridiculous answer, that's what you were doing, not why you were late," Lexa challenged, her eyes brimming with friendly fire.

How will he answer? She fed the flames hoping not to be burned if Dan blew everything and blurted out that they slept together. Though unsure why she did something so risky, part of her must know if he would say anything.

"Brushing my teeth and, no, that isn't what I was doing. It is why I came in late," Dan countered. *Sexy Lexie is testing me—I'm certain of it now.*

"You prioritize brushing teeth over food? Explain your answer. We're going around in circles." Lexa arched her brow.

"Yes, teeth brushing is imperative, because I couldn't WOW you with my beautiful smile without my pearly whites, now could I? I arrived late because I fell asleep unexpectedly before setting my alarm. So the cause for me arriving late is that I overslept ... therefore sleeping." Dan waited for the explosion from his cocky statement.

Bulls-eyes achieved by both. For Dan, his wowing her with his incredible smile comment garnered a flashed glare from Lexa which conveyed, *'I can't believe you said that.'* He gave her a lopsided grin and relished in the flame flickering in the golden flecks of her exquisite eyes. For Lexa, his explanation for being late solidified he would be discrete. The teasing about his smile fed right into it, too. Ray and Loki teased Dan about his toothy grin sometimes and suggested women found it irresistible.

Lexa bit her lip. *Now, what am I going to do?*

Dan's stomach roared again, and the begging commenced. This morning he didn't take the time to replenish his stock of power bars—he forgot all about them in his rush. Dan knew Lexa also kept some in her bag, so he pleaded with her to give him one.

Over the next few minutes, Lexa found all kinds of reasons not to share the energy bars as Dan petitioned her. She should've offered him some, but it was too much fun to see how he would try to wheedle them from her. As they arrived, Lexa grabbed two from the door pocket and tossed one to him with a smile.

A muffled, "Thanks," through a mouthful of the chocolate covered bar, came from Dan before they exited the truck.

Lexa laughed as she noted he shoved the whole bar in at once. *He must be starving. He did use a ton of energy in the past seven hours—not to mention last night—and it doesn't appear we'll be getting a break any time soon.* She planned to eat the second one, but as an afterthought said, "Hey, Soldier, think fast," and chucked the bar to him.

Dan's huge grin showed off his pearly whites as he caught the package.

The little devil sitting on Lexa's shoulder cackled, and Lexa ducked her head as she headed to the command truck so Dan wouldn't detect his smile did in fact, WOW her.

Sara's in Danger

13

July 15
Outside Bennie's Gas Station – 12:15 p.m.

Loki parked the command vehicle near the rear of the station and popped into the back. The team, except Nick, converged at the truck to determine their plan of action. Loki already tapped away on the keyboard working to link into the security cameras and capture images of those inside. Finding their identities would assist Boss with negotiations ... until then they remained blind as to how to deal with the subjects.

Jon doled out the tactical assignments. "Due to the kids, we need to go less lethal. No flashbangs or CS gas either. Loki's working on eyes in to find where the hostage's locations. Dan, in the truck with Loki. Need you studying those blueprints and finding us options for entering undetected, if possible. Lexa, we need info about subjects and hostages. Boss is getting status reports from the units. Ray and Bram, make sure patrol secures the perimeter, group the parents together, and have them move the news crews back further. We don't need the same media fiasco we dealt with at Playful Minds."

A chorus of, "Copy," resounded and all proceeded to their assigned tasks.

Nick updated them, "According to Constable Wiener, at least one subject appears to be high on drugs, as his behavior is erratic. The second subject is less erratic. They have been holed up in there for twenty minutes."

Outside Bennie's Gas Station – Command Truck

Loki got access to the station's cameras. They were fixed in place, creating several blind spots of the interior. The most concerning blank area appeared to be the one closest to the back door. One camera provided a full view at the front of the short hallway which led to the bathrooms, but anyone currently occupying the restrooms could slip out the back door unnoticed.

Once Loki located the hostages, Dan studied the layout of the mini-mart, noting several options for entry based on the tech wizard's assessment.

Relaying details to the team, Loki said, "They grouped the kiddos near the candy case to the left of the hall. The jittery subject armed with a semi-automatic pistol is guarding them. The calmer subject is carrying a rifle and herded the cashier and chaperone behind the counter on the other side of the store. Dan's sure it is a single-shot hunting rifle."

Studying both groups on the monitors, Loki pondered aloud, "Why would they separate the adults and kids?"

"Good question. Suggestions anyone?" Nick put forth to his team.

"Tactically smart on their part. Splitting them makes our entry options more difficult. We'll need to cover two areas instead of one. Also, if an adult isn't keeping the children calm, they may panic and bolt into the line of fire. Subjects might know that limits our tactical options," Dan stated.

"Agreed. Dan, determine an entry plan based on this intel." Jon grinned at Dan's assessment, which mirrored his own.

Although Dan reviewed many options, he remained unhappy ... none presented a fool-proof scenario ... too many variables with kids involved.

Outside Bennie's Gas Station

Nick peered at Jon who stood near the command truck with him. "So, we need a talk solution."

Jon nodded. "Hard tactical might end badly if any kids spook."

"Any progress yet on our subjects' identities?" Nick asked.

"Still running facial recognition," Loki responded.

After learning the name of the cashier from the station's owner, Lexa approached the woman which a patrol officer identified as one of the daycare chaperones. "I'm Lexa McKenna with TRF. Can you tell me your name?"

Wendy clutched a folder in one hand as she bit the fingernails on her other hand and stared at the mini-mart with a fretful expression. She turned her eyes to the officer. "Wendy Glines. They're only little kids. You're gonna make sure they come out safe, right?"

Lexa calmly said, "We're working on that. Wendy, can you tell me anything about the children?"

Wendy shoved the file at Lexa. "Their details are in here. We bring pictures of the children when we go on field trips in case any of them go missing. Please save them. They're so young. We shouldn't have let them go in to pick a treat, but Gayla said it would be a special thing. Our boys are so rambunctious, usually hard to make them sit still for long, but today they behaved so well I agreed with Gayla. Please, you must get them out unharmed."

"Is Gayla the other chaperone?"

Wendy nodded. "Gayla, Gayla Fines."

Opening the manila folder, Lexa scanned the details before asking, "Anything you can tell me about them which isn't in this file?"

Renewing the nervous assault on her nails, Wendy became thoughtful. "Ava and Sara are sisters. Um ... Ava, Ava has asthma. The boys, they can't be still for more than thirty minutes before getting ants in their pants. Sweet, active boys ... I should've never let them out of the van."

As the woman broke down, Lexa waved over one of the paramedics on standby. "We'll do all we can to ensure their safety."

Wendy nodded and allowed herself to escorted away from the crime scene by the medic.

Lexa moved towards the command truck as she filled in the team with what she gathered. "Wendy Glines, the chaperone outside, gave me names and pictures of all six kids involved. I'm bringing them to you, Loki. We have one five-year-old girl, Ava Clarry, who suffers from asthma, so definitely no CS.

"Gary Burns, Todd Olsen, Kenny Rescher, and Paul Vorhees are all four-year-old. Wendy indicates they are high-spirited, and it is hard to keep them still for long.

"The last is a three-year-old girl, Sara Clarry, who is Ava's little sister. The caregiver inside is Gayla Fines. And the cashier is Lonnie Beam, according to the station owner."

Outside Bennie's Gas Station – Command Truck

Dan finished evaluating options. "Jon, got an entry scenario. Not ideal, too many factors. No clear Zulu positions. The plan requires two of us to enter the front door to apprehend the subject holding the adults. To contain the other subject, one of us needs to do a drop entry from the ceiling vent, and two need to approach from the back door. Loki can maintain overwatch via the cameras to alert us of any movement before we execute. Again, it's not perfect, with the chance a kid might spook and dart. Would be better if we talk them out."

"Boss, I found IDs for our subjects," Loki said. "They both are career criminals with long histories. Mostly petty robbery and smash and grabs at computer and jewelry stores. No record of using weapons in previous incidents. This one appears to be different from their usual."

Jon griped, "They escalated to armed robbery, freaking wonderful."

Nodding, Loki affirmed. "Yeah, their rap sheets show involvement in many crimes together. Our calm subject is Chance Bigalow, and the jittery one is Ted Jitters." Loki smirked and chuckled at the last name. "Wow, that's funny. What are the odds?"

Outside Bennie's Gas Station

"Any more information, Loki?" Nick inquired.

"No, Boss."

Nick picked up the megaphone and called out to the station, "My name is Nick Pastore with the Police Tactical Response Force. I would like to talk to you. I'm going to call the landline. Please pick it up so we may speak easier."

The team all breathed a slight sigh of relief when Chance answered the phone and began a dialog with Nick. Boss learned Chance didn't want to rob the station with guns. He preferred to smash and grab, but Ted wanted to try it for fun.

Jon's pride in his team grew. They worked fast to pull together the intel and develop a plan. He decided to position them based on Dan's plan, but with one change which would piss off his rookie … Dan, not Loki, would be manning the cameras.

He doled out the assignments. "Ray, you're with me, entry through the front. Bram and Loki, enter from the rear. Lexa, enter via the vent since you're small enough to fit. Dan, you're in the truck on the cameras. Need you to inform us if anyone moves."

A chorus of, "Copy," sounded off as everyone moved to comply.

Outside Bennie's Gas Station – Command Truck

Dan wanted to object, but he bit the insides of his cheeks to keep from mouthing off. *Why did he bench me? The medic cleared me for duty. It is my plan, yet instead of being allowed to follow it through to completion, I'm relegated to the role of an observer.*

Is Jon questioning my abilities? He didn't even put me as a backup on the rear door. Dan's anger rose. *Why the hell am I being benched? Loki is always in the truck. He is the technical guy and should be monitoring the video feed. I'm a sniper and tactical. I should be in Loki's position.*

Pacing back and forth in the truck, being stuck here, ticked Dan off for a couple of reasons. He hated being in the restrictive, equipment-filled cabin. Not only could he not protect the team from this position, but the confined space caged him in, allowing him only three steps each way … a reminder of another cramp place filled with degradation and pain.

Dan struggled to curb thoughts of THERE, but his emotions surged, coming out in anger as he clenched his fists.

Outside Bennie's Gas Station

Nick continued to talk to Chance, trying to resolve the crisis without the team having to do a hard-tactical entry.

Jon heard Dan's pacing through the headset as he and Ray positioned themselves to move in if needed. Ordinarily an example of graceful stealth, Jon realized the volume of his rookie's movements now revealed his rage. He would grant Dan a few more moments to burn off his resentment of being put on the sidelines for this one before redirecting him if need be.

Jon hated to do this to him, confident Dan would view his actions as a lack of trust in his abilities, but a change in position was for Dan's well-being. Someone must keep an eye out for Dan. Jon also comprehended if Dan discerned the real reason, he would still be upset. *Whew, thankfully I didn't need to pull the TL card.* The squeak of the chair and lack of stomps told Jon that Dan dropped back into the seat.

Outside Bennie's Gas Station — Command Truck

Unfortunately, in the few moments Dan became subjugated by his ire, he failed to notice Ted's irritability escalating and the youngsters becoming antsy and moving around. When Dan checked the monitor, he recognized what his short tantrum cost them. *Shit! I screwed up!*

"Jon, subject two moved behind the kids ... no longer in front of them. I only count five now. Sara is no longer in camera view." Dan's stomach flipped as he frantically scanned the displays. *Where is Sara?*

"Where is she?" Jon asked.

"I messed up. Not sure. I missed her moving," Dan said, self-loathing dripped from every word.

Outside Bennie's Gas Station

"Keep scanning, Dan. Tell us if she comes into view." Jon castigated himself. *Well, this is just peachy! My attempt at protecting Dan backfired one hundred percent. I should've told Dan to sit when he started pacing. If anything happens to the little girl, Dan is gonna blame himself. Hell, I'm the responsible one ... this is my fault. How messed up can this day get?*

About fifteen minutes later, Dan's concerned voice came over their headsets loudly, "Jon, Boss! Ted grabbed Kenny and is shaking him hard."

"Chance, what's Ted doing to Kenny?" Nick asked.

Gaping at his buddy Chance said, "Ted, don't! Sweet Jesus! Ted, don't ... he's just a little boy. Leave him alone. No, no, you don't want to do—"

Dan's commanding tone overrode Chance's, "Jon, you gotta go NOW! Ted's got Kenny on his knees with the gun coming up. He's gonna kill Kenny."

"Go, go, go," Jon gave the order.

The entry team executed the plan as the sound of a gunshot reverberated through the air.

Inside Bennie's Gas Station – Cashier Area

Jon and Ray stormed through the front door, weapons raised. Directing them at Chance as Jon bellowed, "TRF, drop your rifle, drop it now."

Startled Chance only stared.

The cashier and chaperone screamed.

Jon moved swiftly towards Chance as Ray covered him. "Put your weapon down now, put your hands up, on your knees now," Jon commanded. As Chance moved to comply, Jon grabbed the rifle and handed it off to Ray then moved forward to cuff Chance who went down as instructed.

"I'm sorry. I'm so sorry. I think Ted shot the kid." Chance kept apologizing between broken sobs.

Lonnie continued screaming as her entire body shook. Ray approached her, placed a hand on the cashier's shoulder, and using a calm tone, said, "You're okay. You're alright now."

Overcome by the thought of Kenny being killed, Gayla promptly fainted. Ray barely caught her and proceeded to lower her to the tile floor.

Inside Bennie's Gas Station – Back Area

At the same time, Jon and Ray made their entry, Lexa kicked out the vent cover and fast-lined to the ground, landing behind the children. Weapon raised, she yelled, "Police, TRF, weapons down." Lexa scanned for Ted and checked the position of the youngsters.

Bram and Loki stormed through the back entrance as Lexa dropped from the ceiling. They moved to the candy section with MP5s at the ready, shouting, "Police, drop your weapon," as they searched for the subject and hostages.

Ted was no longer where he had been only a split second before entry. Four little ones huddled together, crying. Kenny lay in the middle of the aisle, bawling at the top of his lungs. Three-year-old Sara was not among them.

Mere seconds is all it took for the team to enter and absorb all these details. Intuitively, they divided the tasks at hand. Lexa being closest to the clustered kids moved to cover them. Loki went straight to Kenny as Bram sought out Sara and Ted.

"Subject two and one hostage location unknown," Bram said.

Loki dropped to his knee beside Kenny and explored his little body for the wound he expected. He checked all over and didn't discover one, nor did he find any blood on the floor. "Hostage is unharmed. No harm to Kenny," Loki said with a huge sigh of relief as he gathered the small boy to him.

Bram caught a flash of movement at the back exit. "Subject on the move. Took a hostage and is exiting rear. In pursuit, could use some backup," Bram conveyed as he ran after Ted who grabbed hold of Sara.

Outside Bennie's Gas Station – Back Alley

Dan exited the command truck at top speed. "Bram, covering your six." He sprinted to catch up to Bram in the alley behind the station.

The two ran in the direction Ted took, rapidly cornering him in an alley with no outlet. Both slowed, prepared to contain him until Boss could negotiate since Ted had no escape route.

In his drug-induced frenzy, Ted wildly sought an exit. Realizing he boxed himself in, he turned to face the TRF officers with Sara held tight to his chest, facing outward, using her tiny body as a human shield. His other arm, the one with the gun, twitched uneasily at his side.

"You let me leave, or I swear I'll blow her brains out," Ted hollered as his hand holding the pistol jerked violently.

Dan scanned his surroundings with a skilled eye, honed from years of experience where situational awareness meant the difference between life and death. Sara, a tiny slip of a thing with long, blonde hair wore a pink and green polka dot sundress with a pink bow in her hair. Framed by golden lashes, no tears filled her big, green eyes. She remained quiet as Ted's arm around her little waist trapped her against Jitters.

As his gun aimed at Ted, Dan's focus returned to Sara's delicate face. Emerald orbs locked on to sapphire ones. An innocent soul met a suffering soul. Trust shone brightly from her eyes as Sara smiled sweetly at Dan. Her short, thin legs dangled, and Dan noted the absence of her shoes.

Dan's heart splintered into small, sharp shards as the memory of his little sister smashed savagely into his head.

SARA—SWEET—SMILE

SCREECH—SLAM—SILENCE—SHOELESS

SCREAM—SORRY—SAVE

SOLUTION

BANG!

Three bodies crashed to the asphalt.

You're Safe Now

14

July 15
Inside Bennie's Gas Station

As Bram ran out the back door in pursuit, the team overheard Dan tell Bram he had his six and they trusted those two to handle the situation in the alley. The rest of them began dealing with the bedlam going on inside the station. They needed to contain a distraught subject, soothe five frightened children, calm a hysterical cashier, and obtain medical help for the overwrought chaperone who now lay on the floor.

Ray squatted next to Gayla, checking her pulse, finding it strong, but fast. "Boss, I need EMS in here now. Gayla collapsed."

Nick proceeded towards the store, trying to listen to the chatter over the comms. He couldn't make out Ray's words over the shrill screaming in the background. "Ray, repeat please."

Ray swiveled to peer at the weeping cashier. He stood and placed a hand on her shoulder once again, applying slight reassuring pressure. "Lonnie, I need you to calm yourself, please. You're fine so quiet down, so I can help Gayla," he said in a smooth tone.

Once Lonnie hushed, Ray repeated, "Require EMS inside. Gayla fainted. Her heart rate is too rapid."

As Nick entered with the medics and strode towards Gayla, Jon attempted to pull the blubbering, distressed Bigelow to his feet. Jon needed to place him in the custody of uniforms outside, but the man wouldn't rise.

Chance kept bawling, "I'm sorry. I didn't want to hurt anyone. Sorry."

Frustrated, Jon's gut told him Bram and Dan needed him in the alley, but couldn't go until he handed off Chance. Jon snapped, "Kenny is fine. Get up now. On your feet. Let's go." Yanking the now compliant subject up, Jon escorted him out.

As Ray, Jon, and Boss dealt with their issues, Loki and Lexa focused on calming the terrified children. They must shepherd them outside to be checked over by medics before delivering them into the arms of their anxiously waiting parents. Ava clamped tightly to Lexa's leg, refusing to let go. Kenny, now being comforted by a slight rocking back and forth on Loki's lap, still cried, but no longer wailed bloody murder. The other three boys ceased bawling and nervously hovered close to Lexa.

Lexa gazed down at Ava with compassionate eyes. "Ava, sweetie, everything is alright." She glanced at the boys. "You all are okay. You're safe now. Shall we go to your parents?" With that, Ava put her arms up wanting to be held. Lexa scooped her up into a tender embrace, gently stroking the little girl's blonde curls. Loki stood with Kenny still ensconced in his arms. The seven of them started for the front exit.

BANG!

Five Alpha Team heads jerked up, and eyes widened in shock as the sound of a single gunshot ricocheted in their headsets.

"Bram? Dan? Status?" Nick urgently called, rising from where he knelt next to Gayla. He hurried towards the rear door of the station.

His repeated calls for status were met with only silence.

Outside Bennie's Gas Station — Front

Jon's gut now raged. "Guys, status!" Jon growled as he approached the constable who would assume custody of the subject.

Silence.

"STATUS NOW!" Jon roared as he handed over Chance.

The patrol officer flinched at the ice-hard tone, steel set jaw and lightning flash in the TRF officer's eyes which dared anyone to defy his command. *Damn, he's scary, Glad I'm not the one who didn't respond. They're gonna receive a big-time ass chewing.*

Silence.

Jon spun on his heel and stormed to the alley, alarmed neither Bram nor Dan answered. *This is not what I wanted for a unique day.*

Outside Bennie's Gas Station — Back Alley

Nick and Jon skidded to a halt, taking in the perplexing scene before them. They found Ted lying dead, a bullet through his head. Dan supine on the asphalt and unmoving with little Sara clinging to his chest and sobbing. And Bram appeared to be in shock, down on his knees, hands lying limp on his thighs, head shaking slightly back and forth with faraway eyes and a dazed expression on his face.

"What the hell?" bellowed Jon as his eyes roved from Dan to Bram to Ted. No response.

Sharing an apprehensive glance, Alpha's leaders recognized something terrible occurred, but didn't know what yet with both their teammates unresponsive. Nick assumed control as he directed, "Jon, I'll check Sara and Dan. You deal with Bram."

Jon moved closer and placed a hand on Bram's shoulder, assessing his unfocused eyes. "Hey, talk to me, buddy."

His mind fuzzy and his eyes out-of-focus, Bram remained trapped by the disordered thoughts swirling in his head. *One report, Dan killed Ted. If Ted is dead, why is Dan lying unmoving too? It doesn't make sense. He should be standing. Ted's dead … hey, that rhymes. How did Sara get over to Dan, and why is the little one holding him? So tiny and helpless. She's crying. Why?*

"Buddy, what happened?" Jon tried again.

Bram's voice came out in a whisper, "Dan shot Ted?"

Recognizing the inflection used made Bram's words a question, not a statement, Jon asked, "Bram, are you okay? Tell me what occurred."

The confusion continued to spin in Bram's mind. *Ted's surely dead, then why isn't Dan moving? Is he dead too? Did both fire at the same time? Did I miss a report? No, a sole loud bang. Only one, a single shot, just one, and it came from Dan's gun. I'm sure it did. Dan aimed and fired so fast. Too fast? No talking, only shooting. Why didn't he talk first?*

"Dan shot Ted." This time his words came out a statement, not a question.

Nick knelt to check Dan's pulse. *Steady, but not too rapid, the increase is likely due to adrenaline.* Finding a spot of blood near Dan's head, Nick carefully probed the rookie and found a slight lump and a small cut on the back of his head. *Appears minor, but will likely give him a headache.*

Not finding any other injuries, no bullets to the vest, nothing, Nick concluded Dan must've fallen and striking the ground knocked him unconscious. *But how did he fall? Perhaps slipped while taking cover or trying to save Sara.* Though Nick realized Dan should be examined by a paramedic, he must first calm Sara and move her away from this disturbing scene.

Slowly shaking his head, Bram repeated, "Dan shot Ted."

Loki, Ray, and Lexa all overheard what Bram kept repeating and wondered why Dan didn't say anything. Lexa and Loki remained busy with the kids, but Ray was now en route to the alleyway.

Arriving, Ray stopped dead in his tracks. *Shit, this isn't good.* With Boss and Jon dealing with his teammates, he went towards Ted to secure the weapon lying near the dead subject. Ray glanced at Dan, then Bram on his way as he projected calm into his tone, "Subject neutralized. Loki, we need EMS in the alley. Dan's unconscious. Bram appears to be in shock."

Outside Bennie's Gas Station — EMS Rigs

Carrying Kenny, Loki arrived at one of the three emergency medical service vehicles which responded as Ray requested medics for Bram and Dan. Handing the child to a lanky but muscular paramedic with short, light ash brown hair, Loki noted the nametag on the uniform shirt read, J. Shea.

Loki said, "We've got two officers in the back alley who need assistance. One is dazed, and the other is unconscious."

Jim stopped his assessment of the crying boy for a moment and inquired, "Any GSWs?"

Clenching a fist, praying for a no, Loki asked, "Boss, either one shot?"

"No, Unsure what transpired, but Dan has a slight lump and small cut on his head." Turning his gaze, Nick studied his stupefied entry specialist. "Bram's dazed. Truly no idea what caused their conditions."

Loki relayed the information, grateful Dan and Bram had not been shot … cause quite frankly if Dan had been, twice in one day was too darned much. *This profoundly unique day is turning out far from awesome. Wonder if the omen might be more of a curse.*

Jim did a quick scan of the five children they needed to tend as he listened to the constable. "Since their injuries don't sound life-threatening, someone will be there after we finish examining these kids." Refocusing his attention on the young boy going into shock, Jim said, "Trey, we need to move."

Loki observed Shea push the gurney in the rig and hop in the back after which his partner closed the doors then raced to the driver's side. As the ambulance pulled away, Loki said prayer Kenny would be okay. He glanced at Lexa, giving her a sympathetic smile as she tried to extract herself from Ava. The little one was afraid to go to the medics, but Lexa calmed her and coaxed her into allowing the female paramedic to come close. *Lexa interacts so well with kids. She'll be a fantastic mom someday.*

He informed Boss, "EMS is dealing with the traumatized children they'll be there as soon as possible."

Nick replied, "Copy. Dan's still out cold, but it appears to be only a minor head wound so focus on the kids."

"Copy." Loki refocused on helping Lexa and the paramedics with the distressed kids.

Outside Bennie's Gas Station — Back Alley

Nick lightly placed a hand on the back of the tiny, sobbing girl. She lifted her golden head and peered at him with tears running down her face. "Everything is okay. Will you come to me?" Nick's heart wrenched, observing such distress in the girl's expression.

Sara shook her head and held onto Dan.

"Please?"

Another shake no.

"It'll be alright. You're safe."

Sara's sobbing increased as she held Dan tighter.

"Please? I can take you to your mommy." Nick wondered why Sara vigorously refused to release her hold. "Why don't you want to go?"

"Safe," a tiny voice said.

"Yes, you are safe now," Nick confirmed.

"Safe," and a forceful head shake along with sobbing is how Sara responded.

Baffled by her reaction, Nick took time to assess the situation. *She's only three and unmistakably traumatized. Perhaps her one word means she feels secure with Dan. Pulling her away from him will likely increase her distress. How do I communicate to her she is also safe with me?*

During Nick's exchange, Jon placed his arm around Bram and attempted to break through the haze. "Buddy, come on. Shake it off. Bram, look at me. Where are you, man? Focus on my voice. Talk to me."

As Jon continued to speak, Bram's eyes began to focus and come back to the present, regaining control as his brain exited the miasma. *Why did Dan shoot Ted without even trying to talk? Why would he do that?*

The answer came to him. *Ted shot Kenny. He was an active shooter. Dan neutralized Ted before he could kill Sara, too.* Bram gave his head a sharp shake and blew out a ragged breath before inhaling a deep cleansing one and exhaling gradually as his mind became crystal clear.

Bram gazed at Jon with ferocious determination carved into his features. The expression might be read as a father protecting his young as Bram stated in a rock-hard voice, "Dan saved Sara."

Not expecting such a forceful comment from his long-time friend, Jon questioned, "He saved her?"

"Yes!" Bram nodded with conviction before abruptly standing and going kneel beside Dan. He clasped Dan's left bicep and squeezed. In his fatherly voice, he said, "She's safe. Dan, you saved Sara. Wake up. Everything is alright now. You protected her. Sara isn't hurt, and you're okay."

Bram's actions shocked not only Nick and Jon but him too. Unsure what drove him to react this way, Bram's heart sensed he must communicate to Dan little Sara remained alive and well.

Sara continued to sob, still clutching Dan with all strength she possessed, as her emotion-filled tiny voice chanted, "Safe, safe."

Nick needed to find out what transpired. There might be a clue which would allow him to help this little girl. He could forcefully remove her, but he believed he would cause more trauma. For now, she would stay with Dan.

Everyone grasped something unusual occurred. Otherwise, Dan wouldn't be unconscious with no apparent injuries. Something caused him to collapse. They would need to understand the facts before they could begin to figure out how they might help. Jon and Ray now stood behind Nick, all three staring at Bram with expectant expressions hoping he would shed light on this situation.

"Tell us what happened," prompted Jon.

Bram recited facts, "Dan caught up to me after I exited the rear door. We both ran flat-out after the subject. Ted held Sara to his chest, facing outward. With no outlets in the alley, we boxed him in. Dan and I positioned ourselves where we could see each other. I stood over there."

He only pointed out his location because Ted and Dan still lay in their original positions. "Using Sara as a shield, Ted turned around facing both of us, but more towards Dan. Ted registered solidly in the red-zone when he realized he couldn't escape. A frenzied look came into his eyes, and his body movements remained jerky and unpredictable. As Dan scanned the area, assessing tactical options," Bram peered at Jon, "the calculating expression crossed his face."

Jon nodded, they all were acquainted with Dan's cold, emotionless façade as he assessed critical situations.

"Yeah, well, when Ted shouted he would blow Sara's brains out if we didn't let him leave, Dan's gaze locked with Sara's for the briefest moment. And this sounds weird, but I got the impression two souls conversed. Their gaze broke as Sara smiled sweetly at Dan."

"Although fixated by her smile, in my peripheral vision, I glimpsed Dan glancing down. A fraction of a second later he neutralized the subject. We didn't identify ourselves or tell Ted to drop his weapon." Bram shifted his view to the dead man before moving back to Dan.

Jon shared a glance with Nick, both thinking, *'This might be a problem with NRB.'*

Bram continued, "Everything occurred so fast. Dan must've caught some movement or threat I missed in the split-second before he fired. Maybe something indicated Ted intended to follow through on his threat to kill Sara. After all, Ted already fired inside the station."

Both leaders sighed in relief and communicated silently, *'NRB problem averted. Ted was an active shooter.'*

Still bewildered by it all, Bram's eyes moved between Boss and Jon. "Ted lost his grip on Sara as they both fell. Then Dan was on the ground with Sara sobbing on top of him. It stunned me. I only heard one shot. My mind got lost for a bit trying to decipher how Dan could be down when there was only one report, and how or why Sara ended up on him bawling. That's when you guys showed up, I assume."

As Bram finished, Lexa and Loki approached after ensuring the kids were okay and safely with the paramedics and their parents. Lexa peered down at Dan—concern written in her eyes. She turned her attention to Nick. "Boss, the units have taken over the scene for mopping up. EMS is still busy, probably another ten minutes or so."

Nick nodded, endeavoring to sort everything in his head. This call went from good to bad to weird.

Still puzzled by what transpired, Bram's gaze returned to Dan. "I still can't figure out what caused him to collapse."

Loki knelt and placed a supportive hand on Bram's shoulder as he scrutinized Dan's face and the crying girl clinging to him.

Dan's eyelids started moving as he struggled to open his eyes. He groaned as his hands clenched into fists and released several times. Then his right hand reached out as if he held something. It jerked and dropped limply to the ground as if he lost hold on whatever he had been grasping. He began to regain consciousness, much to the team's relief.

Their relief proved fleeting and turned to alarm when Dan uttered in a small and scared tone, "Sara, oh God, please no. Her shoes. No shoes. Sara, don't go. Why not me? Hurts! Sara, no, no. Don't leave me, Sara. Not her, take me. Sorry, sir, I failed to protect her. Just gone. Didn't save her. Sir, I'm sorry. Stop, don't hurt me. Sir, don't, please stop, it hurts. Yes, sir, no crying allowed. Should've been me. My fault she's gone, sir."

They all exchanged horrified expressions and remained immobile as Dan appeared stuck in some godawful memory or nightmare.

Dan's eyelids flew open as he cried out, "SARA," in a voice filled with abject desolation. He stilled, his eyes staring into the sky, but wholly unaware of his surroundings.

What happened next astonished the team. Tiny Sara lifted her head and scooted her body to peer into Dan's eyes. Locking her teary eyes with his forsaken ones, seemingly searching for something, she repeatedly whispered, "Safe," to him in a soothing, lilting, child's voice as she placed a little hand on his cheek.

Dan blinked, once, twice, three times. The world began to take shape around him, and Dan registered he laid flat on his back on the ground. Lovely green eyes locked onto his deep blue ones, drawing his attention. A comforting, soft voice kept repeating one word … safe.

He blinked again—an innocent soul consoled a tormented soul. *She's safe. I'm safe.* Burning tears gathered in his eyes and threatened to spill out. Dan's muscular arms wrapped around the tiny slip of a girl and held her close in a protective embrace.

Nodding into her hand, Dan murmured, "Safe."

The blonde-haired girl with pure emerald eyes breathed a soft, "Safe," before she kissed his cheek.

Two sets of eyes closed as they both sighed. Sara scooted back down and settled her head in the crook of Dan's shoulder. She moved her tiny hand, laying it over his heart. "Safe," she mouthed one last time before drifting into an exhausted sleep in his arms.

Silence reigned. Seconds ticked by, but no one dared move a muscle—afraid to shatter the sanctuary the sweet girl built for their friend. Dan's glistening eyes blinked open again, and a single tear escaped.

Dan peered at his teammates, locking gazes with each of them for a few seconds as he searched for something. What he sought they couldn't begin to fathom, but whatever he discovered seemed to reassure him because Dan sighed as a serene expression settled on his features, and he silently mouthed, "Thank you."

A kindhearted, fatherly countenance appeared on Bram's face as gazed at Dan and softly said, "Safe."

Dan nodded. "Safe."

Each team member, in turn, calmly repeated, "Safe."

They all remained motionless and silent for several more minutes, each striving to regain their composure, mentally processing what occurred and contemplating its meaning. By unspoken agreement, no one commented on what transpired. Whatever happened appeared to be cathartic for Dan, evidenced by the respite now reflected in his expressive eyes.

Jon moved first. Drawing everyone's attention to him as he adjusted his stance to one of authority. A hint of mischief entered his gray eyes, and a broad grin appeared as he sternly said, "No napping in alleys either, Broderick."

Dan couldn't stop the grin from growing. He realized the unacceptable nap location list would most likely become quite lengthy if this kept up. "Copy."

As he started to rise, cradling a sleeping Sara in his arms, six pairs of hands reached out to help him up. Dan's face lit with happiness as his heart warmed with a sense of belonging and the acceptance shown by his chosen family.

A Matter of Trust

15

An impressive sight greeted the onlookers as seven TRF constables in full tactical gear rounded the corner out of the alley. Flanked by three teammates on each side, a handsome, young blond constable cradled a sleeping girl in his arms. They strode with purpose and conviction towards a distressed couple who were busy consoling their other daughter, five-year-old Ava.

Loki, Ray, Lexa, Jon, Bram, and Nick stopped a few paces back from the girl's parents as Dan approached the mother and carefully placed Sara into her waiting arms. He leaned in close and spoke softly so only Mrs. Clarry heard. "If Sara ever asks, please tell her Dan Broderick is safe because of her. Sara's soul is beautiful and pure."

He stepped back slightly as he smiled down at Sara before reaching out to lightly stroked her hair. Dan bent over and placed a gentle kiss on her forehead and whispered, "Thank you, Sara." Pivoting, Dan strode towards his chosen family. As he approached them, Lexa and Loki each grabbed one of his arms and redirected his trajectory. Confused, he halted. "What?"

Lexa eyed him with an arched brow and pursed lips. This man scared her twice today. As he lay on the ground both times, emotions stirred in her, things she never felt for a man before. Lexa pushed the uncharacteristic reactions down and took a deep breath. "You were out cold for several minutes. You need to be checked out before going with NRB."

"Exactly!" Loki's grip increased … holding on. He would follow through on the vow he made only a short time ago.

Noting Loki's anxious demeanor and Lexa's concern for his wellbeing, Dan allowed them to steer him towards the EMS rig where he sat on the edge of an empty gurney … their smiles his reward for complying.

In truth, he not only conformed for them, but for himself too. Though he detested being examined and didn't believe it to be necessary for the small bump and headache, he loathed dealing with Dick Donner more. He decided to fight one aversion with another and enjoy a slight reprieve before having to discuss two shootings with the abhorrent NRB agent who now glared at him from a distance.

After Loki and Lexa delivered him, they moved off when Boss beckoned them. A glance around at the children being treated indicated it would be several minutes until a medic would be available to give him a once over. While waiting, Dan mulled over what happened in the alley. He realized the team must be wondering about his reaction, but they wouldn't force him to explain. Their expressions while he searched their faces, revealed unspoken respect for his privacy.

A part of Dan didn't want to hold his secret in anymore. He hoped they wouldn't judge him too harshly if he shared with his team how he was responsible for the death of his sister Sara. He wondered how they would react if he explained when he noticed Sara Clarry had no shoes on, the horrible memory of his Sara's death slammed him, and in that instant, he couldn't allow tiny, sweet Sara to be killed by Ted.

Sighing, for once, Dan was genuinely appreciative of his lightning-fast reaction time. If he had not seen in that fraction of a second Ted raising the gun towards her head, little Sara would be dead now. If that occurred, Dan feared he would've been irrevocably lost and broken.

Perhaps my chosen family deserves to know. Can I trust them with this memory? Maybe. Apprehension and anxiety, born of past hurt snuck back in, causing him doubt. *Am deluding myself, is naïveté clouding my judgment again? Will trusting them backfire on me again? I'm tired of being hurt … but TRF is different … isn't it? Yeah, … their eyes told me I'm safe with them.*

To the casual observer, Dan's decision might seem such a small thing, but in actuality, he made a huge step forward. *How do I go about revealing something like this? Starting a conversation with … hey, guess what, I killed my sister, probably isn't the best way. Finding the right words is hard. One reason I never told my unit about Sara. Hell, the only one I ever confided in is Brody, and that was only after we got shitfaced drunk.*

Dan chuckled as his thought prompted another from left field. *Crap, I'm gonna go broke … I got hurt again. I'll be buying the first round tonight at the Pond for sure. Will they consider this to be two times and will I be responsible for two rounds?*

He sobered as a solution came tonight. *After a few beers, I'll be more relaxed. Perhaps it will be easier to tell them how I failed to save my Sara, and that is the reason I don't like to talk about my family. Well, maybe not that last part.*

Still considering how much to tell the team, the same paramedic who checked him at the bank arrived and began asking questions, drawing Dan from his deliberations. As Brad did his thing, Dan distractedly watched the scene around him and wondered at all the news crews. *Must be a slow news day to cover a gas station robbery.*

Several minutes later, as Brad completed his assessment, Dan spotted Boss and Jon approaching. *Great timing.* Dan rolled down his sleeve before buttoning his cuff. "I'm okay."

Nick eyed him and grinned, but turned to the paramedic. "How's my guy?"

Brad reported, "I disinfected the cut. No concerns regarding the lump on the head, no signs of concussion, although it might be tender for a bit. Offered pain meds for the slight headache, but he refused. Sergeant, my opinion is he is fit to return to duty."

Dan slid off the gurney. "Thanks." He turned to Boss and grimaced. "So, off to NRB now?"

"Alpha Team, Echo Team, all-hands-on-deck, Charlie Team needs backup now," Tia sounded off in their headsets.

"What's the situation?" Nick asked.

"Charlie is on scene in Rouge Park, responded to shots fired call. Sergeant Harmon is reporting a gang war in progress. More than two dozen active shooters dispersing in multiple directions," Tia explained.

"Alpha en route. Call in any available members of Bravo and Delta. With so many shooters and the size the park we'll need all available officers," Nick commanded as his team raced to the vehicles.

Outside Bennie's Gas Station – Near NRB Vehicle

NRB Agent Richard Donner glared furiously at the back of Dan Broderick and silently fumed. "I'll bring the cocky son of a bitch down a notch or two. He doesn't deserve to wear a TRF uniform. He's nothing, but a killer," he muttered under his breath.

Kendall Stevens, who stood nearby, overheard Donner say something but couldn't make out the muted words. She ambled over to him. "Quite a day they've had, huh? And it sounds like it might get worse with this new situation. Their job is hard. I'm not sure how they do it, but I'm glad we have constables like them to keep us all safe."

Richard narrowed his gaze on Stevens. He didn't like her much. Tamping down his hatred of Broderick, hiding it from view, he said, "Our job is difficult, too. We keep the police accountable. I'm afraid some of the TRF officers think their badge is a license to kill."

Eyeing Richard carefully, Kendall asked, "Why do you think that?"

Donner turned towards the car, opened the door, and sat. "Cause some kill a lot of people."

"Who?" Kendall asked not believing the vitriol coming out of Donner's mouth. He spat out statements which raised her hackles.

"Broderick, for one. He's been with TRF only a year and racked up more kills than any other constable. He likes to tell all the gory details when I interview him. Goes on and on, says he needs to paint the picture. He enjoys the kill so much … it's sickening. I swear, if he weren't a cop, he would be a mass murderer." Donner pulled the door closed, effectively ending the conversation.

Kendall shivered as Donner drove off. His words about the blond constable possessed malice. She wondered why Donner disliked Broderick. *Is there a basis to support Donner's words? Is Broderick a bad seed?*

Realizing the team would be busy with the gangs for quite some time, Kendall decided to return to the NRB office and do a little investigation into the interviews of Constable Broderick. Her impression of Broderick didn't jive with Donner's comments.

Afghanistan – General's Office – 11:30 p.m. (3:00 p.m. Toronto)

General Broderick paced his office, noting the late hour. He impatiently waited for confirmation from Mike of Pletcher's apprehension. The cat and mouse game went on for far too long as the man managed to evade them for over three months.

William wanted him captured and brought to justice for hurting his daughter and for selling military secrets. He wanted Pletcher never to spend another day outside the walls of a prison. Well, … if being honest, part of him wished Pletcher dead for what he did to Becca, but he would settle for lifetime incarceration.

He tried several times to contact Daniel to inform him Pletcher might be in the area, but every call went straight to voicemail. Unable to reach his son, or soothe his churning gut, he rang Walter to give him a heads-up, but it went unanswered as well. Although concerned by the lapse in time, *three hours and still no callback*, and the possible implications, *no, not everything is about Daniel,* William understood his friend wouldn't ignore him lightly. Unease pervaded his thoughts as he reconsidered asking Erik to phone Daniel to warn him.

Realizing his rather vague call-me-back request didn't communicate the urgency of the matter, though William couldn't say much on the sensitive topic on an unsecured line, he decided to try contacting Walter again. After pulling out his phone and with his finger poised to select Gambrill's number, he halted when the cell began ringing.

Hoping for the call to be from Walter, the caller ID revealed it to be Galloway. His disappointment paled with the import of this call. He pressed accept and answered with a crisp, "Broderick."

Mike didn't relish making this call, but avoidance was not an option. "Sir, we confirmed Pletcher landed in Vancouver but lost track of him shortly after he arrived at the airport. I suggest the best course of action is to relocate Hestia and Phoebe."

William couldn't help the smile which came to his face. Mike gave Yvonne the codename of Hestia, the Goddess of hearth and home. Becca's moniker fit her too. Phoebe, the Titan goddess of prophetic radiance, surely matched Becca's features and bright, independent spirit. Though, unlike her namesake, who was spared from being imprisoned in Tartarus, his high-spirited daughter would continue to be locked down tight for her protection until the slippery and treasonous Pletcher could be found and jailed.

The seriousness of the situation reasserted itself and William's grin faded. "Agreed. You say Pletcher touched down in Vancouver?"

"Yes, sir. We have him on video exiting the plane, but then he disappears. Someone must've tipped him off."

William didn't like this one damned bit. "Sounds like we might have a mole. If Pletcher got wind we were zeroing in on him, someone on the inside must've warned him. I want your full unit in charge of Hestia and Phoebe. No communication to anyone except your unit, Sutton, and myself. Take them to the Unknown."

Cognizant of where the general wanted him to take Mrs. Broderick and Becca, Mike nodded. Codenamed Unknown, the Guardian's safe house near Yellowknife, remained a closely guarded secret. The location obscured, with access limited to those who needed-to-know ... and currently, only the general, Colonel Sutton, and himself were aware of the exact coordinates. "Sir, what about Phoenix?

William thought about Daniel for a moment. If Pletcher went to Vancouver, Daniel would be safe enough for now. "The threat is undefined to Phoenix, and he is capable of covering his six if needed, for the moment. I'm not sure who else we can trust."

Though aware his suggestion wouldn't be popular, Mike put it out there anyway. "Sir, there's always Blain's unit. They're in Ottawa training."

The general's gut twisted when he thought about how Blain, Simons, and Shea turned their backs on Daniel. "I'll keep the option in mind if the situation warrants. Your priority is keeping Hestia and Phoebe safe. I'll talk to Sutton about putting Sergeant Walker's unit onto Pletcher's trail."

"Hammer's unit can be trusted, sir. Excellent soldiers, all of them. If there is a leak, its elsewhere," Mike stated with confidence.

"Contact me only if issues arise with Hestia's health. Otherwise, it will be safer to maintain blackout protocol." For William, his wife's and daughter's lives took priority, even though his heart broke as he accepted their safety, trumped his desire to converse with Yvonne.

"Wilco." Mike disconnected. As he strode to the other room to inform the Broderick ladies that they would be moving again, Mike's mind began working out details on how to transport them out of Vancouver unseen.

An old memory surfaced, and he grinned as he thought, fish bait. Getting Dan out of Makhachkala in the bait box worked well, but wouldn't work here. Ah, but his other idea would. He chuckled as he thought about wild, party girl Becca dressed in a nun's habit. *Miss Fashionista will not be happy with me, but that doesn't matter so long as I kept both ladies safe.*

Priorities, Pendulums, and Planning

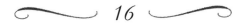

16

July 15
En Route to Rouge Park — 3:00 p.m.

As Nick entered the SUV, he said, "Tia, I'll be switching to channel three in a moment to coordinate with Sergeants Winter and Harmon. The rest of Alpha Team will remain on channel one. Alpha's ETA is twenty-five minutes. What's Echo's ETA and were you able to recall anyone from Bravo or Delta teams?"

"Sergeant Winter says Echo is fifteen minutes out. I reached every member of Bravo, except their rookie, Devon Hodges, he's out sick. I also contacted Aaron, Frank, and Kirk of Delta, but the remainder of Sergeant Turpin's team is out of town on vacation. ETA for everyone recalled is between ten and twenty minutes," Tia replied.

"Copy, switching channels now," Nick replied.

As Dan reached the truck and swung open the passenger door to jump in, he spied a large, brown bag on the seat. After grabbing it, he hopped in and noted **Proper Care and Feeding of Dantastic** written in bold black marker on the outside of the bag.

He turned to Lexa with a quizzical expression. "What the heck is this?"

"Open and find out." Lexa smiled.

Unfolding the top, inside Dan found a double-meat sandwich, two energy drinks, half a dozen power bars, and three bottles of water. On top of all the food, sat two aspirin tablets with a note in Jon's handwriting. **Take these now, Broderick. That's an order!**

Dan grinned. "Aw guys, thanks. When did you get this?" The gesture touched him. Famished, he unwrapped the roast beef and cheese sandwich and took a huge bite. His head, chest, and shoulder did still hurt, though he would never admit as much to the team. So he complied with Jon's order and downed the aspirin with a swig of the caffeinated beverage.

"We grabbed food while the medic checked you over. We thought you might like something, especially since you think brushing your teeth is more important than eating breakfast," Lexa said glibly.

"Yeah, well, ... priorities. Just sayin'." Dan gave Lexa one of his WOW smiles before taking another massive bite of the sandwich. He loved the little flash of fire his grin stoked in her eyes.

He must be careful, though. They were at work, and he didn't know where this new twist might be going. Waking up next to her this morning felt wonderful ... right. But he didn't want to blow his chance with her because he sensed he wanted more than casual sex.

Lexa tried not to react to his smile, though difficult not to. She blew out a small breath and focused on driving as she banished heated thoughts his amazing smile brought forward. However, a few minutes later, Lexa couldn't help but glance at Dan again as he ate. He managed to inhale the whole sandwich, two protein bars, and an entire energy drink. "Impressive!"

"What?" Dan opened a third bar and the second drink.

"How do you eat so fast?"

"Training." Lexa's confusion prompted Dan to explain, "In the field, never knew when the next meal would be or how long I had to eat. It was either go hungry or develop the habit to consume as much as possible as fast as possible when the opportunity presented itself."

"Wow, you've got skill. You could probably win an eating contest." She smiled at him, but a sad thought crossed her mind as he downed the fourth energy bar. *You appear to have way too much practice.* She noted Dan tucked the remaining two bars into his vest and opened a bottle of water.

About ten minutes from the scene, Jon said, "Dano, I think your tactical assessment skills and military field experience will be valuable in developing a strategy in this environment. I want you to join the planning session."

"Copy," Dan responded, shocked, yet pleased Jon requested his assistance. Things improved between them in the past few months, but Jon acknowledging his abilities like this further validated he now belonged.

Today was turning out to be a major study in contradictions with huge emotional swings. Dan experienced the highs of his profound happiness, sense of belonging, and making a difference. He also endured the gut-wrenching lows associated with memories of Brody's death, his torture, Sara's loss, and taking lives. This pendulum ride screwed more than a little bit with his head.

Dan understood he must put everything in a box to deal with later because now he must focus on his job. A gang war in acres of woodlands with over a dozen active shooters would be dangerous and exhausting. He closed his eyes and concentrated on breathing slow, mentally preparing himself.

Rouge Park – Command Post – 3:25 p.m.

Alpha arrived last on scene. Nick, Jon, and Dan went straight to where Commander Gambrill, the sergeants, and the tactical leads converged to discuss strategy. The remainder of the team geared up before wandering over to join the other TRF constables gathered in small clusters.

They stopped behind and slightly away from the three Delta members. Still lost in their quiet mental clearing of the slate, they were slow to register the conversation taking place until they overheard Dan's name.

"What the hell is Broderick doing with the TLs? He's a rookie and doesn't belong," Aaron Plouffe, Delta's sniper, griped.

"Maybe the cocky, ex-special ops guy thinks he knows more than our experienced TLs," Delta's newest rookie, Kirk Henson, parroted things Aaron previously shared about Broderick.

"None of our business. Dan's an excellent officer, and he's been here a year, so he isn't a rookie." Frank Hudson tried to shut down Aaron and warn Kirk to drop the subject. He didn't like the way Aaron continued to bad-mouth Broderick. It was annoying, and he hoped Aaron's attitude didn't taint Kirk like it did Cooper back in April. Luckily, Cooper wised up and changed his mindset. But Kirk had only been with Delta for two weeks, and his chumminess with Aaron might become a problem.

Kirk ignored Frank's hint the Alpha sniper wasn't up for discussion. "If Broderick's so good, why is his tactical lead always pissed off at him? I overheard Hardy yelling at him a few times my first week here. Maybe Hardy's only keeping him on a short leash?"

Aaron snorted. "Personally, I don't think he's good at all. He doesn't belong in TRF. No more than he belonged in Special Forces. We don't need *his* kind here. Broderick's a pretty boy, all show, and no go. My uncle said his daddy pulled strings to get him into JTF2 in the first place. According to my uncle, Broderick was constantly being transferred to new units because none of them wanted to be saddled with a first-class screw-up."

"To be selected for JTF2 you gotta be damned amazing. And Dan's sexual orientation isn't anyone's business but his own," Frank countered and shifted, uncomfortable with the topic.

"Who's his dad and how would he influence him getting in?" Kirk reeled as he put together Aaron's and Frank's comments … 'his kind' plus 'sexual orientation' equaled to Kirk 'gay.' *Dan's gay?*

Frank clenched his jaw. He would let Sarge deal with this when he got back from vacation … set Kirk straight before Lexa dropkicked him like she did Cooper for bad-mouthing Dan. Part of Frank wished Lexa also landed a kick on Aaron; it might've taught him a lesson and shut him up.

"His father is General Badass of Special Forces. My uncle, who's in his command, told me Baby Broderick got kicked out under a cloud. All hush-hush and covered up. He killed a unit mate. Had a lover's spat with his boyfriend then blew him away with a .50 cal. Bet Daddy Broderick is disappointed having such a pansy-assed screw-up for a son," Aaron ridiculed.

"Damn! That can't be true. If he killed someone, they wouldn't allow him to join TRF. Right?" Kirk's eyes flicked over to Dan at the command post. He didn't know what to believe, but Dan was handsome … gorgeous … the type of guy which always attracted him.

Shifting his gaze back to Aaron as he continued to disparage Dan, Kirk recognized he needed to be careful since his teammate sounded homophobic and that might spell disaster. Kirk thought TRF would be different than his previous division, more accepting of him, but perhaps not.

Aaron sneered, "Word is his daddy arranged the position for him with Commander Gambrill, so the general could save face when his son left the military by joining the elite police team. Don't understand how the members of Alpha stomach having someone like Broderick forced on them.

"They had no say in the matter, compelled to work with him. I don't trust him. He was only here a few months when he shot Ray." Aaron laughed. "Lexa KO'd Broderick in the locker room afterward. He's such a wuss. Medics carted Broderick out, unconscious after a girl hit him."

Ticked off overhearing Dan being bad-mouthed in this way, it was not lost on Alpha Team they heard some things they once thought or said. But Dan was now one of them … a proven and valued member of their family and this angered them.

They reminded themselves they were all professionals, and now was neither the time nor the place to engage in a pissing match to set Aaron straight. They all needed to focus on the job at hand and work together. However, recognizing that still didn't make it easy to hear the slanderous remarks, and they would definitely set things right at the proper time.

Although, Lexa did seriously contemplate drop-kicking Aaron to teach him a lesson. Aaron was not new—he had been with TRF the same length of time as Dan, and he should be aware of the respect their team now possessed for Dan. And Aaron damned-well should realize Dan was not just a pretty boy or a screw-up. Dan's record proved many times over he was a damned fine constable.

Having heard enough of Aaron's antagonistic and holier-than-thou attitude, Frank drily remarked, "And you would know all about nepotism, wouldn't you? Didn't I see your great-uncle talking with Commander Gambrill when you tried out for TRF? An RCMP Superintendent, I don't imagine—"

"That's not the same thing!" Aaron scowled at Frank.

"Isn't it?" Frank pinned his glare on Aaron.

The tension between his teammates made Kirk unsure what to think now. *Is Broderick a screw-up or does Aaron only hate Broderick because he is gay? Better to keep my mouth shut until I figure things out. If my teammate turns out to be homophobic, I might request a transfer.* Kirk was so tired of people judging him solely on his sexual preference. *Just because I prefer male bedpartners doesn't make me any less capable as a constable.*

Forcefully, Aaron stated, "No, it isn't. My great-uncle didn't have a damned thing to do with my entry into TRF. I earned my spot. Delta selected me. However, the cocky, worthless, Broderick waltzed in—"

Bram's anger surged. He decided the best way to stop this, for now, was to make their presence known, so he cleared his throat loudly.

Frank, Aaron, and Kirk turned and spotted Bram, Lexa, Ray, and Loki frowning at them. Kirk and Frank appeared embarrassed to be caught gossiping about a fellow officer, but Aaron had the gall to smirk.

At that moment, Nick approached and addressed everyone. "Alright, listen up. This appears to be a turf war between two rival gangs. The Crimson Eagles, headed by Pedro Basto, controls over a third of the drug and arms traffic in the Greater Toronto Area. The Jackals, a fairly new Russian gang, is run by Radoslav Yegorovich.

"They've been moving into Crimson Eagles territory and undercutting them. Radoslav is in custody and said his gang was lured here and ambushed by the Eagles. Basto was sighted on scene earlier. Guns and Gangs would like to bring him in alive if possible, to pump him for information on his network and suppliers."

Sergeant Bailey of Guns and Gangs interjected, "Be warned, Basto is one nasty dude and won't hesitate to kill. He was a champion middleweight boxer before he rose in the gang's ranks. Three years ago, he staged a coup, killed the top ten leaders of the gang, and took over. Basto killed four of them himself … beat them to death, but got off due to technicalities."

Nick added, "You are to use extreme caution. The subjects are heavily armed with a variety of assault weapons. Our goal is to apprehend, but given the risk presented, you're authorized to use lethal force if necessary. Don't take any chances. This will be no walk in the park. Keep sharp and stay safe. Jon will explain the tactical plan."

Jon took over. "Charlie Team apprehended ten members. Based on what we learned from them, we're looking for fifteen subjects. Three are from the Jackals, and the rest are Crimson Eagles. Commander Gambrill, Sergeant Pastore, and Sergeant Winter will coordinate from the command post and communicate between teams using channel one.

"We're mixing it up today, boys and girls. Some of you will be working with different teams. Given the amount of terrain to cover we'll break into seven teams of four. I will lead team one. Team two will be Camden, team three Doug, team four Colton, team five Paul, and team six Carl. Each team has been assigned a specific channel and will search a designated section of the grid and will break their section into four quadrants."

Aaron interrupted, "You only listed six teams. Who's leading the seventh?"

Jon grinned. Happy with Dan's input during the planning session, and the fact his rookie earned the admiration of the sergeants and tactical leads, Jon wanted to provide him with tangible proof he respected his skills. He also recognized Broderick could handle the pressure of leading while hunting down bad guys and believed giving him a taste of leadership TRF style to be essential for Dan's career.

To facilitate his objectives, Jon stated with authority, "Dan possesses the most experience in this type of scenario, so he'll take command of team seven with Lexa, Aaron, and Frank. You'll be searching section seven and be on channel seven."

Dan's expression reflected his surprise, and it morphed into a grin. He gave a small nod to Jon. *Damn, Jon is trusting me to lead. I will do my damnedest to prove to his trust is well-placed.*

Bram, Ray, and Loki glanced at Lexa with *'watch Dan's back'* expressions. None of them spotted the disgust briefly crossing Aaron's features. If they had, they would've spoken up and ensured Aaron was reassigned to Jon's team.

Jon's gaze returned to the group and concluded, "Your TLs will give you further instructions. Kirk, you'll join with Sergeant Bradley's team today."

"Copy." Kirk nodded, relieved not to be placed with either Frank or Aaron today given the tension between them. He wondered how Aaron would react to taking orders from Broderick. Kirk waffled on whether he should say anything but decided if Hardy respected Broderick enough to place a team in his charge, then Dan could handle whatever Aaron dished out.

Walter Gambrill observed as the teams huddled up then headed out. Jon acknowledging Dan's skills, listening to and acting upon Dan's input, and placing Dan in a leadership role pleased him. Nick's team indeed came through as he hoped, and his godson appeared to be doing well now.

He would enjoy updating his friend on Dan's progress when he returned the missed call from William later. Though for now, he must focus on the matter-at-hand, his pride for Dan taking a back seat to the safety and welfare of Toronto's citizens. Walter strode back to the table containing the maps of Rogue Park. *This isn't going to be easy ... we must locate and apprehend multiple subjects bearing assault weapons.*

Assault on Rogue Park

 *17*

Assigned to search the farthest sector from the command post, Lexa, Dan, Frank, and Aaron opted to fast-line into section seven from a police helicopter, ceding the initial advantages of concealment the rugged terrain and dense forest provided. Traveling by shanks' mare might have been safer and drawn less attention, but the stealth provided by hiking in would have exacted too high a price … time.

Foot travel would've consumed a fair measure of the four hours they used to clear three-fourths of their designated area. And with losing daylight in about an hour and a half, that would've complicated matters further because tracking in the dark without night vision gear would be near impossible. The subjects might be able to slip away if they still remained in this area.

Coming to the end of quadrant three, Dan halted and directed his team, "Hold up. Take a short breather and hydrate. I'm switching to channel one for a status check. Back in a second."

"Copy," Lexa responded. She stopped and leaned on a huge rock to grab a drink of water and a quick nibble of a power bar. This section proved to be quite a workout with the constant up and down steep ravines and plowing through dense foliage. She thought a machete would've come in handy as she relaxed a moment, glad for a brief rest.

As she bit into the energy bar and chewed unhurriedly, Lexa smiled thinking how Dan persisted until she took one of the two bars he shoved in his vest. When they stopped for a water break and check-in an hour ago, she realized she was out of bars, after sharing her last with Dan right before the call at Bennie's. Dan graced her with a lopsided grin and said he owed her two from earlier and handed her one.

He gave the second to Frank. When Frank found out it was Dan's last, he tried to refuse, but Dan insisted claiming neither one would want to incur the wrath of Jon if Frank dropped from hunger. The humorous way Dan conveyed his command to Frank caused him to chuckle and accept the offer. Lexa noted Dan appeared comfortable in the leadership role, and later she would privately thank Jon for publicly showing his faith in Dan by putting him in charge of this team.

So much changed in the past year and Lexa believed it to be a good thing. She smiled again for an entirely different reason as her mind wandered. Last night had been fantastic. *Dan is incredible in bed ... a natural there too.* Lexa hoped by sleeping with him once more, it would lessen her attraction, but as she glanced his way, she realized it hadn't. The electric zing continued ... demonstrated earlier when their hands touched as he passed her the protein bar. She strove hard not to react and yank her hand away from the sizzling energy which flowed between them.

Lexa remained uncertain of what to do. Working with Dan would be difficult if she couldn't touch him without experiencing things she shouldn't. *He must be only my teammate ... well, maybe a friend with benefits.* She sighed and tried to put those thoughts away since this environ was neither the time or place for erogenous contemplations. She took a sip of water and put her bottle away before scanning the area.

Motioning to Aaron to stop and maintain guard, Dan switched to channel one. "Boss, Team Seven checking in. Quadrant three cleared. We're moving into quadrant four. How many apprehended subjects so far?"

"Eleven in custody, leaving four, including Basto, still out there if the intel is correct," Nick responded before providing an update on the other teams' progress.

"Copy. Switching back to channel seven." Dan pulled out his water bottle and took a swig as he adjusted channels. "Team, let's move out. Four subjects still to find. Basto is still at large. Team Six finished their section, which leaves only us and Team Three searching our last quadrants. Aaron, resume point."

"Why should I?" Aaron sneered.

Dan almost rolled his eyes and wanted to snap at the man, but said calmly, "I'm team lead, and that's my order. Got a problem with it? Take it up with Jon when we get back. Until then, zip it. We have a job to do."

Aaron's continued defiance of Dan, questioning him at every turn ticked off Lexa. His petulance grated on her nerves, and she began to wonder how Aaron passed the psychological assessment of TRF's qualifications. She also didn't like his sophomoric comments when he asked her to take point, but kept her mouth shut.

Dan switching up partners while they searched quadrant two, made Lexa happy, but she was unsure why he did. Though, the phrase *'keep your enemies closer'* popped into her head as a motive. If Aaron didn't quit his unprofessional behavior soon, Lexa might bruise his bicep to teach him a lesson.

Frank wished Aaron would accept Dan was an excellent officer. He had no clue why Aaron persisted in his negative view. The man Frank perceived, in no way fit Aaron's description of a cocky, pretty-boy with no substance. In his eyes, Dan displayed an aptitude for tracking and tactics. Hardy wouldn't have put him in charge of a team if he didn't value Broderick's abilities. Familiar with Lexa's reputation too, she didn't suffer fools, Frank figured if Lexa respected someone, it meant they possessed skills. Her interactions with Dan today cemented in his mind, Lexa admired Dan's capabilities.

Listening to Aaron's shit became tiresome. *Can't Aaron recognize his uncle is wrong? Aaron is hardheaded, and sometimes it is difficult for him to let go of preconception, but until now, I never realized how jaded his thoughts are. Aaron is not only stupid but utterly blind. I need to talk with Sergeant Turpin soon … this is getting to the point I where I want to deck Aaron.* Frank sighed as he moved out, shelving his thoughts and focusing on locating the subjects.

Speaking of the devil, Aaron remained pissed, with his role in this assignment. He considered himself the most qualified TRF member in this team. *I'm more skilled in tactics than Frank, who spends most of his time profiling. And my tenure with TRF is a year longer than Lexa's and four more than Broderick. I should be the one leading. I'll be talking to Jon about Broderick's poor attitude when we return. Why the hell did Jon put the rookie in charge?*

In his opinion, they moved too slow through the quadrants. If he had been in charge, they would've finished clearing this entire section an hour ago. They would be back at the command post relaxing now like the rest of the teams instead of still trekking through the woods on a wild goose chase.

Aaron glanced over at Frank and Lexa as they moved out, his gaze lingered a moment on Lexa. *It was not too bad when paired with Lexa. At least she is hot-looking, especially her backside. I might be getting married soon, but it doesn't mean I can't still appreciate a nice ass … as long as I don't touch.* Aaron smirked as he recalled asking Lexa to take point because he excelled at covering the rear. *Lexa is so dense, she didn't even comprehend my innuendo.*

Dan's patience with Aaron wore thin as the man continued to test him. Aaron turned out to be as much of a pain-in-the-ass as his uncle. Several months ago, he learned to his surprise Aaron was related to Major Puffy. Aaron cornered him alone in the gun cage and said, 'I know the truth about you and Brody … my uncle, Major Plouffe, told me all about your lover boy. You're such a pansy-assed screw-up. You don't belong in TRF anymore than you belonged in Special Forces.'

Ever since that day, he ignored Aaron's continued snide remarks and innuendos about him and Brody being lovers and he got the job because of the general. Dan conceded the truth of Aaron's claim family connections facilitated his entry to TRF. Though the one pulling strings was his godfather, not his father, and Dan would never reveal that connection … better to ignore the jerk.

Aaron's dislike of him, his juvenile homophobic comments, his arrogance, and his negative attitude were things Dan could handle. He regularly dealt with guys like him throughout his military experience. But Dan drew the line at actions which put the team at risk.

Dan believed Aaron crossed the line when Aaron leered at Lexa's posterior while she spearheaded the search, instead of doing his job covering her back and scanning for the subjects. In his book, absolutely and unequivocally unacceptable behavior. Dan refused to put Lexa at risk with a partner who failed to do his primary task, so he switched up pairings.

Aaron's continual refusal to follow orders also became worrisome. Dan decided to put Aaron on point, ahead of him to keep an eye on him. Tempted to deck Aaron for ogling Lexa like a piece of meat, Dan realized the man was not a bad officer. And although he didn't have to like him personally, the issues Aaron had with him would need to be addressed after this call. Left unchecked, Aaron's impudence and churlish demeanor might put others at risk, and that would never be acceptable.

"Aaron, I said, move out. We've got a job to do," Dan stated forcefully.

Seething, Aaron started moving again. He wanted to punch Broderick in the worst way. He might do it once this was over. Aaron pushed his anger down for now and focused on doing his job.

Rouge Park – Command Post – 7:30 p.m.

Bram, Loki, Jon, and Ray trudged into the command post, having finished searching their section. They went to a table with drinks and food set out for them. After grabbing coffee and a sandwich, they took seats at a circular table next to members of Echo Team. The other teams who finished searching were spread out around the area, many sitting on the ground, flat-top rocks, or logs.

The terrain had not been easy, and everyone appeared dead tired. Ray sat next to Loki and lightly teased, "You survived the woods, buddy. No rabbit snares and not a single arachnid dared attack you today."

Bram and Ray chuckled.

Jon decided to change the subject, not wanting to torment Loki about his fear of spiders and dislike of the woods. "You all did excellent out there. We traversed some rough terrain. Ray, how's the shoulder?"

Ray rubbed his sore shoulder. "Fine."

Loki grinned. "That was some taken down, Ray."

Jon chuckled. "Bagged us four of them gang boys. They never saw you coming, Ray."

Stretching his tired and aching back, Bram pondered aloud, "I wonder how Dan and Lexa are doing."

As Nick poured coffee, he overheard Bram. He ambled over to their table. "Dan just checked in. They're doing well and moving into the fourth quadrant. Doug's team is also in the last quadrant of their section. If both teams come up empty, it appears Basto slipped through our net." Nick sunk to a chair to take a short break with his team.

They sat in silence, relaxing a bit as they consumed their refreshments, each wondering how Dan fared in the lead role. Bram, Loki, and Ray were also curious about how Aaron's mindset as well, would he give Dan a hard time, or would he put his personal feelings aside and be professional? They hoped for the latter.

A very long day, which didn't appear to be quite over, taxed Sean Boulet's energy. The Echo Team techie and explosives expert was bushed. He and most of the other members of Echo, rookie Noel Blythe, sniper Brett Santelli, and their Tactical Lead Carl Buckner, finished clearing section six and arrived at the command post about fifteen minutes ago. They congregated around one of the tables set up for TRF personnel. Sean smiled as his good friend and teammate Trevor McBride walked towards them with a plate of food and a cup of coffee in hand.

He missed Trevor in the past year. His buddy took a twelve-month extended leave to care for his mother while she underwent a bone marrow transplant. Everyone on Echo was glad things appeared to be going well for Trevor's mom, and he was finally back with them. Trevor returned only a week ago and his first week back had been a doozy. Echo ran non-stop every day they were on shift.

"Hey, Trevor, how was your stint with Charlie Team? We missed ya out there. Not gonna lend you out again anytime soon," Sean said in greeting as he pulled a chair over for his friend.

Trevor, Echo's entry specialist, had been parceled with members of Charlie to search section four. "We apprehended two subjects in our section. You?"

"Well, we only found one, just a kid, and he gave up easy. I guess that makes the total count eleven. Only sections three and seven to finish clearing. Have a seat, buddy. You look wrung out." Sean pushed out a chair for Trevor.

"Thanks." Trevor lowered his aching body to the seat. "Not looking so hot yourself. Today's been hell. I don't think any of us, or the guys from Alpha or Charlie want another one like it soon. I'm hungry and exhausted."

"Yeah, been a hell of a day, but I learned some new things."

"Like what?" Trevor asked with a mouthful of sandwich.

"Well, Carl here had us doing some crazy shit out there," Sean replied. "Carl, been meaning to ask you where that came from."

Carl leaned back and lowered his coffee. "Broderick."

"Broderick?" Brett questioned.

"Yeah, the guy sure understands field tactics. Astute and helpful with coming up with today's plan," Carl replied.

"Kinda thought he might when I spotted him with you," Trevor offered.

Four guys stopped to stare at him. Brett asked, "Why did you think that?"

"Because he's had loads of field experience. Happy to see him looking so well for once, almost didn't recognize him. Wanted to stop by to say hello and reintroduce myself, but we've been so busy since I got back, I haven't had a chance. Doubt he would remember me though." Trevor took another bite of his ham sandwich.

"You know Broderick?" Sean asked.

Trevor glanced at Sean. "Sort of. Set eyes on him often while stationed in Kandahar as an MP several years ago. I only talked to him once, but given his death-warmed-state at the time, I highly doubt he'll recollect me."

Taking another quick bite and swallowing, Trevor realized they wanted him to explain further. "I'd only been in the camp for two days and was on my way to grab some chow. I rounded a corner and discovered a guy on his knees, struggling to pull himself up on a crate. I went to assist. Grabbed his arm and helped him sit on the box.

"Covered in dust and grime, he appeared to have just returned from days in the field. Broderick peered at me and mumbled thanks. Man, he was so pale I thought he might pass out." Trevor shuddered a bit at the memory.

"When I inquired where he was headed he said the mess. Told him I was going there too. He only gave a slight nodded and took in a slow breath. I couldn't believe he could make it that far, so I asked him if he required help. He stared at me with a *'Why the hell do you care?'* expression but shook his head and stood. He took several shaky steps before getting his bearing and staggered towards the tent. I followed him in case he collapsed on the way.

"Inside, this massive hulk of a man with a bright smile—never knew his name, but he worked there—well, he took one glance at Dan before he seized his arm, steered him to a table, and guided him down on the bench. As I stood in line to grab my food, I watched the cook return to Dan at with a full plate.

"The place was full, and Dan's table was empty except for him, so I went and sat down. Never witnessed anyone eat so fast. Dan barely finished the first helping, and the big dude returned with another plate. He told Dan to eat, but slower this time or he would toss his cookies.

"Midway through this plate, Dan told me his name and asked for mine. I introduced myself, and we spent the next quarter-hour in conversation. Well, that isn't exactly right. I spent the next fifteen minutes talking. Dan only listened as he listlessly ate. I told him when I separated from the military after the completion of my tour, I planned on returning here and trying to earn a spot in TRF and told him why I was so keen on making it into TRF."

Becoming a little subdued, Trevor said, "As he finished his second plate a guy comes running up to him with a worried expression. The dude was about my height, with brown hair, and striking green eyes. I still remember their intense and cryptic exchange like it occurred yesterday.

"The soldier came to an abrupt halt at our table, immediately wrapped his arms tightly around Dan and hugged him for a full minute, maybe more. When he released him, he tilted Dan's face to his, stared directly into Dan's eyes and said, 'Danny, hold tight, I'm here! How long?' Dan said, 'Seven.' He then asked, 'How bad?' Dan spoke so softly that I almost didn't catch his reply, 'Thirty-two.' He embraced Dan again and whispered, 'Remember the beauty of life,' and Dan nodded once.

"As he held Dan, the green-eyed guy called out to five men who entered the mess, 'Found Blondie, seven and thirty-two. Move now!' Three of them rushed to grab food and water the cook had already packed for them—weird … like he knew what they would need. A lanky guy with light ash-brown hair rushed out of the tent, to where I couldn't guess.

"The fifth guy, a fierce giant by size and appearance … he must've been close to seven-foot and had a nasty scar across his face. He rushed to the table—to tell the truth, he scared me a bit. He swooped in and picked Dan up like he weighed nothing more than a child's rag doll, and started for the exit closely followed by the first dude and the other three."

Shaking his head slightly, Trevor said, "Never did figure out what the numbers meant. Some code for their unit, I assumed. Anyway, saw him around the remote base often, but never had a chance to talk with him again. Usually, he looked like crap as if he just came in from the field. Units would roll in and out, but he seemed to be always there joining another group's deployment. I found it odd … strange, but presumed it must be a Special Forces thing.

"Those six guys were very protective of Dan whenever they were in camp. The grapevine said Dan's skills kept him in demand, constantly deployed and assigned to the most extreme missions. I don't doubt it," Trevor finished as Echo Team sat in silence, absorbing all he shared about Dan.

Alpha team tuned in when they first heard Dan's name mentioned and listened intently to every word of Trevor's tale. They exchanged shocked expression, possessing no words, none … so completely dumbfounded with this insight into Dan's past.

Rouge Park — Section Seven — Near the Clearing — 7:40 p.m.

The team crested another ravine as Lexa called out quietly, "Dan, I think there is movement in the clearing ahead."

"Team hold, take cover," Dan ordered.

They dropped-in-place to conceal themselves. Dan stealthily moved forward and surveyed the little clearing. He brought out his binoculars and zeroed in on the three figures sitting on rocks.

"Lexa, great catch, text the coordinates to Boss' phone," Dan whispered and switched to channel one. "Boss, we have a visual on three subjects. Lexa is sending coordinates. One subject confirmed to be Basto. We'll surround and keep them contained, but we could use backup before attempting an arrest."

Aaron and Frank shared a smile. They would be the ones bringing in Basto … a feather in all their caps. They checked their weapons and prepared to move on Dan's command.

Rouge Park — Command Post — 7:40 p.m.

Bram wondered if the cook in Trevor's tale might be Jarmal. It fits. Jarmal did watch out for Dan. He stepped up without hesitation when Boss asked him to care for Dan back in October.

His thoughts were interrupted when Boss said, "Copy. Starveling's team is closest. I'll notify them and direct them to your location. Then I'll switch to channel seven with you, Dan."

Crispin Winter came over to refresh his coffee and overheard the conversation on channel one. He tapped Nick on the shoulder. "I'll notify Doug, you go ahead and switch channels."

Nick nodded and motioned for the rest of Alpha to tune in to Dan's channel as he mouthed to them, "Basto."

The Chase is On

18

July 15
Rouge Park — Section Seven — Near the Clearing — 7:40 p.m.

Dan relayed to his team, "Boss is notifying Team Three, they're our closest backup. With one subject still unaccounted for, we need to keep our heads on a swivel. Lexa, go left and find a Zulu position. Frank, provide cover for her. Aaron and I will approach from the right. We'll contain them here until Doug's team arrives."

The four moved out quietly, trying to move closer to the subjects without alerting them. With Basto involved, Dan believed it too risky to apprehend them with only four officers. Basto and his men possessed too much firepower and Guns and Gangs wanted him alive, if possible. Waiting for backup would be best. Dan followed Aaron as they moved through the trees.

Lexa found a suitable location, settled in, and took aim on the three subjects. "Dan, I have the solution. How do you want to do this if they start moving?"

Frank stood behind and a few inches right of Lexa, covering her back. Dan's caution played in his head because the last subject could be anywhere. He continued to scan the area as he listened for Dan's instructions.

Rouge Park — Section Seven — Hiding Near the Clearing — 7:45 p.m.

Unseen by the team, Basto, or his goons, two members of the Jackals gang, Damir and Miro, crouched behind a grouping of short trees. They had been closing in to slay Basto when they spotted four cops. Two officers moved into a position a few yards in front of them while two others circled around the other side of the little clearing.

Damir whispered to Miro, "I hate cops with a passion—more than Basto. I wanna kill them first then we can snuff out Basto."

Miro shook his head. "No, we let them kill Basto, then we kill the cops."

"Idiot, they're going to arrest them. We slaughter the pigs then we execute Basto," Damir insisted.

Miro nodded. "Okay, we do this your way, but we need to exterminate Basto too. Yegorovich will reward us well if we take him out."

"Pigs first, then Basto. Agreed." Damir crept forward to obtain a bead on the ones closest to him. Miro stayed hidden in the trees.

Rouge Park – Section Seven – Near a Clearing – 7:45 p.m.

Dan stopped to scan the clearing and the three subjects to answer Lexa's question. About to respond, he glimpsed a flash of sunlight reflecting off metal behind Lexa and Frank. His keen eyes found the subject's gun rising and aiming at Frank's head.

As he sighted the target, Dan whispered, "Down! Gun! Behind you!"

Scanning at Broderick's alert, Aaron located the glint off a weapon. He calculated making the shot from his or Broderick's location would be near impossible. He began moving to find a better position as he worried about his fellow officers.

Both Frank and Lexa spun and crouched down at Dan's warning, searching for the threat. Lexa spied the gun first ... pointed at Frank. She raised her MP5, opening her mouth to tell the armed subject to freeze, as two shots rang out, one on top of the other.

Lexa observed the dead subject fall as Dan's voice sounded in her ear, "Status?"

"No harm," Lexa replied as she turned her attention to Frank because there had been two reports. Frank sat on the ground with a stunned expression.

Frank breathed out, "No harm," as he shook off the shock of the near-miss. The bullet hit the dirt less than an inch from him. *Wow, geez, if Dan had not discovered the shooter, I would be taking a dirt nap now.*

"Subject neutralized," Lexa said as she moved forward and picked up the weapon, before turning back to the clearing.

No one spotted Miro slipping away into the shadows.

Shocked, Aaron stood still as he comprehended the second discharge came from Broderick. *How did he make the shot? It isn't possible. Is it? I wouldn't have been able to make it. Frank would be dead if not for Broderick.*

Rouge Park – Section Seven – Clearing – 7:45 p.m.

Alerted by the gunfire, Basto took off running, one of his guards bolted in the opposite direction, while the other sat on a rock with a scared expression on his face, frantically searching for the source of the reports.

Dan pursued Basto ... unwilling to allow the gang leader to escape.

Still unseen by anyone, Miro ran in the same direction as Basto and the blond cop intending to execute both.

Lexa and Frank raced into the clearing to secure the subject on the rock. Frank moved forward and disarmed the bewildered man while Lexa provided cover for him.

Aaron ran after the fleeing guard. He raised his gun and yelled, "TRF, POLICE. STOP WHERE YOU ARE."

The out of shape guard, exhausted from trudging through the woods, decided to make his stand here. He turned partway with his hand on the trigger. *I'm gonna take a few cops with me to the grave.* Spotting a female, he adjusted his aim, preparing to fire.

"I SAID, STOP," Aaron declared. "Lower your weapon. On your knees."

"NEVER!" The guard took aim.

Frank finished cuffing the third subject when he glanced towards Aaron. The subject's intent and where the gun aimed clear as day to him. He launched himself at Lexa, as he roared, "DOWN!"

Squeezing his trigger was the last action the gang member took in the world. Aaron's bullet hit him in the temple, and he was dead before he hit the ground.

Frank landed on Lexa and rolled as searing pain radiated in his left arm. He was hit, but if he hadn't thrown himself towards Lexa, the bullet would've pierced her in the head. *Fair trade as far as I'm concerned.*

Lexa got to her knees and spotted blood seeping through Frank fingers where he gripped his arm. She checked the restrained subject and found him cowering behind the rock. She peered at Aaron and hollered, "SUBJECT NEUTRALIZED. GO BACK UP DAN!"

Aaron sprinted in the direction Basto and Broderick took. *Damn, I should've fired sooner. Frank got hit because I didn't register the man's intent. Dammit to hell. I should've seen the desperation.* He ran flat out following an easy trail created by Basto barreling through the woods. *Broderick is alone and following a known murderer—I need to cover his back.*

"I'm okay." Frank grimaced.

Lexa shook her head, ripped open his shirtsleeve, pulled out her pressure bandage, and applied compression to Frank's arm. Fortunately, it appeared to be only grazed. A deep one, but a graze nonetheless. Though, the wound probably burned like hell.

"Lexa, status?" Dan called.

"One subject contained and one dead. Frank requires EMS, applying pressure to a wound on his arm. Aaron's on your six," Lexa responded.

"I'm fine, it's only a scrape. My cat scratches me worse." Frank winced and hissed as Lexa pressed more forcefully to stop the bleeding.

"You he-man macho types are all alike. It's gonna need stitches." Lexa grinned at Frank, and he smiled back before she became serious again. "Thanks, Frank."

Frank nodded. "What we do at TRF … we're all on the same team, we've got each other's backs."

Lexa joking with Frank eased Dan's mind, as did Frank's steady and clear voice in return. Dan acknowledged Frank's statement, "Copy," and poured on more speed as he pursued Basto. *The man isn't making it easy to catch him.*

Rouge Park – Section Seven – In Pursuit of Basto – 8:00 p.m.

Getting tired of the chase, Basto possessed more stamina and speed than Dan expected. But Dan knew he had a lot in reserve and he would wear Basto down or take him to the ground. However, to do so, Dan needed to get close enough to him, and that proved to be a bit of a challenge.

"Lexa, Basto must be part rabbit. Damn, he can move fast," Dan said with a laugh as he took another turn following Basto's jagged path.

"Wile E. Coyote, haven't you caught the roadrunner yet?" Loki quipped.

Dan chuckled. *So, the rest of the team switched to channel seven. They must've finished with their section.* He jested, "I could use some help. Wanna ship me an Acme rocket so I can catch up to him faster?"

"Nah, you don't need one. Watch yourself out there. Nothing good ever happens in the woods." Loki's nervousness at being surrounded by trees increased as he recalled all the bad things. Then the conversation overheard at the command post coursed through his mind. With them going after a man as dangerous as Basto, he sincerely hoped Aaron wouldn't let Dan down.

Though sprinting at max speed through the underbrush, Aaron realized the gap between him, Broderick, and Basto continued to widen. *Broderick is more like a roadrunner. Shit, he's fast. Where the hell does he get all his energy?*

"Boss, Basto, his two guards, and the unknown shooter make four subjects which brings the total to fifteen. That's all of them according to the intel, right?" Dan queried.

"Yes, no additional subjects indicated," Nick replied.

"Great. Once I catch Basto, Loki can guide me out of here. Taken so many twist and turns, not sure where I'm at anymore," Dan joked.

"Dantastic, you couldn't get lost even if you tried, but I've got your back. Transponder emitting a strong signal," Loki said.

"Go careful, Dano. Remember, Basto is dangerous," Jon chimed in.

"Got it, Jon. Napping in the woods is off-limits," Dan wisecracked.

"Dan, I'm serious. Got it? Be careful, no unacceptable risks. That's an order," Jon sternly reiterated.

"Yes, sir. Copy," Dan replied, only a little winded.

Unable to keep up, Aaron fell further behind. Pissed off his breaths came in ragged gulps while Broderick joked around without sounding winded as he ran, Aaron begrudgingly conceded Broderick possessed another useful skill. Within five minutes, Broderick and Basto were beyond his visual range.

"Lost sight of Dan and subject, but still following their trail." Aaron stopped to catch his breath, panting and pressing a hand on his side, struggling to recover enough air to continue. A few minutes later, he started to jog, searching for signs of which way they went. Luckily, the route remained easy enough to follow because neither attempted to hide their movements ... broken saplings, disturbed leaves, and footprints galore indicated the direction traveled.

Dan grinned as Basto slowed, the man appeared no longer able to maintain the grueling pace. After traipsing up and down ravines for hours searching and now pursuing Basto at an exhausting speed for the past fifteen minutes, Dan wanted to end this chase and get the guy into custody. He called out loudly, "POLICE, TRF. STOP NOW. NOWHERE FOR YOU TO GO."

In top physical condition, Basto usually left everyone in the dust when running, but now he breathed heavily, ticked off the cop kept up. *Damn, fucking robocop is on my tail. He isn't even winded. How the hell is that possible? I'm not gonna fucking outrun this guy.* Making a decision, Basto came to an abrupt halt, inhaled sharply, raised his gun, and turned.

Dan closed the gap when Basto stopped cold. As the man began to turn, Dan launched himself in the air for a flying tackle.

Basto fired.

Unable to change his course mid-flight, the bullet ripped through Dan's right bicep. His body impacted Basto squarely in center mass and his arms wrapped around the subject's body taking Basto down.

Rouge Park — Section Seven — Clearing — 8:00 p.m.

Hearing the gunshot, Lexa called out, "Dan, status? Aaron?"

"I heard it, still don't have visual of them," Aaron answered, digging deep for more speed as he raced down and then up another ravine. *Dammit, I should've been closer.*

Lexa discerned sounds of impact along with grunts and other vague noises. She requested status again when the headset went silent except for Frank's labored breaths. Torn, Lexa debated whether to run after Dan and Aaron or stay here with Frank. Gazing at Frank, Lexa determined she must remain here. Though unsure what occurred out there, she needed to be here to back up Frank if Basto somehow returned. She hoped Aaron wouldn't leave Dan hanging.

Coyote versus Roadrunner

 *19*

July 15
Rouge Park — Section Seven — Ravine — 8:00 p.m.

The force of the tackle sent Basto and Dan over the edge of a steep ravine. Bodies slammed into underbrush, logs, and rocks as they traveled down the eight-foot embankment before coming to a stop at the bottom. Both men landed on their backs … dazed and struggling to catch their breath.

A deep, gash over Dan's right eye, received when he struck a sharp rock, and the gunshot wound in his right arm both bled freely. Basto's cheek suffered as jagged cut from a tree branch. In addition to the lacerations, both sported various minor abrasions to their faces.

Basto recovered first. After getting to his knees, he spied the blond cop and quickly straddled him—pinning him to the ground. When the damned officer attacked him at the top of the ravine, Basto dropped his PP-2000 submachine gun. He reached back to grab the Sig Sauer P229 compact pistol he tucked in his waistband right before all hell broke loose and he bolted into the woods earlier today when TRF arrived. *Damn! It is gone.*

Angry, Basto slammed his hammer-like fist into the cop's jaw when he began to stir. Glancing around, attempting to locate his weapon, he spotted the P229 halfway up the gulch. *Damn, he'll shoot me before I can reach it, unless …* Basto smashed his knuckles into robocop's face again for good measure causing the dazed man to grunt.

Satisfied by inflicting pain, Basto grinned. *Been a while since I beat the shit out of anyone.* Basto desired to beat him senseless before putting a bullet in his head. After unhooking the MP5 from the clip on the vest, Basto tossed it to the side, then rammed two punches into the man's abdomen. He pulled back a moment to gaze at the pretty-boy face he wanted to pulverize. *You won't be so pretty after I'm done. Hell, your own mama won't recognize you.*

The blows to his jaw stunned Dan, and a grunt of pain slipped out. He gasped for air when two hits pounded into his solar plexus. Gathering his wits afterward, he blocked the next strikes. Dan took Basto by surprise as he unexpectedly bucked, twisted, and heaved the gang boss off him.

Gaining his feet, Dan assumed an attack position. He ignored the blood dripping into his eye, and the burning pain radiating from his right arm. Dan started to reach for his sidearm with his left hand when Basto stood and came at him with fists flying. He unlatched his holster but didn't have time to draw his Glock before he needed to block the onslaught of strikes.

Basto threw multiple punches, but most were deflected, and his adversary landed one or two rock-hard hits. Basto changed his strategy, deciding to use his weight and size to his advantage. He plowed forward, grabbing his opponent's midsection, driving him back with the power of a freight train.

Unable to dodge Basto, propelled backward as the subject rammed into him, Dan's back slammed into a tree forcefully expelling all air from his lungs. Sucking in a breath brought sharp pain from bruised and abused ribs, but Dan couldn't give in to the pain, or he would be dead. Luckily, adrenaline now coursing through his veins helped.

As Basto pulled back to strike, Dan lashed out faster. He connected with Basto's chin first and followed with two more facial blows. Basto's nose crunched under his fist. When the gang boss lurched backward from the agony of a broken nose, Dan landed three solid hits to Basto's abdomen before placing a well-aimed roundhouse kick to his kidney.

Basto staggered back at the onslaught. Then the cop hit him with a forceful kick which nearly sent him to the ground. As blood gushed from his nose, Basto decided this dammed cop would learn a lesson. As a middleweight champion, Basto believed the lighter and smaller man didn't stand a chance against him. He went on the offensive again, his massive hammer fists targeting the blond's face and kidneys.

Grunts and flesh-meeting-flesh sounded over Aaron's headset as he ran, in addition to Lexa's repeated calls for status. He couldn't respond to her because he was too out of breath to speak. It sounded like Broderick was in a fight for his life, and Aaron forced himself to sprint faster than he imagined possible. Reaching the top of a gorge, he stopped, sucked breaths in and blew them out raggedly, thoroughly winded.

Aaron's view of the fight taking place confirmed his worries. Both men were a bloody mess. *Crap!* He aimed his MP5, but couldn't acquire a clear shot because Basto was too close to Broderick and the two combatants moved around too much. Concerned he might end up shooting Broderick, refusing to risk a fellow officer's life, even one he didn't like, Aaron continued to wait, hoping for an opportunity to intervene.

As the battle carried on, Aaron realized Broderick held back a lot in their sparring sessions. What he witnessed now definitely embodied Special Forces training. In awe, Aaron saw Basto stagger from a power-packed blow delivered by Broderick's left fist. Lightning fast, Broderick followed up by spinning and landing a kick which propelled Basto back several feet.

Christ! Broderick possesses real skill ... he isn't worthless. As they fought, Aaron began to question what his uncle told him. He recalled some joint team calls and measured them against his uncle's negative words ... things didn't quite add up. *Did I let uncle's words color my judgment of Broderick instead of making my own assessment like Dad and Dylan implored me to do?*

As the blinders he wore fell away, Aaron accepted he had been wrong about Broderick. *I did it again. I need to stop parroting my uncle's attitudes. It is time to start opening my eyes and taking the time to make my own assessments.*

Aaron wanted to call out for Basto to freeze as the skirmish continued, but worried his voice might distract Broderick at the wrong time and get him killed. Frustrated he couldn't do more, Aaron searched for the right moment to make them aware of his presence and help apprehend Basto.

Dan blocked most of the strikes, but several hit their mark and whipped his head to the side as they landed on his jaw. The blows to his kidneys hurt so bad it made Dan want to double over and curl up, but he couldn't. He wished Aaron would arrive because he could really use some backup.

A sickening thought crossed Dan's mind. *Did Aaron leave me hanging out to dry like the guys in the Fourteenth?* He refocused on Basto and swiped the blood from his brow again as Basto took a small step back. *If so, I'm alone and must change my strategy. Basto is stronger than me, and I'm at a disadvantage given my current physical state.*

In Dan's head, he listened to Ripsaw's coaching. *"Blondie, you'll never win head-on against him. Evade, piss the guy off, make him unbalanced mentally, so he becomes sloppy. Protect yourself and strike only when he's open. Let him tire himself out coming for you. Conserve energy. Once he's drained, go in for the kill."*

So, Dan weaved, ducked, dodged, backed up, twisted, spun, blocked, and threw a few strikes and kicks when Basto left himself open. Every one Dan landed and each one Basto failed to connect, enraged Basto more and caused him to increase his barrage. Dan did as Ripsaw trained him, and as the former boxer spent his energy, he became sloppier.

As his own energy dwindled and blood dripped into his eye again, Dan didn't block Basto's fist in time. The powerful punch landed on his cheek, whipped his head to the side, and he staggered, trying to remain upright. Worried his stamina would wane before Basto's, Dan drew in a painful breath and barely spun out of the way of a kick aimed at his knee.

Aaron noted Broderick struggling to right himself after the last blow. He still didn't have a clear shot, but now would be the time to let Basto know he didn't stand a chance—backup had arrived. He opened his mouth, prepared to shout for Basto to freeze, but stopped when a gun barrel pressed to the back of his head, and cold words whispered in his ear.

Miro shoved his gun into the pig's sweaty hair and hissed, "You're dead if you move a muscle. Let's view the show a moment longer, shall we?"

Aaron swallowed hard as many thoughts flashed in his mind. *I should've been more attentive to my surroundings and moved down to Broderick as soon as I arrived. If I had, the damned subject wouldn't have gotten the drop on me. I would've been able to react. Dammit, I screwed up ... a rookie mistake. I need to tell the team what is going on. Maybe Lexa or Frank can assist.*

Taking a considerable risk, Aaron said, "Broderick versus Basto isn't much of a fight. The score is ten to seventy-eight."

After the constable spoke, Miro recognized the police code and noticed the earpiece. He ripped the communications device off and chucked it into the trees. "Damned pig. I'm not stupid. A 10-78 tells the others you're in trouble. Well, if they come, they are dead, too." Miro struck the officer with the gunstock on the head hard enough to send him to his knees.

Stars burst before Aaron's eyes as he dropped. The subject's gun settled against his temple. As his vision cleared, Aaron watched as Broderick and Basto exchanged more cringe-worthy blows. *For damned sure Broderick will be hurting after this.* Aaron craved to do something other than kneeling here as a fellow officer got the crap beat out of him. *There must be a way out of this situation.*

Aaron focused on finding a solution. As he thought of and discarded one idea after another, Broderick appeared to be gaining the upper hand against Basto. He wanted to cheer him on, let him know he was not alone, but the tide turned as Basto knocked Broderick to the ground.

Dan landed a series of fast strikes and several kicks when Basto left himself wide open. He blinked as blood dripped into his eye again, and that became his downfall. In that split second, Basto moved in and swept his right leg out from under him, and he landed hard on his injured arm, causing pain to shoot up and down his limb.

Rotating off his arm, Dan ended up on his back. Too late he spotted the boot coming down and couldn't move out of the way before Basto's foot slammed on his chest. Pain reverberated across his torso. The stomp stole his breath, and Dan labored to draw in air.

Basto panted as he leaned over, placed his bloodied and bruised hands on his thighs, and glared at robocop with contempt. Basto spat a mouthful of blood and a tooth on the constable. *Damn, he has a mean left punch. I'm gonna enjoy taking payment out of his hide.*

The bloody mess he made of the blond cop's face and the fact he struggled to breath pleased Basto. He straightened and wiped the flowing blood from his own nose with the back of his hand. *The damned cop is gonna pay for busting my nose, too.* Near the end of his endurance, Basto recognized he should end the cop's life, but decided to kick the mangy dog one last time. He pulled his leg back, preparing to ram his boot into the ribcage with all his might.

Dan hurt like hell. Taking in a searing breath, he caught sight of Basto's movement. *If I don't move now, my bruised ribs will surely break.* Pulling on his reserves, Dan rolled as he reached out and grabbed the leg in motion before it could connect with his bones. Yanking hard Dan knocked the gang leader off balance. Spinning his body on the ground, Dan held tight to Basto's leg.

The technique didn't work as intended. Instead of Basto falling backward, he fell forward. The full weight of the heavier man crashed on top of Dan's chest, and his left wrist bent unnaturally. Agony washed through him, and he wondered if his wrist and ribs broke. *If not busted they're at least cracked.*

Doing his damnedest to ignore his pain ... now becoming difficult to do ... Dan managed, helped by another little surge of adrenaline, to push Basto off and roll, before lurching upward and gaining his feet. Unsteadily, he assumed his ready stance, preparing for Basto's next attack.

With significant effort, Basto pushed himself up too. *Damn, I never faced an opponent this tenacious or fierce.* He growled, "I'm going to enjoy killing you."

Having a hard time breathing, Dan recognized he couldn't take another solid hit or a rib might splinter and puncture a lung if they were already cracked. Basto was not coming at him like before ... only standing there with one hand behind his back. Dan spat out the blood filling his mouth as he reached for his sidearm. *My holster is empty. Crap!*

Grinning wickedly, Basto asked, "You looking for this?" as he brought his hand from behind, raised the Glock, and aimed.

Shit! I'm gonna be killed with my own damned gun. No! I'm not gonna let that happen. Dan glanced around and spotted his discarded MP5 a short distance from him. *I can save myself if I can only dive for it, but I need a distraction.*

Aaron couldn't bear to watch Basto blow Dan away without at least trying to help. *I'm probably gonna die for this ... hell, I was dead the moment the other subject put the gun to my temple.* Aaron noted Dan's eyes glance at the submachine gun in the dirt.

Deciding his last act would be one of valor, Aaron would give Broderick a moment's distraction, and hopefully, his brother-in-blue would be able to save himself. Aaron shouted, "TRF. DROP YOUR WEAPON! NOW!" as he lifted and pointed his MP5 at the Crimson Eagle's leader.

Basto turned and glanced up the ravine—shocked to find two men.

Dan didn't bother to turn towards Aaron. He used the split second to dive for his weapon. *Damned glad Aaron showed up*. He hit the packed dirt hard, rolled, and came to his knees with the MP5 pointed at Basto. Dan's adrenaline pumped furiously, and his survival instinct blotted out all physical pain as he yelled, "DROP THE WEAPON, BASTO."

"GODDAMNED COP! YOU'RE DEAD!" Basto roared.

Dan swiped away blood which dripped down, obstructing and blurring his vision as a new voice bellowed from above, "YOU'RE DEAD, COP."

Aaron dove down the ravine—his only option to try to save his own life.

Basto stared for a moment at the cop rolling down the slope.

Startled for only a second, Miro fired at the tumbling pig.

Dan wiped blood out of his eye again and fired.

Miro dropped.

Both Dan and Basto fired.

Basto crumpled to the ground.

"Officers down," Dan uttered before keeling over.

Ten Seventy-Eight

 *20*

Trevor and the rest of Echo halted their conversation when Sergeant Pastore said, "Basto." Leaning over to Bram, Trevor asked, "What's up?"

"Dan's team located Basto," Bram replied.

Echo Team also switched to channel seven to listen to their exchange. They all muted their headsets so background sounds wouldn't interfere with Team Seven's communication. Everyone concentrated on the action taking place in Dan's sector.

They tensed when two almost simultaneous gunshots filled their ears, and relaxed as teammates called out 'no harm' and 'subject neutralized.' Stress returned when two more shots sounded, and Lexa relayed Frank had been wounded. Heavy breathing came across the line as Dan and Aaron chased after Basto.

By this time, all TRF officers at the command post tuned into the channel. Non-Alpha Team constables chuckled at the Dantastic and Wile E. Coyote nicknames and became perplexed about the napping comment, but found it funny. Alpha sure had an interesting dynamic.

Tension resumed when reverberations from a fifth shot came with no response from Dan after both Lexa and Nick called for status. The noises of someone possibly crashing through underbrush followed by a shaky intake of breath preceded grunts, groans, and sounds of flesh-hitting-flesh. Bram, Jon, Ray, and Loki surged to their feet as they assumed Dan engaged in a fistfight with Basto—a middleweight boxing champion who beat four men to death.

The men of Alpha paced short distances, wanting badly to do something to assist. Distress clearly displayed in their taut features. Jon grew more fractious as he repetitively requested status and silence permeated the airwaves.

His face awash with anger, Loki bit out, "Where the hell is Aaron? He's supposed to be covering Dan's back."

But he and everyone else froze as an unknown voice came through their headsets. "You're dead if you move a muscle. Let's just view the show a moment, shall we?" Aaron's response alerted them to the fact he arrived, but his embedded ten seventy-eight distress code told them he couldn't assist and needed help himself.

Nick shouted over to Winter, "Direct Starveling's team to Dan's location now! Officers need assistance."

Crispin had been monitoring both channels and responded, "They can't reach from their current position, they must backtrack and use a different route. They also have three subjects in custody. Our intel on the number of subjects is wrong."

Commander Gambrill began reviewing the maps. He needed to deploy officers there quickly. Dan's team searched the farthest section from the command post and in the roughest terrain. He slammed his fist on the table as he listened to channel seven and began plotting the fastest path to their location. Formulating a plan, he got on the horn to arrange for a helicopter to drop more officers in the area.

Everyone stilled and became quiet when an unidentified voice growled, "I'm gonna enjoy killing you." A brief silence followed … broken when the same man said, "You looking for this?"

Slight relief came when Aaron's distant voice said, "TRF. Drop your weapon! Now!"

Relief increased when Dan spoke. "Drop the weapon, Basto."

But an unknown voice, which they now assumed to be Basto, screamed, "Goddamned cop! You're dead!" before the other male voice coldly stated, "You're dead, cop."

The report of four rapid gunshots sent ice into their veins and suppressed all noise until Dan's labored, "Officers down," followed by dead silence spurred an uncontrolled and uncharacteristic emotional outburst from every member of Alpha Team.

Jon roared, "DAMMIT! NO! DAN, STATUS? REPORT NOW, THAT'S AN ORDER!" He flipped a table on its side, sending the contents flying.

Bram flung a chair. "CHRIST! SHIT! NO!"

Loki slammed a fist on another table. *Bad things always happen in the woods!* "HOLD ON, DAN. I'M NOT LETTING GO."

Ray threw his coffee to the ground. "FUCK NO!"

Loud and clear over the headset, Lexa verbalized her reaction as she clenched her fists, and her body became rigid with worry "DAN, RESPOND. DAN! ANSWER ME, NOW! DAN!"

Nick went silent, his face contorted in anguish. He ripped off his hat and with force, hurled it into the dirt. Repeatedly, he clenched and released his fists, striving to gain control of his emotions.

Rouge Park – Ravine – 8:15 p.m.

Dan roused after blacking out. *I need to check on Aaron.* Urgency galvanized his first coherent thought. Clamping his jaw shut, trying to control his pain and not cry out, he somehow managed to rise and shuffled towards Aaron. When Dan arrived where Aaron lay, he spotted the blood-soaked dirt under his teammate's upper thigh.

Dropping to his knees, Dan confirmed what he already suspected, the bullet hit Aaron's femoral artery. Despite recognizing the wound would prove fatal, Dan still pulled out his compression bandage intent on slowing the bleeding. He pressed down hard with his left hand and grimaced as the sharp pain in his wrist increased. He tried to move his right arm, but couldn't due to the intense burning pain. Dan wavered in place as the accumulation of his injuries took their toll. His vision grayed at the edges, and he held on to consciousness by sheer force of will.

Aaron's lids flew up at the pain caused by pressure on his leg. Spotting Dan above, he voiced his fears in a mere whisper, "How bad?"

Dan stared at the soaked pressure bandage … staunching the flow of blood … wholly impossible. Help wouldn't reach them before Aaron bled out. Unable to say the words to Aaron, Dan allowed his lashes to flutter and close, as he sucked in a jagged breath.

"That bad," Aaron whispered. Dan's reaction told him he suffered a mortal wound. *I'm TRF and excel at talk before tactics, but the grim reaper doesn't negotiate.* Weak from blood loss, but needing to clear his conscience, Aaron struggled to lift his hand and place it on Dan's.

As a hand landed on top of his, Dan opened his eyes and connected with Aaron's eyes. Guilt crashed down on him like a huge boulder. It bowed his shoulders and threatened to crush him. Dan murmured, "I wasn't fast enough. I tried but failed. I'm sorry."

Aaron shook his head slightly as he maintained eye contact. A tear slipped out of the corner and ran down his temple into his hair. Shed for Broderick's unfounded expression of guilt and because he would not be able to say goodbye to his fiancée or meet his unborn child.

His voice grew softer and weaker as his life's blood continued to gush out and soak the earth, "I pegged you all wrong … sorry for being an ass." Aaron gasped for air, all too aware death approached. Using every last ounce of his lifeforce, Aaron breathed out, "Tell … Tammy … I love …"

Dan stared at Aaron's unseeing eyes for a long moment, viewing his failure. *Aaron died because I failed to save him.* Physically and emotionally spent, Dan sat on his heels. His head bowed as the weight of everything became too much to bear.

He spied his headset dangling at his waist. Dan reached for his comms earpiece and clumsily fumbled with it trying to insert the tiny plastic into his ear. His fingers didn't want to cooperate, but he eventually managed to install the device. A cacophony sound greeted his success. So many voices, all yelling at once created a disorienting buzzing, making it impossible to decipher words. Dazed, Dan didn't even attempt to try, allowing the noise to flow around him for several minutes.

The pulsing pain in his right arm caused Dan to turn his gaze to the source. Recognizing he must stop the flow of blood, he lifted his left hand and covered the wound, only to experience a deep throbbing ache in his wrist and fingers. The sharp pains intensified and shot through the damaged joint as he attempted to apply pressure to his bleeding bicep. With no strength remaining and his agony spiking with each squeeze, Dan let his limb listlessly drop to his side.

Dan's enhanced adrenaline levels crashed, obliterating the protective cocoon the stress hormone provided him until now. As intense aching surged forth, he became aware of all his injuries. Pain rolled relentlessly through his entire body, and he was unable to prevent a hiss and moan from escaping.

Rouge Park – Command Post – 8:20 p.m.

Nick briskly rubbed his face as he strained to pick up something … anything at all from Dan or Aaron. His team's demeanor continued on a downward spiral, the anger and yelling persistent. Nick barely caught a soft hiss followed by a moan.

"QUIET!" Nick shouted, pinning a glare on his guys. Calming his tone, he asked, "Dan. Dan, is that you?"

"Mmm," came across the comms scarcely audible.

"What's your status?"

"Alive," Dan faintly uttered before moaning. He swayed on his knees, endeavoring to remain upright, but his strength faded with every second.

"Injuries?"

"Lots."

"Hold on, buddy. We're coming. You stay with us, alright?"

"K." Dan didn't waste what little energy he possessed to form the entire word.

Nick didn't like Dan's single word responses … they didn't bode well. "Can you tell us Aaron's status?"

Dan used the last of his reserves to reach out to shut Aaron's lifeless eyes. Guilt and pain overwhelmed him, and he forgot to breathe. When the need for air burned his lungs, Dan sucked in a ragged breath.

His tone imbued with remorse, Dan answered, "Dead."

"Subject?"

"Dead," Dan let out a breathy moan, "and dead." Dan's vision grayed again and began tunneling into a pinpoint as his chest burned with each breath.

"Do you mean two subjects neutralized, Dan?"

"Yes," a wispy hiss came before Dan said, "Boss."

"Yeah, Dan?"

Through seeking to hide his agony, Dan couldn't stop another hiss and moan escaping. "Tell ... Jon ... sorry ... gotta ... nap." Swaying again, this time unable to remain upright, Dan toppled over, landing on his right arm. "AAAARGH!" pierced the air before blackness claimed him.

Nick's intonation reflected his worry, "Dan, you hold on. Help is on the way. We're coming, buddy. You stay with us, okay?"

Silence.

While Nick talked to Dan, the remaining TRF officers went into high-gear, organizing resources and equipment. Alpha would focus on rescuing their injured teammate. The other teams would take care of escorting EMS to Frank, securing both shooting scenes, and recovering Aaron's body.

Although the constable's miens exhibited varying degrees of shock and grief at Aaron's loss, their actions confirmed their resolve to the living and the 'Priority of Life.' Now would not be the time to grieve, they must concentrate their efforts on preventing the death of another colleague.

Loki pinpointed Dan's location using the transponder. Reaching the site by traveling overland would take them more than an hour, and given the possible severity of his injuries, as the lack of communication suggested, it might prove to be more time than Dan had.

Providentially in the brief interim, Commander Gambrill procured a police helicopter which would allow Jon, Loki, Colton, and Paul to fast-line to Dan's position in about thirty minutes. Once there, Jon and Loki would handle the extraction plan for Dan. Sergeant Colton Harmon and his tactical lead, Paul Miller, would secure the scene until additional officers trekked in.

Rouge Park – Section Seven – Clearing – 8:30 p.m.

Lexa paced the clearing as she visually assessed their situation. Frank sat on a flat-top rock with his gun trained on their restrained subject. Though Frank's non-life-threatening wound caused him discomfort, it did not prevent him from guarding the subdued criminal.

Recalling Jon's words, she took them to heart. A half-hour to reach Dan, in her mind, would be way too long. If Dan had been shot, like Aaron, he might bleed out before anyone arrived. *You need to go to him now and ensure he is alright … keep him alive until help comes.*

"Hey, Loki," Lexa called out over the headset.

"Yeah?"

"Is there a direct route from this clearing to his position? If so, how far is it? I might be able to get to him in less time."

"Great idea! Why didn't I think of that? One second, let me map it." Loki brought up both transponder signals and plotted a path.

Nick said, "Lexa, we can't leave Frank alone. He's injured."

Frank chimed in, "It's only a scratch. I'm fine. Not my gun arm. We don't know the extent of Dan's injuries, but I'm sure he's worse off than I am since he's unresponsive."

Lexa glanced at Frank with appreciation. He nodded with concern written on his face. He hated the idea of Dan being out there alone.

"Are you sure?" Nick inquired.

"Positive. The subject is restrained. Starveling's team is on their way. I'll be fine. Lexa should go."

Loki stated, "Lexa, sending you the route. Arrival depends on your speed, but figure your ETA to be about ten minutes."

"Copy."

Frank gave Lexa a thumbs-up. "Go."

Lexa took off at a flat-out run, calling to Nick, "Boss, on my way to Dan. Frank has the clearing under control."

Rouge Park – Command Post – 8:35 p.m.

As Jon secured his harness, preparing for the upcoming rappel while waiting for the helicopter, one of the paramedics on standby approached him.

"I understand you are fast-lining to gain access to your officer."

"Correct." Jon tightened a strap.

"I can go with you," the slim yet muscular medic stated.

Bram double-checked Loki's harness. "Are you experienced?"

"You got the equipment, I got the experience. Former Army medic. Did my fair share of rappelling."

"Ray, lend him your gear." Jon offered his hand and noted the firm grip as they shook. "I'm Jon." He motioned to the other men. "And this is Bram, Loki, Colton, and Paul. Much appreciate you coming. We have no idea what our teammate's injuries are. All he communicated before we lost contact with him were lots and alive."

The paramedic assessed the tall, well-built, bald TRF constable. The aura of authority reflected in the intense, gunmetal gray eyes indicated a well-versed leader. "I'm Senior Paramedic James Shea. You can call me Jim." He shook hands with the rest of the officers before the one named Ray arrived with rigging for him.

After meeting Jim, Loki nervously rechecked his gear. He usually loved rappelling, but not so much, tonight. As he scanned the surrounding trees, Loki fought his phobia. *Nothing good ever happens to me in the woods.* He sucked it up and pushed down his fear because he would not let anything stop him from reaching to Dan. Loki turned to Shea. "Dantastic's a bit like Wile E. Coyote ... injury prone. I hope you know your stuff. He's important to us."

As he geared up, Jim reassured the nervous and worried officer. "I promise to take excellent care of your teammate. I have tons of practice dealing with an injury-prone buddy. He kept me on my toes for six years."

Loki nodded. "Okay. Okay."

Rescue in Progress

21

July 15
Rouge Park — Section Seven — Ravine — 8:40 p.m.

Dan began to rouse. Hazy yet becoming more aware of the damage to his body, he remained immobile after he found any movement hurt. Employing sniper breathing to manage his pain, he kept his eyes shut and stayed perfectly still, concentrating solely on breathing for several minutes.

After establishing a modicum of control, he started an injury assessment. *Headache with a dash of nausea—possible concussion. Right arm burns—bullet wound. Blood loss might be part of the reason for my fuzziness. Cut above my eye, a split lip, my jaw and cheeks ache. Hell, my whole face stings.*

Searing pain in my chest accompanying each respiration, the level of which indicates I now possess several battered and cracked ribs. My flanks ache from kidney punches—undoubtedly bruised, hopeful no internal bleeding. And Lastly, my left wrist throbs—sprained or quite possibly broken. Conclusion? Nothing life-threatening, only damned painful.

Next up, assess his surroundings. *In the woods in a ravine. Almost dark. Basto? Neutralized. Unknown subject? Neutralized. Aaron? Dead.*

Now mental status. *F.I.N.E. really, really F.I.N.E.* A few tears rolled out unbidden as an anvil of guilt for Aaron's death fell upon his shoulders and in his heart. *I'm the reason Aaron died. I failed to protect someone under my command and safeguard one of my own. Aaron's blood is on my hands—literally and figuratively.*

Dan's insecurities pervaded his thoughts. *My team, my chosen family, will abandon me now. I didn't save Aaron. I should've fired faster. Should've seen the other subject sooner. The team will never forgive me. They will no longer trust me. How can they? My failures are always rewarded with abandonment. This time will be no different than any other in my past.*

I failed to protect Sara, and I lost my family. When we arrived home, the general made me stand at attention in the corner of the room for hours as he dressed me down. He made it crystal clear I abandoned my duty to safeguard my little sister. My father berated me and told me I should've pushed Sara out of the way, and I was nothing but a total and utter disappointment. He cast me out of the family because I didn't measure up to Broderick standards and didn't belong.

The most hurtful words uttered came when he said he wished I had been killed instead of Sara. When I started to cry, he harshly told me to man-up and forbade me to express my grief because if I cared so much about her, I would've done more to save her. From that day forward, my loving, caring family didn't exist. They didn't acknowledge or accept me. I had no value or worth to them anymore because I allowed Sara to die on my watch.

I failed Brody. I lost all my brothers the day I shot him. No one would look me in the eye or speak to me. They blamed me—as they should. Brody's death is my fault. The brother of my heart always protected me. I should've relied on my senses when I caught the jade flash and recognized Brody's eyes. Blaze, Winds, Patch, and Mason don't trust me now. They don't care because I'm not worthy of them. I killed a brother. I broke solidarity. I'm no longer a Guardian and don't belong.

And now my newly chosen family will reject me. I gambled a third time and lost again. Overwhelming pain, both emotional and physical, washed over and through Dan as he retreated into the comfort of oblivion.

Lexa panted as she stopped at the top of the gorge. A gruesome sight greeted her. To her left a deceased, unknown subject with a bullet hole between his eyes. Near the bottom of the ravine was Basto with another perfect kill shot to the head. Aaron's body rested at the base with a blood-soaked pressure bandage on his thigh. So much blood, too much blood, she realized the bullet must've hit the femoral artery. The applied dressing and lack of blood on Arron's hands made it clear Dan revived long enough to make an attempt to save Aaron before he passed out from his own injuries.

Her eyes moved to her teammate next, afraid of what she would find. Dan lay unmoving on his back, and she couldn't tell if his chest rose or fell from where she stood. Blood covered his face and hands. Her heart missed several beats. Lexa shook herself out of her stupor recalling head wounds bled a lot, and the crimson on his hands was most likely Aaron's.

She hurried down the steep incline, almost tumbling when her boot snagged on a root. Lexa knelt beside Dan to check his pulse. *Reassuringly present, if not overly steady.* Her vision blurred for a moment as liquid welled in her eyes. *He's alive. Dan is still with us.* Lexa brushed away her tears because they wouldn't be of any help to Dan. She needed to start a field assessment and render aid without moving him to avoid causing more harm to unseen injuries.

His appearance matched what they overheard on the headset … he had been pummeled severely by Basto, and his face appeared to have taken the brunt of the blows. Searching for the source of the smeared blood covering his facial features, Lexa located a deep gash above his right eye and noted the cut already began to clot. He suffered a split lower lip and a multitude of smaller nicks and abrasions across his face, painful but not lethal.

The right sleeve of his black uniform shirt appeared darker and glistened with moisture. Finding opposing bullet holes in the fabric, Lexa realized he had been shot and the nature of the wound. Ripping open his sleeve, she found the entry and exit points, and unlike the laceration on his head, it continued to bleed too much and needed to be stopped. Having used her bandage on Frank, she reached for Dan's but gathered he used his on Aaron when she spotted his open pocket on his pants.

She moved to Aaron and unzipped the pocket on his left leg, taking the unused dressing, grateful they all carried them in the same location, so she didn't need to disturb his body further. She laid a hand on Aaron's shoulder as grief over his loss rushed in and gripped her heart. Although he bad-mouthed Dan, he didn't deserve to die. Lexa rose, returned to Dan, and applied the compress. *At least the doctor won't' need to dig out a bullet.*

Having taken care of the most critical matters, Lexa reported, "Boss. Found Dan and Aaron. Aaron is gone—he bled out. Dan is alive but messed up bad. Unconscious, his pulse is a little thready, and breaths are shallow. Applied pressure dressing to a gunshot wound in his right arm, the bullet went straight through. He lost a lot of blood, but the bleeding is slowing. The visible injuries are not life-threatening, but I can't tell if he suffered any internal ones.

"He's at the bottom of a steep ravine. By the state of his face, he tumbled down, and Basto used him as a punching bag. I'm not moving him until EMS arrives in case there are internal injuries," Lexa's voice cracked with emotion. The gasps and sighs of her team as they listened conveyed their concern.

"Copy. Jon and Loki are ten minutes out. A paramedic with rappelling experience joined them. Keep our guy safe for now. We'll be there to help soon," Nick said.

Lexa nodded as she replied, "Copy. I'll keep him safe. That's what we promised him earlier today. Dan isn't only family. He's an amazing and selfless man who protects those who can't protect themselves, often at great risk to himself."

"Yes, he is." Nick smiled as the heart of their team spoke his thoughts.

Adjusting her crouched position, Lexa maintained pressure to his wound but now could also stroke her fingers through his hair. She realized this was the second time today she offered comfort to him in this manner, and a part of her wished terrible situations weren't the only time she could.

An image of his WOW smile entered her mind. His ruggedly, handsome features typically drew the attention of many women. Though his present bloody mess might repel some ladies, and bring out the nurturing in others when his bruises turned every shade of the rainbow.

As for her, his intriguing sapphire blue eyes drew her. In the past few months, she came to realize Dan possessed multiple layers and didn't fit any known molds ... a unique and fascinating man. She wondered if Dan would be the marrying kind. *Where the heck did that thought come from?*

She sighed. Today had been one for the record books. She couldn't remember one with so many highs and lows. No wonder her mind began delving into areas she never thought of before with any man. Her disjointed thoughts the result of a stressful day and should be discounted.

Lexa noticed Dan beginning to stir. "Dan, hey, it's Lexa. Help is on the way. Hang in there. You're going to be okay. Can you open your eyes?"

Dan could, but wouldn't. *Is her tone truly one of concern? No, it can't be, and I'm not ready to view the condemnation for my failure in Lexa's eyes.* Dan remained still, keeping his breathing pattern slow, not giving any indication he regained full consciousness ... a skill he learned years ago and sadly, used often.

He languished in his thoughts, not ready or able to deal with the emotions, only physical pain. To counter the agonizing pressure on his right arm and chest with each breath he took, Dan drew on the comfort Lexa offered as she lightly stroked his scalp ... the tingling sensation providing him a degree of relief.

Startled out of her musings when a helicopter dropped low over the trees, Lexa jerked. She lost her balance, and her knee landed on Dan's chest.

Pain, hot and intense, radiated through him, and Dan couldn't stop the groan from escaping or his grimace.

"Dan, I'm so sorry. Are you okay? Dan? Oh my ... sorry, sorry," Lexa murmured, feeling awful she caused him more pain. She peered up at the helicopter, relieved help arrived.

Blackness claimed Dan, blissfully taking him to oblivion again.

"Ready, Jim?" Jon called to the paramedic as they prepared to exit the hovering police helicopter.

"Yeah, been a few months since the last time I fast-lined from a helo, but this is a skill you don't forget." Jim adjusted the medic bag on his shoulder and rechecked his line.

Jon, Loki, Colton, Paul, and Jim rappelled to the ravine's crest. After unhooking their lines Jim, Loki, and Jon rapidly descended, sending rocks tumbling down. Colton and Paul followed; their pace more sedate. Crouching near Aaron with saddened expressions, they wondered about the chain of events which left one teammate dead and the other in serious condition.

Jim reached the female officer and his patient, noting her tears, which to him, indicated she cared about this guy. *No duh, for the entire flight here I listened to the four guys in the bird talking about this officer. Two of them are extremely anxious to arrive and ensure Dantastic is okay. The man is important to them, more than only a teammate.* Jim had known a few guys who engendered a high level of affection and commitment from others. Six such guys Jim would readily give his life for—correction, only four now, the other two were gone.

He turned his attention to the patient. Though Jim had been informed of the injuries, he took a moment to take in the position of the body searching for any visible indications of trauma.

Yes, 'the body' not 'his body.' His heart previously shattered by being too close to those he worked on before, Jim now needed to remain detached and deliberately used impersonal terms to keep the injured at an arms distance. There was a time in his life when he allowed everything to become too personal and being unable to save his brothers nearly destroyed him. Jim viewed nothing indicating broken limbs. He squatted to assess for head injuries as his gaze shifted to the officer's face.

"Blondie," expelled on a faint wisp of air as shock coursed violently through Jim. He couldn't move as his mind processed the image in front of him. "NO! NOT BLONDIE!" Jim shouted in anger and disbelief. Barriers he constructed to protect himself exploded and crumbled in ruins, exposing his heart.

Surprised by the paramedic's reaction, Jon and Loki locked gazes and soundlessly mouthed, "Blondie?" Less than an hour ago, they listened to Trevor's tale of Dan where he had been called Blondie. Both wondered if the medic knew Dan from the military? Lexa appeared to be as confused as her teammates, but for a different reason, wondering what the color of Dan's hair had to do with anything?

Jim shook himself out of his stupor a second later. *It is Blondie and not a figment of my imagination. My brother … and he's hurt again. Criminy, hasn't he been through enough?* Shifting into a different mode, one well-worn and sadly all too familiar, Jim began to assess Blondie's condition.

Well-acquainted with his body, having done too many field exams, stitched several wounds, and cleaned numerous thin gashes, Jim understood how Blondie reacted to injuries and how much pain he could endure before blacking out, so his brother's insentient state worried him. "How long has he been unconscious?"

"About thirty-five or so minutes since he responded to anyone. Not sure if he was out the whole time or only unable to speak. He appeared down for the count when I arrived but began to rouse before …" Lexa's voice trailed off as guilt surged again.

"Before what?" Jim prompted.

"Right before you came down the lines. I shifted, and my knee knocked into Dan's chest. He groaned, and his face scrunched up but became slack again," Lexa finished guiltily.

"Help me remove his vest. I need to check his ribs," Jim requested, silently hoping for broken bones, easier to mend.

Lexa and Jon carefully moved Dan as they helped Jim strip off Dan's armor. Jim cut open his shirts and probed with deft fingers. He noted Blondie sported a torso covered in beautiful shades of red, blue, and purple. A small smile crossed his lips. *The kid always did bruise magnificently. Some of the contusions on his left shoulder and left upper chest are already turning blackish. Those must be hours old. This isn't his first injury today.*

"What caused these older contusions?" Jim needed general details to assess Blondie's current state fully.

"Took two bullets to the vest early this morning. Left shoulder and chest area. Knocked the wind completely out of him, but the medic checking him out gave him an all-clear." Jon stared at the dreadfully bruised chest.

Loki added, "This afternoon he hit his head, and was out for a bit. The paramedic said no concussion, but Dan ended up with a lump on the back of the head. No one knows why he collapsed after he took the shot and saved little Sara. We think he might've had low blood sugar or something. He hadn't eaten today. Medic cleared him for duty then too."

"Yeah, I'm sure it was the hunger. You should've seen how fast he devoured the lunch we got him," Lexa said.

Jim's probing didn't find what he hoped. "Shit, not broken, wish they were," he growled, not realizing he spoke out loud.

Disturbed by the words and tone the medic used, ice laced Jon's tone when he responded, "Just what the HELL do you mean?"

"What?" Jim glanced up, caught off guard by the question and tone. He registered a set jaw and a fierceness which conveyed *I can kill you.* Scrambled to figure out what caused the reaction, Jim realized he must've spoken out loud and how it would sound to someone who didn't know of his history treating Blondie. *Crapola! How to explain?*

"Relax, please. I know him, I'm aware of how his body reacts. I hoped for broken ribs." The glare intensified. *Double crapola, not the right words, shouldn't have said hoped.*

I'm dead, figuratively, if not literally, if I can't make them understand. Jim explained, "Unconscious, fractured ribs, easy to fix, and I would expect him to be insensible, especially if someone accidentally knelt on his chest. Not broken means this must be something worse." *Whew, success. Jon's demeanor changed from I'll kill you to worried.*

"Explain!" Jon crossed his arms, still not satisfied but willing to listen.

"Blondie, err, Dan, to you, possesses a high pain threshold. His injuries would need to severe to exceed his ability to tolerate and become unconscious. Really bad either physically or ..." Jim didn't finish. He didn't want to share *or emotionally* with them, not his place to expose Blondie's issues, so he tried to deflect. "With all the bruising on his stomach and kidney area, I'm worried about potential internal hemorrhaging."

"Boss, we need air-evac NOW, possible internal bleeding. The police helicopter can't get him out. There's nowhere to land, no clearing large enough, and it isn't outfitted with a hoist," Jon said in a tightly controlled voice, although inside he churned with concern.

"Let me find out air-evac ETA, hold tight." Nick switched to the proper channel to communicate the need and didn't like the answer. "Are you sure? Nothing else is available? Any others from surrounding areas with a faster response time? Do what you can, we have a badly injured TRF officer with probable internal injuries."

Frustrated and upset, Nick returned to channel seven, "Jonny, bad news. ETA is two hours. They're busy with an eight-car pileup which includes a busload of high school kids. They say they have nothing closer with the capability to extract without landing."

"We need options, guys ... fast," Jon replied.

The team began discussing possibilities, none happy with the limited alternatives, each one would result in a significant delay in getting Dan to a hospital, which might be deadly for him.

Found Blondie, It's Bad

 22

July 15
Army CH-146 Griffon Helicopter – 2050 Hours

Corporal Nathan Simons removed his headset and peered at his unit commander. "Captain Blain?"

"Yeah, Winds, what's so important you're using titles?" Blaze asked, recognizing something was up. His best friend, a communications specialist and second-in-command, rarely addressed him formally, and when he did, it usually indicated something out of the ordinary was happening.

"Blaze, been listening to local chatter. There's a situation not far from us. The Toronto Tactical Response Force dealt with a gang war, and an injured officer needs air-evac. A paramedic who rappelled to his location reported possible internal bleeding. The civilian medical flight ETA is two hours, backlogged dealing with a multi-vehicle crash. The TRF need a bird with a hoist to reach the officer because of rough terrain. No aircraft with the proper equipment is available sooner. Thought we should help," Winds explained.

"We're finished with the training op. I'll check with the major for authorization. You locate who I need to chat with at TRF if he approves." Blaze keyed his radio to communicate with Major White at the Ottawa base to obtain permission to assist.

Once he obtained authorization, Winds patched Blaze through to the right frequency. "This is Captain Blain, with Canadian Special Forces. May I speak to Commander Gambrill or Sergeant Pastore?" Blaze asked.

Sergeant Winter glanced up to find the commander engaged with the head of Guns and Gangs, so he motioned for Nick. "Hey, toggle back to channel one, a Special Forces captain wants to speak with you."

Nick changed frequencies. "This is Nick Pastore. I'm a bit busy. What is it you need?"

Blaze got right to it. "We would like to lend a hand with your situation."

"How can you help?" A loud whir in the background piqued Nick's curiosity.

"We finished a training op in the vicinity and understand a downed officer requires a medical airlift. We're currently about fifteen mikes from your position. We're experienced in extractions, and our bird is outfitted with a hoist and basket. If you want our help, we're authorized to provide transport."

"Thank you. We genuinely appreciate your assistance." Nick took a deep breath, relief sweeping through him before providing Blain coordinates and directed the captain to switch channels to seven to synchronize with Jon.

Rouge Park – Ravine – 9:00 p.m.

Jon, Loki, and Lexa stood a little away from Dan and the paramedic, still trying to come up with options, but found no suitable solutions. All three grinned when Boss said, "Jon, help is about ten minutes out. I'm patching in a Captain Blain so the two of you can hatch a plan."

Blaze and Jon communicated to define a strategy. When the helicopter arrived, Blain would send down two of his unit with a backboard, basket, and four harnesses. Loki shared a relieved glance with Lexa, glad they would be able to transport Dan to the hospital sooner with the help of the military.

After rechecking Blondie's vitals, Jim set up the IV, hoping to finish before Blondie regained consciousness, not wanting to spark his phobia. Concentrated on his task, Jim didn't notice the sapphire eyes opening.

Dan's lashes fluttered up, and he attempted to focus. His head turned to the right, and he spotted Jon, Lexa, and Loki talking. "Ow!" Dan jerked hard at the prick of a needle. Every muscle in his body constricted, and he strove to pull away.

Panic grew, and his pain intensified with his jolting movement. Memories of being *THERE* flooded in and threatened to overwhelm him. Seeking control, Dan panted as he flicked his gaze to the left to discover who jabbed him with a damned needle.

His vision blurred and swam as he stared at a man he would never forget. *There is no way in the world Patch is here … not here, not now.* Though Dan blinked several times, the same image always presented itself when he opened. Patch's compassionate brown eyes, light ash-brown hair, and expressive mien, all so familiar but the uniform was all wrong.

Dan supposed he must be dreaming, or worse, hallucinating. It couldn't be the medic who saved his life numerous times … but his arm was trapped under the man's knee, as Patch sometimes did when he required an IV. *How can Patch be here?* Dan spoke a faint, hoarse, "Patch?"

If the 'ow' or his name didn't provide him a clue, Jim would've known Blondie awoke by the rigidity of his entire body. He hated to start IVs on his brother when he was awake, but Jim possessed enough experience in doing so that he reverted to his tried and true method, using his knee to trap Blondie's arm while he inserted the intravenous line. He finished taping the tubing in place before turning to meet the scared and questioning gaze.

Jim smiled. "Yeah, Blondie, it's me. I'm surprised to see you too. Missed ya a lot, brother. Hold tight. Evac is a few minutes out. Rest now. I'm here. I'll take care of you like always." He placed a hand on Dan's left bicep and applied light pressure as he did way too many times.

Dan didn't know what to think. *Patch said he missed me. How is that possible? He hates me ... they all do. No one wanted to speak or look at me in the hospital. They left me alone and never visited my cell.* Dan recognized the gesture, a squeeze of his arm, one which often comforted him in the past. Patch told him once, years ago, he did it to let Dan know he cared.

Why did he squeeze my arm? Patch doesn't care about me anymore. How can Patch miss me or care? I did the unthinkable ... killed our brother. Unable to comprehend, his mind too jumbled, in too much physical pain, Dan merely stared at one of his lost brothers, no hint of emotion showing.

Jim's conversation attracted the attention of the team. They hurried over and knelt close.

"Dano, happy you're awake. You promised me no napping in the forest and no unacceptable risks. Do we need to review the definition again?" Jon said strictly, but with a smile as he patted Dan's right leg.

"Got you a cool ride. No regular air-evac for you, Wile E. Coyote. Got an Acme bird on the way ... special ordered. Only the best will do for our Dantastic. But seriously, you gotta stop this. Three times in the same day. This isn't what we had in mind for a profoundly unique day. Just sayin'," Loki wisecracked needing to ease the tension.

Lexa stroked Dan's sun-kissed hair, caressing him. "You scared us. Lie still and allow us help. You'll be okay. We'll keep you safe," she said softly with grave concern. Worry etched on Lexa's features as Dan's emotionless eyes glazed over. He didn't respond to any of their comments, and his blank gaze terrified her.

Dan began shutting down. Uncertain how to handle this ... all this too foreign ... they didn't act as he expected. Experience told him they would yell and condemn him, flay him alive with words for killing Aaron. His mind grappled for an explanation. *Perhaps I'm unconscious and only dreaming ... my mind creating the acceptance I so desperately want. But the pain in my head, chest, and arms is all too real.*

Too many conflicting emotions warred for supremacy … too much for him to cope with at the moment. Overwhelmed mentally by guilt and physically by the trauma to his body, Dan retreated into blackness, eyes shutting right as a CH-146 helicopter appeared overhead.

Jim rechecked Blondie's vitals, finding his heart rate rapid and still thready. Relieved the evac arrived, Jim recognized something was significantly wrong with Blondie. He suffered physical injuries for sure, but the lack of emotion scared the hell out of him. He wished Brody or Blaze were here, they would know what to do. Brody and Blaze always pulled Dan back from the brink of oblivion. Jim wanted Blaze here now because the emotional shit was not his forte. His skill lay in treating Blondie's physical wounds while Blaze and Brody took care of Blondie's psyche.

Two soldiers rappelling down interrupted Jim's train of thought. He bent down, rechecked the IV, and readied Blondie for transport—physical needs first. *Perhaps I can call Blaze from the hospital. We've all been searching for Blondie ever since he left Kandahar. The guys will be shocked to find out the kid is in Toronto and on the police force.* He hoped Blaze remained in-country training with his unit and would be able to take leave because Blondie sure as hell needed help Jim couldn't provide.

Jon and Loki went to meet the soldiers and help with the basket and gear. "Captain Blain?" Jon shouted over the noise of the helicopter's engine as he approached the Army captain.

"That's me, but call me Blaze, everyone does. This is Winds," Blaze responded even louder, reaching out to shake Jon's hand.

Jim's head shot up and peered in their direction.

"BLAZE? WINDS?" Jim bellowed, not believing they were there.

Everyone turned and stared at Jim.

"PATCH?" Blaze questioned as he took in the sight of his buddy. He could always read Patch. An open book to him, fear, concern, and relief displayed with equal measure on his former medic's mien.

"FOUND BLONDIE, IT'S BAD!" Jim yelled as he pointed to the TRF officer on the ground.

"HOLY SHIT!" Blaze roared as he spotted Blondie and processed what Patch said. The medic's four words rang in his ears way too often, and meant action now, questions later.

Blaze called out commands, and in record time they strapped Blondie on the spine board, secured him in the basket, and hoisted him to the helicopter. Blaze, Patch, Winds, Jon, Loki, Lexa, and two other soldiers silently scrutinized the unconscious man as the helo started for the hospital.

St. Michael Hospital – ER Information Desk – 9:00 p.m.

Heather Barkley disliked working the emergency room, which was why she transferred to the surgery department long ago. But Nancy begged her to cover her shift tonight so she could attend her daughter's ballet performance. Heather reluctantly agreed to do it this one time.

The blood and gore of emergency didn't faze her, in fact, she enjoyed being the nurse using her skills to help critical patients. However, she loathed being assigned as the ER waiting room nurse … the one family and friends came to for status on their loved one. The anguish and sense of helplessness exhibited by those awaiting updates and viewing them crumble upon receiving bad news tore her heart. As her luck, *bad luck,* would have it, that is what Nancy's shift had been assigned to today.

While wallowing in her own little pity party, Clare, another ER nurse, approached and asked if she had seen the news. Heather shook her head. She had been too busy dealing with a group of firefighters waiting for word on their buddy. Luckily, he ended up with only a simple leg fracture and a couple of second-degree burns which wouldn't require skin grafts.

They left only moments ago wearing grins, but the hour or so they paced and waited for the update had been arduous. Heather possessed a soft spot for firefighters and constables. She shared an affinity with them, they all focused on saving and protecting life. The only difference, first responders put their lives on the line every day to doing their jobs.

How the teams rallied together when one of their members got hurt always amazed Heather. Most teams consisted of concerned friends and professional buddies. But a few, an exceptionally rare few, became more like families. In those unique teams, she witnessed bonds stronger and more profound, rivaling any natural family bond. They chose each other … not bound by birth. She found it challenging to be an eyewitness when those extraordinary teams dealt with the painful realization, they couldn't protect one of their own.

Clare pointed to the TV. "I can't believe something like this happened here. A full-scale gang war in Rouge Park. The newscaster said almost every TRF constable had been called in to deal with the situation. They tracked down more than a dozen armed gang members. Took them hours and hours, but they apprehend them all …"

Heather no longer listened to Clare as video footage of the command area grabbed her attention. The repeated loop showed a group of officers in full tactical gear going off the wall. Definitely not an everyday occurrence. TRF officers tended to be calm and in control, even in the worst situation. A couple of constables yelled and threw things, unmistakably in distress, while another group behind them stood watching tensely.

Something terrible must've happened. She recognized the officers. They were the ones who saved everyone the day when Adalyn Slater's husband stormed into the dialysis department and took Dr. Reynolds and Adalyn hostage. Graham Slater threatened to kill Adalyn and Reynolds because he believed them to be having an affair.

The TRF negotiator talked Mr. Slater down, and the sad truth of the matter came to light. No affair existed. Adalyn visited Reynolds only in a professional capacity. She didn't want to reveal to her husband that her diabetes progressed to the point she required dialysis. Heather tuned back into Clare but only caught the tail end, "... injured one is coming to us."

"Sorry, I didn't catch all you said." Heather waited for her to repeat.

"Well, if you'd take the cotton outta your ears, I said the injured officer is being air-lifted here. I overheard dispatch tell the ER doctor to prepare for a gunshot wound, head trauma, and possibly internal bleeding. Hope the constable makes it, they already lost one guy today. I'd hate for them to lose two brave officers because of stupid thugs." Clare sighed.

Heather sat heavily in her chair, placed her head in her hands, and sighed. She wondered who had been injured or killed. *Which one is missing from the news footage? I didn't see the female officer, Lexa. Hope it isn't her, she possesses courage and heart.*

Who else is absent? Oh, the cute blond guy who wanted to shoot to solve the hostage issue. They shut him down. Oh, I really shouldn't have laughed at the blond when the tall, bald officer asked the one with wavy dark hair, Loki, yeah, Loki, for duct tape.

She recalled Loki produced a roll and the bald constable proceeded to rip off a piece and threatened to put it over the blond's mouth if he didn't shut up, sit, and watch how the big boys resolved a situation without killing everyone. Lexa and Loki snickered when the blue-eyed, blond clenched his jaw, sat, and glowered at them. *They didn't seem to like their teammate too much, and the sentiment appeared to be mutual.*

Wait, Clare said they lost one guy—male, not female. The only team going berserk must be the one with the causality and injury. So very sad the young blond is dead. He might've been a bit of a jerk, but he lost his life protecting others.

Heather deduced Lexa to be the wounded constable by the overemotional reactions shown. *What terrible injuries did she suffer?* Accepting she would be dealing with one of those rare teams which formed unbreakable bonds, Heather steeled herself, taking a deep breath and hurried to meet the inbound flight with the triage team.

A Man of Many Names

 *23*

While en route to the hospital, none of the occupants on the flight spoke, all lost in private thoughts. Blaze's head bowed, fixating his gaze on Blondie in the basket at his feet. An image reminiscent of the last time they rode in a helicopter together. The day Brody died, and they almost lost the kid too. Like that horrific day, Blondie lay unconscious, and he read fear in Patch's expression, but unlike then, the man he considered a son suffered significant physical injuries, but he didn't believe that is what caused Patch's fear.

Yes, Blondie's injuries concerned Patch, but their medic treated the kid in worse shape. More dead than alive when they found him in the terrorist compound, the physical damage wouldn't be enough to make Patch panic. His former medic never feared to treat Blondie's wounds, well, except for when they rescued him, and when Savelievich poisoned him, but even then, Patch handled things without undue anxiety.

Blondie lived today due to the magic Patch worked in the field and the kid's stubborn tenacity to live. Taking care of physical issues never caused Patch unease, it was the other which scared the shit out of him. Brody dealt primarily with Blondie's emotional needs, and Blaze assisted.

Based on the dread in Patch's eyes, Blondie needed him now. Blaze questioned his ability to do it alone since Brody had always been there to help. Now, as the last time, when he failed Blondie, the task appeared to be solely his, and guilt still ate at Blaze.

Caught up in his grief over Brody's death, he failed miserably when the kid needed him the most, and he lost the man he considered a son. Blaze spent the past year searching for Blondie, wanting to rectify his error and provide the support he sorely needed. Finding him in a ravine in Toronto boggled his mind.

What kind of blackout protocol is this? What is General Broderick up to this time? Blaze pushed all his questions about how Blondie came to be here and a member of the TRF to the back of his mind. He would figure that out later, but now his primary focus must be Blondie. The kid needed him, and Blaze vowed to somehow make things right between them.

Blaze spoke to his pilot, "Hal, Winds, and I are staying with Blondie. We can't leave him. You're in charge until I return. If Major White requires a reason, tell him we're staying to retrieve our supplies … the backboard and shit. We'll return when we can."

"Roger." Warrant Officer Halverson understood Blaze's and Winds's desire to be there now. Although their Guardian unit was still fairly new, Hal was no rookie. Blain and Simons had been together for years, and though he never met Blondie personally, he knew of General Broderick's son. Also, Winds shared some exploits of past missions, and Blondie played a significant role in the tales. Most anecdotes involved how the kid did crazy shit to save their asses when things went south.

Never at a loss for words, Winds became speechless when he saw the TRF officer needing help was Blondie. It knocked the wind right out of him when Patch said, 'Found Blondie, it's bad.' Those words he never wanted to hear again in his lifetime.

He had no idea why, but his mind went back to the day the kid joined them. Blaze's seasoned unit had been down two men due to retirement, and they got two rooks fresh out of Guardian Unit training. Winds thought someone played a joke on them when a blond-headed kid, yes kid, hopped out of the jeep and gave the guy with him a lopsided grin as he grabbed his sniper rifle and headed towards the command tent. Blondie didn't appear much older than twenty—too damned young to be in Special Forces.

It was no joke, though. Blondie, at only twenty-one, was the youngest Guardian ever. With the name of Broderick, Winds figured the general pulled strings to get his son in early. At first, they all worried they might've been stuck with a pretty boy playing soldier to impress the girls.

But the next day, they were sent on a mission with Blondie positioned as the unit's sniper, and the other new guy, Brody, as his spotter. All assumptions and doubts about his abilities dissipated when things went to hell in a heartbeat. They all would've been dead—several times over—if Blondie had not been there covering their asses.

Blondie took out twelve targets, several in rapid succession. The kid proved his mettle, damned fast on the trigger and accurate. He had their backs, and they vowed to have his. Blondie repeatedly drew combatant fire to himself to the point Blaze wanted to turn him over his knee and tan his backside for some of the stupid risks he took to keep them safe.

Winds returned to the present, and relief coursed through him as he watched Blondie's chest rise and fall. *Blondie's alive.* He harbored fears Blondie wouldn't survive Brody's death. A small part of him believed Blondie would've eaten his gun.

He voiced his concern only once to Blaze and received a black eye for his trouble. Winds instantly forgave his best friend because Winds knew how much Blaze cared for Blondie. Blaze already lost his entire natural family, and couldn't stand the thought of losing his surrogate son, too.

Ecstatic Blaze's son still lived; Winds smiled. *Blondie might be a little worse for wear, but we found him among the living. Now I can begin to make amends with Blondie, and perhaps the kid will forgive us for the way we handled things after Brody died.*

None of them had known what to do, and in the end, did nothing, which turned out to be the worst decision in Winds's life. Guilt shrouded Winds in a suffocating cloak. So much so when Mason started in on them after he returned from the field and found out they lost Blondie, he didn't raise a hand in defense. He stood stock-still and allowed Mason to give him a well-deserved thrashing. Unfortunately, the pain delivered by Mason's massive fists didn't discharge the anguish he felt for letting Blondie down.

However, beating the shit out of those who attacked Blondie before he left had been a small redemption. Winds didn't mind being demoted to private when he let loose and told Plouffe precisely what he thought of him when the major had the nerve to dismiss all assault charges against Murphy. The piece of shit Murphy didn't belong in Special Forces, but Plouffe favored Murphy, never disciplining him and even promoting him to sergeant.

Watching both Dan, aka Blondie, and the guys named Blaze, Winds, and Patch-Jim, Jon grinned slightly at all the damned nicknames. He got the sense they knew Dan quite well. He couldn't miss the protectiveness exuding from each of them and the worried faces they all wore as they scrutinized Dan.

Jon assumed them to be Special Forces buddies. Otherwise, they wouldn't have called him Blondie. *Maybe they are the ones Trevor referred to earlier. But the giant man and green-eyed one aren't present. Wait, Dan's best friend Brody was probably the green-eyed man. Jim, err Patch, the paramedic, used the same phrase 'found Blondie' that Trevor related. The words sent the captain into immediate action mode. Damn, they're fast at extraction.*

Their speed made Jon happy. He had been angry when the air-evac communicated their ETA would be two hours. He worried they would lose Dan. The team needed him. Dan had become an integral part of their family. They smoothed off some of the soldier edges, and the rookie continued to prove every day he fit well with Alpha Team and TRF.

Today, Dan nailed negotiating—he truly connected. As painful as that must've been for Dan, he did it to save others in pain. He saved Jason and Marty. Too bad about Garth. Jon realized they couldn't reach everyone. *Some people are like Garth and too far gone, but Dan also protected little Sara today.* Jon recalled what occurred in the alley and realized a few key personal elements were missing. *Perhaps one day, Dan will share.*

Jon pondered the four shots in the ravine. *What order did they occur? Was Dan in a position to help Aaron? Did Dan neutralize both subjects, or did Aaron shoot one?*

One thing Jon accepted with absolute certainty is Dan would've done everything within his power to protect Aaron. Although he conceded, Dan would likely claim fault and beat himself up over Arron's death. Jon would need to set Dan straight. He determined to remind Dan that sometimes they did everything right, and things still turned out bad. This would always be one of the cruelties of life—one of the things they must live with as TRF officers.

Loki hated seeing Dantastic laid out on the floor in such terrible condition. It physically hurt, and he wanted—no, he needed—Dan to be up and about, joking and flashing the smile which made ladies swoon.

Today had been profoundly unique. *Did I jinx us with the omen crap this morning? No, that is an absurd thought—but then again ... No, no, it is stupid. It is as ludicrous as the name Blondie.* Loki smirked. *Where did that thought come from? Guess Blondie is okay, but Dantastic is much better.*

Loki's thoughts turned serious again. Dan's blank stare before he closed his eyes troubled him. *There must be more than physical pain at play. Dan is an enigma and hides emotions too well when he wants. Dan can be open and fun—I like that guy. He's been happy a lot more often in the past few months ... ever since we got our heads on straight and started treating Dan properly.*

After peering into Dan's soul at the bank, Loki determined to hold on tight and not let go. *I'm going to figure this out and to be the person to ... what did Dan say? Oh, right ... to pull him back to the beauty of life.*

This vow Loki would always honor. One, he would keep no matter how long it might take, and no matter how many corny jokes he had to tell. He would help Dan to laugh again and bring the mischievous light back into his eyes. *Dantastic is my brother by choice. I'll always be there for him.*

Lexa reflected on the sensation of Dan's hair between her fingers and brooded over why she focused on something so trivial. As she itched weave fingers though his locks again, Lexa recognized this guy with a WOW smile somehow wormed himself into places she didn't realize existed within her.

She stroked his hair three times today. Twice in front of the team, which wouldn't go unnoticed. She hoped they viewed her action as one of offering comfort to a teammate. *That's what I'll claim if they give me any crap.*

The little devil on her shoulder challenged her. *"Would you ever do that to any of the other guys? Be honest, Lexa."*

No, I wouldn't, but that doesn't mean I care more or less for them. They're all family. Why is Dan different? Why does he evoke these unconscious actions?

Though unsure when it happened, Lexa realized Dan carved a little niche in her heart and took up residence. She cared about him and would walk through hell to save him ... like any of her teammates. And if the expression on his face, actually the lack thereof, a few minutes ago was any indication, she might have to do just that. Whatever Dan needed, she would provide, even if it meant exploring emotions better left in the dark recesses of her mind.

Unsettled by her uncharacteristic reactions to Dan, Lexa reflected on all she learned about him the past year. It seemed like she only scratched his surface, and she comprehended a complex man lived beneath his skin. An unexpected shiver ran through her as the thought of raking her nails down Dan's back as he pleasured her popped into her head. Lexa shook her carnal thoughts away. *This isn't the time or place for them.*

Patch continued to mull over everything since rappelling into the ravine. Though the physical injuries were severe, Blondie's psyche concerned him more. Shocked and relieved when Blaze and Winds showed up, Jim believed a guardian angel must be watching over Blondie, and perhaps it was Brody. If so, Brody sent the one guy who would be able to help their brother ... Blaze.

Upon spotting his former CO, Patch automatically said the four words which communicated everything necessary. Blaze would make it all right again, he and Brody always did. A little thought started to niggle at the back of his brain. *Perhaps Blaze isn't the only one who can help now.*

Patch didn't miss Blondie's new teammates' reactions. Jon showed concern and protectiveness through words and actions ... his gentle pat on Blondie's leg and strict admonishment about not taking risks, which prompted a question that needed to be answered. *Does Blondie still offer himself a sacrifice?*

Next, Jim considered the female officer. *Lexa showed a warm heart by caressing Blondie's hair. Wonder how she knows that gives him comfort?* Jim glanced at her, noting her eyes still fixated on Blondie. *She's a petite, delicate woman with auburn hair ... Blondie's physical type. Wonder how she stacks up on his other criteria?*

Jim shifted his eyes to Loki. *Funny nickname.* He almost smirked. *Patch isn't much better.* As he studied the Italian officer, Jim envisioned Brody. The two didn't match physically in any way, but he used humor like Brody did when talking to Blondie. Brody could always make their brother laugh with his antics, and he believed laughter healed the soul. *With the blank expression on Blondie's face, Blondie's soul needs restoration. Perhaps his new team can help.*

St. Michael Hospital – Air-Evac Pad – 9:15 p.m.

The door sliding open jarred everyone from their thoughts, and they realized they landed at the hospital. They jumped out and assisted in transferring Dan to the hospital's gurney, and then the medical team whisked Dan away from them to the elevator.

Heather Barkley waited as they unloaded the patient. Her eyes rounded with surprise to find Lexa among those helping. Relief and confusion sweep through her, but then she glimpsed the blond man and lost her breath at the sight of him and his condition.

Goodness gracious, she wanted to be the one to help—to fix him—but that was not her job today. She turned towards the group of three TRF officers, one paramedic, and two soldiers standing near the helicopter. All of them wore expressions of distress and anxiety.

She approached them but directed her query to Lexa. "My name is Heather. I'll be your contact in the ER. Can you tell me the name of the injured officer for my records?"

"Dan." "Blondie." "Broderick." "Dantastic." When six people gave her four answers simultaneously. Heather gaped at them. *Oh, my stars, their vigil will be painful. He must've forged strong bonds with them. I hope he makes it.*

"Shit! I should've gone with the doctor. I need to speak to him now. He needs to be made aware Blondie reacts badly to several medications," Patch said as he sprinted after the gurney.

Recomposing herself, Heather noted the rigidity in the remaining people, like they would break into tiny pieces with the slightest bump. The paramedic's words alarmed them, and she wondered what he meant by 'reacts badly,' but she needed to do something to ease everyone's tension.

They unintentionally gave her the perfect solution when they gave her his name. Heather smiled and laughed lightly, "Ok, so can we agree on a name? Blondie's certainly descriptive, but Dantastic is an awesome name. I'd love to see that up on the chart board."

Her tactic released the pressure a little but didn't completely erase it.

Jon said, "His given name is Daniel Broderick. Let's go with Dan for now. I'm his TRF Tactical Lead, Jon Hardy."

"Okay, Dan, it is. If you would please follow me, I'll take you to a room where you can wait," Heather said.

They followed her, and on the way, she showed them where they could find coffee and pointed out her desk if any questions arose. She realized they could use some privacy since they were in full gear. They didn't need people gawking at them at a time like this, so Heather ushered the group into a private waiting room instead of directing them to the general waiting area.

Breaking the Ice

 24

July 15
St. Michael Hospital – Private Waiting Room – 9:20 p.m.

A quiet tension hovered in the air like a dense fog as Blaze, Winds, Jon, Lexa, and Loki nervously paced the room. The frequently glanced at each other, wanting to start a conversation but remained unsure what to say to one another.

Heather returned, carrying a clipboard with several papers and a pen. She handed them to the bald TRF officer. "We need these forms completed for our records."

Jon peered at the sheet with a multitude of empty boxes a moment and back at the nurse. "Don't you have his details already?"

"Sorry, no. He's never been a patient here."

"But Dan's been treated at several hospitals in Toronto. Can't you pull his records from them?"

"Which hospitals?"

Pinching the bridge of his nose, Jon closed his eyes in thought. His gaze returned to the blonde, brown-eyed nurse. "Mercy and Centenary."

"Sorry, our system isn't connected to their database. Please, fill out what you can for now, and we will finish later."

For several moments Jon only stared at the blank form as he fiddled with the pen Heather gave him. When he sat, others followed his lead and found chairs as the silence remained.

Patch entered the room several minutes later. They all turned to him expectantly. He shook his head, indicating no update on Blondie. "Didn't see him, only provided the doctor with necessary info."

He headed to Blaze and Winds, who waited on one side of the room and gave them bear hugs. Huddled together, they began conversing in soft voices that couldn't be overheard.

BELONGING: HOPE, TRUTH AND MALICE 147

They put their questions on how Blondie ended up in Toronto and on the police force on hold and gave priority to discussing how to help him once Patch explained what happened in the ravine. Each agreed the emotional shutdown was familiar, but the catalyst couldn't the same as in Kandahar. They observed three dead bodies, which included a TRF officer.

Blaze speculated Blondie might've formed another friendship like the one with Brody and loss could've flipped the switch. The one thing each understood, it would take something significant to knock the kid off-kilter. With no idea what the past year entailed, they wondered if a single trigger or an accumulation of things caused the shutdown.

All three decided they must talk to someone on his team, but needed to ascertain which one. The agreed to do some recon to discover who if any of Blondie's teammates might be trusted to supply them insights and help their brother through this turmoil.

Winds offered to assess because regardless of what he told Hal, Blaze must communicate a status report to Major White and inform him why they stayed behind. White liked Blondie and had been his Special Forces Guardian training officer, so would understand their reasoning. And though Patch's shift technically ended, he must contact his partner Trey to furnish details for their shift log and tell him not to bother picking him up because the patient turned out to be a friend and he would be staying.

As he covertly observed the three TRF team members, Jon, Loki, and Lexa, according to Patch, Winds endeavored to choose which one to approach. His gaze settled first on Lexa. She sat in a far corner well away from her teammates with her elbows on her knees and face planted in her palms. He detected a slight shake of her shoulders.

Winds found it interesting she tried to hide her crying. He contemplated whether she believed tears would be perceived as a weakness in a male-dominated field, or if she cared about Blondie. *Patch said something about her telling Blondie she would keep him safe. She might be a possibility.*

Across from Jon, the raven-haired Loki stared up at the ceiling while one knee bounced vigorously, and his hands repetitively clasped and unclasped. The emotions written on his face indicated distress. Loki appeared to be in physical pain, yet he oddly exuded a sense of purpose. *Patch indicated Loki joked with Blondie, calling him Dantastic and Wile E. Coyote. A fascinating mix and another possibility.*

Jon's appeared as taut as a strung bow and continued to scowl. Winds recalled the same expression on Blaze more than once over the sixteen years they served together. He assumed, based on his experience with Blaze, Jon may well be pissed at himself for some perceived failure and trying hard not to explode. Understandable with one dead and one injured.

A fiery mien, the precursor to a nuclear explosion, is how Blaze had gotten his nickname. When his buddy couldn't contain his fury, Blaze would erupt with red-hot with rage and torch anyone and anything in his path.

The last time Blaze wore that expression, Mason told them the guard who denied them access to Blondie had been one of the guys who beat the crap out of the kid as he prepared to leave Kandahar. If only they were aware Blondie was going home, they would've been in the barracks, but Major Plouffe ordered them to the gun range.

If he hadn't, could've talked with Blondie as packed up his belongings. They could've prevented Murphy and the other assholes from beating the shit out of their brother. Four against one was not right, although, Blondie did hold his own and pulverized Murphy's face ... served the bastard right.

Winds shifted his gaze to Blaze as he re-entered the room. His best friend struggled with deep-seated guilt. Heck, they all did for how they reacted after Brody died. Though Blaze carried the most and keenly believed he failed both Blondie and Brody. He relayed shit-for-brains Plouffe's fire order. They lost two of their brothers all because the idiot major didn't ensure the entire recon unit exited the target zone before he gave the order. Winds laid the blame squarely at Plouffe's feet.

In the days following Brody's demise, they visited Blondie in the hospital. They almost lost him when he collapsed after finding Brody's body. If not for Baboon starting CPR, Blondie would also be dead and gone.

Brody's death devastated them all, and they couldn't bear to make eye contact with a grieving Blondie—too heartbreaking. Though unjustified, Blaze took the responsibility for the desolate, shattered pain reflected in Blondie's eyes. It physically hurt Blaze to view the agony he caused, and he vomited after each visit. His brother possessed a cast-iron stomach, but Blaze couldn't keep anything down for a week after Hunter perished.

It was too painful for all of them to witness the bleak wasteland and anguish in the kid's sapphire eyes, so they avoided looking at him. None of them found the right words to soothe Blondie's tormented soul and shattered heart, so they said nothing. They realized too late after he left, they should've said something, anything. Sadly, when Blondie needed them most, they unequivocally fucked up. Winds vowed never to fail the kid again if given a second chance. God, he hoped for another chance with all his heart.

Winds turned his gaze back to Jon and noted the tactical lead appeared to be losing his battle with control. *Jon is undoubtedly gonna blow soon. What he explodes about will be telling. It might give us the opening to talk to him. Funny how rage often opens doors faster than smooth talk ... probably because anger is pure, hard, raw, intense, and hard to fake.*

Jon only filled in Dan's name and where he worked. He stared at one particular box on the form, unable to provide the detail and berating himself for how badly he messed up when Dan joined the team. *I should know the answer, but I don't. I memorized everyone else's details. Why not Dan's? What does this say about my leadership abilities?*

Heather opened the door to allow Bram and Ray to enter the waiting room when Jon hit the tipping point of his anger. Jon stood and threw the clipboard with all his might, slamming it into the far wall as he raged, "Dammit, Dan. I'm sorry! You cover our backs every single shift, and I never took the time to learn your damned DOB!"

Loki, Bram, Ray, and Lexa cringed at Jon's outburst. Guilt rushed through them, realizing they never bothered to discover Dan's birthdate either.

However, Blaze, Winds, and Patch burst into uncontrolled, deep, rolling laughter. This caused all five TRF members and Heather to turn and gape at them like they lost their minds.

Winds struggled to regain control and tried to explain between gasps of laughter, "Shit, the kid did it again. Sorry, don't mean to laugh, but it's too damned funny. This exact thing happened to us the first time we took Blondie to the base hospital. Blaze raged and hurled a clipboard across the room for the same damned reason."

Getting himself under control, Winds shared, "Blondie had been with us almost four months, saving our butts more times than we could count, and we never knew his birthday. We felt like shit for not knowing … like we failed him somehow. But Brody told us he didn't know the date and they'd been thick as thieves for a long time. We resorted to hacking into his file to find out his damned birthdate."

Blaze shook his head, still chuckling. "Surprised the hell out of us when we discovered his age. His field skills were so impressive we thought he must be older than he appeared, like twenty-six to thirty. We were wrong. He truly was only a kid. Blondie was twenty-one, just shy of twenty-two."

"So, when was he born?" Lexa asked, still somewhat shaken by the outburst and realization.

"Should make you hack it too, would make this sense of déjà vu complete. But I won't … February ninth. That makes him twenty-eight now," Winds supplied with a smile.

The ice now broken, members of TRF and Special Forces introduced themselves. As they waited for word from the doctor, they laughed and joked about the crazy, embarrassing, and astonishing things Dan did. It helped each of them push away the fear and helplessness hanging over them. They found a unique way to cope for now, and it solidified in the minds of Blaze, Winds, and Patch they acquired new allies who cared for Blondie.

Heather stayed in the room and listened for a while. She was amazed at how they were all helping each other through this terrible time. They did it with humor—forging new friendships and connecting through memories of one remarkable man.

The impression she now held of Dan didn't match with her first one. He now appeared to be a rare man, one who went above and beyond to protect others. Heather could tell he was special to them, and they all cared about him. She hoped he would be okay. Quietly she left the room and went to the ER nurses' station chart board. With a broad smile, Heather erased BRODERICK and wrote DANTASTIC. *Yes, that's more appropriate!*

David and Genevieve Plouffe's Home – 10:20 p.m.

Nick and Walter exited the home of Aaron Plouffe's parents. Informing Aaron's parents of their son's death was a difficult and emotionally draining task, but they deserved to told in person.

They had no official information to share yet. The NRB interviews and statements must be taken and reviewed before relaying any details with his family. Not that they knew how Aaron died. The only person who could tell them that remained unconscious at the hospital.

Nick rubbed his face as he and the commander made their way down the sidewalk to the SUV. Nick couldn't push the image of Aaron's fiancée collapsing into David Plouffe's arms. Nick hoped the stress of Aaron's death didn't cause Tammy any problems.

Images of Lillian, Jon's late sister-in-law, came to mind—she couldn't handle Joe's death, and Joey became an orphan because of it. He hoped Tammy fared better. She seemed to have a support system in place with Aaron's family, but he left a number for a well-respected grief counselor, too.

Sadly, families of officers had to cope with a lot. Their loved ones put their lives on the line to help others every day. When they went off to work, there were no guarantees they would return home. It was hard on families, especially spouses, which is why so many officers ended up divorced. Not everyone effectively handled high levels of stress and uncertainty.

Nick grasped no one was guaranteed to come home at the end of the day. His wife and son were gunned down outside Martin's daycare in a random act of violence. Gangs caused another death today. If he could obliterate gangs and their violence from this world, he would. Nick knew tonight he wouldn't sleep. Thoughts of Aaron, his wife, his son, and Dan would plague him.

He was so ready to head to the hospital to find out how Dan fared. He hoped his rookie didn't suffer internal bleeding. Today had been profoundly unique … not in a good way … nope, not at all.

So lost in his thoughts, Nick didn't notice a man approaching and bumped into him. He stopped, looked up, and his eyes landed on a man in uniform. Nick took in the nondescript features, brown hair, eyes, average height, but noted the man wore the insignia of an Army Major and the tan beret of Special Forces. "Excuse me. I wasn't—"

Major Plouffe cut off the man. "You're with the TRF, aren't you?"

"Yes. I'm Sergeant Nick Pastore." Nick motioned toward Walter. "This is Commander Gambrill. And you are?"

Squaring his shoulders, Plouffe assumed a hard tone. "Major Nigel Plouffe. What can you tell me about my nephew's death?"

Nick said, "Not much until after the investigation. He died in the line of duty. I'm sorry for your loss. Aaron was an honorable man. He will be missed."

"Is that all?" Plouffe stated.

"I'm afraid so. Aaron's parents will be notified once the official investigation is complete and provided full disclosure," Nick responded.

Walter observed the interaction closely. Though not privy to the details, he recalled William mentioning some concerns about a major named Plouffe. The surname name was common enough, so he never connected Aaron Plouffe to Major Plouffe.

But now Walter's gut churned uneasily. *He is Arron's uncle. Should I inform William? It is currently six-thirty in the morning in Afghanistan. A decent enough hour to call, but perhaps I should wait to call until I understand Dan's status. William will want a complete report on his son's condition first. The major being related to one of my TRF officers is secondary.*

One Overwhelming Day

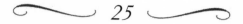

25

July 15
St. Michael Hospital – Private Waiting Room – 10:45 p.m.

Bram continued his story about Dan, "... and while we wrapped things up, Loki handed off a box of munitions to the bomb disposal guy and turned to talk with Ray. The guy stumbled and dropped the box. A grenade fell out, and somehow, the pin got pulled in the process. It rolled towards Lexa and some children who didn't see the explosive coming towards them.

"Dan shouted, 'GRENADE.' Everyone ran for cover except him. He raced forward and threw himself on it right before it exploded only a few feet from the kids and Lexa. Damned glad it was only a concussive, not a fragmentation device. Dan's ears rang for a couple of days after the incident. Mostly from Jon yelling at him for taking unacceptable risks," Bram finished.

Everyone laughed as several others came into the room.

Jon stood and walked over to speak with the newcomers. "Commander," Jon acknowledged Gambrill and nodded in greeting to Nick. He noticed NRB Agents Stevens and Donner and a patrol officer.

"Jon, any word on Broderick?" Gambrill asked.

"Not yet, getting worried. Dan looked terrible when we airlifted him. He's been in there for an hour and a half now and not a single update. Are things all wrapped up at Rouge Park?"

"Yes, and we notified Delta Team and Aaron's family also. Sad day, don't want to lose another officer today, especially not Dan." Gambrill sighed.

Nick gave Gambrill a curious look. He never allowed partiality to color his speech before. Nick began to wonder yet again, how well Gambrill knew Dan.

"Are those the guys who swooped in to help? I want to personally thank them, if they are," Walter inclined his head in the direction of the soldiers, who had their backs to them currently talking with Ray and Bram.

"Yes. I'll introduce you." Jon called out as they walked towards the two Special Forces soldiers, "Blaze, Winds, our TRF Commander would like to meet you."

Blaze and Winds stood and turned to the newcomers.

Halting Jon made the introductions. "Commander Gambrill, this is Captain Blain and Corporal Simons. Gentlemen, this is Commander Walter Gambrill and Dan's sergeant, Nick Pastore."

Nick grinned and shook hands with the men. "Thanks. We truly appreciate your help. Dan's important to us."

Gambrill stared. He knew those names. *Good grief ... what are the chances of Daniel's unit CO being the one to respond?* Walter kept his shock to himself as he extended his hand. "We grateful for the help today. I'll be sending a formal recognition of your efforts to your commander expressing our appreciation. I'm sure General Broderick will be thanking you, too."

Blaze hid his disgust. *Like hell, the general will thank me. The man holds no concern for his son. He will likely be pissed off that we used military resources to help Blondie.* Instead of responding to the comment about General Badass, Blaze shook the commander's hand. "Happy to assist. Never would've guessed in a million years we'd be rescuing Blondie. I owe the kid my life."

Jon noticed the immediate change in the demeanor or Blaze and Winds with the mention of Dan's father. He cataloged the stiffness present in both men now. Turning to Nick, he asked, "Speaking of the general. Nick, did you contact him yet?"

A slight grimace crossed Nick's face. "Sort of, I called before we went to inform Aaron's parents. I spoke with his aide, Corporal Merrill, in Afghanistan. He said he would pass on the message to General Broderick when he got into the office and indicated it would be unlikely the general would be able to come at this time. Apparently, he is swamped at the moment."

Walter inwardly cringed. *Damn, I didn't realize Nick called William. I hope Merrill didn't wake William to tell him about Daniel's injury. William doesn't need to be pacing, waiting for word.*

"Good," muttered Winds under his breath, drawing puzzled eyes from Nick. Recognizing inquisitiveness, Winds stated, "Might be my commander, but I can't stand the man. Better for Blondie if he doesn't come."

The animosity-filled statement astonished Gambrill. He always thought the soldiers respected William and found the remark quite perplexing.

Blaze put a hand on Winds's shoulder. "Not here. Not now."

Further inquiry halted as a doctor entered the room. "Family of Constable Broderick," Dr. Fraser asked, peering up from his clipboard.

"Yes," six TRF officers, two Special Forces soldiers, and one paramedic stated at the same time.

Overwhelmed by the volume of the response and the laser intensity of nine pairs of eyes trained on him, Fraser took a small step backwards and brought the clipboard up to his chest protectively. "I'm Dr. Malcolm Fraser. I'm in charge of treating Mr. Broderick.

"Unfortunately, he's sustained quite a few injuries today, most accompanied by various degrees of bruising, but he is currently stable. The gunshot wound through his upper right arm caused minimal damage. Although he lost a fair amount of blood, the transfusion he is receiving will replace the lost volume.

"He sustained a mild concussion and a large hematoma on the back of his skull. The x-rays of his torso revealed five cracked ribs, but none fully broken, and the left clavicle shows a hairline fracture. In addition to various minor lacerations and abrasions on his face and knuckles, he required six stitches above the right eye.

"Superficially, there's extensive bruising of his left shoulder, chest, and stomach from blunt force trauma. There is also a significant discoloration on his back, arms, and legs. Scans revealed minor contusion of his kidneys, but the liver appears undamaged. Initially, we worried about internal bleeding, but haven't detected any signs.

"His lung and heart function appear robust, but proper breathing will be difficult with his fractured ribs. We'll watch for signs of congestion to prevent complications. Last but not least, we found partially torn ligaments in his left wrist. We consider the damage to be a grade two sprain, which should heal without surgical intervention.

"All in all, Mr. Broderick is one lucky man. He needs a long rest for his body to heal, but I expect he will recover with no long-term adverse effects from any of his injuries."

Sighs of relief sounded all around until the doctor's expression told them he had more to say, and they wouldn't like hearing it.

Dr. Fraser paused a moment before continuing, "However, I'm concerned with his mental well-being. Constable Broderick regained consciousness but hasn't responded in any way. He's awake, and his brain functions are normal, but he will not speak or move and stares blankly.

"It's extremely troubling. For this reason, we'll be keeping him in the ICU for observation instead of moving him to a standard room. I understand he received these injuries on the job. Perchance, did something happen, which may help us understand his current mental state? Perhaps he experienced emotional trauma or shock?"

Alpha Team shared the same thoughts. *Hell, yeah, something happened today, which could affect Dan's emotional state.* They turned to Nick, waiting for him to explain.

"Well, you could say Dan's had an overwhelming day." Nick drew in a breath. "We handled four critical calls today with no break between them. We were on the move since seven this morning until Dan was injured about eight tonight. I will say it's been an emotionally and physically exhausting day with several civilian deaths, the rescue of six children, losing a colleague under his command, and using a dark episode in his past to connect with three Army veterans who appeared to be suffering PTSD. I'm sorry, I can't elaborate more at this time. Protocol prevents full disclosure of Dan's activities."

Fraser nodded. "Well, with the little you shared, which is significant in itself, I grasp it would be quite taxing on one's psyche. Can you tell me if he was involved in the death of any of the civilians? It will remain confidential."

Gambrill stated, "He is the subject officer in at least one of the deaths."

"Having to take a life could have this effect," Dr. Fraser supposed, his mien thoughtful as he considered the impact of killing a person.

"Doctor, you gotta understand … this isn't Blondie's first rodeo," Winds interjected.

"Blondie?" asked Dr. Fraser.

Ray smiled. "Dan has many nicknames, including Blondie and Dantastic."

Fraser focused on the soldier who spoke. "So, you're saying Mr. Broderick wouldn't be affected in this way by killing someone?"

Blaze matter-of-factly stated, "No, he wouldn't. Blondie is ex-Special Forces. Six years as a sniper. He's resilient. Though taking a kill shot isn't easy for him, it wouldn't put him into the kind of emotional shutdown you're describing."

Loki remembered the expression on Dan's face in Central Bank. He turned to Blaze and asked in a slightly unsteady voice, "Would talking about when he was held captive cause this? He … he looked so pained when he connected with the soldiers and …"

"Oh shit! That *was* him!" Patch exclaimed as tears filled his eyes. He recalled what he overheard when he treated one of the bank subjects. His voice cracked, "No, no … Blondie worked so hard to lock the memories of his torture away. Brody worked harder to heal the kid's soul than I did to repair his body … and Blondie was a bloody pulp."

Patch peered at Blaze, his eyes fearful. "Blondie couldn't … it would've … ah shit, he did." Steading himself a bit, Patch redirected his gaze to Dr. Fraser. "Letting those memories out might cause the effect, Doc."

Blaze put his arm around Patch's shoulders. Memories of that horrific time haunted all of them. They found Blondie more dead than alive, and it took all their effort and months of work to help Blondie recover from the physical and emotional wounds of his three-month captivity in the hands of sadistic bastards.

Winds's other hand settled on Patch's back in brotherly support. *Bringing those gruesome memories to the forefront would impact their lost brother. Damn.*

Fraser stared and nod at Patch.

Bram turned to Dan's former unit. "Does the name Sara mean anything to you guys?"

All three shook their heads, but a quick intake of breath from Gambrill caused everyone's eyes to dart to him.

Walter gazed at Bram. "Why do you ask?"

"It is the little girl's name ... the one he saved in the alley. He collapsed afterward. I only wondered if there might be some significance."

Shaken, Walter closed his eyes as he remembered the nine-year-old boy stoically attending his seven-year-old sister's funeral. Dan appeared so lost and alone, it hurt almost as much as losing Sara.

Still in disbelief, Walter lifted his lids and focused on Fraser. "Truly one hell of an emotional day for Dan. Sara is his younger sister's name. Dan was only nine and Sara seven when she died in front of him. He was holding her hand when a car hit her so hard it knocked her out of her shoes. The guy driving was cited for DUI, drunk at eleven o'clock in the morning. Senseless death. I didn't think Dan would ever smile again."

Nick glanced at Jon sharing similar thoughts. *Gambrill knows Dan better than he let on, especially if he is aware of events from Dan's childhood.*

Shocked to learn details of Dan's sister's death, Ray wondered about it ever since he overheard Gambrill in Dan's hospital room when Dan had bronchitis. But he didn't think this was related to now, or at least not entirely associated to Dan's current condition.

Winds's eyes rounded in surprise as he peered at Blaze. *Blondie had a sister who died? Holy shit! The kid still has secrets.*

Patch's mind worked in another direction. Blondie was okay when he found him—he'd been able to operate from call to call. Blondie only went blank after recognizing him in the ravine. "Blondie took one look at me, and his mask descended. He blanked out because of me ..."

Peering first to Blaze pleading for help, Patch choked up, unable to say any more, before turning away to cover his face with his hands, hiding the tears threatening to spill as sorrow and fear leeched out of every pore.

"What?" chorused from Alpha Team.

Blaze understood. With watery eyes, and grief lacing every word he said, "What Patch means ... the final piece in this hellacious day and what probably threw Blondie over the edge is the last time Blondie saw Patch, myself, and Winds was three days after Blondie accidentally killed his best friend. Not his fault. I gave the all-clear to fire, unaware Brody remained in the target zone."

Winds moved his hand from Patch to Blaze's arm. "Not your fault, either. You only relayed the signal to Blondie."

Blaze turned to Winds, appreciative of the support, though he disagreed. Winds would forever insist he bore no blame, but Blaze would always carry the guilt. Always.

"I see," is all Dr. Fraser said. It appeared his patient had been through one heck of a day.

With fire and sadness in her eyes, Lexa's voice came out unsteady, "What can we do to help?" Not wanting them to witness her welling tears, she pivoted away from the guys as she brushed at her face.

Bram's arms wrapped around Lexa and pulled her close. He understood she bottled-up emotions, and notoriously she tried to hide her soft side. Lexa used anger as her default shield, but Bram perceived the dings in her armor, comprehending the events of the day added up and overwhelmed her. Her day had been almost as psychologically taxing as Dan's.

Lexa neutralized a man who wanted to commit suicide. Bram recognized she would still be beating herself up because Garth fired at Dan before she took the shot. Then she viewed Dan's scars for the first time and dealt with several traumatized children.

Three cherries topped this shitty sundae. Lexa had been the one tasked with watching Dan's back after Aaron bad-mouthed him. She had nearly been shot twice with Frank taking a bullet, which would've killed her. And Lexa arrived first, finding Aaron dead and Dan unconscious at the bottom of the ravine.

A lot for anyone to deal with, and now Lexa needed his support ... she needed a hug. So Bram held Lexa close, providing the comfort a father would to a hurting child. He appreciated her willingness to accept his embrace and the emotional support ... if only for a moment to recompose herself.

The rest of Alpha Team and Dan's former Special Forces unit exchanged glances, vowing without words to help Dan find his way back.

Nick calmly spoke for them all, "We need to see him. Dan needs to know we're here. We promised him today to keep him safe."

They started en masse towards the door when a voice halted them.

"You can't, he's a subject officer in five shootings and now a potential suspect in the murder of Constable Aaron Plouffe. He is sequestered! You will not see, nor speak to him. He is under my jurisdiction as of this moment," NRB Agent Richard Donner stated with a venomous glint to his eye.

We've Got Your Six

 *26*

July 15
St. Michael Hospital - ER Information Desk — 11:10 p.m.

Sitting at her desk, Heather finished giving information to an older gentleman about the condition of his wife. A sudden sonic boom of rage and pain-filled yelling exploding from the private waiting room shattered the usual hush of the waiting area.

With so many roaring voices on top of one another, she couldn't comprehend anything except thundering noise. Heather launched out of her chair and raced for the room with one thought. *Oh my gosh, Dantastic died!*

St. Michael Hospital — Private Waiting Room — 11:11 p.m.

Heather threw open the door, stunned to find the room's occupants in absolute chaos, and oozing uncontrolled rage. Everyone shouted, and the target of the rain of fury was a fearful man pushed up against the far wall.

Bram, Loki, Ray, Patch, and Winds urgently tried to disengage Blaze and Jon from the man as they all bellowed. Blaze's hands encircled the guy's throat, while Jon firmly gripped the front of the man's shirt in his fists as he pushed him hard into the wall.

Nick paced in a tight circle, raking his hands through his hair and yelling at Gambrill, who shouted back at Nick and waved his hand in the direction of the scared man pinned by Jon and Blaze.

Lexa stood with her feet shoulder-width apart, hands on hips, fists clenched while screaming at another woman who appeared shocked as she shrieked back and gestured at the man being accosted.

Dr. Fraser hid behind a patrol officer in the corner, and both appeared a bit shell-shocked by the pandemonium around them.

Heather began to register individual comments, but not who said them. *Goodness gracious, what the heck happened?*

"JON, STOP! THINK MAN."

"YOU'RE FUCKING KIDDING ME."

"I WILL SEE HIM! YOU CAN'T STOP ME."

"YOU'RE A DEAD MAN, DONNER."

"BLAZE, NO, GOD NO! STOP!"

"YOU FUCKING BASTARD!"

"STOP THIS NOW!"

"HE CAN'T DO THAT, CAN HE?"

"YOU SON OF A BITCH!"

"I WON'T LET THIS HAPPEN!"

"HE ISN'T A MURDERER!"

"DAN NEEDS US NOW!"

Realizing this wouldn't be the reaction if Dan had died. Heather's wondered how to diffuse this unexpected and emotionally charged situation. *I could call security, but how would they handle a group of Special Forces soldiers and elite TRF officers on an emotional rampage? Several of them are still armed. Sweet mercy, it's a miracle no one has pulled a weapon—yet!*

The last word knocked around in her mind then receded. As she stood there with the door open, a crowd started to gather behind her. Heather needed to act, and now, otherwise, there would be repercussions for the officers, and she wouldn't allow that. She would deal with the on-lookers, assuming the constables would come to their senses and regain control of themselves. Heather closed the door and turned to the gawkers.

St. Michael Hospital – Private Waiting Room – Outside – 11:15 p.m.

Heather Barkley plastered her emotionless nurse face on as she faced the inquisitive group. "They received some bad news about a fellow officer. The one injured in the gang war today. Please, move away and give them the privacy they deserve." Her statement gave them something to chew on, which would both explain and excuse the behavior they witnessed.

Especially since the newscasts had run accounts of Alpha Team's day all evening. The news found out who the injured officer was and reported on his exploits today. Someone also supplied them with video of one of their calls.

The footage showed a handsome young officer flanked by six teammates, carrying a sleeping child in his arms. Dan carefully put the little girl into the waiting arms of her mother, whispered something that made the mother smile, then stepped back. He smiled down at the tiny child, tenderly stroked her golden hair, and kissed her forehead.

The video ended with his teammates protectively surrounding him as they walked away. 'Ahs' were heard from the women in the room every time the clip was replayed. Newscasters called Dan a hero, claiming he saved the girl from a drug-crazed gunman.

They also interviewed a manager who had been a hostage in a bank robbery who recounted how Dan saved two men from committing suicide by talking to them. The middle-aged man appeared to be too shaken up to give many details, only saying the officer showed him the beauty of life that morning.

Reporters delved into his history and related he was ex-Special Forces and served with distinction before joining the TRF's best of the best Alpha Team. The stations also repeatedly played a short clip of the unguarded, volatile reactions of the team when they learned a fellow officer had been injured. Newscasters contended, he must be special to garner emotional responses like that from teammates who typically remained highly composed even in the worst situations.

Heather believed if they only knew the price the young man paid today to save others, they wouldn't be all smiles. They wrapped their stories up in fancy paper and pretty bows. The reality was ugly, bloody, and agonizingly brutal. As the violent storm inside the room began to blow itself out, Heather remained at the door, acting as a guard for their privacy.

St. Michael Hospital – ER Treatment Room – 11:17

Dan knew only two things for sure, he was conscious, and in agonizing pain. His eyes may or may not be open, but all remained blackness, and only a deafening silence roared in his ears. He couldn't detect if he was alone or surrounded. He didn't know where he was. Nothing, absolutely nothing in the physical world registered—except pain, excruciating pain.

Time held no meaning. Dan had no idea how long he lay here suffering. It seemed infinite and unrelenting. His head throbbed mercilessly as spikes drove through his skull. Breathing brought searing fire. Pulsating pain followed any movement. Pain is all his world consisted of now.

Why can't I just stop existing? It would stop my pain. Why won't oblivion take me back and end the torment? Must I always be in agony? Am I such a bad person I deserved this hellish punishment? I wish I could just slip away and be released from this torture.

"Please … oh, God, please … stop the pain," Dan screamed in his head, but it came out as a scarcely audible whisper.

"Doctor!" Nurse Clare called out as she quickly searched for the attending doctor. Not finding him, she grabbed the closest orderly. "Where's Dr. Fraser?"

"With the family. I think in the large private waiting area."

St. Michael Hospital – Private Waiting Room – 11:20 p.m.

Clare hurried down the hall and noted Heather standing outside the private room's door. She motioned her to step aside, jerked open the door, and said, "Doctor Fraser, you're needed. He spoke!"

The tempest in the room instantly stilled. No one moved a muscle. All sound ceased.

Clare blinked, not believing the scene in the room.

Dr. Fraser's years of emergency room experience kicked in as he did a quick step towards Clare. "What did he say?"

"It was so soft and choked, I almost didn't hear him, but he said 'Please, oh God, please stop the pain,'" Clare reported as Fraser reached the exit and followed him toward the emergency room at a rapid clip.

"Shit!" Patch cried and raced after the doctor. *If Blondie is begging them to make his pain stop, he's in overwhelming physical agony.* Patch understood Blondie ordinarily possessed a high threshold to pain, but sometimes his senses overloaded, and he couldn't manage, locking him in an agonizing world.

Shit, shit, shit! This shouldn't be happening. I told them exactly what and how much to give him to prevent it. Why didn't it work? Is something different? This always worked in the past, and Blondie was right as rain in a few hours as his body adjusted. Patch needed to get to Blondie now, and he wouldn't let anyone even the goddamned NRB guy stop him.

When Patch cussed and rushed out, Blaze and Winds comprehended the severity and didn't hesitate to follow. They would remove any barrier, be it doors or people, in Patch's way. They'd done it before and would do it again. Blondie needed Patch and needed him now!

Alpha Team realized something significant must've happened. From the few stories Dan's former unit shared, it was clear they didn't possess the same knowledge the Special Forces guys had with Dan. Sure, he'd been in the hospital with bronchitis and when the glass impaled his ass, and they did know he didn't do well on pain meds. They'd seen him loopy after the SUV crash, but mostly he had been checked out at the scene and deemed fine.

Donner be damned—they all followed Blaze, Winds, and Patch. Their teammate needed help. They figured Patch understood what Dan needed after being the team medic for six years. They'd ensure Patch got the cooperation he required to care for Dan properly.

Commander Gambrill watched the eight men and one woman exit, and a tight smile briefly crossed his face. Dan would be alright; those nine would ensure it. Walter decided to stay and deal with the asshole NRB Agent Richard Donner. He would set the man straight. Dan wasn't a murderer and for the agent to even imply that infuriated Walter.

As he pivoted to face Donner, Agent Stevens stormed over to her coworker and icily said, "Just what the hell do you think you're doing? I already started the process to lodge a formal complaint against you. You'll be lucky to still have your job by tomorrow.

"I reviewed your interviews with Constable Broderick. You're disgusting! How you behaved is deplorable. *He* insisted on painting the picture? *You* were the one asking for all the details. You're a sick man, Richard. I intend to ensure you are fired. You'll regret the day ..."

As Agent Kendall Stevens went on and on, verbally lashing out at Donner, Gambrill took a position slightly behind her. He donned his best stern command stance and countenance to provide solid, but silent support to Stevens. What she said twisted his gut, wondering how this agent got away with treating one of his officers so poorly.

Walter swallowed hard. *Another thing for William to ream me about. Damn, keeping his distance and watching over Dan is a hard job.* His stomach turned to stone when he realized he inadvertently shared about Sara. *Damn. Pastore isn't a stupid man. He will work out there is a relationship between Dan and me. Double damn. Today just can't get worse.*

Officer Marc Fargusson moved to a chair and sank as he listened to Agent Stevens ream Agent Donner. *Wow! This is one profoundly unique day. Never seen one like it in all my decades on the force.*

Marc wasn't sure what to expect when Ms. Stevens requested him as protection detail, but it certainly wasn't this. He still was unsure why she needed him here. *She is doing a damned-fine job of protecting herself. Maybe it isn't her who needs my services?* Marc decided to wait until she finished tongue-lashing the idiot agent before he asked.

St. Michael Hospital – ER Treatment Room – 11:23 p.m.

Nine people stormed through the emergency department, searching for Dan. The fierce expressions made everyone move out of their way. They arrived at Dan's bedside only shortly after the doctor and nurse.

Patch pushed passed the ER doctor to assess Blondie. Anger flared when his worst fears were realized. Dr. Fraser's description of blankly staring had nothing to do with a mental state. Infuriated, this was not Blondie's blank, emotionless mask from the ravine—this was the result of intense physical distress.

Blondie had to be in so much pain he contracted every muscle to prevent movement, which would cause even greater misery. His agony was most evident in his wide-open, soul-revealing sapphire eyes. Pleading orbs—not blank and empty. *Why the hell couldn't they see the difference?*

Everyone's hearts fragmented when they heard low, hoarse sounds barely distinguishable as words. The words were desperately slow as they escaped his dry throat with the minimum possible movement—intense pain showing with each syllable.

"… please make it stop … I can't take … any more … no more pain … please stop the pain."

"Blondie, I'm here, I'll stop your pain. Hold tight. It'll go away soon, I promise. I'm sorry I wasn't here. Relief is coming, brother," Patch crooned as he lightly squeezed Blondie's left bicep.

Bram watched Patch's natural, warm, and gentle motions as he spoke so compassionately to Dan. The rookie's reaction to being touched there started to make sense. The affection Patch held for Dan clear and visible on in his facial features, as too was rising fury.

Patch turned and pinned Fraser with a death glare as he demanded, "What and how much did you give Blondie for pain?"

Dr. Fraser grabbed the chart and handed it to Patch.

Patch swiftly scanned the chart. His indignation increased, and his face turned red with rage. "WHY THE HELL DIDN'T YOU ADMINISTER WHAT I TOLD YOU? I KNOW WHAT HE NEEDS! CAN'T YOU IDENTIFY AGONY WHEN YOU SEE IT? DAMN YOU!"

"Per protocol, I prescribed the standard dosage based on his weight," Dr. Fraser replied defensively.

Blaze flamed hot and fast as he got in the doctor's face. "BUT BLONDIE'S NOT STANDARD ISSUE. HE'S EXCEPTIONAL! YOU WERE TOLD HOW TO CARE FOR HIM BY SOMEONE WHO KNOWS BLONDIE'S BODY INSIDE AND OUT AND KEPT HIM ALIVE FOR SIX DAMNED YEARS!

"BUT YOU ARE TOO HIGH AND MIGHTY TO LISTEN TO A MERE MEDIC. HOW DO YOU FEEL NOW THAT BLONDIE'S THE ONE WHO SUFFERED FOR YOUR PRIDE AND ARROGANCE?"

Alpha Team all took a deep breath. They now understood why the guy had been nicknamed Blaze. None of them wanted to be in the enraged man's crosshairs. They learned a fast lesson in how much Dan meant to these men.

Patch reined his anger, shifted into medic mode, and outlined what would relieve and control Blondie's pain.

Dr. Fraser gave a curt nod of agreement when Clare looked to him for direction. His patient suffered due to his pretentious attitude and disregard of the medic's information. A very humbling experience he vowed never to repeat with patients under his care.

As Clare rushed to comply, she felt ashamed she failed to recognize her patient's misery. Within minutes, Clare returned with the requested medication and began to administer it via the IV port.

After the medication was given, Patch leaned in close to Blondie. He placed one hand on his left bicep again and gently squeezed. Patch murmured in his little brother's ear, "It'll be okay in a moment, rest now, brother. Close your eyes. Stand down. We're here, we've got your six, Blondie. Pain will fade soon. It should be easing now. That's right. Lower your lids, rest. Your agony will go away. Rest. I promise, no more pain."

Lexa stood at Dan's right side, softly threading fingers through his sweaty, golden locks as she whispered, "We're here. Not going anywhere. There's no place I'd rather be. Sleep now. You're safe. I'll keep you safe. We'll protect you now. Time to rest. That's it ... let your eyelids close."

As Dan's lids slowly drifted down, tension released from his body. Patch and Lexa lifted their heads and locked gazes. Both sets of eyes filled with unshed tears of compassion, and both mouthed, "Thank you." Each sighed and straightened up, but Lexa kept stroking Dan's hair, and Patch kept his hand on Blondie's bicep.

"How long was he awake?" Dread colored Winds's voice, not really wanting to know the answer.

"About an hour and a half. Why?" Clare replied.

Winds didn't answer, he only hung his head, and brushed at tears which started to drip. He turned away and crouched, hiding his face in his hands, his heart shattering as he realized the agony Blondie suffered. *The kid's suffered way too much. Enough is enough. This shits gotta stop.*

Nick perceived the reason for the question from Winds's tone and body language. He responded wearily, "Because that is the length of time your patient was stuck in a world of unbearable pain, unable to communicate, and none of you noticed."

A horrified look took over Clare as liquid welled in her eyes. "I'm so sorry, so very sorry. I ... I ... no excuse." Clare covered her mouth as a sob escaped, and she rushed from the room in tears.

Dr. Fraser turned and went after Clare. *It isn't her fault. It's mine, and I'm going to make sure she knows.*

Nick, Jon, Ray, Bram, Loki, and Blaze all moved towards Dan and reached out to lay a comforting hand on him. They didn't touch him before, not wanting to cause more pain. Winds wiped his eyes, stood, and pivoted to join the group around Blondie. They stood silent, surrounding the bed, watching him sleep as each became lost in their thoughts.

Relieved by Dan's relaxed body, Loki studied the downcast faces of everyone around Dan. Hoping to break the thick tension, he said, "Kinda figured Dan's not standard issue. Think our Proper Care and Feeding of Dantastic manual needs some additional details."

When Alpha Team chuckled, Blaze, Winds, and Patch stared, wondering what they found so funny.

"What kind of manual is that?" Blaze asked.

"I think the nine of us should sit down and have a serious exchange of information, and then a long talk with Dan," Jon replied.

Eight heads nodded in agreement. They discussed when and decided to meet at TRF HQ tomorrow morning. The team would be off duty, but the briefing room would accommodate everyone and provide them privacy for the discussion.

A little while later, Dr. Fraser cleared his throat to gain their attention. Heads as one towards him, but bodies didn't move. They created a protective barrier and wouldn't allow anyone close to Dan at the moment.

Contrition etched into his features, Dr. Fraser said, "We must move him to ICU now. Jim, I confess I should've listened to you. I would very much appreciate consulting with you on proper dosing for Constable Broderick. I want to enter necessary details into his permanent medical records here, so we never repeat this inexcusable episode. I would also like your opinion on giving him more sedative to help him sleep tonight."

Bram stated in a voice that would brook no defiance, "We go with him to the ICU."

The doctor nodded as he and Patch stepped away for their discussion. The rest opened ranks to allow the nurses to prepare to move Dan. They encircled the gurney as they escorted him to the Intensive Care Unit and waited outside the glass-paneled room as the nurse attached the necessary monitors. Patch rejoined the group as the head nurse explained they couldn't remain in the hall, and they needed to relocate to the waiting room.

After the Storm

27

July 15
St. Michael Hospital – ICU – Outside Room A – 11:55 p.m.

With the room only large enough for two or three visitors at a time, the group of nine discussed who should enter first as Commander Gambrill, NRB Director Reed Caldwell, and the patrolman approached them.

Director Caldwell stated, "First, I apologize for Agent Donner's behavior. He overstepped bounds and will be dealt with appropriately. And I assure you, no assault charges will be brought against Constable Hardy or Captain Blain."

Gesturing to the patrol officer, Caldwell explained, "Constable Fargusson is now assigned as protection detail and will be stationed outside Broderick's room. I will allow each of you a moment with Broderick to assure yourself of his well-being, but you must leave afterwards."

Reed focused on the TRF team. "You're to consider yourselves sequestered. As such, you are not to discuss today's cases with anyone until after your statements are given. We will convene for interviews tomorrow at one o'clock at TRF headquarters. Any questions?"

Blaze asked, "We're not TRF, does that mean we can stay?"

"Unfortunately, no. In the case of an injured subject officer, the compassion protocol states only family may stay." Caldwell noted the dismay and a bit of challenge in their expressions.

"He is our brother?" Blaze declared as Patch and Winds nodded.

Understanding how close military men became, the NRB director clarified, "Biological family or spouse. Neither of which qualify for anyone here."

Not one to give up easily, Patch tried, "Can we remain outside the room without speaking to him, so if he wakes, he isn't alone?"

"No. It is doubtful he'll wake tonight. Dr. Fraser gave Broderick a sedative to help him sleep and recover," Caldwell replied.

Gambrill understood the team wouldn't like this but would comply. "You've all had one hellacious day. You're dead on your feet. Go home, eat, and sleep. That's an order. Broderick will be alright. I need you clear-headed and focused tomorrow."

Everyone realized they had no choice at this point, and all agreed they were running on fumes. Dan would be okay now. Patch assured them the proper medication had been administered, allowing Dan's intense pain to subside, and he now slept. Patch also indicated when Dan awoke, his pain level would be manageable since he briefed the doctor on Blondie's unique needs and agreed to follow the recommendations.

July 16
St. Michael Hospital – ICU – Inside Room A – 12:01 a.m.

Blaze, Patch, and Winds entered first. Patch went to the left side and placed his hand on his brother's bicep, but remained quiet, wishing they found him sooner.

Winds stood at the end of the bed and gripped the footboard so tight his knuckles turned white. "He looks like shit. I hoped never to see him beat to a pulp again. What happened? Where the hell was his backup?"

Blaze gently laid his hand on the kid's thigh as he studied Blondie's bruised and abraded knuckles. A small chuckle emitted. "He sure put up one hell of a fight. I glimpsed the face of the dead guy. Blondie gave as good as he got. Maybe more. The guy's nose appeared to be flattened."

"Ripsaw would be proud." Winds grinned despite the situation.

Patch nodded. "He's been here for a year. A fucking year. And we never knew. How come we couldn't find him?"

Blaze shook his head. "Don't know. This isn't like any blackout protocol I've ever encountered. Something isn't right."

A hard edge entered Winds's voice, "The general. He did this. I'm sure of it. That heartless, cold bastard. He has resources at his disposal to make it impossible for us to find Blondie."

Shifting his gaze to Blaze, Winds declared, "I'd give the bastard a piece of my mind and a taste of my fists if it wouldn't get me court-martialed. I don't give a damn about me, but ..." Winds released his left hand and peered at the thin white scar. "We need to be where we are now to fulfill our oath."

Blaze nodded and turned his palm up. The scar, a reminder of their blood oath, to kill every last animal who tortured Blondie. A vow not to leave the field before they kept their promise. "Hey, kid. I've seen you worse. You're gonna heal, and we're gonna have a long-overdue talk. We won't fail you again. I promise. Rest now, kid. We'll be back tomorrow."

Patch grinned. "Actually, we'll be in later today, little brother." He squeezed his bicep again. "Sleep well."

Winds patted Blondie's leg. "Fate finally dealt you a decent hand, kid. What are the odds you end up a constable in the same city where Patch is a medic? Catch ya later, Brother."

The three turned and headed out, unhappy they couldn't stay, but for now, they wouldn't make waves. Blondie would be safe here. When Loki, Ray, and Jon entered for their short visit, Patch invited Blaze and Winds to stay at his apartment since they were planning to meet with the TRF team in the morning to discuss additions to the *Proper Care and Feeding of Dantastic* manual.

Jon studied the mass of colorful bruises on Dan's face, glad he was no longer covered in blood. He cleared his throat. "You did good out there today. I'm glad you survived, and you're on this team."

Loki cautiously grasped Dan's right hand—the left now ensconced in a brace. "Still holding on and not letting go." He couldn't think of anything else to say to the unconscious man.

Still reeling on the inside, Ray understood the real possibility Dan could've died today, like Aaron. He hadn't seen the ravine, but Loki described the scene to him. *If Jon, Loki, Bram, or I had been with Dan's team instead of Aaron, would this have happened? By sounds we listened to, the damned fight went on a long time. What took Aaron so long?*

Regardless of his inner turmoil, Ray used his calm tone as he said, "When you are better, you owe us all a round at the Pond."

Jon chuckled. "More than one."

The comment caused Loki to grin. "Yeah, my count is three. Two in the vest and one in the arm. Maybe we can add one round for each injury."

Ray shook his head. "Nah, we don't want him to go broke. He would pick up extra shifts to pay for it all and be in the same boat again."

"We'll be back later. Rest easy, Dano." Jon patted Dan's leg.

Loki released Dan's hand to follow Jon and Ray out. He turned back for one last glimpse and sighed. *What a difference a year makes.*

Nick, Bram, and Lexa entered at last. Bram headed straight to Dan's left side and lightly gripped his bicep. He had stopped Patch outside when he came out of the room and asked about the gesture. Though prying, Bram wished to understand the meaning.

Patch peered at his hands and didn't offer anything at first. Bram shared he made an identical gesture a few times and received an interesting reaction from Dan, which prompted Patch to disclose he did it to convey his concern whenever Blondie was severely injured. The simple touch communicated comfort and love for his brother without words.

Bram had been right in his assumptions. It would be something he would adopt since Dan responded well when he did it. Bram blew out a breath. "Looks like Allie used all her crayons on you. When you're released, I want you to come stay with Kellie and me. The girls will take excellent care of you. I promise not to let them paint your fingernails while you sleep."

Nick stood still at the bed's foot. Yesterday had been an ungodly day. The day started with such promise with Dan's smile lighting his eyes. Nick released a long sigh. *It could've been worse. We could've lost two officers.*

He wondered what happened in that ravine and the four shots in rapid succession. If Aaron failed to back up Dan, Nick would never forgive himself for allowing them to be paired. Sighing again, he observed Lexa stroking Dan's hair. She had such a gentle heart, which she hid from view of most everyone. Lexa's day had been terribly stressful, too.

Nick put his hand on her back and whispered, "Dan's going to be okay. You did well yesterday. I don't want you thinking about all the would've, could've, and should've. You did as you were trained, and absolutely none of this is your fault."

Lexa stopped her hand. She didn't realize she was doing that again until the Boss spoke to her. *Oh man, this is bad. What did Boss observe in my actions? Did I give away the fact Dan and I slept together?* She blew out a breath and dropped her hand to her side. She decided to use his words to cover her real thoughts, which were nowhere near contemplating fault. "I'm aware, but thanks for saying so. He's strong, and he'll come back to our team soon."

Nick grinned. "That's the spirit. Positive thoughts."

Dr. Fraser entered to check his patient. "It's time to go. Dan needs to rest, and you all do, as well." He stepped forward, guilt eating at him for failing to recognize his patient's pain and not heeding the medic's words. The events of tonight were a wake-up call he would heed. He would never again allow something like this to happen to any patient in his care.

After Lexa and Bram left the ICU room, Nick paused in the entry and turned back to address a concern. "Doctor, I'm his medical proxy. Please call me if there is any change."

Fraser nodded. "I have your number in the records."

Surprised to learn that piece of information, Gambrill wondered when Dan listed Nick. It made him both happy and sad. Although Dan's family loved and cared about him, they remained estranged. However, he found this new knowledge proved he had been right about Nick—he would help Dan heal.

He was also shocked to discover Captain Blain, Corporal Simons, and the medic Jim Shea. Dan's old unit buddies certainly didn't act like they turned their backs on him. William would be pleased—although he wouldn't be pleased with the rest of this.

After everyone but Officer Fargusson and Reed Caldwell left, Gambrill turned to Director Caldwell and stated, "I don't like this at all."

Reed shook his head. "It's just a precaution. I really don't think anything is going to happen."

Marc Fargusson agreed with the commander. He didn't like this at all—not one bit. But he pulled a chair near the entrance to Constable Broderick's room, took a seat, kept his thoughts to himself, and sighed. His gaze followed the two men down the hallway until they rounded the corner. *Nope, I don't like this one damned bit.*

Lexa's Home – 12:30 a.m.

Though worn-out both physically and mentally, Lexa opened her door, then sluggishly closed and locked it behind her. Right now, the physical aspect was her biggest problem. She climbed up and down so many ravines today, her leg muscles resisted every movement.

The stairs to her bedroom might as well be Mt. Everest, and she was not capable of scaling another mountain, so she headed directly to the living room couch. As she lay down, tucking one of the couch pillows under her head and pulling the throw blanket over her, Lexa decided to shower in the morning. Sleep is what she needed now.

As Lexa settled in, her mind wandered and landed on the thought of her stroking Dan's hair in front of the guys. *Will my actions give us away, or will they attribute it to a caring gesture?* Part of Lexa hoped they would tease her about it so she could play it off as if it didn't mean anything.

But she knew better—it meant something—but what that something would become, she was not in a fit state to even begin to analyze. Before falling into an exhausted sleep, Lexa had one last conscious thought. *Glad my bedroom wall is the same color blue as Dan's gorgeous eyes.*

Loki's Home – 12:35 a.m.

Loki quietly let himself into the house. He didn't want to wake his ma. Today had been unparalleled to any he had before. He reset the alarm and headed for the kitchen.

He spotted the note on the fridge before opening the door. *What a wonderful mother she is, she always takes care of me.* A huge dinner plate ready for reheating looked delicious, but he was too wrung out to eat.

Loki had lots of questions for the Special Forces guys. Things the team should know but didn't necessarily want to know. He needed to be well-rested to deal with the raw emotions that would come with the answers he expected. He decided to take a quick shower then sleep.

Ray's Apartment – 12:38 a.m.

Ray sat at the kitchen table, finishing off a sandwich. He'd been in a lot of bad situations in his youth, did things he wished he hadn't, things that still hurt today if he thought too closely about them.

He wanted desperately to be something different, something better, to help people instead of hurt them. Thinking over the last few months as they began to learn about Dan, Ray recognized those same feelings reflected in Dan.

Tomorrow should be interesting. Talking with Dan's old unit buddies will give us insight so we can help Dan if he ever wants to talk to anyone. Though I doubt Dan will. He and I are alike in that manner. My past is the past; it doesn't belong in the present. Forward is the only direction.

Ray switched off the light as he left his kitchen and headed for bed. It would be a short night's sleep, but Ray being so exhausted, he would sleep like the dead. He grimaced at that analogy as he thought about Aaron. Although Ray didn't know what happened at the ravine, part of him blamed Aaron. *Plouffe should've been there to cover Dan. What took him so long? Why wasn't he there to back Dan up sooner?*

Bram's Home – 12:40 a.m.

Sluggishly Bram shuffled down the hall and opened the door to Allie's room—the last of his four daughters to peek in on before heading to bed. His sweet little girl lay nestled safely under her covers. As he watched her sleep, he thought about what he said to Dan before leaving.

Dan is unquestionably welcome here anytime. *Kellie and the girls adore him and will want to take care of him.* The only part concerning Bram would be Allie's reaction to Dan's condition. His face would still colorfully show the damage, and it would break Allie's little heart.

He stepped into her room, kissed her, and tucked her favorite blanket around her. Bram consoled himself with one thought. *At least Dan's alive. I don't have to tell my girls Dan died today. Allie would be devastated—they all would if he perished like Aaron.* He smiled. *Dan will be here for the team BBQ next week—only a little more colorful than usual.*

After he showered, Bram slid carefully into bed so he wouldn't wake Kellie. He scooted in close and placed his arm over her. *She is my rock, my port in the storm, which allows me to do the things I must and still feel safe and cared for.* As sleep gradually overtook him, Bram wondered if Dan had someone like Kellie in his life. Dan tended to be closed-mouthed on his personal life—it was possible. If he didn't, Bram hoped Dan would eventually find a loving woman.

Jon's Home – 12:40 a.m.

Jon rearmed the alarm after entering his home. Jennifer had fallen asleep on the couch, waiting for him tonight. He found the muted TV on and a rerun of last night's news playing.

Dan's official TRF picture flashed on the screen, followed by an amateur video taken at the gas station incident. He grabbed the remote, increasing the volume, as he sat dumbfounded.

Man, I hate the inane commentary. How much of this garbage did Jennifer and Kent watch? He switched off the television and delicately shook Jen awake. She peered at him with sleepy eyes, smiled, then wrapped her arms around him and said, "Bad day?"

He only nodded, drawing comfort from her warm embrace as they stood and walked towards the stairs.

Nick's Home – 1:00 a.m.

Nick lay in bed, the grime of the day cleansed from his body but not his mind. He couldn't have ever imagined what happened to the team today. They dealt with emotionally charged situations all the time, but nothing in his history compared to today.

He hoped nothing would ever come even remotely close to this again. They endured so much today, and except for two times, they acted professionally. There was nothing to forgive for those times—his team and he were human and possessed emotions. *Our team is family, and we protect one another. I so proud of each one of them.*

His thoughts shifted to Dan and what he discovered about his rookie today. *He lost a sister in front of him at the tender age of nine. He was held captive and tortured. He killed his best friend. He witnessed a fellow officer die. His family won't bother to come visit him when he is badly injured. All this is just so very sad.*

Right before sleep claimed him, Nick thought, *I'd be proud to have someone like Dan for a son. General Broderick is a pathetic man if he can't understand and accept his son.*

A Baited Trap

28

July 16
St. Michael Hospital – ICU – Inside Room A – 1:00 a.m.

Dan woke gradually keeping his eyes closed and his breathing steady—a habit born of need. *Ookay dokey time to me assess—wait, order wrong—assess ne, ne, ne, ne, ne, me. Ah hell, should be fun.*

Physical? Injured? Yep! Feels like I went ten rounds with my hands tied behind my back—not fair, not fair at all. Wait ... I did, sorta. Wrap ... mean crap, Basto got the drop on me after we shared such nice little trip down the ravine. Sucks. I'm a mummy, wrapped in too much gauze.

Deep breath in, crap ... that hurts. Shallow breaths it is. Hey, I got new holes in me, great! Ooh and stitches too. Gonna lose the pretty boy face if I keep gettin' stitches there. Not much pain now, well ... no shit Sherlock ... pumped full of the good shit ... loopy ... sucky weird feeling. Think no straight. Hey, the only part that doesn't hurt is my ... wait ... nope, my ass hurts, too. Ah crap ... hate this loopy shit.

Where the fuck am I? Hospital, fucking hospital. Damned incessant beeping ... not great for sleeping ... beep, damn beep, beep, beep, damn beep. Shut the fuck up! IV ... uncomfortable bed ... nicer than ravine ... not by much.

Ok, mental? Yeah, I'm mental alright. Status? Well ... that'd be up fucked! Can't worth think shit. Yeah, gonna leave this ... sleep now ... sleep good ... nighty night. Dan drifted into a light sleep.

St. Michael Hospital – ICU – Outside Room A – 2:00 a.m.

A brown-haired, brown-eyed man of average height and nondescript features wearing a hospital janitor's uniform stopped to talk to the officer. "Long night?" he asked.

"Had longer," Fargusson replied.

"No fun—pulled many nights of guard duty when I served in the military. On my way to grab coffee, would you like one?" the man queried.

"Kind of you to offer. No cream, three sugars please," Fargusson answered.

"Be back in a few."

Five minutes later, he returned, carrying two foam cups of steaming brew. Handing the officer his, the janitor initiated a short, benign conversation about mundane things before leaving. Marc leisurely took a sip of his coffee.

St. Michael Hospital – ICU – Inside Room A – 2:55 a.m.

A man slipped into Dan's room unnoticed by the now sleeping patrol officer. Slipping him the sleeping powder had been easier than expected. The idiot would be out for hours and never even know it. Some people were just so trusting. "Now to take care of this cocky son of a bitch," he whispered.

St. Michael Hospital – ICU – Outside Room A – 2:55 a.m.

Officer Marc Fargusson feigned sleep. He thought the coffee sure tasted weird at the first small sip. After decades on the force he learned to listen to his gut. Something kicked it into high gear this morning.

As he engaged the janitor in everyday conversation, nothing out of the ordinary and highly forgettable, as he probed for information. "So, if I need another cup of joe, where would I find it?"

The man happily told him where and said anyone on the floor was welcome. That, in fact, he just met another haggard guy grabbing a cup and said no one ever appeared rested in the ICU.

"Thanks. I'll let you get back to it," Marc said with a smile and a nod as he sat down in the chair and pretended to take another sip.

As the custodian walked away, Fargusson thought, *I have a job to do, protect the sleeping young officer from whatever is coming.* Although uncomfortable with the plan, he realized it was not his call to make. They wanted to catch the guy in the act to make the charges stick, whatever they might be.

Shortly after Alpha Team and those other guys ran into the ER, Agent Donner stomped out of the hospital like a baby whose candy had been taken away. Only he, Agent Stevens, and Commander Gambrill remained in the waiting room. Gambrill made a phone call and a short time later Reed Caldwell, the Director of NRB, arrived.

Gambrill and Stevens expressed concerns over Donner's behavior. Stevens said she reviewed all his interviews with Broderick and they were wholly out of line. Caldwell confirmed he possessed concerns after a lawyer named Gibbson reported several incidents to him.

Dale Gibbson didn't understand the hostility Agent Donner continually displayed towards Constable Broderick. Gibbson shared the incidents with Caldwell since his first encounter with the guy—when he found how far off protocol Donner went with Broderick—he made sure he was always there before Broderick arrived if the agent-in-charge was Donner.

The lawyer told Caldwell that Donner seemed to go out of his way to make Dan review every grotesque element in excruciating detail multiple times even when they were irrelevant to determining if it was a justified action. Stevens's review of the transcripts corroborated his observations.

Stevens stated a TRF officer's job was hard enough, especially when forced to end a life. They didn't need to be interrogated by the likes of Donner. Caldwell agreed with her. He believed TRF constables were men and women who wanted to save people and it hurt them when they couldn't. The interview process was necessary to maintain accountability, but shouldn't be used as a weapon to inflict more pain on the officer.

Caldwell, Gambrill, and Stevens discussed what to do about the situation. Donner had not done anything illegal—pushed protocol, yes—but nothing that warranted any legal or official action like dismissal. Stevens voiced her concern that after the altercation tonight Donner would probably do something to Broderick while vulnerable. She said Donner had become unstable over the past few weeks and would often rant in the office about a 'cocky son of a bitch.' Donner never said a name, but she now believed he meant Broderick.

They devised a plan. Fargusson would've preferred it to include Broderick's teammates, but Gambrill rightly insisted they were too exhausted and too personally involved to stay objective. He also indicated Donner would recognize any TRF officer so they must use detectives in plain clothes so as to not tip him off if he showed up. They needed to let it play out, well not quite all the way, if the situation turned deadly. Donner's irrational behavior led them to believe things might go awry.

When Fargusson thought something might be in play after tasting the coffee, he alerted the others via the agreed upon signal, rolling his head and rubbing his neck. He was fairly certain the night janitor was an opportune tool used by Donner, but the others would detain him and investigate to be sure. He pretended to take another drink of the likely drugged-laced coffee, set the cup on the floor, leaned back, relaxed, and closed his eyes as if he nodded off.

However, he remained fully alert. Forty-five minutes later, Donner entered Dan's room. Marc now listened intently as the others watched nearby, waiting for Donner to reveal his intent.

St. Michael Hospital – ICU – Inside Room A – 3:00 a.m.

Happy an easy opportunity presented itself for him slip past the guard, he covertly added the sleeping powder into the coffee as the friendly janitor turned to obtain sugar packets. The unsuspecting guard would be out for hours and he could take his time with the cocky son of a bitch.

Richard would bring Dan down this time, torture him with emotions, and finish him off the best way possible. All those interview questions had a purpose—they showed him how to hurt him the most. *Broderick will pay for what he did all those years ago.* Donner laughed quietly and maliciously as the SOB slept. *I'm going to enjoy this. All I need now is for Broderick to wake.*

Senses instantly alert—danger, his gut told him, Dan realized someone entered his room. Breathing kept steady to not alert the intruder to his awareness, the quiet, cruel laugh unnerved Dan. *Who is it?*

Better to remain as is and gather my strength and wits. Damned glad my thinking is clearer now. The pain meds must've worn off enough. He had not surveyed the room when he woke earlier. Not that it would've helped— having been too loopy before to even recognize anything close that he might use to protect himself.

Dan conceded he was not doing great at the moment, but his pain appeared to be manageable. He accepted his exhaustion and recognized hand-to-hand combat would be near impossible his current weakened state. Dan hoped things didn't progress that far, so he waited, allowing the person to make the first move.

"Guess I'm gonna have to wake this bastard up," Donner sneered after ten minutes in the room. He threw his empty paper cup at Broderick's head. "Wake up, asshole."

Damn, okay maybe I should've opened my eyes sooner. Dan allowed his eyes to open and adjust to the dim lighting. "Ow, what the hell?" he said aloud as he peered at the person who threw something.

"Naptime is over, Broderick." Yes, Donner read the transcripts of today's calls and thought the nap jokes were stupid.

"Donner, what the hell? Why are you here?"

"Well, I'd like to sleep, too. You were the subject officer in six kills today including the murder of an officer under your command. I need information and I'm not waiting any longer," Donner snarled.

"Five lethal actions, not six. I'm aware of NRB protocol. This can wait until I'm released. Don't you read your own manual? Or do you like interviewing me while I'm undressed?" Dan replied irritated. He couldn't help adding the last remark. Not the best idea to antagonize him, but Dan hurt and he didn't want to put up with the man's shit tonight—he didn't possess the stamina.

Donner only glared.

Tired of the staring contest, Dan said firmly, "You've been on my case since the first time we met. I don't know what your problem is with me. But for now, you need to get the hell out and let me rest."

Damn, my display of bravado used up most my strength. Dan realized it was a stupid thing to do. *Crap, I'm so tired.* He carefully scanned the area. He noticed the patrolman outside his door leaning back in a chair. *Why?* Then he recalled protection was protocol for injured subject officers until after the interview. *Yeah, backup if needed.* He relaxed a bit, but stared directly at Donner and waited for him to leave.

He noted hatred and something else disturbing flare in Donner's eyes. *Whatever this is, it won't end well. The guy is on a razor's edge.* About to call out to the patrol officer to remove Donner, the agent took a menacing step toward him, and Dan tensed.

Donner ranted, "You're a destroyer. You ruin everything in your path. You always have. There's nothing in your life left UNTAINTED. Today, in the span of thirteen hours you murdered SIX PEOPLE! But that's only a small portion of the blood on your hands. You're not worthy! You destroy families! You should've died years ago! Why didn't you DIE? If you would've DIED, people would be safe."

Taking another step towards Broderick, Donner taunted with malice in his voice, "Your best friend Brody would still be alive. How many more friends did you MURDER? How many heads did you BLOW off from long distance and smile as their bodies fell—BLOOD splattering everywhere?

"You're a killer, that's all you've ever been. That's all you'll ever be. KILLER! MURDERER! You can't save anyone. Everyone you care about DIES because of YOU. No one's safe. You should fucking DIE."

Dan reeled from the onslaught with no shields to protect himself. His walls remained down and unfortified. He lay wide open to attack. Venom laced words entered his bloodstream—the poison rapidly pulsed toward his heart.

Donner continued to slash into his soul. "SIX! SIX, BRODERICK! DO YOU HEAR ME? SIX PEOPLE YOU KILLED TODAY! WITHOUT A SECOND THOUGHT. IN COLD BLOOD. YOU MURDERED SIX INNOCENT PEOPLE!

"YOU'RE SO SURE OF YOURSELF, SO COCKY, TOO FAST ON THE TRIGGER. YOUR BADGE ISN'T A LICENSE TO KILL. YOU MURDERED AARON—YOU'RE A MURDERER.

"HOW CAN YOU EVER BELIEVE YOU'RE FIT TO BE A TRF OFFICER? YOU PUT YOUR TEAM AT RISK EVERY TIME. WITH EVERY PERSON YOU KILL, YOU PUT BLOOD ON THEIR HANDS TOO!"

Dan fixated on one word 'murderer.' *I only did my job. Am I a murderer?* White-hot pain perforated his soul and it started to bleed.

VILE WORDS CONTINUED TO SPEW FROM DONNER'S MOUTH. "YOU NEED TO die AND SAVE THE WORLD FROM ALL THE HARM YOU CAUSE. YOU SAY YOU WANT TO PROTECT, BUT ALL YOU DO IS KILL.

"I KNOW HOW MANY PEOPLE YOU HAVE murdered. YOU'RE WORSE THAN ANY SERIAL KILLER EVER KNOWN. YOU DESERVE TO DIE. YOU DON'T DESERVE TO BE SAFE. MURDERER!"

Slammed hard, powerless to make him stop, thoughts swirled in Dan's head. He had killed so many. Every single one created a rip in his soul—it was almost completely shredded. So much blood stained his hands and now his soul bled and he couldn't staunch the wound. Emotional pain so visceral engulfed him as he turned and vomited violently.

Horrifying glee entered Donner's eyes viewing the impact his words had on the evil spawn. The loss, agony, and self-loathing in Broderick's expression right before he hurled delighted Donner. He would make him suffer, repayment for all the pain Dan caused. Richard laughed as Dan vomited several times until nothing was left, but dry heaves.

St. Michael Hospital – ICU – Outside Room A – 3:05 a.m.

Officer Fargusson itched to go in and put a stop to this cockup after the first comments. Caldwell kept telling him no, they didn't have anything they could charge Donner with—verbal assault is not illegal. *Now the kid is retching. How much longer can I hold back? No one can stay objective listening to this madman's rant. Alpha Team would've already gone in.*

On the brink and about to pull the plug, the ability to charge the asshole with anything be damned, Gambrill endeavored to remain professional. But Walter didn't want to put his godson through anymore. Dan suffered too much for one person to bear. He would not allow Dan to drown in the cruelty of the words spewed forth.

St. Michael Hospital – ICU – Inside Room A – 3:05 a.m.

Survival instinct tried to kick in. Dan puked again then gagged out, "Why? Why are you doing this?"

Entirely lost to his psychosis, Donner lashed out, "YOU KILLED MY FAMILY. YOU MURDERED MY DAD. I WAS THIRTEEN AND YOU MURDERED HIM. YOU DIDN'T PULL SARA OUT OF THE WAY. YOU'RE THE REASON MY DAD IS DEAD!"

"How did I kill your dad?" Dan moaned as his stomach rolled again, not able to comprehend.

"YOU FAILED TO SAVE SARA. YOU PINNED YOUR SAD, LOST EYES ON HIM. YOU MADE HIM COMMIT SUICIDE. YOU DESTROYED MY FAMILY!"

St. Michael Hospital – ICU – Outside Room A – 3:06 a.m.

Gut-wrenching understanding hit Gambrill. He gasped out, "My God, he's the son of the driver who hit Sara. The driver took his life a week later. Couldn't live with the fact he killed a little girl. Dan doesn't know anything about that. We never told him."

Caldwell and Stevens stared at Gambrill.

Everyone's attention returned to the room as Donner started to hysterically laugh.

St. Michael Hospital – ICU – Inside Room A – 3:06 a.m.

Rocking back and forth on his heels, Richard shoved his hands into his jacket pockets.

Reaching the end of his physical endurance as he finished retching again, Dan turned sad and confused eyes on Donner.

Richard screeched, "NOW I KILL YOU!" as he pulled a gun from his pocket and aimed at Dan's head.

BANG!

Help Me Brody

29

July 16
St. Michael Hospital — ICU — Inside Room A — 3:10 a.m.

All hell broke loose in Dan's ICU room as people ran in to help. Donner's dead body lay on the floor of the room. One second the gun had been pointed at Dan's head. A fraction of a second later, Donner turned the weapon on himself and blew his brains out.

Crimson pooled on the floor near Donner's head. Richard stood so close to Dan when he pulled the trigger, that his blood and brain matter now covered Dan, splattering across his face and chest, dripping from his arms and hair, and coating both hands. A gruesome sight.

Dan's mind seemed to be lost at sea, floating somewhere off the coast of eternity. He held his breath. *I'm always at the wrong place at the wrong time. How many moments until my next wrong time?* Dan simply stared. His gaze riveted to his hands. *How appropriate, my hands are literally and figuratively bloody.*

Everyone stopped instantaneously and listened keenly when Dan spoke with a very fragile voice. "Brody, I'm losing my fucking mind. Don't let me disappear—help me. Brody, I'm falling. Please hold on to me. Nothing's left, Brody. My safe place is in ruins. Help me rebuild the walls. I'll hear your voice always. Help me, Brody—help me."

Only Dan heard his brother. *"Hey, Danny, I'm right here. Hi ho, hi ho, it's off to work we go."*

A small chuckle emitted from Dan.

"Brody, wait for me. I'm coming. I'm ready to go." Dan's face paled, vision narrowed, and muscles slackened as he drifted into a sea of nothingness, cradled in Brody's arms.

Walter leaned in close to his unconscious godson and spoke in an urgent whisper for Dan's ears only, "Don't break. Be strong. I'm here for you."

"Sir … Sir!" Gambrill finally registered someone called to him. He turned and spotted a young nurse and several others. "Sir, we need to take care of him now." He nodded and shifted so they could do their work.

They needed to clean Dan and move him to another room away from the memories and bloody crime scene. A nurse came over with a cloth, prepared to wash Dan, as an Inspector stepped into her path.

"Hold. We must take photos first for the files," Inspector Davis said formally.

Aghast, the nurse gaped.

Rage surged in Walter. He wouldn't allow it. He wanted no tangible images of Dan like this. It hurt too much, and if they ever found their way to the media, he'd be dead. He refused to allow pictures of Dan in distress ever to be released again. William would be sure he died painfully if this happened a second time— not that he didn't deserve a tongue lashing after this fiasco.

In an authoritative tone, Gambrill stated, "HELL NO! No pictures will be taken of Constable Broderick in this state. The general won't allow photos."

"I'm only following procedure, Commander. What does a general have to do with this anyway? This is a police matter," Davis retorted.

How did I let that comment slip out? Walter scrambled to make up something plausible. "The constable is former JTF2 and the son of General Broderick. Any photos, if ever leaked, would compromise his security. There are enough witnesses to gather statements from, so photos aren't necessary, and none will be taken. Nurse, please proceed and remove that damned man's blood from my godson!"

Inspector Davis peered at Gambrill. *General? Godson? Special Forces?* He decided to accept the flimsy, hastily formed reason. His skill told him there is more to this than meets the eye, but Gambrill was right, there were enough witnesses, and he would let this go.

The nurse swiftly complied, setting to her task, delicately washing the blood from his body and rinsed it from his hair. She left no trace of gore on the young constable. One of the orderlies stripped off the soiled gown and placed the garment in an evidence bag. He started to put on a clean one when Gambrill stopped him.

"A favor, please. Dress him in pants of some sort and a t-shirt. Danny will be more comfortable and feel more in control. It's important," Walter implored, his gaze directed at the nurse in charge.

Jerry, the orderly, hesitated and turned a questioning eye at his superior, who nodded as she said, "I'll find something, scrubs perhaps."

She was about to go when Jerry piped up, "We're about the same size. I have a clean pair of comfortable sweats and a t-shirt in my locker. I don't mind. It's a small thing I can do."

Dan's nurse smiled and nodded as Jerry trotted off to retrieve them. They knew who this officer was from the news accounts, and after everything he went through yesterday, they wanted to assist him in any way possible.

When Jerry returned with the clothing, they transferred Dan to a clean bed, then dressed him in a pair of soft, dark gray pants, a black t-shirt, and a pair of warm socks. Jerry grabbed the socks out of his locker because as he left to grab his extra garments, his hand brushed against the officer's ice-cold feet.

Socks were another small comfort he could offer this officer. Jerry learned that sometimes little things made the most significant impact. After finishing, he covered the patient with a warm blanket before pushing Dan's bed to another room so the nurse could reattach the monitors.

St. Michael Hospital – ICU – Outside Room D – 3:25 a.m.

Officer Fargusson stood out of the way, observing. Once the staff settled Dan in the new room, he moved the chair to the front of it and promptly took up position. He would only allow the medical staff entry—no one else, not even the commander. The kid needed rest and quiet, and Marc would make sure he got it—even if it cost him his job or his life.

Gambrill remained off to the side in the hall, his thoughts running many directions. A cold, leaden pit settled in his stomach. *Dan is too young to endure this much pain. I thought him coming here would ease his suffering, not add to it.*

Until now, Gambrill successfully concealed Dan was his godson and had known him since birth. He didn't want to cause Dan any issues at TRF like those experienced in Special Forces being the son of the general. Walter realized let the cat out of the bag earlier tonight by giving details of Sara's death. Nick would surely ask him about it. And now the associate would be the record of this incident. He prayed it wouldn't cause Dan more problems.

With Director Caldwell, Stevens cautiously approached Gambrill. Like herself, she perceived the events of tonight deeply affected the commander, though the salt-and-pepper-haired man managed to maintain a poker face.

The haunting words Dan spoke before passing out hit Kendall the hardest. Dan spoke to his dead friend, the one he accidentally killed, asking Brody for help. The meaning of *'Wait for me. I'm coming,'* concerned her most. Did Dan intend to join Brody? She hoped not.

Gambrill said, "Alpha Team will want our hides, and I don't blame them. We promised he would be safe and made them leave. We nearly got him killed. Dan would be dead now if Donner didn't turn the gun on himself."

Kendall struggled to maintain her composure, aware she shouldered part of the blame. "Sir, I'm so sorry. It is clear Donner lost control, but I never imagined this scenario. We screwed up."

"Walter, if we can be of any help, let me know. This is so, so ... hell, I don't have the words for what this is. I had no idea Donner had gone so far over the edge. What did you mean he is the son of the driver who killed Sara?" Caldwell asked guardedly.

"Caldwell, we may need to push the interview sessions out a day or so. I trust you will allow my team and the Special Forces men access to Broderick. I'll be assigning Alpha as protection detail beginning tomorrow. Consider the soldiers as Dan's family," Gambrill stated decisively choosing to ignore his question about Sara, for now at least.

Realizing he wouldn't receive an answer to his question, Caldwell nodded. "Although outside protocol, given what occurred is beyond compare, I'll agree on the condition they don't speak with him regarding the shootings until he has been interviewed. We must talk with Broderick as soon as possible because he is the only one who can shed light on how Constable Plouffe and the two subjects died. Aaron's family deserved to be told what happened."

"Agreed, but I won't push Dan. He's in a fragile state, both mentally and physically. His well-being is my priority." Walter's mind shifted gears to the dreaded call he must make to William.

Caldwell and Stevens studied a sleeping Dan for a few moments before reluctantly taking their leave. Stevens said she would check in at one to determine if Alpha Team would be available for interviews and if not, she would reschedule them.

Gambrill pulled out his phone and dialed a number from memory. It rang three times before being answered.

"Broderick."

"Hello, Will."

"Walter, is that you? What are you doing calling at this hour? Is Daniel alright?" William glanced at his clock, calculating it to be zero three-thirty in Toronto and noted Walter's voice sounded strained.

"Yes, it is Danny, and he isn't doing well. He talked to Brody."

"What do you mean?" William rose and started to pace in his office.

Gambrill gave William a synopsis of the full day, including what occurred with Donner.

William stopped pacing mid-way through the dissertation and stared out his window at the barren desert. His heart ached. His voice came out calm and held no reflection of his inner turmoil, "My God. Daniel, my son. Will it ever stop? Why does all this happen to him?"

The general didn't expect an answer to his rhetorical questions, and Walter didn't offer any platitudes. They both comprehended what Daniel endured in his twenty-eight years—more than any one person should have to bear and it all started when Daniel was only a child.

William took a deep breath. "So, physically, he will mend. It's the emotional aspect you're concerned about."

Walter stared at Dan through the glass. "Yes, although I believe his team will help him. Dan is resilient, but ... Will, I never knew. If I had, I would've told you, but I didn't."

"Walter, what is wrong? You're rambling. I can tell you're concerned about something else." William raked a hand through his short hair.

"Yes, I'm concerned. We might have a problem."

"With his team?"

"No. That is resolved. They have his back. You should've seen them in action today. Quite impressive," Walter stated with both pride and exhaustion imbuing his tone.

"Explain, please."

Walter walked to a quiet corner so he wouldn't be overheard. "This is related to what you shared with me—your suspicion about a certain person. The pit of my stomach is roiling, but I have nothing tangible to back up my hunch. If your intuition is right, Dan might be at risk. I only found out something today when I visited the parents of my slain officer."

"I'm not following you, Walter. How are my suspicions related in any way with one of your officers? And why do you think Daniel is in danger?" William returned to his desk and slumped into his chair.

So many things ran through William's head. Pletcher was last seen in Vancouver yesterday morning. He could've traveled to Toronto by now. Hammer's unit trailed him but had not gotten a solid lead yet.

Walter leaned heavily on the wall for support. "The constable who died ... is related to the person you're concerned about."

William surged to his feet. *The officer is related to Major Plouffe!* "What is the relation?"

"My constable was his nephew. Will, I swear I didn't know. Plouffe a common enough surname."

William started to pace as pieces of a puzzle struggled with for years began to fall into place. He opened the bottom drawer and pulled out a folder. He flipped it open and stared at the photo on top. "How did you find this out?"

"I saw him as Sergeant Pastore, and I left the officer's parent's home after informing them of his death. I only made the connection because he wore a uniform with a tan beret," Walter explained.

Gambrill rubbed the back of his aching neck as a stress headache formed. "I'm going to have Dan's team assigned as protection detail after they get some sleep. I have a patrol officer on his room for tonight. Do you think I'm overreacting?"

William stared at the words on the note that accompanied the last picture. His gut churned. "No, I don't think so. In fact, I'm going to send a unit to safeguard Daniel. Something is seriously wrong here, and my gut is telling me he's involved. Like you, I have no proof, but I'm not about to leave Daniel vulnerable. Someone is targeting him. I'm sure of it. I just don't know why or who. It might be related to the villain who went after Becca, too."

"Will, the unit which provided the air-evac … that was Captain Blain."

"You're kidding me?"

"No, I'm not. You should've seen them tonight. Plus, the first paramedic to reach Dan is also an old unit mate —Jim Shea."

"Patch is there?" William leaned heavily on his desk. Disbelief flooding in. "What do you mean I should've seen them? Were they indifferent, hostile? Do I need to send—"

Walter cut him off. "William, stop. It's all good. All three of them were so protective. Amazing to witness. Blain nearly strangled Donner when he called Dan a murderer and said they couldn't go to Dan." Walter smirked. "Damn, I should've let him strangle Donner."

William chuckled. "Not your style, you save, I kill. If what you say is true about Blain? I'll make the arrangements to assign Blain and Simons as protection detail."

Walter blew out a breath. "I'm going to have to tell Dan's team. I can't have them in the dark. They need to be aware of the possible threat. You realize they're proficient at investigating things. Pastore and McKenna would do a profile for you. Baldovino and Palomo are excellent at digging out information. Hardy and De Haven, well, I think they'd give any of your SF boys a run for their money in tactics.

"There's the added benefit that they're invested in Dan. And … and this is a huge one … if you do have a problem in your community, they are free of taint. They're outsiders with only Dan's best interests at heart. You can trust them implicitly."

Every one of the damned photos he received arrived in conjunction with a classified mission. With no way to determine friend or foe inside Special Forces at the moment, aware a leak must exist since someone had inside information, William listened and made a decision.

"Send me their full names and personnel records. I need to obtain security clearances before I can involve them in this. You can inform his teammates there is an undefined threat, and Daniel is now under protection."

William sighed deeply. "Walter, take care of my boy, please. I screwed up at every turn with him. Someday, I hope he can forgive me. I'm flying to Toronto. Brief your team and Blain at zero six hundred, and I'll provide more detail when I arrive. I should be there by eighteen hundred."

"I'll do my best, William. I'll see you soon." After exchanging goodbyes, Gambrill disconnected. Although beyond weary, he wouldn't be going home anytime soon. He needed to send William the requested details so he could bring Alpha Team up to speed.

He said a silent prayer to keep Danny safe before taking a deep breath and straightening up. Walter strode with purpose down the hall and stopped at his godson's room. He peered at Dan, who now slept peacefully.

Shifting his gaze to Constable Fargusson, Walter directed, "If Broderick wakes and wants to leave the hospital, he will find a way. Of that, there is absolutely no doubt even if it's against medical advice. If he attempts to do so, you're to inform him he is under orders to appear at HQ for debriefing immediately and is not allowed to go anywhere else. TRF headquarters is the only place you're allowed to take him. Understood?"

"Yes, Sir. But may I ask you something?"

"Yes."

"Why would that work? And why TRF HQ?"

"Broderick always follows orders—an ingrained behavior. Be sure you use the term 'ordered.' This is for his protection. He hates hospitals, and in his current condition, he needs protection. We can ensure his safety at HQ."

Gambrill took one last glance at Dan, sighed deeply, then started to leave. An afterthought struck him and turned back to the officer. "You are on protection detail until you're relieved by someone from Alpha Team only, or you drop him off at headquarters. Do you remember what they look like?"

"Yes, Sir. Never will forget their faces." Fargusson wouldn't ever forget them. The events of the past day seared the images in his mind.

"Excellent. Please keep him safe." With that, Gambrill turned and left. *Tomorrow, well, actually in a few hours. I must face Dan's team and fill them in on this ugly situation.*

Building Walls

30

July 16
Patch's Apartment — 3:40 a.m.

Blaze lay on the couch in the quiet, dark living room of Patch's place, staring at the ceiling. He couldn't sleep because his mind remained too active. Finding Blondie in a terrible situation brought back so many memories, and his gut screamed something was not right, but try as he might, he couldn't put the pieces together.

After arriving at Patch's home several hours ago, their former teammate lent them a pair of sweats, not the greatest fit, but something to wear while they laundered their uniforms. Both he and Winds much appreciated a hot shower and a shave after the long, hot, grimy day training and evacuating Blondie.

While Winds started the laundry and Patch whipped up something for them to eat, Blaze checked in with Major White again. When he updated the major on Blondie's condition and requested a two-day leave, White granted it without hesitation. He found it a bit odd, but the officer liked Blondie. The kid had people in his corner, despite the general's disdain for his son. Patch also called into his boss to request the next week off. After explaining why his superior approved the leave, surprised Patch knew the now-famous Constable Broderick.

Blondie's face filled the news coverage reruns. Blaze's sense of pride increased as he viewed the clip of Blondie carrying the little girl to her mother. Blondie possessed a soft heart for children. His first glimpse of that had been their mission to rescue Dom's girls.

Listening to the bank manager say 'beauty of life' nearly undid all three men. Brody always talked about finding beauty. They shared a glance, understanding they must make Blondie understand Brody's death was a tragic accident, and they didn't blame him.

Once they finished eating, he and Winds stretched out on the couches, and Patch went to his bedroom. Winds's soft regular breathing indicated he dropped off to sleep long ago, but Blaze couldn't shut down his thoughts.

His mind kept returning to the Blondie puzzle. The kid lived here for a year, and the whole time, they couldn't locate him. Someone must be manipulating information. In the waiting room, Loki shared he did a search on Blondie after he joined the team and came up blank. Loki blushed when he revealed invading Blondie's privacy in an attempt to learn about his new teammate. The techie appeared to be an interesting mix of Brody and Patch—funny and an open book—easy to read.

Loki's outcome meshed with the results received by Blaze when his contacts searched for Blondie. On the surface, this appeared to be standard operating procedure for blackout protocol. But never had someone blacked out been left in the open unguarded, or allowed to have his image, name, and details splashed all over the news. That isn't how the Guardian units worked. If someone was on blackout, they entered protective custody, and all trace of their lives would be wiped out of every system.

A strictly enforced Blackout protocol is the reason why Blaze never learned what happened to Daphne. His sister worked in covert ops. When she failed to report in, everything buttoned down tighter than a drum, and within a day, his little sister no longer existed.

When informed Daphne had been declared dead, it hurt like hell. She was the last of his natural family. He had been more of a father to her than brother—having raised her after their parents died.

Blaze still missed her but pushed thoughts of Daphy down for now. He returned to his current dilemma—Blondie. Blaze had experience with blackout protocols, and something didn't jibe, which burned his gut.

What the hell is General Badass doing? Blaze sighed. When no answers came to the forefront, Blaze realized he the solution remained out of reach for his fatigued brain. Blaze forced himself to slow his breathing and relax. Blaze's eyes barely closed, sleep within reach, his phone vibrated and set him on edge.

Blaze picked up the cell, noted the time displayed 03:40, and answered, "Captain Blain."

"Blaze, this is Colonel Sutton. Sorry to wake you at an ungodly hour."

"Colonel, what can I do for you?"

Although Tom Sutton reeled from what William shared with him before the general raced out to catch the transport, his voice remained professional, "You and Corporal Simons have been given a new priority assignment."

Sitting up, his mind turning all business, Blaze stated, "Yes, sir. Details?"

"You two have been placed on protection detail."

"For who, sir?"

"Constable Daniel Broderick," Tom stated and waited for the shock or explosion.

Blaze stood, his tone reflecting disbelief, "Blondie? We are protecting Blondie?" He got a hold of himself. "Yes, sir. Why?"

Tom briefly explained, "There's a credible threat to his life based on an incident he was involved in with the TRF yesterday."

"What type of threat?" Blaze asked as he reviewed Blondie's day—things gleaned from the TV coverage rather than shared by Pastore or Gambrill.

Is a family member of one of the targets he killed after him? He took out a hostage-taker on steroids, a crazed druggie, and three gang members. The gangs ... yes, they might seek retribution. Blondie killed the leader of the Crimson Eagles, and the other gang possessed Russian ties and might seek vengeance. Why is the colonel putting Blondie under protection? Wouldn't this fall to the police department? Blaze's mind whirled a moment with possibilities.

Tom simply stated, "Broderick was present when Constable Aaron Plouffe died."

Blaze blinked, more confused now. "I'm aware. Why is that relevant?" Plouffe popped into his head, and a proverbial lightbulb turned on. "Wait ... any relation to the major?"

"Yes. Aaron was his nephew. I can't divulge details of at this time. The general is en route and will arrive today at approximately eighteen hundred hours local. Blaze, I would tell you more, but I can't."

Blaze understood why his gut seized. *Blondie is in danger, but what is the threat? General Broderick or Major Plouffe?* "He's coming here? Are we to meet with him?"

"Yes, and he will brief you, Simons, Commander Gambrill, and Broderick's team after he arrives."

"Where?"

"General Broderick will join you at TRF headquarters."

"Got it. When do we start?"

"You are to meet with Gambrill at TRF HQ at zero six hundred local, and he will transfer Daniel into your custody. Understand this is a GU assignment, and you must proceed with all caution. Communications only through the general, Gambrill, and myself."

Blaze nodded, surprised the guardian unit protocols would be invoked. More questions plagued him. *Is this the reason for the non-standard blackout protocol? Did Blondie actually leave the military? Is the kid on some covert mission?* He halted his thoughts; answers didn't matter at the moment. "Understood, sir. One question. Since GU applies, and he is in the hospital and vulnerable, who is covering Blondie now?"

Sutton grinned. He liked Blaze a lot—one of the best-damned unit COs ever, who could easily transition into the leadership role if he would consider leaving field operations. "Yes, he is being guarded by a local patrol officer."

Not wanting to chance Blondie's safety, Blaze asked, "Can we go sooner?"

"No, the constable is under orders to only cede his position to members of Alpha Team at the hospital or to escort Broderick to TRF HQ if he attempts to leave the hospital."

Blaze chuckled. *Blondie will never change—the kid still hates hospitals. If Blondie could walk or crawl, he would leave.* "Roger. Any additional details?"

Tom rolled his shoulders, trying to release the building tension. "No, Blaze. Your sole task is to take care of Blondie. I don't want to have to face the general if his son is killed on our watch."

Like General Badfather would give a shit. Blaze wanted to rage, but he calmly responded, "Understood."

As he ended the call, Blaze sank down to the couch again. He checked the time, three forty-five. They needed to be at TRF HQ by six. Forcing himself to quiet his mind for a one-hour nap, Blaze closed his eyes and drifted off with one last thought. *Who's trying to kill you now, kid? Can't you catch a break?*

St. Michael Hospital – ICU – Inside Room D – 4:00 a.m.

At the four o'clock shift change, the young ICU nurse who cleaned away all the blood from Dan briefed a grandmotherly nurse on the patient. They shared a sad look and sigh—working ICU is difficult most days, but tonight ... beyond compare.

When the previous nurse left, Lois started her vitals and status checks. She noticed her patient's eyes rapidly moving behind closed lids. Lois smiled, glad her patient appeared to be enjoying a pleasant dream, given the slight upward tick of his lips. She firmly believed REM sleep helped people sort things out, and after the day Mr. Broderick experienced, he needed to dream.

Sitting on a flat rock, Brody called out to his brother, "Hey, Danny, Danny. Yeah, you. Come sit, take a break. I want you to listen to this song. Come on, buddy. Don't roll your eyes at me. Give it a chance. You 'love' the mellow sounds of easy rock." Brody laughed.

Becoming serious, Brody continued, "Just listen. Sit and listen now. It'll help you. You need a break, brother. We're done rebuilding your walls. Always hard work, but your safe place is rebuilt, and everything is back inside."

Exhausted by his efforts, Dan sat beside Brody.

Brody put his arm around Dan's shoulders as he said, "I realize you still gotta sort through everything. Not gonna lie to ya, it'll be hard. But you can do it. You did it before. You'll get through this again.

When Dan dropped his face in his hands and started to cry, Brody pulled him closer, holding tight. "Let your emotions out, Brother. Let the pain go. I know this all hurts real bad, so rest a moment. Sit with me and listen. I want you to remember this when you wake."

Brody held his brother close and secure, offering comfort as they listened to 'Defending Our Lives' by Jon Heintz.

When the song finished, Brody lifted Dan's head and made eye contact. "What I need you to recall, Danny, is I won't let you down. I will defend our lives. You need to smile into the faces of our enemies. Remember, you are who you are, and you're perfect to me—flaws and all. Remember the beauty of life and keep striving to find it in the world around you."

His face reflecting the love he had for his brother, Brody said, "Live for us, live for me. Live for you! I'll always be here in your heart and in your mind. I will always be the defender of your soul. I will never desert you."

Brody stood. "Hey, Danny boy, I gotta go now. Time for you to nap. Remember, you promised me to be strong, to heal, to live, to laugh, and to smile. You won't let me down, and I won't let you down. I'm always here—always."

Dan reached for Brody as he faded—not ready for him to leave, but his hands grasped only air. "Thanks, Brody. I give you my word to live and seek the beauty in life."

As she finished her checks, Lois noticed his body relax as the REM halted. He would now be in a deep healing sleep. Lois gently stroked his blond hair, gave his forehead a gentle kiss, and whispered, "Thank you. You're an amazing man Dan Broderick, find your peace. My granddaughter Sara says your soul is safe." Lois Clarry smiled and left the room.

TRF HQ – Dispatch Desk – 4:00 a.m.

Peter glanced up when the elevator dinged. Thank goodness things had been quiet after the gang war yesterday. A noticeable pallor hung over everyone after receiving notice of Aaron's death. Everyone wanted to understand the sequence of events leading to his death, but only Dan possessed the information.

He spotted the commander. *Man, is he ever wiped out.* Peter offered, "Commander, is there anything you need? I can grab you a cup of coffee."

Walter stopped at the desk and shook his head. "Thanks, but no on the coffee. I need you to pull the files listed here for me and send them in encrypted form to this email." Walter slid a piece of paper to Peter.

Rubbing his neck, Walter continued, "I need you to text Alpha to notify them they need to be here at six a.m. instead of one p.m."

"Sure."

With fatigue etched in his features, Walter added to his request. "I also need a printed copy of the gang war transcript and Aaron Plouffe's personnel file. Lastly, I need the team rotation schedule to make some shift changes. Alpha will be off regular rotation for the time being. I'll be in the briefing room."

Peter nodded. "Yes, sir." He perused the note and found the list of files required included the entire Alpha Team roster. And the email address had a military extension. "Which do you want first?"

Seeking to dispel his tension, Walter rubbed the back of his tight neck again. "I'm going to grab some coffee. Send the files first, then provide me the transcript and Aaron's file, then text the team. And on second thought, I'll deal with the schedules later, only make sure you notify Charlie Team they'll be covering for Alpha tomorrow."

"Right away," Peter said as he pulled up the personnel files to send them. Though he wondered why Gambrill wanted Alpha Team's files to Colonel Sutton, he didn't ask.

As he headed to the break room to obtain what passed for coffee, Walter wished he had the foresight to stop at Timmy's. Though the office brew tasted terrible, it would provide him much-needed caffeine, since he would not be seeking his bed for many more hours.

Walter dreaded the potential repercussions of the disclosures he made last night. Facing Alpha and revealing his connection with the Brodericks might throw a wrench into the team's dynamics. Though he sincerely hoped when the extent of his relationship with William and Daniel came to light, they would understand why he chose to keep their association private.

Chewing on Glass Shards

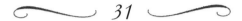 *31*

July 16
TRF HQ – Dispatch Desk – 4:45 a.m.

Nick received a text about forty minutes ago, indicating the change in meeting times. Unable to sleep, he spotted the message as soon as it arrived, so he got up and ready to come in at his usual time, although the team technically didn't need to be here until six.

Coming to a halt at the front desk, Nick grinned at Tia, and handed her a cup of coffee. "Morning."

Tia smiled. "Thanks. How'd you guess what I needed?" She took a long slow drink. "Ahh, coffee, the true nectar of the gods. You're in early. Peter told me Gambrill said you guys weren't due until six."

"Force of habit, five a.m. workouts and all," Nick replied as she gave him an 'I don't believe you' expression. "Actually, I wanted to catch the commander before the meeting. Is he here yet?"

"Gambrill is in the briefing room. He was here when I came in about fifteen minutes ago. Peter said Gambrill showed up around four after he left the hospital."

"Thanks." He nodded and headed towards the conference room. Nick wanted to ask Gambrill a few questions before the team arrived. First, why did he move the time up from one in the afternoon to six this morning? His exhausted team needed time to recoup.

Second, how well did he know Dan? Gambrill's knowledge of the incident with Sara implied he and Dan had been acquainted a long time. Nick never pushed for an explanation of why Dan joined TRF with a top-down approach and no input from the team, but now, Nick decided he needed to understand more about the rookie's past. He needed more than the few crumbs in Dan's personnel file.

TRF HQ – Briefing Room – 4:50 a.m.

As he came to the entrance of the briefing room, Nick found Gambrill seated in a chair with his arms folded on the table and his head on his arms—asleep. The man appeared drained and wrung out even in sleep. Quite understandable, with the day all the officers under his command experienced yesterday. The weight of leadership pressed heavily when officers, whether injured or deceased, became casualty statistics.

Nick never spent much time with Aaron and couldn't speak to the man's character, but didn't like learning Aaron said foul things about Dan and questioned Dan's commands, putting the team at risk. However, Aaron had been a TRF officer, a man who put his life on the line to help others, and in the process, made the ultimate sacrifice.

Aaron would still be considered an honored member of TRF. His behavior would be forgiven—everyone experienced a bad day on occasion. They were human, after all, and many shades of gray colored life.

Had this occurred been a few months ago, everyone on Alpha, sans Dan, could've been vilified. Luckily, they got the opportunity to fix their errors with Dan. Nick would like to think Aaron would've too if he had the chance. Nick hoped Aaron's parents would heal from the loss and find solace knowing their son protected others.

Nick stood in deep in thought for several minutes, deciding whether or not to wake the commander as Jon sidled up next to him.

"He looks awful. We should let him sleep until absolutely necessary to wake him," Jon murmured.

"How do you always know what I'm thinking, Jonny?" Nick responded with a smile.

"Guess I'm special," Jon intoned with a quirk of his head and glint of mischief in his eyes. "Let's talk in the locker room." He pivoted started down the hall.

TRF HQ – Men's Locker Room – 5:00 a.m.

When Nick and Jon entered the lockers, the rest of the team, including Lexa but minus Dan, were sitting on the benches in Alpha's aisle. Some appeared more rested than others, but each still exuded fatigue. Nick recognized they all were creatures of habit—all here before five as they would be on any regular day. However, Nick's spidey-sense told him today would not be another normal day for them. He only hoped whatever today brought, didn't cause his family more pain.

"So, I guess the debriefing puts our Care and Feeding discussion with Dan's buddies on hold," Loki stated.

"Looks that way," Nick responded.

"Any idea why they rescheduled for so early?" Lexa queried. Her emotional upheaval after receiving the text still lingered. The time change ruined her plans to swing by the hospital to check on Dan.

"None. It's odd. I wish I had time to check in on Dan." Nick noted nods from everyone, indicating they also planned to peek in on him. "Perhaps Tia can get an update for us while we debrief."

Loki and Lexa peered at Nick with hopeful eyes as they nodded again.

Bram shifted on the bench. "I hope she can. Been worried about Dan all night." Another round of bobbing heads showed they all shared the same concern. "That was one awful day for him. I can't figure out how he does it?"

"Does what?" asked Ray.

"Processes his emotions, and tucks things into slots. Must be a Special Forces thing. I'd be a wilted mess—would lose my friggin mind if I went through everything he did. I'm particularly sad it occurred yesterday. Tainted what should've been a Dantastic day," Bram said, shaking his head.

Loki's eyes scrunched in confusion. "What do you mean?"

Bram studied each person and noted recognition in Jon's and Nick's expressions, so clarified for the others. "Did you notice Dan wore a real smile yesterday morning? Not the surface one he puts on, but one which reflects in his eyes."

Looks of contemplation crossed their faces, followed by more nods.

"I think he finally believed we accepted him as a true member of this team, part of the family, and he belonged. It was like he already figured out how the day was totally awesome and unique. Dan's countenance shown with profound happiness as we all offered up ways things might be uniquely different. Then the day happened. I'm worried what that did to him," Bram finished.

Everyone remained silent for a long time as they contemplated their own thoughts. None of them slept well, and everybody decided to come in instead of hanging out at their own homes—seeking comfort to be among family.

Bram's words rang in their heads. Only twenty-four hours ago, Dan truly smiled. Bram was right; there had been a light in Dan's eyes that had not been there before. Somehow, they broke through his shields. They should be ecstatic for Dan, and they were—except they didn't know what cost yesterday would exact. How did someone deal with all of that?

Lexa broke the silence. "Dan's gonna need us even more. He's going to need us to support him regardless of what happened in the ravine. We must be there for him."

Loki's knee started to bounce. "I'm worried. You didn't see his face when he was in the bank, but I did. What I witnessed … raw torment. I think it really hurt him to bring out those memories."

Ray put his hand on Loki's knee to stop the bouncing and to offer silent support to his best friend. "None of us can begin to understand what Dan went through—those scars …" Ray used his other hand to absently rub the scar on his own thigh, one of several he got from the Blooddrop Crew when he refused to murder Father Lopez. "I'm sure the scars on his chest are not the worst ones he bears. Three months of torture … the invisible wounds will be worse."

Jon, Bram, and Nick shared a cheerless look. They knew all too well about invisible scars—each bore their own. Ray, Lexa, and Loki were right.

Nick said, "We're family. We're stronger together. Whatever Dan needs, we will be there for him."

Loki grinned and tried to lighten the mood. The atmosphere had become so thick like they were planning Dan's eulogy instead of being elated Dan is very much alive. "All for one and one for all. We're the seven musketeers. Dan is D'Artagnan because he's young, foolhardy, brave, and clever. Can you imagine Dantastic as a gallant musketeer and in a sword fight?"

They all chuckled, leave it to Loki to break the heavy tension.

Lexa brightened up as she conjured up an image of Dan as a swashbuckler wielding a sword to defend a damsel in distress heroically. Interestingly, the damsel looked a lot like her. Lexa shook the image from her head and sighed. Dan sure seeped into her mind and made her think things so out of character. *I'm no damsel in distress, and I fight my own battles.* But her smile increased. *Yeah, Dan would be dashing dressed as a musketeer.*

Jon smirked. "I think Dano would miss his Remi."

"Nah. Allie calls him Prince Charming." Bram chuckled.

Ray grinned. "He'd certainly have all the ladies swooning for him. I mean, the nurse last night changed his name to Dantastic on the board."

"I know, right? Dantastic is a way better nickname than Blondie," Loki said with enthusiasm.

Brett Santelli, Echo Team's sniper, strode into the locker room and came to a stop near them. "Hoped I'd find you in here. There are two guys in fatigues and the medic who rappelled with you yesterday at the desk. They're asking for you. The captain said he was ordered to be here at o-six-hundred. By the way, how's Dan?"

Checking the time, Nick wondered why Blaze, Winds, and Patch would arrive forty-five minutes early. They'd planned to meet at eight today. Nick stood. "I'll go in a moment. As for Dan, he should be okay. He's a bit beat up, but thankfully nothing life-threatening."

Nick shared only the basics since full disclosure was not anyone's business. "The doctor decided to keep him overnight for observation. We're hoping for an update soon."

"I'm glad. He was all the news talked about last night." Brett chortled. "Bet he's gonna love all the ladies swooning over him. My sister and a few of her friends came over last night. They all gushed on and on about how sweet Dan must be to kiss the little girl. They all fought over who would be the best girlfriend for him."

Everyone except Lexa chuckled as they thought Dan would probably get a kick out of the attention.

Instead of laughing, Lexa tensed up—for some reason, the comment made her angry. She didn't understand why. So, Lexa forced herself to smile as she stood. "I'll come with you."

The others rose also, and the team moved as one to go meet with Dan's Special Forces buddies.

TRF HQ - Dispatch Desk — 5:18 a.m.

Blaze spotted Blondie's new team as they exited the locker room, and he extended his hand to shake Nick's "Sergeant Pastore, you're looking a bit rested this morning. Is Commander Gambrill around? I'm a little early, but I'm hoping to be briefed on the new situation as soon as possible."

To Nick, Blaze sounded exhausted, and he exuded a high level of concern. The captain carried his body stiffly and formally—different from last night's ease. He also asked directly for the commander and expected a briefing of some sort. This worried Nick. He would bet the situation involved Dan.

"Commander Gambrill is in the large conference room. How about Jon shows you where to grab a cup of our wonderful coffee, and I'll inform Gambrill you arrived." Nick turned to Jon. "Would you pour one for the commander and me while you're at it?"

Jon nodded and led the way to the break-room. He understood why Nick sent them for coffee, to give him privacy when he woke Gambrill.

Outside TRF HQ — 5:30 a.m.

Gathering the courage to face his teammates, unsure of the reception he would receive, Dan peered at the entrance. *Will I be accepted or reviled? Will they condemn me as a failure and murderer for Aaron's death?*

He worked extremely hard with Brody guiding him to rebuild his safe place, the thick-structure that held all his hurts. Although he remained very confused and needed to sort his emotions and conflicting thoughts, Dan complied with the order to come to HQ for debrief if he left the hospital.

And though facing them terrified him, Dan wouldn't run away. He was no coward. He promised Brody he would be strong, so Dan would shoulder the blame for all the blood on their hands.

If the team hated him, he would walk away. He would find somewhere else to belong because he also promised his brother to heal, to live, to laugh, and to smile. Dan understood being rejected again would hurt, but somehow, someday, he would find the beauty of life. Though he desperately hoped it would be here.

His hand on the door, Dan reminded himself, *breathe, just breathe ...*

TRF HQ - Briefing Room – 5:30 a.m.

Commander Gambrill and Nick stood next to the windows as the team plus Dan's army buddies entered. Alpha Team dispersed around the table and took their normal seats. Winds and Patch chose chairs at the back of the room at the end of the table while Blaze stood behind them.

Utterly exhausted, running on an hour's restless sleep, and on edge, Blaze decided to come straight to TRF instead of waiting around at Patch's place. His gut screamed at him Blondie needed him—needed them. The unanswered questions in his head were numerous, and he didn't like the fact he was not covering Blondie already. He refused to fail the kid again.

Patch leaned over to Loki and grimaced. "Your wonderful coffee tastes like boiled boots. Worse than any field coffee I've ever had."

"That's why we usually take turns on Timmy runs. It was Ray's and my turn yesterday. Dan and Lexa were up for today. Things changed, so we gotta make do," Loki shared as he took a sip and scowled. *Boiled boots? Yep, quite descriptive.*

Walter cleared his throat to gain everyone's attention. *This isn't going to be easy.* He took a deep breath and exhaled. That, combined with a mien of someone chewing on glass shards, made everyone tense even before Walter began speaking. "I want to start by saying Dan is resting securely again."

They all registered 'again,' but held their tongues.

Gambrill proceeded to explain every wretched detail of what happened to Dan after they left the hospital. The expression of fury and worry were in line with what Walter expected, but he also expected the room to roar. The dead silence disconcerted him.

Jon, Nick, and Blaze shared glances all leaders would understand. The guilt of failing someone under their charge etched deeply on their features.

Bram and Winds locked gazes. Warriors of different styles, but both fiercely trying to find the right words to describe the brutal emotions surging within them—and both coming up blank.

Dumbstruck, Ray stared with his jaw clenched. He liked being 'less-lethal Ray,' but oh, what he wouldn't give to go back to the waiting room and kill Donner to prevent him from attacking Dan.

Patch's and Loki's faces revolved through so many emotions—outrage, disbelief, sadness, worry—it would be hard to pinpoint one.

Lexa's expression hardened to razor-sharp fury. Ferocity rolled off her in waves and threatened to engulf everyone in the room, but she targeted the commander. If the golden shards in her eyes could actually cut, Gambrill would be sliced to the core and bleeding out.

TRF HQ – Outside Briefing Room – 5:50 a.m.

Dan entered the building, and ever so slowly climbed the four flights of stairs to the TRF headquarters floor. Only able to take one or two steps at a time before stopping to breathe, it took Dan ages to reach his destination. He accepted his decision to take the stairs instead of the elevator as more a tactic to delay the debrief than his usual habit of avoiding small, metal boxes.

Panic rose the closer Dan got to the fourth floor. He found fear of the team's rejection hard to combat and strove mightily to gain control over his anxiety. Sweating and shaking, he gradually pushed on the door's handle.

He stepped out, and the automatic door closed behind him. The loud click, like a nail being driven into his heart, spiked his dread again. Breathing became difficult as Dan tried to tamp down on the panic—but fear got the better of him, and Dan started to turn back to the stairwell.

Crap! I can't do this! I can't.

His body shook, and Dan clenched his right fist midway in his turn. The pain of his swollen knuckles surged, causing him to release his fist. He whispered, "Brody, help me. I'm afraid they'll reject me. I don't want to be alone anymore."

Brody's voice tickled his ears, *"Small steps. Everything will be okay. I'm here. You are never alone. One foot in front of the other, brother."*

Dan turned in the direction of the briefing room again. His head bowed, he noted his sock-clad feet. When he awoke in the hospital, Dan was glad to be dressed in sweats and a shirt instead of a hospital gown. These comfortable socks weren't his, and they weren't the normal hospital booties. He wondered where they came from.

Though Dan attempted to put on his boots, he found the task impossible. He couldn't pick them up or bend over, and there was no way in hell he could tie them. The officer offered to put them on, but that was too embarrassing. So, he left his shoes at the hospital. *Comfy socks, gonna buy some of these.*

His mind recognized he delayed again and refocused on Brody's words. Brody encouraged him many times to break things down into little steps when overwhelmed and needed to conquer physical or emotional obstacles.

Brody murmured, *"Small steps, one after another, and you'll reach your goal."*

Watching his feet, Dan hesitantly took a step forward as a bead of sweat trickled down the side of his face. Dan took another tiny step and continued to focus on his shoeless-feet as until he reached the dispatch desk area.

Dan lifted his eyes and discovered the dispatcher's desk empty. *Tia must be in the copy room.* Dan noticed the briefing room windows were opaque, but the door remained open. He started forward, inch-by-inch, and stopped several feet outside the conference room. No one noticed his noiseless approach.

He spotted his team and the commander. He didn't comprehend why they were all quiet, but glaring at Gambrill. It reminded him of his first day—minus the yelling. That day, the team clearly and loudly let him know he wasn't wanted.

Will today be the same? Will they forsake me? Will I be alone again?

Dan stood stock still and focused on Lexa. He glimpsed the fire in her eyes, but his presence continued to go unnoticed by the aggravated occupants.

Unvarnished Truth

32

July 16
TRF HQ — Briefing Room — 5:55 a.m.

Lexa held her tongue for as long as possible, but she couldn't contain her fury and exploded. She stood and slammed her fists on the table as the golden flecks in her hazel eyes lit like a raging inferno, and she laser-focused her attention on Commander Gambrill.

"WHAT THE HELL WERE YOU THINKING TO PUT HIM AT SUCH RISK IN HIS CONDITION? USING HIM AS BAIT WHEN HE COULDN'T DEFEND HIMSELF. YOU LET THAT SICK, TWISTED, SOB HURT DAN. YOU ALLOWED DONNER TO STAB A VIRTUAL KNIFE IN HIS HEART AND SOUL. THAT IDIOT ALMOST KILLED HIM.

"YOU SHOULD'VE TOLD US! WE WOULD'VE PROTECTED HIM. WE PROMISED TO KEEP HIM SAFE. HE'S FAMILY. WE PROTECT FAMILY! YESTERDAY DAN RISKED HIMSELF TO SAVE SO MANY. HE TOOK A HORRIBLE BURDEN ON HIS SOUL TO SAVE OTHERS."

Gesturing to her teammates, Lexa yelled, "WE'VE EXPERIENCED THE AGONY OF TAKING A LIFE. DAN WILLINGLY ACCEPTED THAT PAIN TO SAVE OTHERS FIVE TIMES YESTERDAY. HE SAVED NICK. HE SAVED TWO WOUNDED SOULS. HE SAVED A LITTLE GIRL. HE SAVED FRANK AND ME, AND HE NEARLY DIED TRYING TO SAVE AARON."

Tears of fury streamed down her face. "WE NEED HIM! HE IS FAMILY. WE TRUST HIM. IT IS A TRUST HARD FOUGHT FOR AND ONLY WON YESTERDAY MORNING. IF WE LOSE HIM, IT'LL BE ON YOUR HANDS. WE BETTER NOT LOSE HIM. DAN BELONGS HERE!"

All her vehemence and energy spent, Lexa dropped into her chair and mournfully said, "I promised to safeguard him. I need him to be safe." Lexa put her hands over her face as tears welled in her eyes.

TRF HQ – Outside Briefing Room – 5:58 a.m.

Dan listened to the raw, unvarnished truth and passion in the ferocity of Lexa's rant. His mind translated the meaning—acceptance, family, hope, trust, redemption, solace, and, most importantly ... BELONGING. His heart and soul were gently immersed and soothed by her words.

Into the deafening silence, Dan spoke quietly and calmly, "I'm good. Nowhere in the world, I'd rather be."

His team's heads whip towards him, each displaying shocked expressions. A beautiful smile grew on Dan's face, and a light shone strong and bright in his clear sapphire blue eyes.

Cocooned in warmth, Dan reached his physical limitations. He would be safe here—he belonged. As he collapsed to the floor, the smile never left his face even when his eyes fluttered closed.

Ten people rushed forward as Dan crumbled to the tiles.

Lexa reached him first, followed by Patch and Loki. The three dropped to their knees around him. Patch checked his pulse. Loki grabbed hold of Dan's hand and squeezed as he silently begged for his eyes to open.

Cradling Dan's head in her lap, Lexa stroked his hair softly as she whispered, "Beautiful smile. Intriguing eyes. Rest now. You're safe." Lexa didn't give a damn that she stroked his hair in front of the guys yet again. The light in his eyes and the smile on his face elated her. She agreed wholeheartedly—*Nowhere in the world I'd rather be.*

Everyone else circled them, wearing concerned expressions, waiting as Patch assessed Dan.

Patch released a heavy sigh. "Blondie's sleeping. He took his body to the end of his endurance, and it forced him to rest. He'll be okay." Patch sat back on his heels and grinned at Blaze and Winds. "He found a new place to be."

Blaze nodded awash in profound relief. Blondie's eyes were not blank like Patch described to him last night. Whatever emotional turmoil rolling around in his head had been sorted out if Blondie presented that smile. It soothed him to view the spirit in the kid's eyes. Blaze feared the light extinguished forever after Brody died.

A collective sigh resounded at Patch's words. Being so focused on Dan, Alpha Team failed to notice his collapse drew the attention of the others in headquarters. However, the deep reverberating audible breaths surrounding them should've alerted them.

Nick became the first to notice all the members of Bravo, Charlie, and Echo teams plus Frank and Tia, standing stock still around them. He reasoned Lexa's outburst initially brought them forth. They probably witnessed everything and were as relieved as him by the paramedic's report.

Colton Harmon, Charlie Team's sergeant, smiled. *Good, they're whole, and they're a family now. It is time to give Alpha privacy.* Colton turned to the others. "Alright, everyone, let's move. You've all got jobs to do." He clapped his hands and made a shooing motion to make his point to leave.

Turning to rejoin his team at the gun range, he nodded to Nick, his former sergeant. Although Colton sometimes missed being on Alpha, he enjoyed being a sergeant of his own team. Plus, with his move to Charlie's top spot five years ago, the slot opened, which allowed Jon to become the tactical leader. Despite his reservations about accepting the promotion, it had been the right move to make. Jon made a great tactical lead.

After assuming leadership of Charlie, Colton tried to instill the same sense of familial bond with his teammates but hadn't achieved it yet. He concluded it took a unique set of people to build a family, and not every team would succeed. Until today, Colton wondered if Dan would ever truly become one of Pastore's family, but the events he just witnessed, fortunately, proved him wrong.

The remaining group continued to gawk at Dan until Jon shook out of his stupor and said to no one in particular, "Gotta find him a proper place to sleep. The floor outside the briefing room is an unacceptable nap location."

Laughter—pure, deep, and cleansing—burst from all.

"Man, he's in terrible shape. His face looks like some kid spilled their paints on him," Ray snorted as he gained control of his laughter.

"Either gonna repel the ladies with his ugliness or garner their sympathy. Who wants to bet it will be sympathy?" Winds said.

"I'm with you on sympathy, especially after those news reports yesterday and the reactions of Brett's sister and her friends," Bram added.

"Who's Brett, and what reactions?" Blaze asked.

Bram explained it to the unit guys, and more laughter followed.

"So, where do we put him to rest? Any ideas?" Loki inquired.

"Must be where I can safeguard him," stated Blaze firmly and all business. "Do you have a cot or something we can put in the briefing room? Blondie can't leave my sight. He's under my protection."

That got everyone's attention. Peering at Blaze, Nick asked, "Does this have to do with the new situation you referred to earlier? We were wondering why you are here so early."

"Yes, it does. Winds and I are officially assigned as Blondie's personal security detail. My orders are to meet with Commander Gambrill at zero six hundred to ensure the kid's safety."

Everyone turned to Gambrill.

Walter drew in a deep breath. "Let's settle Dan. Then we can deal with the rest. First up, we need some sort of bed or mattress."

Not having moved off with the rest of the spectators, Tia offered, "We have they gurney in the storage room … the one we use for training."

"Perfect. Where is it?" Winds asked.

Ray motioned to Winds as he started to move. "Come with me."

"I wish I had ready access to my med-pack. Blondie appears dehydrated, and he's gonna need pain meds here soon. Shouldn't be out of the hospital, but I understand full well, no one can keep him there when he wants to leave, even when it isn't in his best interest. Hospitals freak him out," Patch shared.

"Sounds like one more thing to add to the Proper Care and Feeding manual," Loki said.

Lexa couldn't stop herself from continuing to gently stroke Dan's hair. "If we contacted Dr. Fraser, would he send over what you need?"

"Worth a try. The guy was mired in guilt last night. I think he'd do anything to try and make up for his screw up. I'll call him." Patch rose, walked a little away, and placed a call to the hospital to get a hold of the doctor. He doubted Fraser would still be on duty, but perhaps they would give him his personal number.

After a few frustrating minutes of conversation, Patch remained unsuccessful in convincing anyone to provide the detail. "Dammit, stupid regulations. They won't give me Dr. Fraser's number."

Loki popped up to his feet. "Give me a few seconds. I'll get it." He went over to the computer at Tia's desk. "Mind if I use this?" He grinned at Tia as he raked his errant lock of hair off his forehead.

Wow, Tia is so beautiful, and her perfume is real nice too. Loki wondered what fragrance she wore as Tia scooted out of his way. Within seconds, he obtained Fraser's home number.

"Success," Loki hollered then cringed, realizing he shouted. He handed the number to Patch. To Tia, he said, "Thanks for sharing," before he stood and returned to Dan. Loki glanced back at Tia. *Man, she's so far out of my league it isn't funny, but a man can dream. Yeah, very interesting dreams.*

Patch spoke to Fraser and explained what he required. Fraser was more than happy to help and offered to bring the necessary items personally. Patch hung up and turned to the group. "Dr. Fraser will be here in about twenty to thirty minutes, depending on how long the pharmacy takes to fill the order."

Ray and Winds returned with the gurney, a pillow, and a blanket. Winds, Jon, Blaze, and Patch carefully lifted Dan and settled him on the thin, plastic-covered foam mattress. Loki slid the pillow under Dan's head.

Bram noted Dan's socks and smiled. "Where are his boots?"

"Hospital, I suspect. No way with his injuries would he be able to put them on himself," Patch spoke with knowledge.

Lexa nodded as she covered Dan with the blanket as studied the man who confused her so much. She was glad he smiled. Lexa tried to turn away, but she couldn't. Her gaze focused on his bruised face. She wanted to kiss his pain away. Lexa took a quick step back as if burned. *My God! Dan truly causes wild thoughts to emerge. This doesn't bode well for me at all.*

TRF HQ – Briefing Room – 6:20 a.m.

As they moved Dan into the conference room, Nick suggested, "We are all still disconcerted by the events of yesterday. I suggest we wait until after the doctor arrives with the medication, and Patch is satisfied Dan is situated before we begin our discussion. I suspect we all need a break to sort our thoughts."

"We could all use some coffee that doesn't taste like boiled boots, too," Loki added, drawing a smile from Patch. "I suggest we make a Timmy's run. Maybe grab something for everyone to eat? I'll go, anyone want to join me?"

Ray and Winds offered to go with him and as they were about to leave, Lexa piped up, "Hey, Loki, grab Dan his favorite iced capp. He might not be awake to drink it for a while, but don't want him to be left out when he wakes."

"Make it decaf. I don't want to flood his system with caffeine. Blondie needs his sleep," Patch directed.

"Copy," Loki replied before he started towards the elevator.

Timmy's – 6:50 a.m.

As they waited in line at the busy Timmy's, Loki kept glancing at Winds. He finally asked, "Why is a military protection detail assigned to Dan?"

Winds shook his head. "I don't rightly know yet. All Blaze told me is an undefined threat arose. Something connected with yesterday's events. The damned general will be here to brief us later today."

Loki noted venom in Winds's voice. "Dan's never said much about his family. None of them ever came to visit when Dan is injured or hospitalized. Does his father care nothing for him, is he truly so callous?"

Winds clenched his jaw and fists. *Hell yeah, General Badfather is a heartless bastard and more.* Recognizing it was not his place to talk about Blondie's familial relationship or lack thereof, he relaxed his muscles. "I'll only say, respect for the position has nothing to do with respect for the man."

About to probe for more detail, Loki halted as Ray said, "Not our place to pry, brother. Dan will share with us what he wants."

Venetia finished with the customer and then turned up her smile several watts to greet the next one. Most of her customers were grumpy until they got the first shot of coffee. So, a happy smiling face in the morning helped everyone's day start better.

Her smiled waned when she recognized Loki and Ray as yesterday's news came to mind. Out of uniform, she hadn't recognized them right off the bat. Her voice soft and sad, she said, "I'm so very sorry for your loss. Aaron was a nice guy. It is terrible to learn of his death and Dan's injuries. How's Dan? I hope he isn't hurt too badly. The news only said a military helicopter airlifted him to St. Michael's."

Ray quietly replied, "Thank you, Venetia. Dan is going to be fine."

Taking a cleansing breath, Venetia brightened her smile. "What can I make for you today?"

Loki answered, "Alpha Team special, but make Dan's iced capp with decaf." He turned to Winds and asked, "What do you guys want?"

Winds grinned at the young lady. "Three large, strong, black coffees."

Venetia smiled back at the handsome soldier. Tall, dark brown hair and the most amazing amber eyes. The deep, rich yellow-copper color held her spellbound a moment. Shaking off the enchantment, she turned to Loki. "Decaf iced capp? I didn't think Dan liked unleaded. Are you trying to pull a prank on him? That wouldn't be nice after yesterday."

"No." Loki's expression sobered, thinking about the reason.

Winds noted Loki's deflation. The officer was so easy to read, much like Patch. "Blondie's gonna be okay. He only needs some rest. Patch will take excellent care of him and knows exactly what to do to help Blondie physically. He's kept our little brother alive for years."

Ray turned to Venetia and added a few things to the order before pulling out his wallet to pay. When Winds went for his, Ray stayed his hand. "We got this. A small way we can say thanks for all you did last night."

Winds nodded. "Thank you, though it isn't necessary. I … we would gladly do that and more for the kid. Been a long year without him. I only hope he still trusts us and can forgive us for losing him."

Loki opened his mouth to ask but caught Ray's slight shake of the head. He pursed his lips and retrieved his billfold to leave a generous tip for Venetia. The guys gathered the trays of coffees and bags of food without further conversation and headed back to headquarters.

An Inquisitive Mind

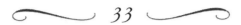

33

July 16
Toronto's Special Victims and Homicide Division – 7:00 a.m.

Inspector Davis remained troubled by the incident last night at the hospital. Sitting at his desk, several questions niggled at him. Most would simply chalk it up to a deranged man picking a target and attacking. But there was more to it. He had many, many questions.

What is the connection between Broderick and Donner? Why did Donner first point the gun at Broderick, but then turn it on himself? Why does a general care if pictures are taken of a crime scene? Gambrill's flimsy excuse about being a problem for security didn't hold water with Davis. It seemed more like a father trying to protect his son. But Davis found still found that odd.

Why is Broderick's boss so concerned? Wait, one answer, Gambrill called Broderick his godson. What is the business about Sara? Who is Sara? Who is this driver that killed himself after killing her? How is that connected to Broderick? Who is this Brody Broderick referred to before he passed out? The name freaked out Commander Gambrill every time Broderick said the name.

Davis's mind generated so many questions he couldn't sleep so he headed to his office and started digging for answers. His excavating led him to several things. He discovered Richard Donner wrote a blog, and from the posts, learned Donner was under the care of a psychologist, Dr. Carter.

The blog stated Richard moved to Toronto from Ottawa to live with his aunt after being orphaned at thirteen. On Donner's site, Davis also found a scanned copy of an old newspaper report on a car accident in Ottawa, where seven-year-old Sara Broderick died. The Sara connection answered. Sara had been Dan's younger sister. With that piece of information, he contacted an old buddy who worked the Ottawa Police Department, which led him to the police report. His buddy scanned and emailed over the entire file to him.

It contained several photos, one of which he suspected, caused Gambrill to insist no photos be taken. With the details in the report, he located a follow-up news report about the suicide of the driver, West Donner.

That led him to another police report, which his friend sent to him as well. However, try as he might, Davis had not unearthed anything about anyone named Brody.

Davis hoped the call he would make in a bit—he waited for a more reasonable time of day—would shed the final light on this incident. Tragic, truly tragic, and so many people had been hurt by this. Davis would try to put the pieces of this puzzle together, and perhaps it would be helpful to Broderick.

Last night, Constable Broderick's expressive eyes communicated his utter confusion. The vomiting, disassociation, and plea for help confirmed for Davis, the young officer had been affected by Donner's words.

Davis also recalled Gambrill indicated Dan didn't know anything about the suicide of the truck driver. Depending on what Davis concluded, perhaps Broderick should be told.

Before making the call to Donner's psychologist, Davis once again reviewed all the facts he discovered.

Nineteen years ago, a car accident killed seven-year-old Sara Yvonne Broderick. The vehicle hit her so hard she was knocked out of her shoes. Daniel William Broderick, nine-years-old, witnessed his sister's death as she was wrenched from his grasp at the crosswalk.

The driver responsible, one West Donner. Richard Donner, thirteen at the time of the accident, was West's only child. The police cited West for driving under the influence, but it turned out he wasn't drunk as the officer believed at the scene.

Toxicology reports instead showed a high level of anti-depressants—still grounds for citation, though. West had been a paramedic. West's wife, who was six months pregnant, died in a collision two weeks prior to the one that ended Sara's life. Sadly, West was the first responder to his wife's crash. Both his unborn daughter and wife died in his arms when she bled out.

The day of Sara's death, Richard Donner rode in the car with his father. West Donner picked his son up from summer camp early because Richard had attacked and injured a kid after being teased about being a momma's boy. *Ouch, that had to be harsh having lost his mom only a few weeks earlier.*

Back to facts. Okay, so the officer in charge of investigating the accident … Inspector Walter Gambrill. *Dang, must've been hard on him, especially with Dan being his godson. He would've known Sara, too.* Davis flipped through papers. Records showed Gambrill transferred to the Toronto Police Department two years later. *Okay, so there is the connection to Gambrill.*

So now about the pictures. One of the crime scene pictures got leaked to the press, and a damned tabloid printed it. Viewing the picture, Davis wished to find the idiot who decided to run it. He wanted to punch their lights out— no kid should be photographed in such a state. Bad enough, the kid experienced something so horrific, but for some asshole to immortalize Dan's intense agony in a photo was downright cruel.

The picture in question showed a little boy kneeling next to his dead sister— two golden blond heads. The little girl's blood coated the boy's arms, hands, shirt, shorts, and face. He clutched a pair of pink sandals to his chest. The boy must've hugged her tightly for that much blood to transfer to him.

However, the most disturbing thing ... the photographer caught the grieving boy in the moment of an agonizing scream. His little blond head tilted slightly upward, mouth open, and face contorted with unfathomable pain, forever frozen in time. His tear-filled blue eyes appeared so tormented and lost. Davis's heart hurt, gazing at those expressive eyes. This absolutely explained why no photos were allowed last night.

The follow-up article said West Donner left a suicide note. Inspector Davis read West's lengthy and extremely detailed note. He included exacting descriptions of how he felt in the week after the girl's death. He wrote down the things he said to Dan on the day of the accident. He couldn't live with himself for causing such agony and torment and indicated the boy's eyes pierced him to the soul. West became consumed with guilt for ending a beautiful little girl's life

He repeatedly wrote she deserved to live, and he tried to beg forgiveness from the little boy, telling him he wished he could die to bring her back. In what amounted to a written account of seeking absolution from the child for killing his sister, West claimed he wasn't worthy, and it was all his fault. As a paramedic, he was supposed to save people, not kill them. West pleaded for mercy because he failed to save the girl, and he was so sorry.

Donner went on to say at the scene he begged the boy not to cry, to stop crying. The child's shrieks tore West apart, but the inconsolable child was in a state of shock and kept screaming for Sara. The police report noted no one could get Daniel Broderick to respond to them. Daniel was so locked in his anguish over his little sister he wouldn't allow anyone to touch him or take the shoes. Donner admitted seeing what he caused devastated him.

The death note also detailed what happened when the children's father, General Broderick, arrived on the scene. The grief for both his daughter and son expressed by the general was so intense. Donner said he felt remorse no one could stop the boy's wails or coax him into relinquishing his hold on his sister. He only stopped and released her after his dad yelled at him in a booming voice, ordering him to let go.

It was the only thing that worked. Prior to the shouted order, the dad pleaded with his son, cried with him, and tried soft-spoken words, but nothing penetrated the child's grief barrier. The pain Donner witnessed on the dad's face as he bellowed and then tried to console his child ate away at West's soul. The distraught man couldn't live with what he did, so decided to end his life. He shot himself in the head late one night.

The investigator's report said West's son woke from a nightmare and went to his father for comfort. Richard walked into the room right as his dad pulled the trigger. "Aw hell, that would screw anyone up!"

Davis checked at the clock, noting it was still early, but hopefully, Dr. Margaret Carter would be in her office. He dialed the psychologist and waited. When she answered, Davis, explained why he contacted her, leaving out names other than Donner's. At first, reluctant to discuss a patient Dr. Carter offered information after Davis reminded her Richard Donner took his life.

Richard had been a long-term patient. She started treating him when he was thirteen after his father's suicide. The boy possessed deep-seated guilt, believing his father wouldn't have been driving if he had not been fighting at summer camp over his mother.

The boy believed he destroyed his family. Richard eventually found the published photos. After viewing all the blood on the little boy, Richard developed a fixation on gory details. For the most part, Richard was able to operate in the world. He did possess thoughts of ending his life in the same manner as his father.

Carter then said something changed in the past year. Richard no longer blamed himself. Richard never gave the doctor a name, but for some reason, Donner now believed someone else was responsible for his father's death. She shared that Donner spoke a lot about eyes, lost eyes, and she suspected that had something to do with the change in her patient.

She also disclosed Donner's suicidal fantasies changed. He began indicating he wanted to do it in a way that made the responsible person live with the same pain he endured. When Davis described how Donner killed himself, Dr. Carter said it made sense.

Apparently, Richard never planned to actually kill the person he blamed. He only wanted to kill them in the sense Richard had died years ago. He wanted to make the person watch as he committed suicide like Richard watched his dad do. Davis thanked her and hung up.

Davis wondered if he would cause more hurt to Broderick if he shared this or if it would help Broderick. With nothing to base a decision on, Davis decided to contact Gambrill since Broderick was his godson.

TRF HQ – Dispatch Desk – 7:45 a.m.

When Ray, Loki, and Winds returned, everyone except Patch stood near the dispatcher's desk while Dr. Malcolm Fraser did a full checkup on Dan. They handed out the cups, and everyone milled around waiting for the word as they sipped their coffees and ate the breakfast sandwiches the guys brought from Timmy's. As time wore on with no word from Fraser, their worry increased.

When Malcolm finished his exam, he stepped out of the briefing room and approached the anxious group. "Jim is finishing inserting an IV. I still can't believe Constable Broderick left the hospital in his condition. He should still be there, but I understand from Jim that isn't possible at the moment. Luckily, his fall didn't cause additional injuries. I provided Jim my personal number and directed him to call me any time day or night if Dan requires anything or if his condition deteriorates in any way."

Gambrill nodded. "Thank you for coming. We appreciate it."

Malcolm shook his head slowly. "No thanks needed. I owed him this and more after last night's debacle. Please call if he needs anything, anything at all. Also, have him follow up with me in a few days so I can monitor his progress."

"Will do," Nick stated.

As the doctor left, the rest wandered into the briefing room. Loki took a quick detour and put Dan's iced capp in the breakroom fridge.

Easy Money

34

July 16
TRF HQ – Briefing Room – 8:00 a.m.

Coffee in hand, everybody returned to their chairs to ready to focus on the business of protecting Dan. Loki passed the bag of timbits around and handed Patch one of the breakfast sandwiches they bought for everyone.

Patch grinned. "Thanks, Loki." He took a sip of his coffee and sighed. "Much better than boiled boots, much better."

Loki smiled. He liked Patch. It made him happy Patch took such excellent care of Dan. With as often as Wile E. Coyote got hurt, Loki figured it would be a real advantage having him as one of Toronto's paramedics.

Nick sat and studied Gambrill. *Time to understand the new situation and obtain some answers.* As everyone settled into seats, Nick asked, "Okay, so what do we need to understand about this situation?"

Gambrill took a steadying breath. "The circumstances are related to something in Dan's past." His phone vibrating interrupted him. Checking the displayed number, Walter recognized the first three digits as ones reserved for police. He held up his hand to the group indicating 'hold' as he answered.

"Good morning, Commander. This is Inspector Davis of Special Victims and Homicide. I did some investigation and discovered several things. Got a moment to talk?"

"Kind of busy. Is this important?"

"Might be. Last night, several things didn't add up. Got my brain into overdrive. I just spoke with Dr. Carter, and she shed some light on Richard Donner, which you might find interesting and helpful."

"Who is Dr. Carter, and why would she have anything to do with last night's events?" Gambrill's comment perked up the ears of everyone in the room, except the sleeping Dan.

"She is a psychologist and treated Donner for years. I think you should listen to what she shared with me. It might be important for Broderick, too. Perhaps helpful for him to know, but I don't want to cause more problems for him. I'm unfamiliar with the man, so I'm seeking your opinion."

Gambrill put together Donner was the son of the driver, and wondered if something more was going on. "Davis, I'd like to hear what you learned, but I want to do it in person. There are a few others who may need to be made aware, so if you can come to TRF HQ, that would be best."

"Will do. Heading out shortly. It'll take me a while to get there. I'm all the way across town." Davis disconnected, then gathered all the reports and slipped the papers into a file folder.

Walter looked at the expectant faces. "That was Inspector Davis, who worked the incident with Dan last night. He is bringing information to share."

Nick directed his gaze at Gambrill. "Sir, before he arrives and we start the briefing, I have a question. I planned to ask you in private, but this centers on Dan and his past. We need some facts I believe only you can provide."

"I'll answer what I can," Walter responded warily.

Ottawa – Scott Broderick's Home – 8:30 a.m.

Leaning down, Scott Broderick kissed Lily. *Wow, my wife. She married me. I'm the luckiest man in the world.* Lilyanna would always be his one true love. It took him years to find her, and then a few years to gather the nerve to ask her to marry him, but now his world was complete.

Lily smiled up at Scott, "You're gonna be late."

Scott grinned. "Don't have to be in until nine today. I have some meetings in the afternoon, but I should be home in time for dinner tonight."

He sat back down on the bed and gazed into Lily's baby blue eyes. He reached out and touched the short, silky tresses of her dark chocolate brown hair. Scott couldn't get enough of her. They had been married for only three months.

Tomorrow would be officially three months. April seventeenth is a day he would never forget. The entire family came to witness their marriage vows and celebrate their happiness. His face fell slightly—not quite everyone.

"What's wrong?" Lily reached up and caressed Scott's face.

"Nothing." Scott shook his thought away and smiled.

"Scott Erik Broderick, don't you start lying to me. I can tell something is bothering you. Perhaps I can help?"

Scott chuckled. "All three names. Makes me seem like an errant little boy."

Lily smiled. "Changing the subject isn't gonna work." She took his hand and held on. "Let me share your burdens if they're not of the secret type."

He squeezed her hand. "No, not secret. Only sad. I was thinking of our wedding." At the flash of hurt in Lily's eyes, Scott clarified. "Best day of my life. But it would've been better if Dan could've been there. I found out yesterday Dan's been in Toronto this whole time. If I had only known … I would've gone to visit him."

"Dan means a lot to you, doesn't he?"

"Yeah. I feel like I let him down. I should've done more. I should've tried harder. He became so lost after Sara died. And then he was just gone. I never agreed with what Uncle Will did. Though only seventeen at the time, I should have done something more. Dan is the younger brother I wanted for years. I was lucky to have him before my brother Kyle was born. Dan and Kyle are so different, but each one of them means the world to me."

Lily smiled. "All your siblings and cousins are important to you. I'm glad you're all so close. This is the large family I always wished I had. Growing up, it got lonely with only me and my dad after Mom died. Neither of them had any siblings, and both sets of my grandparents were gone.

"So it makes me happy you have such tightknit relationships with your sisters, brother, and cousins. Now that you know Dan is in Toronto, maybe we can visit him. I would love to meet your twin eight years younger." Lily chuckled. Scott and his male cousins loved to tease her about a twin cousin. She knew they were pulling her leg, but she enjoyed being included in the teasing and bantering of this large, loving family.

Scott grinned. "Now that you're safely married to me, I can introduce you to my doppelganger. But meeting him will have to wait. Dad shared some disturbing news with me last night. He's working with my uncles to coordinate emergency leaves for all of the guys so we can visit Dan for a long-overdue Broderick intervention. Dad will inform me of the date, but it should be within the next few weeks.

"There are things that must be addressed. Dan needs to understand we care, and we didn't abandon him." Scott blew out a shaky breath as he recalled what his dad told him about Dan's mail being intercepted. With the investigation ongoing, Scott couldn't share the details with Lily yet. It made him sick to think Dan believed the family had forsaken him and no longer cared enough to write.

It was quite the opposite—Scott had written more often. He hoped whatever caused Dan to stop writing to him would be resolved. But now Scott comprehended Dan never stopped either. Scott wanted to hang whoever was responsible from a yardarm by his balls.

Lily sat up and wrapped her arms around Scott, and kissed his cheek. "I love you so much. You have a heart of gold. I can wait to meet Dan. You and your family will sort things out. I have complete faith in you."

Scott hugged Lily and began to kiss her. He got lost in the sensation and only came back to the world when Lily gently pulled back and placed her fingers on his lips. He kissed her fingers as Lily said, "As much as I like doing this, you'll be late if you don't go now."

He chuckled. "I'll gladly take a dressing down to be late because of you, my love."

Lily giggled. "Go. Duty First."

Scott stood and saluted Lily. "As you command, Ma'am."

Her laughter stuck with him as he headed out to work. It made him grin. *I'm the happiest and luckiest man on this earth … Lily is my wife.*

Vancouver Island, BC – Empress Hotel – 5:30 a.m. (8:30 Toronto)

Frustrated, Jorge Pletcher sat at the desk in his hotel room as he worked on his laptop. Things had not panned out like he planned. Fortunately, Plouffe gave him the heads-up the general's security detail tracked him.

He barely slipped away from Galloway and his men. If he had not turned on his phone before getting off the plane, he would've been caught. Galloway turned out to be more of a challenge to evade than he expected.

Distractedly, Pletcher tapped away on his computer to do the funds transfer to Plouffe. Plouffe charged an exorbitant fee for the heads-up, but better than being caught and charged with treason and attempted murder. Had he known Plouffe would become so greedy, he would've never begun a partnership with him. At first, it was small potatoes, but over the years, Plouffe demanded more and more money for slipping him intel.

Thankfully, his clients willingly paid ridiculous amounts for information. He and Plouffe made a significant chunk of money off of a deal he brokered years ago. Plouffe had been so pissed off when Broderick survived being taken captive. The major fully expected and wanted the general's son to be killed.

But that nearly blew up in their faces. Broderick never divulged a single thing in the months he was tortured. It made Pletcher's contacts leery of the quality of his deals and information for some time, but he managed to sort things out over the past few years.

His most lucrative client, Abdul Khaliq Mousa, was still willing to pay outlandish amounts for intel and connections. He introduced Mousa's right-hand man, Anwar Yassin, to Chris Thruston, Junior. Christopher, the son of Christopher Alfred Thruston, Senior, was a malcontent party boy with a penchant for getting into trouble with underage girls. The elder Thruston, CEO of Thruston Group, held several military contracts and were working on an experimental type of explosives. That could prove to be very lucrative for him if it panned out.

His mind shifted back to his near capture, which would've ruined everything. *Damned Brodericks are the bane of my existence. Plouffe's latest scheme is the reason I'm on the run. I can't believe I agreed with this one.*

Becca Broderick turned out to be was a witless, blonde bimbo. She possessed no useful information. Why the major ever thought she would be a source of decent intel, he would never understand. But when Plouffe offered him a bonus to kill her, Jorge couldn't pass that up. He must dispose of her anyway since she knew too much about him.

Jorge also couldn't believe she jumped from his car. He almost turned around to finish her off when he noticed a car stop, and two men hop out. He recognized the general's security men. It meant only one thing—somehow, he had been found out and needed to run.

But Plouffe made him an offer he couldn't refuse. After completion, he would have to go into hiding for years, off the grid, and he needed to stockpile money. Plouffe would pay him a cool million to complete his task and told him Becca and the general's wife were in a safe house in Vancouver.

Pletcher hit the send button to transfer the funds to Plouffe's Cayman Islands account. He would lay low a while and figure out where they took Becca. Then he could figure out how to finish the job.

As he sat back, Jorge blew out a breath. "Damned Brodericks." His phone vibrated, and he received a text on his burner phone.

Double payment if you eliminate my toy soldier.

Jorge shook his head. *No. No. I can't. Too risky with Galloway on my tail.* He texted back. **Not worth the risk.**

Easy money. Sitting duck, in hospital.

No.

Toy soldier no longer innocent, has to pay the price.

No.

Triple payment.

Pletcher hesitated. *That is a lot of money.* **Where's the toy soldier?**

St. Michael's in Toronto.

Okay, but I choose the time and place.

Agreed, but soon, he must pay for what he did.

Jorge blew out another breath. "Damned Brodericks!"

The Error of His Ways

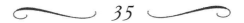

35

Having already discerned the answer to his first question, why the meeting time had been moved up, Nick asked Gambrill his second one. "I read Dan's personnel file, and as blacked out and redacted as it is, it still contains nothing relating to him as a child. Nothing about his sister Sara. How long have you known Dan?"

"Since he was born. Daniel is my godson," Walter replied, garnering shocked expressions, but everyone remained quiet, hoping he would offer more. Silence drawing out, Walter realized he must explain more.

"I picked up William from the base the day Danny decided to be born. Should've seen the panic when William realized Yvonne went in labor three weeks early. William hadn't even put the crib together. He was lucky to be home. He planned on surprising Yvonne, but he ended up being the one surprised. Well, I guess they both were. I drove Yvonne and William to the hospital, alerted family members, and waited for news. I was among the first visitors for the new family and held Danny when he was only a few hours old."

Stunned countenances and more nods implied he should continue.

"I've known William Broderick since we met as young boys on a base in Saskatchewan. Our fathers were both stationed there, and we seemed to hit it off. Two boys couldn't be as different as us—night and day—but we formed a friendship that stuck even as we moved to different bases."

More nodding, and continued silence.

Gambrill chose to provide the essentials, as they might be relevant to the current problem. "Okay. I'll lay it out for you. I comprehend you all care for Dan so I'll tell you what I can. Some of it will have to wait until General Broderick arrives tonight."

His disclosure drew more than a few disgusted expressions. The hatred clearly evidenced on the hard planes of the faces of Blaze, Winds, and Patch surprised Gambrill. Though his friend didn't give a rat's ass what people thought about him and tended to be a hard, stoic military man who he earned his nickname Badass, Walter believed William at least engendered a sense of loyalty in his Special Forces men.

William watched out for them and truly cared about their well-being. *Perhaps Dan's opinion of his father rubbed off on these three men. They do care a lot about Dan.* Still, the intense hatred confused him. He cleared his throat and prepared to give them a little history. "Not sure when Davis will arrive. Let me lay a quick Broderick foundation up to Sara's death, at least."

Several nodded. A few relaxed into their chairs, preparing to listen, wanting to learn more about Dan. While others, namely Blaze, sat tensely near Dan with one hand on the kid's leg and with a fierce expression that if Gambrill had known him better, he would've read, *I don't want to hear anything about the hardhearted SOB who treated his son so callously.*

But Walter didn't know Blaze well, and he interpreted the look to be protective of Dan. Choosing him for this detail had been the right call. The general's concern the friendly fire incident changed their relationship was unwarranted, at least from Blain's perspective.

Gambrill realized Dan probably wasn't even aware Blaze and Winds were here. From where Dan had been standing outside the door, his three former unit mates wouldn't have been visible to him. When Dan had seen Patch in the ravine, he blanked out. It would be interesting to see how Dan reacted when he found out everything they did for him yesterday. Hopefully, it would mend some wounds for all four of them.

"Well, where to start? Okay. So, I was the best man at William and Yvonne's wedding. Still not sure how he got her to marry him. Yvonne is all bright and full of laughter, and William is still a dour man who never really shows his emotions to anyone.

"Dan came along about ten months later, a honeymoon baby most say. Two years later, little Sara blessed them, and Becca four years after Sara. All three kids took after their mother's personality. Bright, outgoing, full of smiles, and mischief. You know, happy kids.

"Dan and Becca have their father's blue eyes, and Sara's eyes were emerald green like her mother."

Bram sharply inhaled as he thought of Sara Clarry's eyes. His teammates glanced at him, likely recalling the same thing, but no one interrupted Gambrill.

"Physically, Dan takes after William in many ways. Rugged features, untold stamina, and hard to kill."

Patch snorted. *Damned straight. Blondie is one hell of fighter. He should've been dead several times. Dr. Pastore called Blondie an outlier ... his survival way outside statistical odds ... thank God!*

Gambrill's remark filled Blaze and Winds with rage because that is exactly what they thought the SOB tried to do, kill his only son.

Unaware of their rage, Walter paused as he peered at his godson. *Too many close calls. Damned hard to kill. Thank goodness!*

"William was a major when Dan was an infant. I'm not privy to the full details, but when Dan was about one, William nearly died in France when his unit handled security for Colonel Grasett while he attended a summit. By all accounts, William should've died, but he didn't. He had Yvonne and Daniel to live for ... a strong motivator for him to fight to hang on.

"During his extended recovery period, William loved spending time with Daniel ... time he hadn't had while on duty. When William returned to active service, he received a promotion to Colonel. Tom Sutton was promoted to Lieutenant Colonel while William rehabilitated. They filled the Special Forces leadership vacuum created by the deaths of both Colonel Grasett and Lieutenant Colonel Elkin.

"William was promoted to Brigadier General shortly before Dan turned five. General Craymuier groomed William to eventually take over his position. That's when things started to change."

Walter stopped as sadness over what they all lost because of William's damned attitude toward raising Dan. He considered what to say next and popped a timbit in his mouth, chewed slowly, and washed it down with a sip of coffee.

Blaze stared out the window, trying to contain his fury. He couldn't care less about the general's meteoric rise to power. Sure, he was the second-youngest man to make full general, but that didn't mean the general was a decent and honorable man. In Blaze's opinion, the cold-hearted soldier didn't measure up to the standards. A man who treated his son like General Badass treated Blondie would never be considered honorable in his eyes.

Trying to recall the positive, Walter thought about the general's pride in his son. "Dan was six when William started teaching him how to shoot—bought him his first rifle that summer. He got a kick out of being able to take Dan to the gun range, Danny was such a natural. He took after William in that manner. William was a sniper when he first joined Special Forces. He preened like a proud papa the day his eight-year-old son bested some of the experienced marksmen in a friendly competition."

Walter chuckled. "I remember him telling me it pissed off some of the guys to be bested by a little boy. But he said most of them took it in stride, and he believed some of the snipers missed on purpose."

Recalling Yvonne's displeasure over the same event, Walter continued, "Yvonne wasn't happy, though. She believed at six Dan was far too young for William to be taking him to the range every weekend. By the time Dan turned seven, they would go several times each week. Yvonne argued with Will over it, but William wouldn't back down.

"William can be stupidly headstrong and insisted it was never too early for a boy to learn the skill and Broderick males are military men, always had been, always would be, generation after generation. William firmly held it was his duty to prepare Dan for life in the military. So, Dan's training must start young so the lessons he taught became second nature to protect him."

Sadness entered Gambrill's voice as he shared, "That is the reason Dan was only ever allowed to address him 'Sir' and had to stand at attention or parade rest when speaking with him. From the time Dan was five, William ruthlessly drilled into him, he must always follow orders, and not doing so was a failure he wouldn't accept or tolerate."

Gambrill stopped to take a drink of coffee. He wondered if he should really be sharing this kind of detail, but decided to continue. "Unfortunately, he was a misguided man and verbally dressed-down Dan like he was a soldier when the boy got into mischief or didn't follow an order. Sadly, Dan learned early on to turn off his emotions in front of his father.

"Dan was smiles and laughter when only his mom and sisters were around. However, he would flip a switch to soldier mode when William entered a room. Truly sad. William's actions originated from love for his son. He simply wanted to prepare Danny for the harsh world of a soldier. But William couldn't recognize his methods were so wrong until it was too late."

Walter sighed and took another drink to compose himself. "The day Sara died showed him the error of his ways. That day he lost not only his little girl but also his son. He finally comprehended he broke the father-son relationship between himself and Dan, and all that remained was a general-soldier one.

"William is a tough and proud man who rarely openly expresses emotions, but he does feel them deeply. He is still guilt-ridden for what he did to Danny and tried so hard to mend things over the years." Walter stopped and focused directly on Blain.

"BULLSHIT! THAT MAN IS A SADISTIC BASTARD, AND IF I WOULDN'T BE COURT-MARTIALED, I WOULD'VE BEAT HIM TO A BLOODY PULP FOR ALL THE SHIT HE PUT BLONDIE THROUGH.

"NO ONE WHO LOVES SOMEONE WOULD DO THOSE THINGS. YOU HAVE NO IDEA HOW HARD BRODY AND I WORKED TO KEEP THE KID'S SOUL INTACT," Blaze roared, having listened to enough. He stood and stormed from the room.

Remembering his duty, Blaze stopped at the door only long enough to say, "Winds, watch Blondie. I need a break," before striding out.

Stunned by Blaze's outburst, Alpha Team remained silent, trying to digest everything, and concluded the relationship between Dan and his father was complicated.

A few moments later, Nick rubbed his face several times. "Let's take a much-needed break. We can continue when Blaze returns."

They all nodded. Nick, Loki, and Bram stood and paced slowly to stretch their legs as their minds churned. Gambrill moved to the windows, and stared aimlessly at the scenery. Ray leaned back in his chair and made his body relax, taking shallow, slow breaths.

Lexa turned to stare at Dan. He had as complicated of a relationship with his family as she had with hers, maybe even more so. Lexa noted Dan appeared flushed, though she found it difficult to tell with all the bruising. She sighed, relieved when Patch rose to check on him.

Patch detected the heat radiating off of Blondie and pulled out his tympanic thermometer. He didn't like the results. Patch mumbled to himself as he reached in his pocket for his phone. He dialed and when the call answered, Patch got right to the point. "Dr. Fraser, it's Jim Shea. Dan is running a fever."

"How high?"

"One-o-two. I'm pretty sure he needs antibiotics and something to bring down the fever. Can you arrange to send them over and a couple more bags of saline? I want to keep him hydrated."

"Are you still at TRF headquarters?"

"Yeah."

"Okay. I'll order an antibiotic and a fever reducer. Though I didn't find any signs of infection, I need you to monitor his wounds closely, especially the bullet wound. Are the rest of his vitals normal?"

Patch took Blondie's pulse, blood pressure, and did a quick physical exam. "No changes in the other vitals, and I'm not observing any redness or exudate. I'll call if there are signs of heat, swelling, or discharge." He spoke with Fraser a few more moments before disconnecting, then started to leave.

When she overheard Patch's conversation, Lexa laid her head on her arms on the table and closed her eyes, thinking sarcastically. *This keeps getting better and better*. She sat up as Patch began to exit the room. "Where are you going? Do you need something for Dan?"

"Want some damp paper towels to cool him."

"I can do better. There are tons of fresh towels and washcloths in the locker rooms. I'll grab a few and some cool water. Also, we have some instant cold packs in our first aid kit. I can bring them if you think they would help," Lexa informed him.

"Thanks. An ice pack for his wrist would be great." After Lexa nodded and left, Patch returned to Dan. "Blondie, you're always giving me trouble. One problem after another. Always testing my skills. It's okay to stop it now," he jokingly said as he squeezed Dan's left bicep.

Winds rose and strode over to Jon, who stood in the doorway, staring in the direction Blaze went. As angry as Blaze, his stomach churned, Winds wished he could storm out, but he understood his best friend needed a break more than he. One of them must remain to protect Blondie.

Stopping next to Hardy, Winds said, "I'm must stay with Blondie, or I'd go after Blaze. I hate to ask, but would you check on him for me? I think you two are a lot alike, and he could use someone who understands how he thinks right about now.

"Give Blaze ten minutes to blow off steam and calm down, then talk to him, please. He's not much of a talker, but he might with you. If that Davis guy shows up while you're gone, we'll make him wait until you two return."

Jon nodded affirmatively and started from the room.

Calming the Inferno

 *36*

July 16
TRF HQ — Rooftop — 8:50 a.m.

As he exited the stairwell, Jon stopped. He searched for Blaze out front, and when he didn't find him, he decided to check the roof. Watching Blaze pacing on the rooftop reminded him of how Dan always came here seeking calm.

Blaze clenched and released his hands several times as he strode back and forth. Each time he stopped in front of the air handler, Blaze seemed as if he wanted to punch it when his fists closed, and his arms came up, but then he released them and pivoted to stride back to the other side of the building.

Jon understood his emotion—the unbridled rage that came when he was powerless to protect the people he cared about. Jon waited for the onslaught of fury to subside. Jon figured he would only end up getting decked if he tried to intervene now.

Gradually Blaze got control of his rage. Calming his inferno, he stopped pacing as he approached the AC unit for the umpteenth time. He turned, leaned his back on the metal, and bit by bit slumped to the ground, ending up with his knees bent and his forehead in his right palm.

Jon checked his watch. *Yep, ten minutes, Winds knows Blaze well.* As Jon approached unhurriedly, he thought again about Dan, and how this was his favorite place to sit. Jon slid down next to Blaze. He remained silent, not pushing, only making Blaze aware he was not alone.

After a long time, Blaze blew out a ragged breath and turned his gaze toward Jon. He studied Jon's features long and hard before he said, "I hate the general so much. For six hellacious years, we protected Blondie as best we could. But there were things beyond our control—my control. The damned general put Blondie through hell repeatedly. I can't accept the man loves Blondie no matter what Gambrill says."

Minutes ticked as he sat silent again with an expression of deep sadness. Blaze eventually spoke again. "Blondie isn't aware that I know exactly how many kills he had to make in those six years. The number would make a stone man weep with despair. When he was with us, we tried to limit the hits to his soul. However, when General Broderick ordered him to join other units, it was very hard on him.

"You see, Blondie had to prove himself repeatedly, putting himself at risk countless times. He carried a target on his back, being the general's son. Many people thought he received special treatment. HA! Yeah, special, my ass! Blondie was used and abused by that damned man. He is a cold-hearted bastard, and Blondie never got downtime. When my unit stood down, he assigned Blondie to another unit temporarily.

"I could do about to stop him. The orders came directly from the top. When Blondie went with the other units, we never knew if they covered his back. Usually, they didn't. He was with another unit when captured by the terrorists. The green sergeant discounted Blondie's input for his perch. He ordered him to an indefensible position and left on his own for three days with no one checking on him.

"Once a unit flat-out tried to kill him. The leader allowed one of his men to choke Blondie unconscious and left him to die. I call it justice; they paid the price for that with their own lives. If Blondie had been with them, he would've alerted them before they walked into the ambush.

"Then, there is the time he was sent out in the field for seven days and had to take out thirty-two targets." Blaze banged his head lightly on the metal box behind him as frustration built again. "That time, the fucking unit *forgot* he was with them. Bastards! From his perch, Blondie saved their asses when they bugged out because they were overrun by a much larger and well-armed group than they'd anticipated. They ran and left without him. Alone, Blondie hiked over sixty kilometers back to camp, through hostile territory, with no supplies left. No water, no food, and no ammo—he used it all, saving them.

"I reported their actions to the major, and the bastards didn't even receive a reprimand. Something like that had to be reported up the chain of command. I still can't believe they got off scot-free for putting Blondie at such risk. He could've died—Blondie was alone, unarmed, and in hostile territory—and the general did nothing to the assholes who left him.

"When we found him in the mess tent, Blondie teetered close to the edge. He eventually told us he didn't tip off the edge because some guy offered to help him and talked to him about TRF before we found him. The kindness shown to him shocked Blondie because no one but us gave a damn whether he lived or died. The kid said TRF sounded like a good place to be."

Blaze put his head on his knees. His doubts and questions resurfaced in his mind. *What kind of blackout protocol is this? Is Blondie on a mission? What kind of op would involve the ruse of Blondie being with the TRF?* A mission was the only thing that made any sense at the moment, but he found it exceedingly difficult to discern the truth.

Jon listened to everything Blaze shared. He sat quietly, assessing all he heard and found his respect for Dan going up many notches. *How the hell did Dan go six years without a break?*

Part of one of the early discussions Nick had with him when his stubborn ass needed to change his attitude towards Dan filtered into Jon's mind. Neither quite knew what Dan's comment meant at the time, but now Dan's statement at least Alpha Team didn't try to kill him made sense. *Shit!*

He wondered about Dan's father too. *Can the general be that apathetic towards his son? It didn't jive with what Gambrill said. Who is right, and who is wrong? Is Walter blinded by an old friendship? Is Blaze misinterpreting things?* Jon had no idea where the truth lay in this puzzle.

But one piece fell into place as words from Trevor's story matched up with words Blaze said. The pieces fit together, and he made the connection. Quietly, Jon said, "So, that's what they meant, it confused Trevor a lot. Gonna have to reintroduce those two."

"What? Trevor? Reintroduce who?" Blaze questioned.

"Yeah, Trevor—he's on Echo Team but has been on leave as long as Dan's been here. He only got back to duty a week ago. At the command post yesterday, Trevor recounted an encounter he had with Dan while he served as an MP in Kandahar.

"Trevor said he couldn't forget the event or people, and it stuck with him because of the intensity. He still wondered what the numbers meant when one guy yelled to others, found Blondie, seven and thirty-two. He thought it might be some unit code.

"You also went into action fast when you heard Patch yell, found Blondie, in the ravine. What a small world—a damned small world," Jon said, shaking his head.

"It was our code. Shorthand for how bad physically and mentally things were for Blondie," Blaze stated flatly.

"So, I gather the first was how many days in the field and the second how many kills he made," Jon replied solemnly, only getting a nod of agreement from Blaze.

Sorrow etched itself on Blaze's face as he confessed, "In the end, even we, his brothers, utterly failed him. Blondie left us because we failed him when he needed us the most. I relayed the all-clear order to him, which resulted in Blondie shooting Brody."

Tears threatened as anger mixed with pain, and Blaze said through a clenched jaw, "I couldn't look him in the eyes and witness the agony I caused him. None of us could. His eyes can be so expressive. We didn't know what to say to help him, to take away the pain, so we remained silent. On the fourth day, we went to the hospital—I finally pulled my head together and knew I needed to say something—Blondie was hurting so badly.

"But when I showed up, he was gone. It took me a day to locate him. They moved him to a special location for the duration of the review board inquiry. I—we—all tried to visit him but were denied. The guard said the general ordered Blondie couldn't have visitors.

"Then he was just gone. We found out that before Blondie left, four soldiers jumped him. One of them was the damned guard who wouldn't let us visit him. I searched for the past year, but he didn't exist. Blondie disappeared. I worried he ran—and he might've …"

Blaze trailed off, not wanting to voice he thought Blondie committed suicide. He didn't want to say it aloud because that would be a betrayal of Blondie's strength, and he didn't want Jon to form the impression Blondie was weak—because Blondie remained the strongest man Blaze ever met.

Instead, he said, "It was all my fault. I gave the order to fire, and I failed to talk to him afterward. I lost him, and I can only hope Blondie can forgive me. It hurts so much to know I failed him. I'm no better than the damned general."

Jon sucked in a breath. *No fucking wonder Dan is still standoffish with us, and it took so long to connect with him. Dan got hurt repeatedly. Bram is right— the shields Dan hides behind were forged over many years.*

He gazed at Blaze. "You're only human, and humans make mistakes. Dan means a lot to you three, I can tell. Given what little you shared, it is clear to me you did well protecting him." With regret in his voice, Jon added, "He's important to us, too. But we also failed him."

Blaze's eyes scrunched, not following Jon. "How?"

"I won't lie. We got off to a rocky start with him. We almost lost him, or more correctly, almost drove him away. We—I—let how Dan joined our team color my judgment. We all did. Gambrill put him on the team. Customarily, teams select their new members, and at the time, the standard number for a team was six. The *Proper Care and Feeding of Dantastic* manual is a result of a meeting the six of us had after we recognized our error.

"It took us nine months to build trust and prove to Dan; we are worthy of him. Yesterday should've been a fantastic day. Nick, Bram, and I recognized Dan truly smiled for the first time during yesterday's workout. He appeared happy and rested, too. So it should've been great, but ended up being a terrible day for him … for all of us.

Jon paused and met Blaze eye to eye. "I promise you, we were there for him yesterday, and we are here for him now. Dan is safe with us. He is family, and he belongs. We won't allow the general hurt him. We won't let him fall."

Blaze nodded, accepting Jon's impassioned vow. *Blondie will be safe with this team … they'll cover his six … that is if the kid is really with TRF and not on some damned black ops mission.* Blaze decided to keep the last bit to himself for now since it was only conjecture. He allowed a small smile to cross his face as he remembered what Blondie said before he started his nap, as Jon called it—Blondie knew it too.

His thoughts halted as Jon stood and offered a hand to him and said, "You know, it's weird, but I have this unsettled feeling I can't quiet. It's screaming there's something more going on here than a crappy father. We've been gone quite a while. Ready to go back and figure out what the hell is going on before it harms Dan?"

Blaze nodded, grabbed Jon's hand, and rose. "My gut's been telling me something's wrong since early this morning. After hearing about what happened at the hospital, I thought that might be it, yet my gut hasn't shut up at all. I'm happy to take all the help I can get to keep the kid safe."

They headed back inside, both glad they had talked.

TRF HQ – Dispatch Desk – 10:00 a.m.

Inspector Davis arrived right after Jon and Blaze returned, and Tia escorted him into the room. She overheard him explaining he was sorry for the delay in getting to TRF. He needed to deal with another case. When she returned to her desk, she found a female waiting and holding two large bags.

The team resumed their seats as Tia reappeared at the door. "There's a woman here with things for Dan. Says she's a nurse."

Patch popped up and went to the desk following Tia. He recognized her from the night before and grinned. "Heather?"

Heather turned and smiled. "Hi, Patch, isn't it?"

He nodded.

She lifted the bags. "I was at the pharmacy picking up something for a friend when I overheard the pharmacy tech trying to figure out how to deliver these to TRF HQ sooner than two hours because Dr. Fraser put a rush on the order. Their second delivery driver is out sick, and the drugstore is backed up. I asked her who they were for, and she said, Dan Broderick. So I offered to bring them over. Why isn't Dantastic still in the hospital? He really is not well enough to be out so soon."

Patch chuckled. "Blondie hates them. No need to worry. I'll take excellent care of my brother. I've got a lot of experience with him."

Heather smiled broader, drawn to the paramedic for some reason. It might be his smile and the sound of his laugh. He possessed kind, brown eyes, and she liked his short, light-brown hair, and his physique. A real hunk!

She found herself saying, "Okay, but let me give you my number. I'm off the next three days. If you need any assistance help with Dantastic for any reason, please don't hesitate to call me."

Oh goodness, what did I just say? I never offer my number to strangers. Heather blushed as she handed over the bags. Embarrassed, she turned to leave as swiftly as she possible.

Patch stopped her as he asked, "Your number? I mean, in case I need something for Blondie." He grinned when she turned to the dispatcher's desk.

With pink heat scorching her cheeks, Heather asked the officer behind the desk, "May I borrow a pen and do have a piece of paper?"

Tia smiled and handed the requested items. She noted the mutual attraction between the two, clearly visible on both their faces. Tia wondered what might come of this chance meeting. She busied herself with nothing in particular as she covertly watched them.

Heather scribbled down her name and number and ripped off a page from the notepad. She turned and handed it to Patch. "I gotta go now. Need to deliver the things to my friend." She turned and hurried out, stopping herself from glancing back at the attractive paramedic.

Patch took the note and peered at her name. *Heather Barkley*. His grin broadened again. *She's cute! Might have to keep this number for later use.*

He refocused on the retreating woman, watching until she stepped onto the elevator and the doors closed. Pivoting, Patch headed back to the room and went directly to Blondie to start the antibiotic and antipyretic.

Moths To A Flame

37

When Patch finished administering the antipyretic, Lexa stood aside to make way for him to sit beside Dan. She wanted to stay next to Dan but she couldn't. She must pull back and strive to hide her desire to be the one taking care of Dan, so she didn't raise Nick's suspicions. Boss possessed an uncanny ability to read emotions, so she needed to be on guard. Lexa returned to her usual chair and after sitting, forced herself not to stare at Dan.

Gradually rising to consciousness, Dan's body shifted between extreme heat and cold. The fluctuating made no sense, and he wondered if he could be in the Afghanistan desert in mid-summer and the Yukon's tundra at the same time. Muted and muffled conversation he couldn't quite discern filtered in, however, the effort necessary to make sense of his environmental puzzle left him exhausted, and Dan drifted off again.

Turning his eyes from Dan, grateful for Shea's skills, Gambrill spotted the inspector standing at the entry. He waved him in, and after introducing everyone in the room, Gambrill handed the meeting over to Davis.

Having scanned the room before he entered, Davis was surprised to find Constable Broderick on a gurney. As he observed the interplay between the occupants, Davis noted the gentle care provided by the medic and Constable McKenna, and the concerned expressions on the others.

Davis found the dynamic fascinating. The injured officer appeared to draw people to him like moths to a flame. Keeping this in mind, he said, "I'll start by explaining what I discovered while investigating Donner."

As Inspector Davis relayed the facts about the accident that claimed young Sara Broderick's life, everyone paid attention. However, it was hard to listen to the tragic details surrounding the child's untimely death.

In a nebulous fog somewhere between stupor and somnolence, Dan's protective reflexes kicked in as insecurity and pain crept in. Not quite aware of his location, he woke in stealth mode. He registered a dull aching throb throughout his entire body, but mostly in his right arm, left wrist, and jaw. The constriction in his chest made it uncomfortable to breathe. His pain remained bearable if he breathed slow and shallow.

The shivery heat plaguing him, which came with a fever, meant he must've developed an infection. As he continued to take stock of his physical condition, he established an IV had been inserted in his arm, which confused him.

I left the hospital, didn't I? Did I make it to HQ? Dan laughed in his head. *Yeah, I did, though I wish I had not given the patrol officer a hard time about needing to leave. I shocked the guy when I complied with the ordered to come to TRF for debrief. Good thing someone dressed me 'cause it would be embarrassing to show up here wearing only a gown with my naked backside peeking out.*

Dan's anxiety level lowered. *I'm at HQ … I'm safe here. But where, here? The light pattern is like the briefing room, but there aren't any comfy beds in there. So, what's going on?*

Quieting his thoughts, Dan focused on the indistinct voices of several people. Some seemed familiar … others not. Dan decided it would be safest to continue pretending to be asleep until he determined who besides his team was in the room with him. Since he had been summoned for debriefing, he surmised the unfamiliar tones must belong to either an agent or inspector investigating yesterday's events.

Unbidden, his mind brought forth all the shit he endured. He took five lives, Aaron died, and he pulled out torturous memories while trying to connect with three soldiers who wished to commit suicide by cop. Two still lived, one had been too far gone. He saved a tiny, green-eyed girl wearing a polka dot dress. An image of her telling him he was safe soothed him.

Recollections of the gang war pushed in. Aaron giving him crap. Fighting Basto. Aaron saving his ass when Basto tried to kill him with his own gun. The unexpected subject. Aaron bleeding out, and he could do nothing to prevent his death. Lexa stroking his hair. Patch taking care of him in the ravine.

Patch? Did I hallucinate Patch? He was unsure. He had been in so much agony and wanted his brother. Patch always took his pain away. *Yeah, I probably hallucinated him. Patch isn't here. He is still with the unit. He wouldn't leave Blaze and Winds. Only wishful thinking on my part.*

Donner memories came next. *The demented NRB agent spewed vitriol and blamed me for his father's death. Why, and why did Donner turn the gun on himself and blow his brains out? I thought he intended to kill me.* Not ready to deal with the crap, Dan pushed those thoughts into a box and slammed the lid.

Switching gears, Dan recalled Lexa tirade at Gambrill. He registered his teammates' expressions as she yelled, and they appeared to agree with her rant. *Damn, Lexa's sexy when she's angry. A little scary too, but definitely sexy.*

Though a wreck, a total mess mentally with many terrible things to sort out, Dan determined he would be able to cope because he had a place to belong again. Yesterday morning, here with his new chosen family, had been a turning point for him ... he belonged again.

Yeah, I'll be okay. I can handle anything with the support of my brothers and sister. Whoa! Wait. Nope! Can't think of Lexa as my sister. Creepy and incestuous. We slept together—twice—and I want to again. No, definitely not a sister. Lexa is something different, better, more.

His thought from yesterday popped into his head. *Friends with benefits. Yeah, that'll do for now. Sexy Lexie is a friend and we enjoy the benefits of mutual attraction. Not the smartest thing to do with a teammate. Hope this doesn't blow up in my face.*

When Davis finished with the facts, he pulled out the picture and asked Gambrill if he should share it with the group.

Walter nodded but declined to look. He experienced the captured moment in real-time. Danny's screams and William's actions and reaction tore his heart out. He couldn't bear to view a reminder of that horrific day.

Davis handed the copy to Nick, whose sharp gasp and distressed expression set the team on edge. The photograph silently passed from Nick to Jon to Bram to Ray and to Loki—each man's face displaying a disquieting effect as they handed it to the next person.

Lexa, the last of Alpha Team to lay eyes on the image, stared intently, absorbing the raw agony and desolation exuding from Dan's eyes. Her heart ached. She began to hand it over to Blaze but stopped as she gazed at the blond man in the snapshot. His expression mirrored Dan's devastation and pain. Briefly, she wondered if it might be Donner, but Lexa discounted the first thought as her eyes registered a familiarity, but in her sleep-deprived state, she didn't connect the dots.

As she handed the print to Captain Blain, Lexa asked, "Who is the man in the photo? He is as devastated if not more than Dan ..."

The voices started to become distinct. Dan recognized Lexa and tried to focus on what she was saying, though it would be easier if he wasn't so damned cold.

"... he seems familiar," Lexa finished.

Her teammates shook their heads. So focused on the distraught image of Dan, none of them noticed anyone else in the picture.

Lexa glanced at Dan and the images merged. *No wonder he is familiar.* She made the connection as Blaze spoke.

"General Broderick," a dazed Blaze exhaled breathlessly. He didn't believe his eyes as he read utter devastation in the general's mien. In all his years in Special Forces, Blaze had never witnessed any expression other than stoic authority or coldness.

When someone mentioned his father, Dan's thoughts went wild. *Shit! They didn't call him, did they? They wouldn't do that to me, would they? The general is hard enough to deal with when I'm at one hundred percent but like this? Wait, they might've called, but he's in Kandahar. He won't come. I won't need to face him and put up with his bullshit. Whew!*

Winds snatched the photo from Blaze, and what he saw left him speechless for once in his life. His focus remained on Blondie. *The kid … aw, damn … the poor kid.*

Patch bolted out of his chair and peered over Winds's shoulder. He didn't want to wait until it was passed to him. "NO FUCKING WAY!" Viewing the total and absolute misery on the general's face overwhelmed Patch, and his legs lost the ability to hold him upright. He crashed down with a loud thump to the floor.

Blaze's and Jon's eyes met from across the table as they silently communicated. *Our guts are right.*

The cussing voice sounded so familiar to Dan. *No, it can't be Patch. Can it? I only hallucinated him in the ravine.* He chalked up the voice to an effect of his fever. *Yeah, I must be having an audible hallucination due to my fever.* But part of him dismissed the assessment, insisting it was Patch's voice, and he would recognize it anywhere. *If it is Patch, what is he doing here?*

He wanted to open his eyes to validate, but he was so drained they wouldn't obey him. So Dan relied on his ears, intrigued when a new voice, one he didn't recognize, started to speak.

Davis cleared his throat. "I'm sorry, that's a grueling photograph to view. I've reviewed many crime scene photos, but this one is by far one of the more emotionally-loaded ones I encountered. Do you need a moment, or can we move on to the suicide?"

What suicide? Oh crap, they're talking about Richard Donner. Dan steeled himself to listen; thankful no one had become aware he woke. He would have a chance to process whatever they said without having to cope with their reactions.

"So, he left an extremely detailed note," Davis continued.

"Inspector Davis, hold on a minute. You're saying he wrote a suicide note? I never knew that," Gambrill interjected.

When his godfather spoke, it confused Dan. *How could you know? It only happened last night.*

"But you were listed as the investigating officer. How could you not be aware?" Davis asked.

"Officially, I was listed, but I recused myself immediately after the accident. I couldn't be objective. Handed the case over to a junior officer—guess they didn't change the name on the file. I was too wrapped up in grief to follow the case." Gambrill paused, then asked in a manner which indicated he didn't really want the details, "So, what does the note say?"

More than confused, pieces didn't fit, and Dan realized they must be speaking about something other than Donner killing himself in his hospital room. *So what is this about? Who's suicide? Perhaps the soldier ... Garth Summers?*

Davis glanced at Constable Broderick as he hesitated a moment. "As I said, it was extremely detailed. The man was devastated by what he had done to the boy and girl. In his note, he spoke of how the girl was so young and how she deserved to live and the overwhelming guilt he felt for killing her. It went into great length about what he said to the young boy at the scene."

"My God, I didn't realize the driver spoke to Dan. I arrived with William after the first responding officer took him into custody and placed in the back of a patrol car. What did he say?" Gambrill's interest piqued but remained wary.

The miserable mix of hot and cold muddled Dan's mind, and though he wanted to pay attention, his body's natural defense to fever kicked in, and he began to shiver. Sensing a movement next to him, Dan tensed when he detected swishing sound followed by water dripping. When someone placed a cool cloth to his forehead, a barely perceptible sigh escaped.

"Blondie? Blondie, you're awake," a voice said close to his ear. "Come on, buddy, I'm well-attuned to your stealth mode. Open your eyes. There are a couple of guys who are eager to see you again. Open up, brother," Patch encouraged.

The others in the room all turned to gaze at Dan when Patch started to speak. When Dan finally got his eyelids to obey, he found eleven sets of eyes staring at him. He registered his team, Gambrill, and an unknown. He blinked several times because he couldn't believe Blaze, Winds, and Patch were all there. *Crap, the fever must be so high I'm imagining them.*

"Hey kid, you scared us bad," his mirage of Blaze said. It rose and walked towards him. It gathered him in a gentle hug and said, "I'm so sorry we lost you. Won't happen again. I won't hurt you again. I'm sorry you thought we blamed you. His death wasn't your fault—only mine. I gave you the all-clear. If anyone is to blame, it's me."

The heat of Dan's face cooled as tears dropped from Blaze's eyes and splashed on his cheeks. *Blaze is holding me? This isn't a hallucination, or is it? Do I want them to accept me so badly I conjured them?*

Unable to stop his reaction, hot liquid welled in Dan's eyes as Winds moved forward and grasped his hand.

"I'm holding tight, Blondie. Not ever letting go. I apologize for hurting you. I couldn't find the words to ease your pain, and couldn't bear to witness the agony in my brother's eyes," Winds choked out as he stared intently at Dan.

I must be hallucinating, right? "Hot, cold, hallucinating?" Dan rasped out in a dry voice.

Reaching for a water bottle and opening it, Patch responded, "Hot plus cold, yes, you have a high fever. Hallucinating? No, we *are* here, Blondie. Drink." Patch lifted the bottle, putting it up to Blondie's lips.

The cool liquid felt good as it touched his lips and slid down the back of his throat. The water and their words quenched a long aching thirst. Dan sighed as he focused on each of his brothers. Each one held his gaze, didn't shift their eyes away and smiled at him.

Do they truly not blame me? Part of him couldn't fathom the concept because he blamed himself, carried the guilt, and probably always would. But Brody had been there for him last night. He unsure how, but it seemed so real it had to be him in some form.

Blaze asked, "You doing okay, Kid?"

Dan smiled weakly, still so tired. "Missed you. Mmm okay. Hungry," and as if on cue, his stomach growled loudly. The tension broke, and light laughter filled the room.

Pulling Blondie into a gentle and careful hug again, Blaze admitted, "Missed you too, Kid. Been searching for you a long time. I'm so happy we finally found you." Blaze tried to recompose himself as he embraced Blondie, a bit embarrassed to be crying in front of the others. But real men cried—he told Blondie that years ago and he held the belief still.

Winds wiped his eyes and turned to the window, overwhelmed with emotions. *We found Blondie alive.* He worried for so long Blondie wouldn't survive Brody's death. *He said, okay. Blondie is okay, not fine.* Winds's world righted itself. *The kid is alright.* Winds vowed to protect him with his life from whatever this new threat might be. *I'm never losing him ever again. I'll not fail my little brother again.*

Davis watched Dan's eyes during the entire exchange. When West Donner's note said the boy's eyes pierced his soul, Davis wondered what the man meant. He now understood. *This guy is multifaceted and intriguing.*

The range of emotion communicated in those blue orbs is astonishing. Confusion, profound grief, hope, guilt, forgiveness, questioning, and acceptance with a sense of peace. Fascinating! Davis sat back with a slight smile on his face as Broderick's stomach announced he was hungry.

The affection Dan's old unit displayed for him warmed Nick's heart. Though he recognized the soldiers and former soldiers needed a few moments to regain control of their emotions. So, Nick said, "It's close to lunchtime. Let's take a break and order some sandwiches or something to be delivered."

When everyone agreed, Jon rose and went to talk to Tia about ordering food for everybody.

Tia was pleased Dan woke and readily agreed to take care of the lunch details. She chose to call Fire Stick Grill; aware Jarmal would send over food Dan would enjoy.

Loki skipped from the room, pulling his wallet out on the way. Stopping at the vending machines, he selected a snack for Dan before going to the breakroom fridge to grab the iced capp they bought for him earlier.

Subtle Compassion

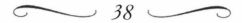 *38*

Loki, with food and drink in hand, bounded back to the room to find Patch adjusted the elevation of the gurney to place Dan in a reclining position. With a huge smile, he enthusiastically said, "Here, Dantastic, got you something to hold you over until the real food arrives."

"Thanks. Exactly what I need," Dan said softly and gazed longingly at the iced capp, eagerly anticipating the flavor and caffeine boost to help him remain awake.

Loki wondered why Dan didn't reach for the beverage but then had a *'no duh'* moment as he recalled Dan's wounds. A badly-sprained left wrist and a bullet graze on his right bicep would hinder his movements. Holding the cup, he positioned it so Dan would be able to sip from the straw.

Dan took a long drink but grimaced. He swallowed, glaring at the offending brew. "Whoa, not right, not what I expected."

Patch snickered. "Sorry, little brother, you hate decaf, but you can't have any caffeine yet. So, either put up and shut up, or I'll make sure you only get green jello and broth for lunch." Patch moved his hand, threatening to take away the snack sitting in Blondie's lap.

Dan pinned him with a *'damn you'* stare, as he said, "Yummy," in a rather sarcastic tone. He tried not to gag and shuddered a little as he swallowed another mouthful. Loki and Patch chuckled, which earned them both glares.

Patch opened the granola bar and held it up to Dan's lips. After taking a bite, Dan chewed slowly due to his aching jaw. When Patch lifted the bar again, Dan shook his head. "Thanks, but no more … a little too hard."

"Lunch should have something softer and easier to chew. Perhaps broth and lime gelatin would be better," Patch replied.

Loki glanced at the crunchy bar and back at Dan's bruised jaw. *Darn, I wasn't thinking. His jaw probably hurt a lot.* He handed the cup to Patch. "I'll go find out what Tia ordered and make sure there's something soft."

After Loki left, Dan whispered to Patch, "Don't want to be rude to Loki, but I can't drink any more of this decaf crappacino. Would rather drink bilge water."

Patch chuckled. "How about some regular water instead."

Dan nodded, and Patch assisted Dan to take a long swig.

Nick observed as the medic coaxed Dan into consuming nearly the entire bottle. Though a task he wouldn't enjoy, as Dan's sergeant, it fell to him to bring him up to date on everything. After moving to Dan's side, he addressed those still in the room, "I need to speak with Dan alone. Would you all please leave the room for a few minutes?"

Blaze shook his head. "Can't comply. Blondie's under my protection. He can't be out of my sight."

"How about a compromise? You and Winds can take up positions on the adjoining doors for this room. There's the main one and the one leading to conference room two." Nick pointed to the smaller entry by the window.

Nodding, understanding of the need to control information, Blaze directed Winds to the secondary doorway while he took up a position at the primary access. Everyone else complied, and soon only Nick and Dan remained.

Nick pulled a chair close and sat. He rubbed his hand across his eyes as he often did when gathering thoughts. Taking a moment to assess Dan's current state, Nick was unhappy with the extreme exhaustion he perceived. Dan required rest, not more turmoil, and certainly no more painful events.

Unsure why Boss cleared the room, Dan remained quiet and studied Nick, as Pastore scrutinized him. Concern reflected in his eyes, and Dan wanted to set him at ease. "I'm okay, beat up and colorful, a little feverish, but okay. Yesterday was a bitch of a day. Won't lie—many highs and lows—like swinging on a damned pendulum. I still need to process several things, but I've experienced worse days. I'm alright. Whatever it is you need to say, spit it out. I can cope."

"Oh, I don't doubt you. The fact you're sitting here is evidence. Whether I want to cause you more anguish is quite another thing," Nick returned.

Dan calmly waited as Boss made up his mind.

"First, how long were you awake? What did you hear?" Nick asked.

"Caught the last word or two of what Lexa said. Think someone said my father's name, and given Patch is actually here, he said 'no fucking way.' Whose suicide are you discussing? Pieces don't fit for it to be Donner's. Why are Blaze, Winds, and Patch here? Why am I under Blaze's protection?" Dan peppered Nick with multiple questions.

Nick liked how fast Dan assessed the situation. "It is Donner's suicide, only a different Donner."

"Huh? I don't follow."

"This is related to what happened last night. I'm sorry they used you as bait. If we'd known anything about their plans, agent Donner wouldn't have gotten within one hundred yards of you." Nick rested a hand on Dan's forearm, communicating the veracity of his statement.

He then proceeded to fill Dan in on events transpiring after his last radio communique, being careful to leave out details that might influence Dan's testimony as a subject officer. Nick concluded, "This is the reason why your buddies are here, and we are currently meeting with Inspector Davis."

Stunned with more to process, but for a change, some of what he learned was pleasant. *My unit brothers and Alpha went above and beyond for me.* Their actions filled him with a greater sense of belonging and warmth.

"So, is this something you want to hear, or would you rather sit this one out? If you're not up to this now, we can apprise you later of any details revealed which shed light on the 'new situation' requiring you to have watchdogs," Nick offered.

Dan weighed his options. Sara's death hit him hard, and most events occurring afterward were blurred. Learning the driver responsible for her death killed himself, and the NRB agent was his son still didn't answer why he became Richard's target. *We were both kids when the accident occurred.*

Though what Donner did in the interviews made some weird twisted sense, the man hated him for some reason. Dick wanted to inflict pain and mental anguish—and he had. Dan understood the possible motivation, but it didn't make it easier to accept what the bastard did. He would need to work on forgiving Donner or at least tucking this event away.

Perhaps the father's suicide note will help me to understand Donner's mindset. "I need to listen to the rest. Don't think it will be easy, but doing so might help me comprehend why Donner targeted me." As Richard's words rang in his mind, the weight of Aaron's death hit Dan again, and he lowered his gaze.

Nick placed his hand under Dan's chin, gripped gently, and tilted his head up, so their eyes met. Nick firmly stated, "Okay, but I need you to give me your word, if this becomes too much for you, tell me, and we'll stop. We're here for you. You don't have to face any of this alone."

"Promise," Dan murmured.

Nick was unsure if Dan's response was an answer or a question. *Did Dan promise to tell me, or ask me if I'm serious about him not being alone?* Nick softly smiled. "Promise." He glimpsed the slight grin and realized Dan's response had been a bit of both and his reply helped Dan.

He stood and went to the door to call everyone back inside. Nick still believed this undertaking might be too stressful for Dan so soon after yesterday, but he would abide by Dan's wishes. When he exited the briefing room, Nick discovered the food arrived during the interim.

Ottawa – National Defense HQ – Naval Intelligence – 12:10 p.m.

Eating lunch at his desk, Marquise set his sandwich down, surprised by what Jarmal shared with him. "Hang on, bro, there's someone who needs to hear this." He got up and hurried to Lieutenant Broderick's office and knocked.

Scott called out, "Enter."

Opening the door, Marquise met Scott's gaze. "Sir, I have news about your cousin." He closed the door and strode over to the lieutenant's desk and put his cell phone on speaker. "Okay, Jarmal, repeat what you told me."

As he listened, Scott's stomach dropped when he found out Dan had been injured. When Jarmal finished, Scott said, "Thanks for the information."

After Marquise left his office, Scott dialed his father, hoping he answered. He needed to fill him in, and would also suggest they move up the Broderick intervention. Danny needed his family now more than ever. Relief surged as his dad picked up, and he launched into the tale.

TRF HQ – Briefing Room – 12:15 p.m.

Everyone reentered the briefing room carrying bags of food delivered from the Fire Stick Grill. As they all gathered around the table to eat, Bram, Patch, and Blaze helped move Dan into a chair.

While Nick spoke with Dan alone, the guys decided to keep the lunch conversation light and fun. Jon started by sharing a story about how his son Joey decided he was a superhero and refused to take a bath because he believed it would wash away his powers.

Winds grinned when Jon finished and switched topics as he said, "Flippin' fantastic to see Jarmal again. Blondie, did you know he settled here?"

Dan nodded. "Yeah, I've eaten at his place a lot."

Patch grinned at the soft cookies included. "I'll be visiting his place often. He did amazing things for us while in Kandahar. Glad he followed his dream to open a restaurant."

Blaze nodded, but changed the subject, aware going further down this path would raise bad memories for Blondie. He brought up hockey, and a debate over which team would win the Stanley Cup this year ensued.

Dan sat quietly, listening. The move from the gurney to the table, even such a short distance, sapped him of what little strength he possessed, and although hungry, he found it difficult to eat.

His braced left hand was useless, his right arm hurt to move, and his jaw ached too much to chew. Added to the mix, the miserable hot-cold fluctuations of a fever always affected his appetite. So, he picked at his food, mostly munching on the soft oatmeal raisin walnut cookies Jarmal included.

Lexa noticed Dan wincing as he moved his arm and chewed. The poor guy didn't appear to be eating much, likely due to the pain, fever, and fatigue he must be experiencing. She wondered how Dan would react if she tried to help him. From all she knew of him, he didn't like appearing weak. He probably wouldn't appreciate any overt assistance. So, Lexa inconspicuously set aside a selection of soft foods for him to snack on later if he got hungry.

Lunch was a long, slow affair. Everyone stole glances at Dan and noticed how sluggishly he consumed his food and, without verbal agreement, chose to prolong the meal, allowing him sufficient time to satisfy his hunger in an unhurried fashion.

Dan peered at Patch, who sat next to him. He hated to ask, this part always bothered him, but he required help. He leaned a little closer to his brother and whispered, "I gotta take a leak."

Patch nodded and murmured, "Can you walk?"

Lowering his gaze to his lap, Dan answered honestly, "Exhausted, would probably face plant on my own."

"I got ya." Eyeing Bram, an image of Mason entered Patch's mind. The way Bram talked about his little girls, and the fact Blondie stayed with him several times, gave Patch the impression De Haven might be a caretaker like Mason. "Bram, can you give me a hand?"

Glancing up as Patch started taking the saline bag off the pole they rigged, Bram comprehended the situation but asked, "Sure, what you need?"

"We need to take a little trip. Can you spot Blondie? I won't allow him to walk alone in his condition."

Dan appreciated the way Patch phrased his comment—didn't make him appear weak in front of the others.

After Bram pulled out his chair, Dan managed to rise without groaning as every aching muscle protested the movement. Bram remained right beside him.

Bram, and no doubt everyone else noticed the effort it took Dan to move. *Damn, he must be in a lot of pain.* Bram considered how he might assist Dan to the bathroom without inflicting more and not causing him embarrassment.

Loki, also aware of the enormous effort Dan used to stand, swiveled in his chair and called out playfully, "Hey, Dantastic, why don't you sit back down? Our seats make awesome race chairs. Let's race to the restroom and back. Ray can push me while Bram pushes you. I'll win, of course. Ray and I hold the championship title against Sean and Heath."

Jon chuckled. "Yeah, and you four got extra duty for your little escapade. Remember?"

Dan recalled their exploits. The race occurred several months ago and ended with one broken chair and all four guys on the floor laughing. Jon hadn't been too happy with them.

"Sorry, Bram's faster than Ray, and racing's in my blood. We'd take your trophy away." Dan responded with a slight smile—all he could manage without reopening his split lip again. As he took a painful step, Dan failed to conceal a grimace.

Loki piped up again, "No way, I would win. Perhaps Bram should take you on a practice lap before we race since me and Ray gots more experience. Otherwise, it won't be fair." Loki brightened as he spied the small upturn of Dan's lips.

Dan took one more agonizing step determined not to appear weak. He glanced at Bram, and his blue-green eyes only showed compassion.

Bram grinned at Dan before he pushed the wheeled chair behind him and held the seat steady. His eyes flicked the chair. "Practice lap sounds like an excellent idea."

His pride be damned, Dan conceded he would never make it to the restroom under his own power. Bit by bit, he sank to the comfortable cushion, as Bram whispered, "Smart choice."

As Bram pushed Dan out of the room with Patch next to him holding the IV bags, Ray patted Loki's back. "Awesome job."

Loki beamed at all the nods of approval he got from Boss, Jon, Lexa, and the commander. He especially liked the grins directed at him from Blaze and Winds. Loki believed he was beginning to understand Dan more. To save face, Dan would've walked although it caused him significant pain. Luckily, he found a way to help Dan by using a humorous approach, and Loki determined to use the method in the future if needed.

If A Picture Could Scream

 *39*

July 16
TRF HQ — Briefing Room — 2:00 p.m.

As Bram wheeled Dan back into the conference room, Blaze glanced at his watch. *Where the hell did the time go?* "It's fourteen hundred hours, only four hours until General Broderick arrives. We better wrap this up so Gambrill can brief us on known details."

Dan's head snapped up. "The general's coming? Here? Now? Why?" Dan croaked with bewilderment plastered on his face.

"Pastore, I thought you told him everything?" Blaze queried.

"My apologies. Guess I forgot one thing. Dan, your father is en route. He'll be here at six o'clock. Apparently, he possesses additional information which can only be communicated in person," Nick said.

"Roger," Dan retorted as his body unconsciously shifted into a more rigid posture.

They all caught the military acknowledgment and noted his more erect bearing and the stoic mask which dropped into place.

Davis inquired, "Are we ready to start?" He directed his gaze at Dan, waiting for his response alone. When he received a slight nod, he said, "Before we broke for lunch, I indicated to the others that Donner's suicide note is quite detailed. I can summarize, or you may review the detail if you wish."

"I'll read." Dan believed it would be easier to process the contents if he read the note himself.

The group remained quiet as Dan reviewed West's missive. They expected to witness sadness or perhaps sympathy for the man who committed suicide. None of them expected Dan's utterly traumatized and confused expression as he mumbled, "No, no this can't be right. No, the general said that! No! God no. He said …"

After he finished reading, a wounded and lost little boy peered up at Gambrill. Dan's voice trembled. "This isn't right, it's wrong. The general ... he yelled them at me ... dressed me down ... he ... no, no ... this is so wrong ..."

The expression on Dan's face scared Gambrill immensely. He reached for the paper, needing to find out what turned Dan into the traumatized nine-year-old boy he'd seen the day Sara died.

Dan laid his head on the table, he ignored—or more correctly, never felt—the physical pain as his arms encircled the back of his skull, protecting himself. His whole body began to shake uncontrollably as a surreal, agonizing howling scream broke free and wouldn't stop as long-ago memories resonated in his mind, and he became aware of the truth of that day.

Bodies frozen in place by Dan's reaction, all eyes turned to Gambrill.

As Walter read the letter, his expression of horror slowly transformed into astonishment. He whipped out his phone and dialed a number, and when the call connected, he shouted, "I FOUND THE KEY. IT'S BEEN UNDER OUR NOSES FOR YEARS. DAMMIT, WHY DIDN'T I EVER LOOK? WE CAN REACH DANNY NOW. THERE'S HOPE. COME STRAIGHT HERE. I'LL KEEP HIM SAFE UNTIL YOU ARRIVE."

General Broderick overheard an ungodly scream in the background. His heart shattered as he recognized his son's voice. Though he missed the first part of what Walter said, he bellowed into the satellite phone, "WHAT THE HELL HAPPENED?"

"Sara ... it has to do with Sara. I need you here as fast as possible. I have the last piece of the puzzle in my hands. Will, there is real hope," Walter explained cryptically, but the line went dead as the signal dropped.

Angry the connection failed, Gambrill went into action. The rest of the TRF didn't need to witness Danny's distress. He moved towards Dan as he yelled, "EVERYONE OUT NOW, SEAL THE DOORS!"

The only one who left was Davis—actually, Jon and Winds forced the inspector out the doorway. The others refused to leave. Nick hit the button to shut the main door and turn the glass opaque as Dan's howling continued unabated.

Military Aircraft En Route to Toronto – (2:10 p.m. Toronto)

The imperturbable General Broderick strode up and down the center of the plane. After the call dropped and he tried unsuccessfully to connect with Walter again, he bellowed and demanded until he became hoarse for the pilots to move quicker. They shaved off some time, but not near enough to appease him. The howling screams reverberated in William's ears and mind. Shrieks like those he never wanted to experience again.

Daniel needed him, but like so many times, William was too damned far away. This time he vowed not to fail his son! Come hell or high water, he would reach Daniel this time and make things right.

Many of the men who lined the sides of the aircraft were scared shitless and sat stock still, endeavoring to avoid being noticed as the general thundered past them. The short call, in which he only asked what happened, turned the man into a total raving maniac. If looks could kill, their pilots would be dead for telling him they couldn't go any faster. Many soldiers wished their destination was closer if only to be out of striking distance of this livid, fuming general.

Corporal Stefano Xenos surreptitiously eyed one brave soul who ventured to communicate with General Broderick. In awe, and frankly a bit thrilled by General Badass's behavior, Stefano now understood how the fierce man earned his nickname. The Special Forces general exuded power, and Stefano couldn't wait to participate in the selection process. Without a doubt, he would make the cut, and this authoritative, inspiring general would soon be his commander. Stefano respected men of the general's caliber, believing the military required hard-wearing and decisive leaders.

Master Corporal Karla Weeks had never seen her superior come unglued like this in all the years she worked in his office. The call truly upset his apple cart. She went into action, trying to facilitate a faster arrival for him to the TRF headquarters in Toronto.

With no fear, aware this had something to do with his son, Karla approached him and said, "Sir, the captain informed me we are at max speed, and he received clearance to land at Toronto International instead of Ottawa. I arranged for a helicopter to be waiting upon our arrival to take you to your destination after landing. Sir, you'll be there in two hours, tops. Please try to calm yourself. There's nothing more we can do."

Corporal Tristan Parsons glanced at his friend Stefano and whispered, "The master corporal must have a death wish. She told a general to calm down."

Stefano shrugged. "She's got guts that's for sure—not a shy, demure creature. She reminds me of my twin sister Cassandra."

Tristen nodded. "Still, I wonder what set him off. He's damned scary if you ask me."

"No clue, but whatever it is, it's gotta be important. I can't wait until we make to Special Forces. Rumor has it they're opening more slots than usual in the next few rounds. I'm positive we're both gonna make it," Stefano stated.

Giving his buddy a slight grin, Tristen wondered if he should drop out ... Broderick as a commanding officer, might be a bit too much for him. But then again, he dreamed of making JTF2 since he was only a boy, and his family would be proud if he achieved his goal.

Sergeant Blake Murphy sat near the back, staring at General Broderick, captivated by the caged lion. He smirked. *It must be something to do with his asinine son. Plouffe is right ... the asshat is the only thing that makes Broderick lose his cool.* Murphy smiled; aware he would earn kudos for reporting this and couldn't wait to contact Plouffe.

Corporal Cody Merrill studied his superior's uncharacteristic unabated rage. He questioned whether another unit had been lured into an ambush, which occurred too frequently recently. The intel they relied on appeared to be wrong and was taking a toll on the units.

Upset they would not be landing in Ottawa, Merrill's thoughts turned to personal matters. The change in destination crimped his last-minute plans. When tagged to accompany Broderick home, he accepted an offer for his hobby. The only problem was the bobble-head was in Montreal—so going to Toronto instead of Ottawa would put a kibosh on him getting his bobble-head. Now he must decline the offer or at least postpone getting it, if possible.

Although William attempted to relax, he couldn't, so he continued pacing. Two hours was too long. He needed to be there now. Daniel needed him now. *Gambrill said there is hope—he has the key to the last piece of the puzzle. Good God, please let there be hope. Let me finally be able to right my wrongs. Please ... I need my boy back.*

TRF HQ – Inside Briefing Room – 2:30 p.m.

The initial onslaught of sound reverberated in the room—nothing anyone said or did penetrated the barrier trapping Dan. Everyone feared for Dan's sanity, and after five minutes of gut-wrenching howling, Patch made a frantic call to Dr. Fraser requesting a fast-acting sedative be rushed over.

Ten minutes passed since, and although Dan's howls shifted to a lower keening, his body continued to shake violently. Patch worried how much more Blondie could take physically. His blood pressure, heart rate, and breathing increased significantly, and his temperature spiked.

A loud knocking at the side door drew Patch's attention. He rushed to the entry and cracked it open. He found Tia, her face pale and expression concerned, holding a bag. She shoved the package at him before closing the portal. Patched raced back to Blondie and administered the sedative via the IV.

Within a minute, dead quiet filled the space. Blondie's body still shook. Patch placed the cause of that on aftereffects of the emotional upheaval and raging fever. He blew out a breath, relieved the heart-ripping sounds stopped. The only other time he heard the soul-shredding noise had been after Blondie discovered Brody's body. That day, if Nils hadn't been there, they would've lost Blondie too.

Although in medic mode, Patch had not been able to tune out his empathetic connection with Blondie. After six years keeping him alive, the bond had rooted in his soul. When Blondie hurt, Patch hurt almost as much. He sank into the chair, wholly spent.

Blaze took a deep breath as silence descended. He watched Patch as closely as Blondie. Aware the kid's desolate cries for the past fifteen minutes completely drained Patch, Blaze understood he must provide support. He moved forward and lay a hand on Patch's back. "How are his vitals?"

The solid and warm hand on his back calmed Patch. He drew strength from his former leader as he inhaled and regained his composure. Patch checked Blondie's vitals. "Still in the toilet, but improving. His pulse and respiration are slowing, and pressure is lowering. We should move him back to the gurney. His current position isn't great for breathing, given his ribs."

Jon, Bram, and Loki came forward to assist Blaze and Patch in moving Dan. Lexa covered him with the blanket and tucked it snugly around him as the room breathed a collective sigh.

TRF HQ – Outside Briefing Room – 2:40 p.m.

Tia sat at her desk and wiped the tears gathered in her eyes. The last twenty minutes had been horrible. The lobby was eerily silent now after the onslaught of Dan's screams.

When his screams started, she'd been alarmed and began to run to the conference room, along with members of other teams, prepared to help with the emergency. All were shocked when Inspector Davis was roughly thrust out, and the doors swiftly sealed.

The howling was disturbing—even muted by the walls. She and the others had no clue what the hell happened. Too excruciating to listen to, Charlie Team rapidly left when they got a critical call. Sergeant Winter ushered Echo out to the gun range, aware Alpha would handle the issue. That left only her and Davis outside the room.

In somewhat of a state of shock, Tia wished she could've left too, but she remained at her post and endured Dan's anguish.

When a paramedic rushed in with a packet saying it was for Broderick, she immediately took it and ran to the ancillary door and knocked as loud as possible, hoping to be heard over the heart-wrenching sounds.

She stood staring at the briefing room until the noises stopped. Then she turned and headed back to her desk. That's when Tia's tears made a path down her face. Regaining some semblance of control, she brushed away the liquid as a small shudder coursed through her body. She wondered what happened and hoped Dan would be okay.

Inspector Davis slumped into one of the chairs in the waiting area and tried to tune out the terrible sound after they impolitely shoved him out. Distraught, he never in his wildest dreams thought Broderick would react in such a manner. He only wanted to help, not hurt him.

If a picture could scream—that's exactly what Davis imagined the one of the little, blue-eyed boy would've sounded like. *Hell, it is that little boy—only nineteen years later.* Immovable now, Davis thanked God the unholy shrieking ceased, and he prayed the young man would be alright.

The Devil's Toy

 *40*

July 16
Grand Citadel Hotel — Lobby — 2:45 p.m.

Finding himself ousted from free room and board, a tired and irritated, Major Nigel Plouffe stood at the front desk, waiting impatiently for the idiot receptionist to check him in. Assuming his brother David would offer him the use of the guestroom at his house, Nigel had made no other arrangements.

He grew incensed when informed Aaron's fiancée would occupy the spare room. David displaced blood and opened his home to a stupid twit. Christ, the girl blubbered nonstop, but he covered his true feelings, played the concerned uncle, and let the witless woman cry on his shoulder for hours.

Perhaps it was for the best, not staying at the house. He needed space and privacy to figure some things out. When he discovered Dan Broderick was in the ravine when Aaron died, he barely controlled his rage. The Brodericks continually fucked with his life … and now caused the death of his nephew … an unforgivable deed.

Growing exasperated with the man's incompetence, Nigel glared at the inept receptionist, which seemed to distract and further fluster him. Turning away, he scanned the opulent surroundings. He deserved to stay in a hotel of this quality.

A splurge, yes, but if anyone asked why he stayed, he would discount the expenditure to grief and need. Being so distraught over Aaron's death and the unanticipated boot from his brother's home, he picked the first hotel on the website. No one would question him spending this much money.

His sorrow was real. Aaron had been the only one in the entire family worth a damn. As a boy, Aaron would sit and listen to his stories with awe. Learning from Aaron that Broderick joined TRF pissed Nigel off at first, but he found a way to use the knowledge to his advantage—via Aaron.

Nigel filled Aaron with vitriolic crap about Dan to ensure his nephew would make life at TRF untenable, and the toy soldier would return to the military. Thanks to Merrill, he gained information about the fast path the general created for his son's reinstatement to JTF2. Plouffe missed being able to manipulate his plaything and desired the younger Broderick back under his control.

But not now. Aaron died, and William's spawn was no longer an innocent pawn in his crusade against his rival. Now Nigel would knock his toy over for good. There wouldn't be another miraculous recovery for the general's mutant offspring.

The receptionist punched more keys and glanced at the major again. Nothing he tried worked. Every time Percy entered in an available room into the computer, the number changed and assigned the major to a room they only rented out to select clientele.

Percy was unsure why they even designated a room with this number. They didn't have a thirteenth floor—it went twelfth floor, concierge floor, and then the fourteenth floor, so they shouldn't have this room number, but they did. Percy mumbled, "God preserve me, not that room again." Percy typed another number and pressed enter for the sixth time.

Getting fed up at the long wait, Plouffe growled, "What's the issue here? Just assign me a damned room."

Swallowing hard, the skittish, thin man glanced up at the scary major through his heavy, black plastic glasses. "Sir, I'm trying, but it keeps changing the room to one we rarely ever use."

"I don't give a damn about the numbers. Just check me in," Plouffe commanded harshly.

Shaking his head, Percy said, "But, sir … it's room six sixty-six."

Plouffe snorted. "Assign the goddamned room. I'm not some superstitious pansy-assed idiot with hexakosioihexekontahexaphobia."

Percy did as instructed and assigned room 666 to Plouffe. He crossed himself before picking up the programmed room cards, placing them in the hotel's embossed sleeve, and handing to the guest. "Um, I'm truly sorry about this. Enjoy your stay with us, sir. If you need anything, please ask."

Nigel grabbed the packet from the weak-minded man and strode towards the elevators. *This world was full of idiots.*

TRF HQ – Inside Briefing Room – 2:50 p.m.

Although the wailing ceased, the ears of those inside the conference room still reverberated. Sorrow permeated the room as each strove to process their emotions after witnessing such an alarming episode. All but one, wondering what in the note had been the catalyst for Dan's reaction.

Walter remained at Danny's side the entire time. Unable to break through, like that fateful day nineteen years ago, he stood lightly patting Dan's back. Memories from the past mingled with the present. Often envisioning the little boy sitting here rather than the full-grown man, Walter fervently hoped this would be cathartic instead of hurtful.

Nick picked up the photograph of Dan and stared at the image again as tension and worry grew. He imagined Dan's scream as an echo of that day. This hit Nick deep. In some ways, it reminded him of the one he released when he found Martin's bullet-ridden body under Janie's. Anger boiled just below his surface. *Son of a bitch, this is precisely what I didn't want to happen. I caused Dan more hurt. What is this all about? How can I ... we help?*

Jon and Blaze continued to bloody their fists, punching the concrete walls in their frustration and inability to cut through the barrier to rescue Dan from his torment. After helping put Dan on the gurney, they resumed storming back and forth, both endeavoring to dissipate the fury of helplessness engulfing them.

Winds remained frozen in his place the entire time. He stood staring out the window, dead silent and unresponsive. *This all too much for my brother. Did Blondie just lose the last piece of his soul? Is this what it sounds like when the body lives, but the soul dies? Did the fucking general finally succeed in killing his son in the worst way possible?*

Lexa sought out Bram's arms for fatherly comfort during the screaming. It crushed and shattered her heart. She screamed like that into her pillow after her mother died. She couldn't bear to view Dan in so much pain. In the past twenty-four hours, he waded through hell and came out smiling.

For him to be laid low now by mere written words confused her. Lexa couldn't fathom what caused his agonizing reaction. After covering him with the blanket and tucking him in, she stood beside Dan, unconsciously stroking his sun-kissed hair as she gazed sightlessly out the glass pane.

Bram drew strength and solace for himself by helping at least one of his teammates as he embraced Lexa. He wracked his brain, desperate to figure out something or some words which might help Dan. When Lexa released her hold on him, he assisted the others in moving Dan to the gurney.

Though well-aware Dan possessed a wounded soul, Bram never imagined his suffering to be so profound. He wondered how much Dan could take. Bram walked to the table and picked up the file folder and discovered other pictures inside. As he flipped through then, Bram found one of a lovely, blonde-headed, green-eyed girl with a beautiful smile. *So, this is your Sara—you have the same smile.* Bram didn't notice the tears sliding down his cheeks as he stared at the cute little girl and grief for a life lost filled him.

Loki pulled a chair next to Dan's bed, sat down, and refused to release his teammate's hand. Silently, he repeatedly told Dan that he wouldn't let go. Deep concern and a bit of fear etched themselves on Loki's features.

Ray placed his hands onto Loki's shoulders; offering added strength to his distraught best friend. He perceived Loki verged on the edge. Dan's howling unsettled him also. The contents of the suicide note hit Dan at the core of his being. Ray wished to take away his brother's distress and pain.

Ottawa — Naval Staff HQ — Commander Broderick's Office — 1500 Hours

Commander Erik Broderick peered up as his aide entered his office, and waited until the sailor came to a stop before he asked, "Have you had any luck with contacting Lieutenant Collins yet?"

"No, sir. They arrived in port last night, and he has a two-day leave."

Erik nodded and noted the folder in the young man's hand. "Okay, try again in about a half-hour. What do you have for me?"

"The paperwork you requested to authorize emergency leave for Able Seaman Kyle Broderick. I took the liberty to fill out almost everything. All it requires is the dates and your signature, sir." He handed over the file.

"Thank you, that's all for now." Erik opened the folio. He wanted everything in order in case he must override Kyle's CO. The man continued to be on a power trip, which forced Kyle to put up with a lot of shit from him in the past few months. Although he preferred to allow his youngest son to fight his own battles, and Kyle desired it that way too, this time, Erik would gladly use his authority to secure Kyle's leave if necessary. Scott's call a few hours ago sharing the news of Dan's injuries might necessitate the uninvited actions.

Trying to reach Will, but failing, Erik contacted Colonel Sutton. Relieved his elder brother was en route to Toronto, Erik decided to wait until later tonight before contacting Will. This interlude would give Will a chance to check on Danny and assess his needs. Once the essentials were covered, they would determine the right time for all the Broderick men to show up.

Of the cousins, only Kyle and Jeff had not secured leave yet. Kyle, because of his CO being an ass. Jeff, due to being unreachable while in the field on maneuvers with his latest group of recruits. Erik glanced at his clock. *Mark will be finished with his conference in an hour or so.* He needed to phone his second eldest brother to bring him up to speed so Mark could contact his son Jeff in person if required.

Erik dialed his younger brother, and when it connected, he said, "Ryan, glad I caught you. I know you're busy. I won't keep you long. The timeframe to visit Danny might need to change. Scott called me earlier, and you're not going to believe what's happened to Danny now."

Grand Citadel Hotel – Room 666 – 3:10 p.m.

Plouffe slammed his laptop closed. "Fucking idiot!"

Nigel prided himself on how he kept his hands clean. No one could trace anything back to him—ever. He was too smart, but Pletcher just laid a trail of breadcrumbs to his door. He fouled up by not using the encryption key when he sent the wire transfer to his account.

If he had not needed Pletcher's contacts years ago, he would've dissolved their partnership. Jorge screwed up in his attempt to dispatch Becca. *How in the world could Pletcher bollix eliminating a ditzy, air-headed, party girl? He should've strangled her to death after screwing her—but no, Jorge wanted to make it appear like an accident, so he took her to France—idiocy!*

Jorge messed up a second time when he left his burner phone out, and Becca snooped and found Plouffe's text, offering him money to exterminate her. *Damned good thing, the phone can't be traced back to me, and the signals bounced through so many tower nodes it would be near impossible to locate the origin.* He destroyed that phone and gotten another one since then.

High and mighty General Broderick will never in his lifetime figure out who made his life hell. Nigel enjoyed making Broderick pay for messing up all his plans—slowly, painfully, many times, and in many ways. Now the general was not the only one who would pay.

Up until yesterday, Daniel Broderick had been only a tool used to hurt his adversary, but not now. *No, now my toy must die. He is no longer innocent … he's the reason my nephew is dead.*

Needing assurance Daniel Broderick would be dead soon, Plouffe texted Pletcher again. **Make the toy soldier your priority.**

The reply came back fast. **No, too hot.**

Nigel typed again. **I want my plaything dead before funeral.**

Pletcher responded. **Not happening. Need to lay low. Galloway is hot on my heels.**

Plouffe fumed and chucked his phone at the wall. "Goddamned, Pletcher!"

He knew Pletcher was not fully under his control—in it for the money only. Now Plouffe must figure out how to finish them off because all his minions were in Kandahar at this time. There was no way to get them here without raising questions. *Dammit!*

As Nigel realized he wouldn't be able to kill the damned toy soldier before the funeral, he flipped over the table, sending the contents flying and scattering across the floor. In his fit of rage, Plouffe didn't notice the sheet of paper that floated under the dresser. If he had, he would've retrieved it instantly.

Puzzle Pieces

41

Everyone remained quiet for quite some time, soothing silence preferable to any sound and anything anyone might say. Winds finally broke out of his near-catatonic state. He turned and aggressively stepped toward Gambrill.

His voice of barely containing his rage, Winds growled, "You damn well better explain something to us now, or I'll be doing some serious bodily harm to the damned general to extract the information when he arrives. I assume that's who you called. You know something about this. I know the general—he'll never explain. So if you want him to live, you'll explain. NOW!"

Hoping the emotional outburst wouldn't require them to intervene to protect General Broderick, all faces ping-ponged between Winds and Gambrill, waiting for the commander to respond.

Walter expelled a weary sigh as he dropped to a chair. He read and reread the note. *It truly is the key, the final piece of the puzzle.* Now upset with himself for not following up on the investigation back then, he spoke, his voice reflective of his emotional turmoil, "It isn't for me to share... but"

Having missed the softly-spoken 'but,' Blaze flared red hot indicative of his nickname. "I DON'T CARE IF IT'S FOR YOU TO SHARE, TELL ME NOW, OR THE GENERAL WON'T BE THE ONLY CORPSE IN THIS ROOM."

"Let the man talk," Jon said as he placed his hand on Blaze's shoulder and lightly squeezed. For the first time, he noted the dried blood on his knuckles. *Damn, punching the concrete wall was stupid. At least I didn't bust my hands.*

The touch and simple words banked the fire in Blaze enough for him to rein in his fury and find the ability to walk to the far corner of the conference room, a safe distance from Gambrill. He leaned against the wall before sinking to his haunches. Jon joined Blaze in a symbolic gesture to their earlier connection.

Gambrill silently sat a moment longer, determining how to explain. "I'm not sure where to start. The whole affair is messy and confusing because human emotions are involved, so it might be best if I begin with a problem statement and try to tie everything back to it."

He scanned the concerned faces for an acknowledgment before starting again. "Simply stated, the problem is … Dan thinks his family, especially his father, forsook him. He believes William only ever wanted him to be a perfect soldier, not a son. Danny also believes his dad holds him responsible for Sara's death, and the entire family shunned him for failing to protect Sara. He thinks he's an outcast, and unworthy of his family's love.

"William's and Dan's relationship over the past nineteen years can be described as one misstep after another. Each tried, in their own way, to fix this, to prove something, but nothing ever worked. Every damned time something went wrong, and they end up further apart."

He paused, giving them time to register his words. "William believes events surrounding Sara's passing are all part of a complex puzzle, but he couldn't find the missing piece. He is aware of how his failures contributed to this debacle, but never understood how certain ideas got into Dan's head. Horrible notions which are unaccounted for by any of Williams's previous words or deeds."

Taking several breaths, Walter controlled his emotions. "I've always believed if we unlocked the mystery, the how or why, William and Daniel would, at long last, be able to mend their relationship. The suicide note gives insight into the final unknown pieces of this damned puzzle.

"I think when Dan read the note, his adult brain recognized the fallacies his nine-year-old mind latched onto and convoluted. I believe what we witnessed is his anguish at comprehending the years lost living under misconceptions. I hope when Danny awakens, he understands the truth."

His tone still a bit shaky, but also now hopeful, Walter stated, "If he now recognizes what actually occurred, Danny might be able to release the heartache he's lived with under the false perception his family rejected him, deemed him unworthy, and held him responsible for Sara's death. There is hope now for father and son to reconcile, for Yvonne to get her boy back, and for Danny to accept the embrace and love of his whole family."

Gambrill paused, unsure what else to relay.

Turning and focusing her eyes on the commander, Lexa said, "If we're going to help Dan, we need to understand the full puzzle."

Walter grabbed a water bottle, opened it, and took a sip before he answered. "Okay, I'll do my best. Let's start with the pieces William is confident are part of the problem—his actions. As I told you, he is a hard man, but he was never cruel."

Blaze, Winds, and Patch all grunted, their expressions reflecting their disgust and disagreement with Gambrill's statement. From their experience, without a doubt, that was a fucking lie. They witnessed the cruelty first-hand, but for the moment, each man chose to keep his mouth shut.

Walter studied Dan's old unit buddies, confused by their reactions. "After the accident, William became fully aware his parental errors contributed to the alienation. He should've never insisted Dan address him as sir, drilled him to follow orders, and dealt with the boy in the manner he did when Danny didn't meet his rigorously high expectations.

"William always expected Danny to behave in an adult manner, even as a child. When Dan erred, the only acceptable responses were 'Yes, sir,' 'No, sir,' 'I'm sorry, sir,' 'My fault, sir,' 'Won't happen again, sir,' or any combination. By the time William recognized his folly, certain behaviors had become so ingrained in Danny they wouldn't change.

"To this day, Dan only addresses William as sir or general. He always takes responsibility when things go wrong. Even if it isn't his fault, Dan thinks he could've or should've done something to change the outcome, and repeating a mistake is tantamount to failure. Sadly, William also successfully embedded in Dan's psyche that he must always follow direct orders from a superior."

Nick nodded. He bore witness to those ingrained behaviors, but he asked, "How did General Broderick determine those are pieces of the puzzle?"

"By how Danny reacted after the accident. When I found out what occurred, I went to William's home to inform him. Yvonne collapsed upon hearing the news. Luckily, her sister Ann took charge of Yvonne and Becca so William could go to Danny. The ambulance pulled up to their house to take Yvonne to the hospital as he and I left.

"When we arrived, the horrific scene greeting us devastated William. His beautiful Sara dead … sprawled on the ground covered in blood. His beloved Danny, covered in Sara's blood, one hand holding onto Sara, and the other clutching her shoes to his chest. Danny howled as he did today, but also screamed Sara's name repeatedly."

After taking several calming breaths, Walter regained his self-control. "The first officer to respond told us Danny had been screaming for about twenty minutes and wouldn't allow anyone near Sara. No one could penetrate his grief. As William approached Danny, a photographer snapped that godawful picture." His finger pointed to the one they viewed earlier.

"William's always been protective of his family and didn't want his son photographed in such torment. Outraged by the man's total lack of compassion, he cold-cocked the guy with one punch. Before going to Danny, he knelt beside Sara, stroked her hair, kissed her forehead, and whispered something to her." Gambrill sat silently, absorbed in the terrible memory.

A soft gasp escaped from Lexa. "Dan made those same motions with Sara Clarry yesterday."

The team all nodded.

Gambrill started again, "William went to Danny, who was still shrieking and holding onto his little sister's hand and shoes. William tried everything to break through and calm his boy. He pleaded so many ways using soft words. William was crying himself—unheard of for him in public. This hit William so powerfully he couldn't control his emotions when faced with his son's anguish and daughter's death. Danny wouldn't release Sara or allow William to embrace him. The only touch he allowed was when his father stroked his hair."

Lexa peered down at her hand as she deftly ran her fingers through Dan's short locks. Something deep inside she hadn't been aware of must've known this motion would comfort Dan. Wanting to give him solace, she continued to caress him.

"After trying with no success for God knows how long—it felt like forever—William resorted to the last thing he would ever want to do. He used his command voice and ordered Danny to stop and to come with him. It twisted William's gut when Danny immediately stopped screaming, dropped Sara's hand and shoes, stood at attention, and replied, 'Yes, sir.'"

Jon softly said, "It's a sickening feeling. I had to yell at Dan at the bank yesterday. It was the only way to calm him so he could breathe after the shots to the vest knocked the wind out of him."

Nodding in response to Jon's comment, Walter continued, "So traumatized, Danny marched to the car and got in the backseat. There were no more tears, and he didn't speak at all—only stared straight ahead. When we arrived at William's home, Danny trooped into the living room and stood at attention in the corner where William usually disciplined him. He stayed there with vacant eyes fixated on a spot on the wall in front of him.

"William endeavored to coax Danny upstairs to wash off the blood and to tuck him into bed, but Danny wouldn't budge. He couldn't bring himself to order Danny again—it hurt William too much to yell at his boy the first time. He didn't want to move him forcefully either, especially after such a trauma. So William decided to wait and to give his child some time to sort through things."

Gambrill stood, walked over to Dan, and placed a hand on his leg as tears threatened to pool. He took a slow breath, willing them to stop, but his eyes glistened anyway. Walter inhaled and exhaled several times before turning to glance at the suicide note lying on the table.

Lifting his gaze, Walter made eye contact with Nick. "This is the part where the missing piece comes into play. Danny stood there for over an hour before he started speaking, but his words thoroughly shocked and confused us.

"He said things like, it is all my fault, sir. I understand I failed her. It's my job to protect, and I'm a failure, sir. Yes, sir, no crying allowed. No, sir, I won't cry—no more crying. I'm not worthy, sir. Failed in my duty, sir. Crystal clear, sir, I should be dead, not her. I'm so sorry, sir.'

"William knelt in front of Danny, eye-to-eye, and countered everything word out of Danny's mouth. He tried so hard to make Danny understand he was not to blame for the accident, and it was okay for him to cry. In vain, William repeated to Danny that he didn't fail, and he would never wish Danny dead. But again, nothing got through. Unfortunately, the trauma of witnessing Sara's demise locked Danny inside his head and jumbled things into an unrecognizable mess.

"William's heart shattered when his little boy insisted he should've died instead of Sara. It is only the second time I ever saw William cry in his life. The first was at the accident scene. William broke into pieces because he couldn't help Danny. Although stern, he is not a cruel man. He loves his kids deeply. They're his world. We had no clue where the words came from—never in a million years would William say hurtful things like that to his children.

"When Danny began shaking uncontrollably and still wouldn't allow his father to hold him, William called the medics. His boy needed more help than we could provide, and we feared Danny might be going into shock. In hindsight, we should've taken him straight to the hospital to be with Yvonne. If we had, perhaps none of this would've occurred."

Visibly shaken by the intense memories, Walter unsteadily shuffled back to the chair, sat, and crossed his arms on the table before resting his head on them. "Give me a minute to regroup."

The tension remained thick and heavy, and no one moved from their spots as their eyes went between Gambrill and Dan.

Several minutes later, Walter took another deep breath and blew it out gradually. After regaining control, and his voice came out steadier as he said, "Danny, appeared as if he might collapse at any second as he remained at attention. His little body shook nonstop, and he continued to repeat those damned words until the medics arrived.

"When one medic touched him, Danny started screaming. He fought like a wildcat, and William forcibly held his son while the paramedic sedated Danny. The whole gut-wrenching scene lasted too damned long. Once the meds took effect, and he quieted, William, unwilling to relinquish his much-loved boy, cradled Danny in his arms and sat on the gurney.

"When we got to the hospital, I went to inform Yvonne for William since he refused to leave his son. William stayed with Danny all night. Early the next morning, while Danny still slept, William decided to visit Yvonne to provide her an update. Her room was two floors below Danny's.

"Gone less than ten minutes, when William exited the elevator on Danny's floor, he heard Danny screaming again. He raced to the room and threw open the door.

"He found two burly orderlies physically restraining a thrashing Danny. A male nurse roughly tried to force pills into Danny's mouth. The men yelled at Danny to quit screaming, stop fighting them, and to swallow the damn pills. William said Danny's eyes were wild and terrified.

"Beyond livid that they manhandled his little boy, William bellowed at them. All four froze, obeying the order to halt. Danny's features reflected his terror, but his body became rigid and motionless. Spotting the red finger marks on Danny's jaw, cheeks, arms, and legs from where the men held him, William let loose a scathing diatribe.

"So enraged by their despicable actions, William ripped them to shreds as he dressed down the men in a booming voice that reverberated through the entire floor. In colorful language, he told them to get out, they didn't belong, and they were complete and utter disappointments to their professions and their families. He scarcely maintained enough control not to strike them, though I'm sure it crossed his mind.

"Dr. Pastore, who is Broderick's personal physician, overheard everything as he started his rounds. Jasper came in, dismissed the others with a hard rebuke for their actions, then sedated Danny. Jasper decided it would be in Danny's best interest to keep him in a medicated twilight sleep for several days.

"William crawled in the bed and held Danny in his arms the entire time. He only put Danny down for the few seconds needed to use the facilities, but even then, William never let Danny out of his sight. When Jasper finally discontinued the sedation, Danny woke with a blank, lost expression. The joyful light in his eyes disappeared … replaced with desolation and grief."

Tears welled and glistened in almost everyone's eyes, whether they recognized it or not as they stared at Dan. So many things swirled in their minds, but each one of them realized this might be why he hated hospitals— he experienced trauma upon trauma in a few short hours at such a young age.

Emotion nearly choking him, Walter cleared his throat. "Things were never the same between William and Danny. Over time, William deduced the shock of witnessing his sister's death, caused Dan's mind to twist events. Warped them to the point Dan believed his father told him the things Danny said in the living room. None of us could determine where those words came from.

"A psychologist also suggested to William that Danny distorted the dressing down he gave the three orderlies. He indicated while grief-stricken and in shock, Dan erroneously interpreted the exchange to be directed at him and came to the conclusion he was unworthy of his family's love and didn't belong.

"Over the years, William approached this problem many ways, hoping Dan would see the truth. Sadly, William never found the right words. He attempted to show his love by actions, but somehow things always got screwed up." Walter blew out another long breath, emotionally taxed.

Nick assessed his team and perceived they were overwhelmed, like him. Striving to comprehend the complex gravity of what he learned, Nick realized they all needed a bit of time to sort out their emotions to deal with this in a level-headed manner. "That's a lot to take in. I think we all need a short break."

"General Broderick should be here soon. We'll resume after he arrives," Blaze stated gruffly. He needed time to work through what Gambrill shared. The general who abused Blondie for six years didn't fit at all with the man described.

Blaze laid his head on his knees, needing to think. *Perhaps Commander Gambrill twisted his memories of what happened or viewed them in the light of an old friend who doesn't want to accept reality. General Badfather is a cold-hearted bastard towards his son—the pieces don't fit together at all. And to top it off, my gut is screaming at me. Something is off—completely off.*

Unable to figure it out, Blaze lifted his head and stood. He went to Blondie and placed a hand on his shoulder. Blaze vowed silently to solve the puzzle and to keep the young man he proudly thought of as a son safe from future harm. *Blondie needs a protector, and I'm the right man for the job. I will gladly sacrifice my life for his without hesitation or regret.*

Deadly Ambitions

42

July 16
Military Aircraft Landing in Toronto – 1610 Hours

After almost two hours of pacing, General Broderick took a seat for landing. Still mulling over the little Gambrill shared. *What is the key? When did Walter locate it? Why was Daniel screaming? How did my childhood friend discover the missing piece after I searched unsuccessfully for so many years?*

William long ago accepted his fault in the scheme of things and regretted his failure to resolve the puzzle. If he could go back and change history, he would, but unfortunately, life continued to move onward. Though now, with the enigma resolved, there came the promise of a future together with Dan. *Hope, is there truly hope?*

The screams, Danny's howling cries, ripped his heart apart again. *I failed my son so miserably. Can I ever truly fix my relationship with my son? I tried and failed so many times before and only succeeded in pushing Daniel further away. I hope this time will be different.*

Exiting the plane, he pulled out his phone and dialed, not breaking stride as he marched towards the waiting helicopter. When Walter answered, he stated, "I'll be there in ten minutes."

Murphy's unit and the off-duty flight crew deplaned to relax during the unscheduled layover. Given a two-hour liberty before continuing to Ottawa, most of the contingent aboard left rapidly, leaving only Murphy and a skeleton crew aboard. Now alone, he pulled his cell, located the entry, and pressed send.

When Plouffe answered, Murphy spoke quietly, not wanting to be overheard by anyone still on board. "I just landed in Toronto. We got diverted after the general received a call. You're going to love what I have to tell you." He proceeded to relay to Plouffe the one-sided conversations he overheard and the general's demeanor on the flight.

TRF HQ — Briefing Room — 4:20 p.m.

A commanding voice bellowing, "WHERE IS MY SON?" startled the room's occupants from their quiet contemplations. Gambrill hurried to open the main door, comprehending his friend would breach any obstacle to reach Daniel. As the rolling door went up, he called out loudly, "William, he's in here."

Blaze moved and placed himself in front of Blondie to bar the general from him. In a flash, Winds and Patch flanked Blaze, creating a solid wall of protection for their little brother.

William ducked under the entry before it opened fully, and strode with purpose towards the gurney he spotted upon his scan of the area. When blocked by the human wall created by Daniel's former unit, he halted and roared, "Move out of my way, now!"

Blaze met his commander's challenging glare head-on with flames burning in his hazel eyes. His voice came out as authoritative, if not more, than his superior officer. "General Broderick. Blondie's under my protection, and no one, including you, is going to harm him."

Winds settled a hand on his sidearm. He would not allow General Badfather to hurt Blondie ever again. He would die before he allowed this poor excuse for a parent another chance to cause Blondie pain.

"I order you to stand aside!" William commanded, surprised at Blain's noncompliance.

The tension palpable, Alpha Team and Commander Gambrill observed the confrontation. When Walter spotted Winds's hand moving to his weapon, he moved forward, prepared to intervene, but stopped when Blaze spoke again.

Blaze continued to glare at the cold-hearted bastard who nearly killed his son by abusing the power of his position. He had no idea what game he played now, but Blaze would be damned if he would roll over this time. His voice still hard, he stated, "I can't do that, sir. Colonel Sutton placed Broderick under our protection. GU protocols, which means I possess the authority to do whatever is necessary to ensure his safety."

"Who the hell do you think ordered Daniel to be in protective custody?" William's ice-cold voice demanded.

"Got my orders from Sutton," Blaze responded with scorching heat.

"And the colonel got them from me. Now move, or you won't like the consequences, Captain."

Blaze, Winds, and Patch remained firmly in place. The others observed two unyielding soldiers square off in a battle of glares. Icy blue met fiery hazel. Neither man flinched nor blinked. General Badass and Captain Blaze both appeared deadly. An undercurrent they were not privy to existed between the two men, and the team wondered if they would come to blows.

"I'm not sure what game you're playing, but I'm telling you here and now, I won't allow you to manipulate or harm Blondie further," Blaze stated, ready to kiss his career goodbye to save the kid. He should've challenged the stone-cold general years ago. *Better late than never.*

Winds sarcastically said, "Great mission planning, sir. Once again, you left Blondie hanging out to dry with no one covering his six."

Jon flicked his eyes to Winds. *Is Dan still in Special Forces?* He blurted out, "What mission?"

William blinked. "Mission? You think Daniel's on an op?"

Blaze stated, "It's the only thing that makes any sense. He's been black for a year. No information to be found on him. I know, I searched. We scoured the country, world, for any trace of him, but Blondie no longer existed—as if on blackout protocol. Yet here he is, in Toronto, left wide open again with no backup. So, what's the mission, and who wants to kill him this time?"

Loki gaped at Ray with disbelieving eyes and whispered, "Dan's on a mission?"

Ray only shrugged, as dumbfounded as his friend.

Lexa stared at Dan. *What the heck? Is he playing me? What is Dan doing at TRF?* She kicked herself for letting her defenses down and being pulled in by him. But then her little devil whispered, *"If he's still in the military that solves your problem. He wouldn't be on the same team."*

Nick noted Gambrill's countenance became a mixture of shock and anger. *Angry at who, Blaze, or the elder Broderick?* He glanced at Dan. *How would he react to what played out before them? Perhaps Dan being sedated is for the best. He doesn't need more to deal with now.*

Bram glimpsed the slight slump in Dan's father's shoulders as a flash of shock crossed his face, only to be displaced by a mien of regret and sadness before an emotionless mask covered his face and he squared his shoulders again. *Like father like son. Both possess expressive sapphire eyes, a rigid military carriage, and both men appear to hide their emotions behind well-crafted shields.*

"You are the ..." William halted. *This is the second time someone accused me of placing Daniel under a blackout. And what the hell is Blain doing mentioning Guardian Unit protocol in public?* He would have to deal with all of this and find out what Walter discovered to make him believe hope existed, but access to Daniel became his top priority.

William locked down all emotions. With calm authority, he stated, "Daniel is not in the military. There is no mission or blackout. Captain, this is the last time I ask you to step aside so I can check on my son."

"No blackout?" Blaze appeared astounded as his gut screamed, *something is very wrong here.*

William's eyes became shards of deep, blue ice, but his voice remained calm and commanding, "No. We'll discuss things later, Captain. Now, I'm ordering you to move aside or you *will* face charges of insubordination."

Blaze and Winds shared a glance before grudgingly stepping aside. Both remained perplexed but agreed they were close enough to take out the general if he tried to harm Blondie. Patch looked to Blaze for direction. Receiving a slight nod, he moved to where his former unit mates now stood. All three kept vigilant eyes on Blondie, and Winds maintained a hand on his sidearm.

When the confrontation ended peacefully, Gambrill breathed a sigh of relief, though he still had many questions. *Why would Dan's buddies think he is on a mission and what is blackout protocol?* For now, the answers must wait because William needed a moment with Danny.

Dan's teammates gathered in the farthest corner to give as much privacy as possible without leaving. All bewildered by what they witnessed, they continued to stare but remained silent.

William's heart ached as he scrutinized his boy's battered condition. He gazed for several moments before engaging in uncharacteristic public behavior. He allowed his paternal emotions free rein as he gathered Danny into his arms, the distress apparent in his expression. Further demonstrating affection for his son, he ignored those around him and held Daniel with one arm, cradling his Danny's head on his shoulder and gently stroked his son's hair.

He whispered words meant for Daniel alone, unaware the room's acoustics carried them to everyone. "Danny, I'm so sorry, my son. I made a mess of things. I promise I'm here for you. I should've realized sooner. Rest now, my boy. No one will harm you again. Your family never abandoned you—they're all coming. We'll work this out, son."

William caressed Daniel's cheek. "You look terrible. You bruise so easily—like your mother. She would want to be here with you, but I'm happy she won't see you like this. It would break her heart."

"My God, you look nearly as bad as the first time in Kandahar—gunshot is in the arm this time, instead of the thigh and hip. I'll never get used to seeing you hurt—it tears me to pieces every damned time you're injured."

Leaning down, William kissed the top of Daniel's head. "Rest, my son. I'll protect you with my last breath."

Grand Citadel Hotel – Room 666 – 4:30 p.m.

Plouffe hung up the phone after talking with Murphy, giddy as he thought about how General Broderick would be hurting again. His adversary must've been informed his son had been injured in the gang war. Plouffe hoped the toy soldier suffered mortal wounds.

Broderick ruined all his ambitions over thirty years ago. Plouffe crafted a strategy to become general one day, and if not for William, he would be leading Special Forces. He should be a general now—not the jackass Broderick. His plans began to fall apart shortly after they were both promoted to major.

At the time, Broderick also horned in on the woman Plouffe wanted—for her fortune more than anything else. He worked for months to gain the attention of Lady Yvonne Loving. The gala to celebrate the promotions would've been the perfect opportunity to make his move on her. She would've been his, but goddamned Broderick showed up at the celebration. The sourpuss never came to those functions, but he attended this one.

The idiot Jasper Pastore also intervened and had a hand in screwing up everything. Jasper believed himself to better than anyone because he went from being a JTF2 medic to a full-fledged doctor. The damned man had the nerve to interrupt his conversation with Yvonne and pulled her away from him, laughingly telling her she must meet someone extraordinary. Pastore introduced her to William of all people.

However, unknown to him at the time, Yvonne's twin sister had been married to Erik Broderick for nearly seven years. So Pastore's words were meant as a dig to him. God, he hated Pastore and made him pay for the insult. He cut the brake line on Pastore's father's car. In the ensuing accident, Jasper's parents and brother all died when their car slammed into the back of a semi. It had been so satisfying when Pastore cried like a baby at their gravesites.

Yvonne, a bright and gregarious woman, didn't belong with a dour man like Broderick, who always seemed to have a stick rammed up his ass. It surprised the hell out of Nigel when the rich bitch actually married the cheerless jackass. Nigel never figured out why she did—they had nothing in common.

Within the first year, Broderick saddled her with a brat. Nigel's plan for swooping in on a grieving widow, wooing her, marrying her, and exterminating the squalling brat before he turned two never came to fruition. The plan to eliminate Broderick and to move up to Lieutenant Colonel at the same time would've worked, but the damnable Broderick ruined it again.

Plouffe worked to achieve his current rank before he met Broderick. Afterward, he worked even harder to use every opportunity presented to him to feed his need for power and control. Colonel Grasett's indiscretion provided him the perfect tool to use to advance his ambitious schemes.

After catching Grasett *in flagrante delicto* with a male enlisted soldier directly under the colonel's command, Plouffe blackmailed him, threating to expose the affair with photographic evidence. Grasett became putty in his hands, giving him prime assignments and even smoothing over a friendly fire incident. It was not his fault the dumbass Jay Pearce moved into his line of fire

At least that's what Grasett's official report declared. To this day, Nigel remained pissed he hit Pearce's leg when he sighted a kill shot. The idiot moved at the last second, then Broderick, Sutton, Washington, Pastore, and Cardillo swooped in, preventing Nigel from eliminating a rival.

Colonel Grasett also expedited his promotions—only right as far as Nigel was concerned. The Broderick family connections allowed William to move up at rocket speed. Nigel's method was no different than Broderick's nepotism.

When both he and Broderick were majors, his plan to become lieutenant colonel almost worked. He succeeded in killing off Elkins, but regrettably, Grasett changed cars at the last minute, ending up in the one with Broderick and Elkins, and he also died. The fact Broderick survived still enraged him.

By all accounts, Broderick should've died—like he should've died countless times before in the field. Broderick was one lucky bastard. General Badasswipe turned out to be as hard to kill as his toy soldier.

With Grasett gone, Nigel no longer possessed any leverage to use for quick upward mobility. Plouffe's confidence rivaled his conceit—certain General Craymuier would promote him to lieutenant colonel when Broderick ended up near death's door. Nigel also believed he could've moved up in rank to colonel in no time. However, much to his chagrin, Craymuier promoted Major Sutton to lieutenant colonel and left the colonel's spot vacant.

Still outraged over the slight, his well-planned schemes took another hit when he discovered Broderick returned to active duty. Not only did the asshat come back, but after a year off to laze around, Craymuier bestowed Grasett's former position on Broderick. So, while Nigel worked his ass off and Broderick played house with his wife and child for an entire year, nepotism garnered his nemesis rank and status he didn't earn.

That is when Plouffe began searching for ways to make the man's life hell. He impatiently hunted for eight years, and by pure accident, he discovered Broderick's soft spot. He picked up the local tabloid and read the article on the death of Broderick's seven-year-old brat.

The picture on the front page showed him exactly how to exact his revenge on Broderick. However, it took several more years of patiently waiting before he could use the information. Getting ahold of his toy soldier thrilled Nigel, and he had a long run with his plaything. Although, all his past attempts to knock over the general's son ended in failure. Plouffe mostly blamed Murphy's ineptness, but also because William's spawn wouldn't fall. He always stood again with the help of his damned unit.

Now he is alone and can't rely on Blaze and the others to save him. He should be easier to kill. Junior asswipe is the reason Aaron died, and I'll have my vengeance. As Plouffe thought about the countless efforts to kill the master corporal, he grinned at the amount of pain he caused both Brodericks.

Plouffe wished he hadn't lost control of his toy because Aaron would still be alive. He never expected that result, and it still burned his gut the younger Broderick didn't eat his gun after killing Hunter. That had been his plan, and Nigel had been confident it would've worked, but for some reason, it didn't, not even after he isolated him.

When Nigel learned from Aaron that Broderick ended up in Tactical Response Force in Toronto, he began to strategize again and feed Aaron lots of misinformation, hoping Broderick would return to the military like when things got tough for him at the Fourteenth Division.

One day, years ago, Plouffe overheard Buzz and Dutch talking to retired Sergeant Wilson Keswick. They discussed the problems Broderick junior experienced as a rookie with the Toronto Police and how they talked him into joining the military. He watched his toy soldier closely ever since he joined the Army and became ecstatic when he requested special dispensation to apply to Special Forces before he met the minimum age requirement.

Eager to get his hands on the means to make the general's life hell on earth, Nigel had been livid when he discovered a clerical error almost prevented his plaything from making the cut. Although the mistake could've cost him his prize, it yielded a more fortuitous trophy, Corporal Merrill.

Over the years, he reveled how his machinations made General Blowhard suffer. It never mattered to him the spawn was innocent—only a tool to be used. But now he was stained with Aaron's blood and must pay.

A satisfied smile formed. The undeserving general would finally witness the death of all his soft spots ... his mutant son, ditzy daughter, snobby wife. Once they are all gone, he would wipe the general off the face of the earth too.

Wait, no. I'll also make him suffer the losses of the rest of the Broderick males one-by-one because they are a blight on the military. The Broderick line will be wiped from history and be finished forever. All that will be left for me to do to attain my rightful position is to take out Sutton.

Plouffe's malevolent grin grew as his mind began to spin different scenarios and options. *I will not fail this time.*

Conundrums

43

With guarded miens, Blaze, Winds, and Patch silently scrutinized the fatherly concern playing out before them. A conundrum they couldn't reconcile given what the general put Blondie through for six years. Gambrill's words painted a vastly different picture of the man. Their experience showed them he always put the kid in harm's way, so much so, Blondie came within a hair's breadth of losing his soul.

Impossible to tune out the words intended for only Blondie as they permeated the deathly quiet room, Blaze mulled over the immense disconnect. He zeroed in on the first time Blondie got injured in Kandahar. The terrible memory flashed into his mind.

Blondie and Brody joined the unit about four months prior. Their mission required Blondie to take up a sniper position, with Brody as a spotter. The rest of them went to recon the two-story house a kilometer away. While he, Patch, and Winds cleared the first floor, Gambit and Mason tackled the second, and everything went as planned until all their comms inexplicably failed.

Concerned by the lack of chatter, Brody and Blondie maintained visual on them. While scanning for tangoes through his rifle's scope, Blondie spotted several strange shapes on the building's exterior. Resuming overwatch, he delegated their inspection to his spotter. Brody checked the devices with his high-powered binoculars and realized someone rigged the structure with explosives. The two surmised false intel lured their unit into a trap.

Needing to communicate the danger but unable to transmit, the rookies decided since Blondie ran faster, he would go while Brody took over as sniper. The kid hauled ass to warn them. As Blondie sprinted towards the building, a barrage of gunfire alerted Blaze to a change in circumstance.

Brody dropped three targets, and the shooting ceased. When Blondie got close enough, their young rookie yelled at the top of his lungs, 'Get out, bomb, out now!' Winds, Patch, and he hurried out at Blondie's warning, but Gambit and Mason hadn't heard him. Blondie didn't stop as he raced in and sped up the flight of stairs, still shouting.

Blondie found Mason and Gambit at the far end of the second level. They raced downstairs, and the three had almost cleared the exit when it blew. First out and thrown clear by the blast, Mason ended up shaken and bruised, but otherwise unharmed.

Gambit came out second. Sadly, he died when a massive piece of the concrete wall collapsed and crushed him as he lay unconscious in the dirt. Losing Gambit hurt like hell, and Blaze still missed him.

They hadn't seen Blondie exit, and when the dust settled, they located him on the ground with blood covering his entire face. The concussive wave blew him forward and peppered him with debris. A sizable chunk of a wall struck his back and pinned his body. A smaller piece rammed into his head above the ear, causing a deep gash, which bled like a stuck pig. A shiver ran down Blaze's spine as he recalled the memory.

At first glance, they all believe Blondie died. It took him, Winds, and Mason to lift the heavy concrete off Blondie. Patch found a pulse, rapid but present … the kid lived. Though relieved, they were all shocked to find two bullets also struck their kid. One round embedded in his thigh, and the other grazed his hip, leaving a long gash. Brody became distraught over allowing shots to be fired and didn't realize Blondie had been hit because his brother never missed a stride in his mad dash to warn them.

That was the first time they rushed Blondie to a hospital. He had lost a lot of blood by the time they arrived—his face beyond pale. While they waited for word from the doctors, they decided the injury to be severe enough to alert the general since Blondie was his son.

Blaze remembered the conversation and boiled even now. *"General, this is Lieutenant Blain, Corporal Broderick's CO. I'm calling to inform you that your son's been badly wounded. We're at the base hospital. He's in surgery now, sir."*

The response he received Blaze never expected from a father. *"Is he alive?"*

He answered, *"Yes, but his condition is unknown. We're awaiting word."*

Ice-cold words spoken next shocked Blaze. *"Inform me if he doesn't make it. I don't have time to run to the bedside of every wounded soldier."*

The cold-hearted bastard showed no concern. He didn't ask about the kid's injuries, only if Blondie died. That day the unit decided they must protect Blondie. With a father like General Badfather, who needed enemies. After that, the kid became everyone's little brother—well, not quite everyone's.

Blaze came to view Blondie more as a son than a brother. He figured the emotion came from the fact he raised his sister Daphy and had become more of a dad to her. And with Blondie being two years younger than Daphy—a fatherly protectiveness grew fairly rapidly in him.

Though grateful Blondie's risky action saved their butts, they were unhappy he got hurt in the process. To show appreciation, concern, and unit solidarity, they all took turns staying at his bedside during his entire hospitalization—never once did they leave him alone.

Thinking back, Blaze shook his head. *That kid surely hated hospitals … Blondie left after only four days.* At the time, Blaze believed his fear irrational, but Blondie didn't possess irrational fears. After learning what Gambrill shared today, he now understood the rational basis—being manhandled as a kid must've created deep-seated anxiety.

Blaze's mind returned to the aftermath of the mission. Luckily, the bullet didn't shatter or break Blondie's femur and didn't do significant damage. The blow to his head caused a mild concussion, and the one to the back resulted in bruised ribs. The grazed hip was relatively minor. The impact of debris and smacking the ground left his face contused, and the bruises turned wildly colorful, like now.

Although only a short walk from his office to the hospital, the general never once came to visit Blondie. Viewing General Broderick holding Blondie and speaking to him in a caring manner now didn't fit the facts he knew to be true, leaving Blaze puzzled. *Damn, none of this makes any sense.*

As he held his son, William thought about the first wounds Daniel sustained while serving in Kandahar. It hurt him to be so cold to Lieutenant Blain when Daniel's CO called. All William wanted to do was race over and check on his boy, but he couldn't display his emotions.

Unfortunately, Daniel paid the price too often for being his son. Every night William covertly visited Daniel. The first night the entire unit sat in the room, so he stayed hidden. The second night, Master Corporal Srònaich O'Naoimhín was the only one there, and while Mason slept soundly, William surreptitiously crept into Daniel's room.

Daniel's appearance shocked the hell out of him. He stroked his son's hair a few times as he whispered gentle words. Though wishing to hold him, William feared the repercussions if someone witnessed the embrace, so he refrained. The next night, finding Brody at Daniel's side made him smile. William liked Brody—the young man had been a true friend to Danny.

As he continued to stroke Daniel's head, William allowed himself to become lost in his memories of each time Daniel suffered an injury. Too damned many times and each instance ripped out a piece of his heart.

Walter cleared his throat and said, "William, General, Sir, we must talk."

Pulled from musings, William took a breath, peered at Danny's bruised face again before gently resetting him on the gurney. Though not ready to release his boy, William recognized he must. He straightened, squared his shoulders, held his general mantle tight, and turned to face the others. Using his calm, steady authority voice, William stated, "I want to thank you all very much for all you have done for Daniel. I understand he's been through a lot."

He took a moment to assess the nine men and one woman in front of him. He noted the dark circles under most of their eyes and tight, drawn expressions. Whatever hell Daniel experienced, they went through with him. These people went above and beyond for his son. Recognizing they were utterly spent, William altered his original plan.

"You all have been through a certain hell the last two days. Although I planned on briefing everyone tonight, it can wait. You all need rest. I will move Daniel to a secure location so he can rest. Captain Blain, I will make other arrangements for his security for the next day or two. In three days, we will reconvene, and I'll brief you on the situation."

Blaze interrupted, "Sir, with all due respect, that will not work. I am Blondie's protection detail, and I don't plan to leave his side until the threat to him is resolved. If you believe I'm insubordinate, you can have my walking papers now. I won't be swayed from this decision. Blondie doesn't leave my sight until I'm certain he's safe," Blaze set his mouth in an unforgiving line and glared at the general.

"I second that, Sir," Winds added forcefully.

William noted Corporal Simons's hand never left his sidearm.

A chorus of strongly voiced, "Copy that" from the TRF officers echoed Winds's declaration. Taken aback by the solidarity his son engendered, William stared, and his jaw almost dropped when the petite, female constable stepped forward and spoke directly at him with fire flashing in her eyes.

"He's our responsibility, sir! He's family, and we take care of our own. We'll keep Dan safe—we promised. Dan belongs here. We'll protect him," Lexa interjected passionately with glowering eyes.

"I see," William said, determining how best to proceed and decided to relent in the face of a potent force. Thoroughly versed in battle tactics, he recognized an outflanking maneuver. Happy Daniel developed stalwart friends ready and willing to lay everything on the line to defend him, another more pressing thought jarred him.

His son needed help. He didn't miss the excessive heat radiating from Daniel, and his boy's screams still echoed in his mind. Daniel suffered both physical and mental trauma in the past two days. *I hope Danny's former unit and his new team can help him weather this storm.*

Prepared to accept their service, William allowed his gaze to rove over each of them. "We must make a plan. Daniel requires proper rest and care. Something more than a gurney in this room."

As the group began to disperse around the room, Walter spoke, "William, I agree, and you are correct, we are all exhausted."

Though unhappy and confused by the alien general in front of him, Winds released his grip on his gun, aware helping Blondie was his priority. He would deal with the puzzle later. "Sir, we can rotate shifts safeguarding Blondie. As for where, I'm not certain, but you're right, this room isn't ideal."

"How about taking Dan to his place? He'd be comfortable there," Ray suggested.

Jon shook his head. "Not secure. If there's a threat against Dan, that would be one of the first places whoever is after him would check."

Patch voiced his opinion, "Not a hospital, either. Two reasons, hard to secure, and Blondie hates them and will sneak out if given the slightest opportunity. Can't keep him in them if he's mobile—and often when he isn't."

William nodded. *He has reason to hate hospitals—those damned orderlies terrorized my boy. I wish I could've done more than dressing them down.* He winced at the thought, realizing what his chastisement of those men caused. Pushing away bad memories, he said, "I'll rent a suite and several adjacent rooms at the Grand Citadel. Captain, would you be able to adequately secure the area?"

Blaze rubbed his weary eyes, aware they all required rest. He found it difficult to be on top of his game while dog-tired. "Yes, sir. With the appropriate resources. I have a request that will solve two issues. Allow me to bring in the other four members of my unit. I trust them implicitly, though we've only been together for a short time. It would give us the manpower required and would allow the rest of us some much-needed sleep."

"That resolves the security aspect, but what about Blondie's physical needs? Patch can't stay up twenty-four-seven, he's about to drop as it is. He's a miracle worker, but ..." Winds trailed off, glancing at his drained buddy with a worried smile.

Patch's expression communicated both, *Thanks* and *What the hell? I'd do anything for my little brother.* While he accepted the truth of Winds's statement, his sleepy brain came up with an idea.

"When Heather brought the supplies earlier, she told me she had the next three days off and said if we needed anything to call her. Perhaps she would be willing to help care for Blondie while I grab a bit of shuteye. She seemed concerned about all of us the other day. Geez, was that just last night? Wow!" Realizing something that might persuade them, a grin teased at the corners of his mouth before he added, "I think Heather likes Blondie ... she changed his name on the nurse's chart board."

"She did what?" asked Loki.

"Heather changed Blondie's name in the ER," Patch repeated.

"To what?" Loki asked, itching to know. The grin on Patch gave him a clue, but he wanted to hear anyway.

"Dantastic!"

"Holy smokes! Told you Dantastic is way better than Blondie," Loki gleefully chortled.

When loud, boisterous laughter erupted from all except William, he appeared concerned. *Are they so tired their minds cracked?* Then he considered the name. *Dantastic, yes, the moniker fits my boy.* William allowed a hint of a smile to cross his face for a fraction of a second.

As the laughter died down, Patch queried, "Should I call and ask if she'll lend us a hand?" When heads nodded, he phoned her. Heather told him she was honored and delighted he contacted her for assistance.

Patch also conveyed a list of provisions to bring with her. He needed supplies to redress the wounds, more pain meds, more saline, and more fever reducer, along with a couple of other items. He instructed her to have the front desk at the Grand Citadel Hotel contact General Broderick's room when she arrived for an escort.

Before disconnecting, Patch asked her to also arrange for more sedative after Blaze suggested it would be best to keep Blondie under for a few days so that his body recovered a little before he dealt with the emotional stuff.

Their plan began to take shape. William contacted the hotel and acquired a block of rooms. The others were surprised to learn he rented out an entire wing of one floor to make security easier, and because he wanted to provide everyone rooms. He explained they would be able to rest without having to be far from Daniel, and believed it was the least he could do as a small repayment for taking care of his son.

Loki spoke with Winds and Gambrill to identify and procure equipment necessary to set up a secure perimeter. Nick obtained Dan's keys from his locker. He and Lexa headed to his apartment to gather clothing and personal care items Dan would need, and to their respective homes to collect the same for themselves.

Blaze contacted Major White in Ottawa and requested the rest of his unit be assigned. The major was hesitant to comply until General Broderick took the phone and resolved the issue. Hal, Angus, Duncan, and Russ would be sent straight away, but it would be a few hours until they arrived. Blaze called Hal directly and arranged for him to bring their kits and change of clothing for him and Winds, along with several items they required to make the room more secure.

Security, medical, personal items, and lodging arrangements made, Bram gazed at Dan and asked, "So how do we move him there? I doubt we want to attract attention wheeling him through the hotel's lobby on a stretcher. Not after all the pictures of him on the news lately. Striding in with General Broderick would also cause people to notice."

Everyone stopped to think, but they struggled to come up with workable ideas. They got stuck on solutions going through the lobby until Ray offered, "Perhaps we can take him through the rear service entrance. If we cover his head with a hat pulled low, no one can glimpse his face. Two of us can sling his arms over our shoulders and carry him in."

Pointing to the gurney, Patch said, "Although I like most of it, I prefer this be the mode of conveyance, but at the bare minimum, we need a wheelchair. Given his injuries, I don't want to put undue pressure on his arm, shoulder, or ribs."

They pondered suggestions for a while longer. Still coming up blank, they decided task Patch, Blaze, Jon, and Bram with devising the plan to transport Dan safely to the Grand Citadel without attracting attention. This allowed Winds, Loki, Ray, and William to leave for the hotel and install security measures before Dan arrived.

Although he didn't want to desert Dan at this time, Walter still had a job to do running TRF. He must rearrange team schedules to allot Alpha extra time to act as Dan's protection detail. It would be challenging with Delta Team still out on bereavement leave dealing with the loss of Aaron.

TRF would now be down two teams, which would mean the other teams would be pulling extra duty, and Walter was unsure how they would react. He also had to schedule the NRB interviews for the two subject officers. Lexa would need to do hers tomorrow, but Dan's would wait until he was able.

Walter handed William a copy of the suicide note. "We'll speak later, and I'll provide you with the full details." After William nodded, Walter exited the conference room and noticed Inspector Davis sitting waiting area. Halting near the inspector, Walter said, "I'd like to find out what the psychologist told you. If you have time now, would you come with me to my office?"

Davis nodded and followed Gambrill. Though he did take a peek into the room as he passed. His inquisitive mind wondered about all the people and activity but realized he needed to let sleeping dogs lie this time.

After much deliberation and many non-workable ideas, the group tasked with getting Dan to the hotel unseen became frustrated. They milled around the briefing room as they endeavored to come up with more possibilities.

Jon yawned as he stared out the window at the traffic below. Inspired by observing a panel truck making a delivery, he smiled, pulled out his phone, and called his wife.

Jennifer, a part-time events planner, would be able to assist him in locating a vehicle necessary to make his idea work. When she answered, Jon said, "Hey, Jen, it's me. I need a favor."

Jennifer answered as Kent and Joey headed out the back door to play basketball. "Hi, Hon. Sure." She recognized the tiredness in her husband's tone.

"Do you know any caterers who would allow us to use their truck for an hour or so?"

Though a little surprised by the strange request, Jen didn't ask why. "You might try Dan's friend Jarmal. He recently started catering. If he can't help, I can give you the names of three others who might."

"Thanks, Jen. I'm sure Jarmal will help if he can. He was quite concerned about Dan earlier today when he delivered lunch."

"How's Dan doing? When will he be released? Oh, and if he needs someone to care for him for a few days, he can stay with us."

"He's no longer in the hospital." Jon sighed and rubbed his tired eyes.

"What?" Jen exclaimed.

"I'll explain later when I stop by home to pick up some things."

Confused, Jennifer asked, "Like what?"

Jon pinched the bridge of his nose. "Would you pack me an overnight bag with a couple days' worth of clothes and toiletries? Sorry, but I can't say more over the phone."

"Sure. Okay. Anything else I can do?" Jen asked with worry in her tone.

"Please call Kellie and ask her to pack a bag for Bram, too."

Jen wondered what was going on. *This is so strange.* "Yes, I'll do that. I'll have your bag ready shortly. Call if you need the other numbers. Take care of yourself. Love you."

Uncomfortable expressing his softer emotions in front of others, Jon answered, "Ditto."

"Oh, you know all the right words to make me swoon." Jen laughed.

Jon smiled and relented as he whispered, "Love you, too, My Queen."

A quick call to Jarmal set their plan into motions. More than happy to assist, Jarmal agreed to prepare the vehicle and alter his schedule to bring his truck over himself. Once Jarmal arrived, they rigged the gurney with poles on four corners, draping it like a food rack—completely hiding Dan.

Jarmal also provided them Fire Stick Grill's caterer's jackets and offered to drive the truck to the Grand Citadel's service entrance at the back and wait while Blaze, Patch, Jon, and Bram offloaded Dan, on the off-chance someone questioned the unscheduled delivery. Afterward, he would transport Jon and the equipment back to TRF so he could pick up his car and make the rounds to his and Bram's homes to grab their overnight bags.

TRF HQ – Gambrill's Office – 5:30 p.m.

Davis finished sharing what he learned from Dr. Carter with Commander Gambrill. "Truly, I'm sorry if my digging caused the Brodericks more anguish. That was not my intention."

Walter sighed as he thought about all he must share with William tonight. Richard Donner was as much a victim of that fateful day as Sara, Danny, and everyone else involved. To Davis, he said, "Tragic all around. The young Donner carried such a heavy load all his life. Perhaps if I'd known about all this back then, things might've turned out differently for so many.

"Thank you for your in-depth investigation, which brought West Donner's suicide note to light. It may not have sounded like it earlier, but I believe this will go a long way in helping to heal old wounds.

"Daniel will be alright, and I'm certain William would want me to express his sincere appreciation for your exceptional work." Walter stood and offered Davis his outstretched hand.

Standing and shaking Gambrill's hand, Davis allowed a slight smile to form. "Not often I solve an old puzzle. I'm glad some good will come from this tragedy. If either Broderick has questions, please provide them my contact information."

Walter nodded. "Again, we appreciate your efforts." After the inspector left, Walter slumped into his chair and took several minutes to regroup, shoving all the should've, would've, and could've thoughts into a box. Inhaling deeply, he held the breath for a count of four before exhaling and pulling out his phone to call Harriet to inform her it would be another long night, but he would be home at some point.

Into Purgatory Again

 *44*

July 16
Grand Citadel Hotel – Dan's Room – 6:00 p.m.

Despite the presence of Dan's unit brothers and his father, De Haven and Hardy decided Jon would go back alone, and Bram would remain in case Dan woke confused. So, after they moved Dan to one of the two queen-size beds, Jon headed out to return gurney to TRF and pick up things from his and Bram's homes.

Manning the now-functioning security hub, Loki answered the suite's phone, and after a brief exchange, he popped into the room and said, "The front desk said Heather arrived. I'll go escort her up."

The others nodded as Blaze pulled a chair beside Blondie's bed and wearily sat. Running on vapors, his mind left everything he learned tonight jumbled. He needed sleep before logically sorting out everything. As Patch readjusted Blondie with the help of Winds and Bram, putting several pillows behind the kid to make it easier for him to breathe, Blaze released a long sigh.

Winds turned to Blaze and recognized as many questions swirled in his best friend's mind as his own. They all had so many damned unanswered queries. However, discussing anything now wouldn't be the best timing with them all dog-tired. Quietly he said, "We gotta talk with Blondie."

Bram scanned Dan's army buddies. "I think you should hold off. He's been through a lot. Give him some space."

Blaze eyed Bram. "We understand what to do. Did it for six years."

"Yeah, well, that may be true, but ..." Bram trailed off. Though not his place to judge, he wondered where they were for the past year.

Patch slipped another pillow under Blondie's left arm to elevate his sprained wrist as he completed Bram's statement, "We've been MIA for a year. That's what you wanted to say, right?"

Bram nodded and pivoted to face General Broderick. He recalled the confrontation between Dan's buddies and father. "No clue why you all abandoned him last year, but he needed friends or family—people he trusted. Yesterday was bad, but the entire year's been tough on him."

William raked a hand through his hair at the slight censure in Daniel's teammate's voice. Blain's words echoed Erik's—both thought Daniel had been on blackout protocol. *I screwed up again. How can I ever begin to make this right?* He cleared his throat. "Constable De Haven, Mr. Shea, if you will please leave the room, I must speak to my men."

Bram didn't want Dan left alone with his father and his former unit mates, mostly because of the extreme animosity exuding from Winds for the general. "Perhaps, it would be better if you took your discussion in the other room. I'll stay with Dan."

"Not leaving Blondie!" Blaze empathically stated.

William addressed Bram. "Daniel will be fine."

Patch shook his head. "I refuse to leave my brother, sir."

William squared his shoulders, hating to do what he must, but couldn't find any alternative in this situation. "Master Corporal Shea, in order for you to stay in this room and your security clearance to be in effect, you must consent to be recalled for a special short-term assignment, effective now. If you decline, you must exit with the constable."

Patch's shoulders slumped and his eyes rounded with shock. *Damn, so much for exiting the military and never looking back. Can this get any worse?* He glanced at Blondie and decided he would willingly pay the cost of admission … he owed Blondie at least this much, if not more. "I agree, sir." Patch gave a curt nod to his general before turning his gaze to Blaze. "He's worth it."

Blaze only nodded as Winds fought hard to keep his trap shut. *How dare he do this to Patch?* His eyes flicked to Blaze. *What the hell is going on?* His intense loathing glare returned and stayed on the man who made Blondie's life hell.

"Sir, is it wise to remain in this room alone?" Bram stated, not missing the open hostility on Winds's face.

William peered at the huge constable. His comparable size and the protectiveness he read in Bram's blue-green eyes brought a vision of Mason to his mind. He wasn't certain what to make of De Haven yet, but he stated calmly, "Please close the door on your way out, Constable."

Grand Citadel Hotel – Main Suite – 6:05 p.m.

Bram slowly shut the door, though he didn't want to. He shifted his gaze to Ray, who glanced up from the security monitor with an inquisitive mien. Bram shook his head. He had no clue what the hell was going on.

Weary, he lowered himself into one of the larger chairs as Lexa entered the hotel suite after storing her items in the room assigned to her.

"Where is everyone?" Lexa asked.

Ray responded, "Jon is with Jarmal returning the equipment to HQ. Loki's getting Heather. Haven't seen Nick, so he must still be in his room. The others are in the bedroom with Dan."

Lexa's gaze went from the shut door to Bram as she took a seat beside him. He appeared worried. "What's going on? Why's the door shut?"

"Not exactly sure. The general wanted to talk to his men privately and told Patch and me to leave. When Patch refused, Dan's dad said the only way he could remain is if he accepted an immediate active-duty, short-term assignment so his security clearance would be in effect.

I swear Patch looked like he might vomit, but he agreed." Bram glanced heavenward, then back at Lexa. "I'd sure like to know what's going on, but he kicked me out of the room. After everything we've overheard and learned, I'm damned confused."

Ray whistled low. "None of this makes sense. What the heck is blackout protocol and GU? At HQ, the general certainly was unhappy when Blaze said that. Whatever's going on, it must be serious to involve putting Dan under the protection of Special Forces soldiers."

After rubbing his tired, dry eyes, Ray noted Bram and Lexa appeared as clueless as him. Shifting his gaze to all the audio jamming devices, he sighed. *Yep, something serious is going on.* He returned to monitoring the camera feeds Loki set up, giving them a view of the hall.

"How is Dan?" Lexa asked as she rolled her tired and aching shoulders.

"Still sedated," Bram answered simply.

Lexa leaned back in the chair as she stared at the bedroom door. Her eyelids became heavy as her body began to experience the toll of the past two days. Thoroughly exhausted, her usually crisp and clear mind no longer fired on all cylinders. Lexa didn't intend to fall asleep, but her lids lowered, and her head lolled to one side as she drifted off.

Bram peered at Lexa and sighed again. *Yeah, we are all running on empty. It will be a good thing when the other soldiers arrive to take over for us.*

Grand Citadel Hotel – Lobby – 6:05 p.m.

Loki gave Heather a huge grin when he met her at the desk. "Hey, let me carry that for you. You're a real lifesaver," Loki said as he lifted a large nondescript box off the floor. "Dantastic's gonna appreciate all your help. In fact, we all do. Were you able to gather everything we needed, or do I need to send someone out to grab anything?"

Heather replied, "Got everything and some things he didn't ask for. I like being prepared. I'm happy you guys called me to help with Dantastic. He's special, isn't he?" She smiled and followed Loki to the elevators.

"Yeah, *quite* special." Loki chuckled.

Several minutes ago, Major Plouffe walked into the lobby and spotted a pretty woman at the front desk. He chose one of the chairs in the opulent lounge and picked up the newspaper to read while waiting for his dinner reservation. Behind him, he overheard the banter between the woman and some man. *Dantastic is a stupid nickname. Probably a mutt or other animal.*

As Nigel half-listened to them, he read about Aaron's funeral arrangements, miffed it wouldn't be until the nineteenth because his idiot brother wanted to wait for some of Aaron teammates to return before they held the service. The fact the damned newspaper allotted tons of space to the injured Broderick and his exploits that day, but barely printed a word about Aaron also angered him.

This isn't right, Aaron was a better man than Broderick. The article should be singing Aaron's praises. Hell, even the dammed gang lord, Pedro Basto, got more attention than Aaron.

Plouffe rustled the newspaper in frustration. He still needed a decent plan. He had gone to the hospital after talking with Murphy to determine Broderick's room number so Murphy could slip him an overdose of morphine, but his toy soldier was not there.

From the little information he gathered from an orderly he spoke to Broderick was not in the best shape. Albeit, before he could kill William's spawn, Nigel had to find him. Plouffe decided to check Broderick's apartment tomorrow, and expand his search if he didn't locate him.

Grand Citadel Hotel – Dan's Room – 6:05 p.m.

William took several moments to gaze at his son as Bram exited the room. Tearing his eyes away, he pulled on his command mantle as his stance and demeanor became authoritative. "Attention."

Blaze, Winds, and Patch all abruptly stood and assumed the rigid position.

General Broderick raked his eyes over the men as he held them at attention for some time. When William spoke, his tone carried an icy-edge. "I am your commanding officer. Your display in the TRF conference room is conduct I never expected from my best unit."

He strode to Winds and halted directly in front of him. Frigid blue eyes met and held the corporal's amber orbs. "Corporal Simons, you are damned lucky you never drew your weapon. You will stow whatever personal emotions you may possess for me at this time and focus solely on your duty, soldier. Your priority is the safety of Daniel Broderick. Is that clear?"

With immense effort, Winds bit back the words that wanted to fly out of his mouth, things he held at bay for years. His voice clipped, he responded, "Crystal clear, sir."

Turning his focus on the captain, William's tone remained icy. "Captain Blain, you were in breach of regulations when you mentioned GU and blackout protocol in the presence of persons without proper clearance. In all the years that you've served, I never imagined you would be so careless. You will also stow whatever animosity you may feel towards me personally and focus on your priority."

Blaze knew he screwed up, but he felt an urge to belt the general here and now. It took all his control to keep his hands at his sides. "Yes, sir."

William pivoted away from the men, as he stated, "At ease." Struggling to quell emotions swirling in him, William hated dressing down men who stood protectively between him and Daniel. They were devoted to his boy, but he couldn't allow insubordination. If he did, it would be a slippery slope, which could lead to the collapse of the command structure.

Blaze, Winds, and Patch all went to parade rest as they stared at the back of their no-nonsense general. They observed his hands clench and unclench, and one hand rake through his hair. Blaze thought for a moment how Blondie's and the general's body movements were so similar. The motions were so like Blondie when he teetered on an emotional edge; if Blaze didn't know better, he might believe General Badfather was trying to recompose himself.

Regaining control of his emotions and locking on his stoic mask, William turned back to his men. "This one time, I will excuse your conduct, given the extenuating circumstances. Now, Captain Blain, explain to me why you believe Daniel is under blackout protocol."

Blaze crisply stated, "We searched for Blondie for the past year and found nothing on him—no trace. As you are aware, we have some rather remarkable resources at our disposal, and I called upon them, but they drew a blank. Furthermore, we were denied access to Blondie during the incident review process. Combined, that points to him being subject to a blackout."

William couldn't completely cover his shock as his eyes widened. "You were refused contact with Daniel during the review?"

Blaze nodded. "Yes, sir. We were told you ordered no visitors. Sir, permission to speak freely?"

"Granted."

"Your order was downright cruel and inhumane. Blondie needed support after Brody's death."

Shaking his head, slightly confused, and his gut roiling, William leaned against the wall. "I gave no such order. I checked the logs frequently."

He straightened, unwilling to display weakness. "If you attempted to visit, it was never recorded as it should've been. I didn't place Daniel on blackout protocol. And to be clear, he isn't on a mission. Daniel has been a member of the Toronto TRF since July of last year."

Weary, William moved to a chair to sit and motioned to the others to take a seat. "We are all extremely tired. There are things we must discuss, but I would like to wait until Daniel is awake so as not to repeat myself. Daniel's experienced a shock related to his sister's death.

"I am expecting you to maintain security for us while Daniel processes this new information. We will address the additional threat and the meaning of this pseudo blackout once Daniel is capable of joining us."

Blaze sat and scrutinized the general's behavior and features—nothing matched with his perceptions. The man appeared weathered, weary, and at a loss. Things Blaze would never associate with General Badass. "Is there anything I need to be aware of to ensure Blondie's safety?"

William took a moment before he peered at Shea. "I'm sorry for activating you. However, it is necessary." He shifted his gaze to Blain. "There are few I truly trust to keep my son safe at the moment. You men are among them. You may trust your other men, but they will stay on the perimeter. You three and Daniel's TRF team will be his primary security."

He drew in a breath and gradually exhaled as he scanned the men. Blaze had level five security clearance, while Winds and Patch each attained level four. He made a decision, one he hoped he wouldn't come to regret. "We have a security breach somewhere in Special Forces. It is unclear who it is at this time. I trust Colonel Sutton, Galloway, and his unit, the three of you, and Sergeant Srònaich O'Naoimhín. Everyone else is not above suspicion."

Patch's eyes widened. *What kind of shit is going down?* "Sir?"

Turning to Patch, William shook his head. "That's all I'll share tonight. When Daniel is awake, we'll discuss further. All of us are too dead on our feet to be effective." He stood and said, "Captain, work with Sergeant Pastore to figure out a security plan. I want TRF mixed with SF on each shift. Gambrill assures me we can trust Daniel's team. However, you are not allowed to reveal we may have a breach in our ranks. I am working on a level of clearance for his team, but it hasn't been granted yet."

Blaze rose and nodded. "You have my word Blondie is my priority. I will not fail, sir."

William strode to the door, placed a hand on the knob, and said, "I'll order something for everyone to eat while you discuss plans with Pastore." As he entered the main suite, William hoped he chose wisely when he shared his concerns regarding the breach.

Winds leaned over to Blaze and whispered, "Shit!"

Blaze chuckled. "Aptly put." He turned to Patch. "Sorry, buddy. I know you needed to leave this all behind."

Patch nodded. "True, but I'd walk through hell for Blondie any day because he's done the same for me."

Winds chuckled. "Yeah, we all would. Looks like we're headed into purgatory again. Hope you wore your fire-retardant boxers."

Blaze slapped Winds's back and grinned because really there was nothing else to do at the moment. *Ah, shit, what the hell is going on? A security breach in SF? Why does the general trust only a select few? If he didn't put the kid on blackout protocol, who the hell did? What is the threat to Blondie?* He needed some sleep to think clearly.

Nothing Adds Up

 *45*

July 16
Grand Citadel Hotel – Main Suite – 9:00 p.m.

Heather reentered the main room, scanning for the handsome paramedic. She found him in a chair with his eyes closed near the magnificent, unlit fireplace. Still in awe of the opulence, Heather paused a moment to behold the beautiful accommodations. Having never been in a five-star hotel before, the massive common area of this suite stunned her.

Her entire apartment would almost fit in the common room alone. Besides the ornate hearth, the area boasted plush carpets, three huge sofas, about a dozen comfortable chairs, a few ottomans, several end tables, and a dining table with space for fourteen people. Heather's eyes settled on the massive desk, one she dubbed command central, due to the security monitors, computers, and an array of electronics she couldn't begin to name setup on it.

Heather noted a smaller desk, had been shifted underneath the huge wall-mounted television. It appeared Loki tapped into the flat-screen TV, which now displayed the camera feeds so more than only the person sitting at the larger desk could view the live video.

The suite also contained a kitchenette with a fridge, coffeemaker, sink, microwave, and a completely stocked bar. Near the dinner table, a double-sized glass patio door opened up to a balcony which contained another large table and multiple lounge chairs. The area wouldn't feel crowded even with ten people congregated in the space, if she didn't include herself, Dantastic, or the four other soldiers outside in the hallway.

As for Dantastic, her patient lay in one of the two bedrooms connected to the suite's central area. Pushing aside her amazement, Heather headed for Patch and crouched to speak softly, "Dan's fever is up to one hundred three. Do you want to peek in on him?"

Though exhausted, Patch lifted his lids, nodded, and pushed up from the chair. With a grim countenance, he followed her into Blondie's room. As much as his brother hated hospitals, Patch believed he should be in one now. But with the current situation, he would be safer here.

Blaze reentered the suite with Master Corporal Angus MacDonald after checking in with his other men. Concerned about their welfare since they traveled directly here from Ottawa without stopping to eat, he took them each several sandwiches and coffee. He didn't want them distracted by hunger, and the caffeine would help them remain alert all night.

He strode directly to the general, who still sat at the table with a cup of coffee. The assortment of food, enough to feed an army, had been moved to the far end. After grabbing a bottle of water, Blaze twisted the cap off and took a seat along with Angus, Winds, Jon, and Bram.

Blaze downed half before he said, "General, we've laid out the plans for tonight. Angus will remain in this suite."

William shook his head. "Not what we discussed."

Blaze took a deep breath. "Sir, reconsider. We need someone with fresher eyes watching the monitors tonight."

William studied Master Corporal MacDonald. Though part of a Guardian Unit, the leak might be anyone, and he must weigh whether he trusted MacDonald with Daniel's life?

Angus had no clue what was going on, but he met the general's gaze dead-on. "Sir, I owe Blondie my life. He served with my unit several times over the years. Me and the boys wouldn't have made it home if not for him drawing fire away from us. Ripsaw and I were tight, and Blondie saved his butt many times also. When Blondie went with my old unit, Ripsaw asked me to watch Blondie's six. I did, sir, and I will again. You have my word. He will come to no harm on my watch."

William asked, "You were friends with Master Corporal Preston?"

Angus smiled. "Yes, sir. Best damned hand-to-hand and explosives expert we had. I was proud to call him my brother. May he rest in peace."

"How do you feel about the fact Daniel returned from a mission Preston didn't?" William inquired with a hard edge as he observed the master corporal closely for any negative reaction.

Angus dropped gaze, before lifting eyes which reflected sadness. "Sir, we never know when our time will come. Although I'm unaware of the details, my heart and gut tell me whatever happened, Blondie tried to save Ripsaw, Buzz, and Dutch. If there had been a way to prevent their deaths, your son would've. Sometimes things are beyond our control, and we can't. So, if you're asking, do I blame Blondie for Ripsaw's death? My answer is, hell no, sir."

William nodded and turned to Blaze. "Okay, Captain, MacDonald can man the monitors tonight. Everyone else needs a night's rest. I think we all should head off to our respective rooms."

"Sir, I won't let you down." Angus stood, pivoted, and strode to the desk. His demeanor relaxed as he introduced himself to the TRF officer, "Name's Angus MacDonald. You can call me Angus."

"Dante Baldovino, but I go by Loki."

"The trickster Norse god?" Angus grinned.

Exhausted and concerned for Dan, Loki only nodded before briefly explaining the camera positions he put in place.

Lexa ambled over and raked the soldier with an assessing gaze. She wondered why Dan's father grilled him and why he didn't want anyone but Dan's former unit and them in this room. Her fatigue made her tone a bit more rough than usual. "You let one hair on his head be harmed, and you'll be dealing with me!" She pivoted and strode out, leaving Loki and Angus staring at each other at the vehemence of her words.

Loki absently rubbed his bicep, where Lexa hit him once after he pissed her off. "Man, no one ever wants to deal with Lexa when she's ticked off. You better follow through if you want your arms to function normally." Loki nodded to Ray and followed him toward the door.

Angus riveted his gaze on the monitors as the three officers left. Although Lexa might be petite, he would do well to heed her word. Like Ripsaw, she epitomized the idiom, never judge a book by its cover. Preston might've been short in stature, but he easily took down men twice his size and weight.

Grand Citadel Hotel – Dan's Room – 9:05 p.m.

Patch finished checking Blondie and instructed Heather when to administer the next dose of sedative. He turned as Blondie's Sergeant enter the room.

Nick moved forward and peered down at Dan as he rubbed the back of his neck. "How's he doing?"

"Resting comfortably. I'll keep a careful watch on him tonight. Don't you worry," Heather assured the worried officer.

Patch answered, "His fever's up, which typically happens with him. Should probably break sometime tonight."

Nick nodded and shifted his gaze to Patch. "How do you know so much about Dan?"

Tired and not up for much discussion, Patch yawned. "Lots of experience and mentoring from an excellent doctor." As he thought about the military doctor, his mind latched onto something, and he pinned his eyes on Sergeant Pastore. "Do you have any extended family members who are doctors?"

"No. Why?" Nick asked.

Patch shook his head and grinned. "Well, sorta interesting, the doctor who helped me keep Blondie alive ... his last name is Pastore. Would've been fascinating if you were related."

Nick tilted his head at the idea of another name coincidence in proximity to Dan. He gave Heather a tired smile. "Thanks for coming to take care of Dan tonight. We all truly appreciate all you're doing."

"My pleasure. I'm happy to help." Heather turned her attention back Patch after the sergeant left the room. Attracted to this man, her heart pitter-pattered being close to him.

"I'm in room fifteen-o-six if you need me. Just call, and I'll be here in a flash," Patch said in a drained voice.

Heather gently laid her hand on his arm. Pleased to learn his real name earlier, she used it now. "Get some rest, Jim. I promise to call if he needs your attention. I also have Dr. Fraser on speed dial. He said to contact him if Dan takes a turn for the worse or if I'm concerned about anything."

Leaning down to Blondie, Patch squeezed his left bicep. "Rest easy, little brother. You have a pretty nurse caring for you tonight." Straightening up, Patch grinned at Heather, noting her slightly blushed cheeks. "Goodnight, Heather. Remember, I'm only a call away."

Heather beamed at Jim. *He called me pretty.* She only nodded because she didn't trust her voice not to come out in a squeak.

William entered the bedroom as Patch exited. He put Daniel in the room with two queen beds because William would not be leaving his son's side tonight. He grabbed his duffel bag from the second bed and said, "I'll be back in a bit, going to shower and change in the other bedroom, but I plan on sleeping in this room with my son."

"Yes, sir." Heather pulled the chair close to Dan's bed and positioned it to give her direct visibility to monitor her patient, but also near a lamp she could use for reading. She settled in and picked up her latest book.

Grand Citadel Hotel – Blaze's Room – 9:10 p.m.

When Blaze and the rest stepped into the hall to go to their rooms, Blaze held Winds and Patch back. "Guys, we need to talk." Not wanting their conversation to be overheard, he added, "Let's go to my room." Several moments later, the three entered his room, and Blaze closed the door.

"What's up?" Winds asked, though certain he knew what Blaze wanted to discuss. The same thing weighed on his mind, and the storm clouds were gathering. He held it together in the general's presence, but now—now the tempest whipped up.

Blaze walked to the window and stared out before allowing the aggravation he reined in all night freedom. "The general. That isn't the man we know. Not the asshole with no regard for Blondie for the six years he served with us, the bastard who kept assigning Blondie to work with other units, when he should've had downtime. Not the stone-hearted gargoyle who refused us when we requested to search for Blondie after he was taken. Hell, none of what he displayed today or what Gambrill shared adds up."

"I'm struggling, too," Patch put in. "The way he held Blondie—can't be someone who is so cold and calculating. Gambrill's words and the general's actions and words don't match to the bastard who made Blondie's life hell. Why would he care if there is a threat to Blondie now? He certainly didn't care when he was tortured for months.

"He only visited once when Blondie was back from that, and all he did was order him not to commit suicide because he put too much into his training— so cold. Why would he do all this? Why does he care now? Which is the true man? Why are they so different?" Patch said tiredly, trying to make his head clear enough to understand.

Bitterness infused Winds's tone, "Re-activating Patch is more like the general we know and hate. Which, by the way, is incredibly wrong regardless of this so-called security breach. However, what isn't like General Badfather and what's bugging the hell outta me was when he whispered to Blondie, 'Look terrible like the first time in Kandahar.'

"How the hell could he know what Blondie looked like back then? All he asked Blaze is if Blondie died. He never even bothered to visit the kid. A solid fact because we were with Blondie the entire time. We never left him alone." Winds dropped down on the bed, working hard to rein in his emotions before he let loose words he might later regret.

Still gazing out the window, Blaze said glumly, "I caught that, too. Made me remember the day. Still miss Gambit. I recall how badly Blondie reacted when we told him Gambit didn't make it—he blamed himself. The fact he saved us three and Mason didn't assuage his guilt.

"He kept telling me Gambit would be alive if he had run faster, spotted the C4 sooner, or avoided getting shot in the thigh, he would've gotten there sooner. I remember laughing when Blondie said the last one. Like he could've controlled the bullet's trajectory.

"At the time, I didn't understand where those kinds of thoughts came from, and only accepted his deep-seated sense of guilt to be a part of who he is. But after today, I believe I comprehend. Sadly, I think the source of his mindset is his sister's death."

Winds slammed his fists on the bed. "How come we're only now learning Blondie had a little sister who died? I thought he trusted us."

Blaze squeezed the back of his neck. "Blondie's always had secrets. As bad as Brody's childhood was, I think Blondie's was worse in some ways. He holds close to the vest things that make him feel vulnerable. The only one who Blondie ever fully trusted is Brody."

Winds snorted. "Maybe not, Brody didn't even know his birthday, and they'd been friends for several years."

Blaze kept quiet. He had his suspicions Brody knew the kid's birthday. A true brother and confidant to Blondie, their bond unique and unbreakable, Brody would've kept all Blondie's secrets—like Blondie's fear of water. So, it stood to reason Brody had known about Sara too.

Blondie never did talk much about his past with them. Blaze knew he'd earned Blondie's trust on the rooftop in Makhachkala, and he was damned sure no one—except perhaps Dr. Pastore—learned the secret the kid shared with him that day. A secret of Blondie's he would take to the grave. After today, Blaze was confident the kid still possessed other secrets.

"I didn't hear that. I was too focused on how the general held Blondie. The expression on the general's face tonight is exactly like the damned photo. Perhaps Gambrill is right … maybe Blondie mixed some things up in his head as a little boy.

"Something like witnessing your little sister die in front of you would be very disturbing. But that still doesn't explain the other stuff. It just doesn't," Patch said unhappily and thoroughly confused.

"So, what the fucking hell do we do about it now? How do we proceed with our version of Dr. Jekyll and General Hyde?" Winds pent-up emotion spiked, needing an outlet.

Hearing that well-known tone in his best friend's voice, Blaze turned and studied Winds. *Oh shit, the storm is brewing. The outburst at Gambrill was a category three. Winds is definitely gathering force again, and if he lets loose this time, it will likely cost him his career, especially after the dressing-down we received tonight.*

Most people believed Winds's nickname came from his specialty as a communication expert, *like talking to the winds.* The unit let others think that, but the real reason was the hurricane force of words he occasionally unleashed. Those 'winds' of words could be devastating to their target, but mostly it ended up costing Winds reprimands and demotions.

That was why he was still only a corporal after so many years in service. The last time he mouthed off, Plouffe busted Winds down to private. This time, General Badass would likely ensure Winds received a Big Chicken Dinner—a bad conduct dishonorable discharge. Blaze wouldn't allow Winds to throw away the military life he valued. Blaze considered the question, figuring a way to dissipate the storm before it developed fully.

Blaze sighed and focused on Winds. "I think it's best, for now, to put it on the back burner. Focus on protecting Blondie while he's unable to do it for himself. Nothing jives at all anymore, and I have more questions than answers at the moment. The one thing we do know is Blondie is no longer under the general command. Blondie's safe at the TRF."

Winds and Patch stared at him with expressions he read as *Are you fucking kidding me?*

Considering Blondie's current condition resulted from activities with TRF, Blaze amended, "Well, at least safer than being under General Badfather's control and in Kandahar."

"Amen to that, brother!" Winds stood, appreciating the way Blaze always looked out for all of them.

With no more words, they gave each other a brotherly hug before Winds and Patch left for their rooms. So exhausted, Blaze didn't bother to pull the covers down or undress as he let himself fall onto the bed. He was asleep within seconds.

Winding Down

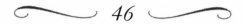 *46*

Loki finished showering and changed into comfortable shorts for sleeping before exiting the bathroom. He nodded to Ray, who currently sat at the desk. They offered to room together so Heather would have a room to herself. "You pick your bed? Window or door? This room's got an awesome view. The city is all lit up. Did you find the coffee pot?" Loki continued talking non-stop as he stood peering out at the scene fifteen stories below.

Aware something bothered Loki since his best friend tended to ramble when he became frazzled, Ray only listened because Loki would eventually reveal his concern. If he let him spew a bit first, he would be able to pinpoint Loki's worry. He grinned as it finally came out. *Ah, there it is, 'Did I set up enough cameras?' and 'I'm not sure I found all the blind spots.'*

Ray interrupted and used his calming voice, "Loki, you did an excellent job. Dan's well covered. Everything will be fine. It's alright to sleep now. I'll shut off the light. You take the window bed."

"Do you think Dan is really the target of someone? I searched for blackout protocol. I didn't find anything on it. What do you think all this means?"

Rising from his seat, Ray went to Loki, nudged him towards the closest bed, pulled the sheets back, and gently pushed him down, so he sat on the edge. "I don't have any answers for you. Time to turn off your brain. None of us has enough mind power now to think properly."

Loki yawned. "Yeah, you're right. We need some sleep. Tomorrow is soon enough to begin sorting all this out." Loki plopped back on the pillows, tugged the covers over him, and closed his weary eyes.

Ray switched off the light and crawled into his bed. His mind as mixed up as Loki's, he hoped tomorrow would provide them the answers they sought. *For now—sleep is necessary.*

Grand Citadel Hotel – Lexa's Room – 9:25 p.m.

Twenty minutes ago, as Lexa reached her room, her cell rang. She glanced at the number and recognized it as Commander Gambrill's. He informed her she would be meeting with Agent Stevens of NRB tomorrow morning at eight in the hotel lobby for the interview regarding her lethal force at the bank.

Lexa rose from the tub she soaked in for the last fifteen minutes, trying to remove the ache from her overused muscles from the trek in section seven. Now less stiff, she toweled herself off, pulled on her short nightgown, and slowly moved to the king-size bed.

A part of her didn't want to be so far from Dan and wished she could've stayed in the other bedroom in the suite. An unpleasant sensation kept her on edge, believing danger lurked all too close to Dan. Though he now rested under the watchful eyes of many, something continued to claw at her mind, urging her to be aware.

Lying down on the soft, downy pillows, Lexa pulled the plush comforter over her body up to her neck as she shifted her thoughts. After she hung up with Gambrill, she had a sense of relief. Her interview would take place here, though she remained upset with herself for having tears in her eyes. The blink to clear them allowed Garth to shoot Dan, and he suffered a hairline fracture of his collarbone because she was not ready.

As she recalled his scars, his appearance in the ravine, and the ungodly howling, waterworks started to flow. Her silent tears turned into quiet sobs, muffled by her pillow. Empathy for Dan filled her. She lost siblings, too. Not quite the same, her four brothers weren't dead, but she understood the pain of his loss. Lexa still missed her brothers and couldn't imagine what it would be like if they died.

Lexa cried for a long time. She rolled onto her back and stared at the ceiling as she chided herself. *Pull yourself together. You don't weep over men—ever.* Out of the blue, images of Dan's expressive eyes, reflecting his various emotions over the past two days, danced in her mind.

Unexpected tears sprung forth and silently rolled down her cheeks, leaving trails of salt. She closed her eyes as she cursed out loud, "Damn! Why does Dan affect me so deeply? I refuse to cry for any man."

She curled up on her side. She hadn't wept since the man who meant the most to her shattered her heart and left a million scattered pieces on the ground. Lexa willed herself to sleep. *I'm only overtired.*

The devil on her shoulder exchanged her horns for a halo and softly crooned, *"Rest now my little one. Remember, you have always been loved."*

Lexa's mind filled with childhood memories, smiling as she baked cookies with her mom, enjoying a time when she felt the love of her entire family.

Grand Citadel Hotel – Main Suite Balcony – 9:50 p.m.

William sat alone, at the table on the balcony, with his coffee in hand as he stared at Toronto's city lights. Being fifteen floors above the sounds below, they filtered up somewhat muted. Though exhausted, he took the time to speak with Walter about the contents of the suicide note and what Inspector Davis relayed regarding what Dr. Carter said about Richard Donner.

After taking a sip of coffee, William allowed himself to grieve. To mourn, for all the years he lost with Daniel and the loss of his son's innocence. To wallow in his sorrow for everything their family suffered, and all his boy endured due to the events of one fateful summer day. To recall his beautiful Sara, whose light had been ripped from them all far too early.

A lone tear streaked down his face. He wished to call Yvonne for her advice on how to proceed. He wanted things to change, yet every time he tried something it backfired. William knew he had so many things he must beg forgiveness for from Daniel. Some actions William fully accepted would be unforgivable—but he hoped.

William pushed those painful memories to the back of his mind as he reached forward and turned on his encrypted phone. Things were FUBAR. He dialed Tom's number as he flicked on the radio frequency and digital audio jammers and noise generator, which would prevent his communications from being overheard, picked up, or recorded by anyone who might endeavor to listen in. When Sutton answered, William stated, "Things are worse than I imagined."

Tom sighed and used the code name assigned to Dan as he inquired, "How is Phoenix?"

"Sedated. Injuries he'll recover from, but I learned several things that give credence to his comment about me trying to kill him. I'm not sure what's going on. I need the security clearances for TRF right away. Also, start paperwork on Patch. I had to activate him under the special assignment clause."

Tom blew out a long breath. "Christ, Oracle, why the hell did you do that? You know why he left."

A chuckled without humor slipped out from William at Tom's use of his old call sign. It had been many years since he'd been called Oracle. "Yes, I do, and I wouldn't have if it was not necessary. He refused to leave Phoenix, so I had no choice if I allowed him to stay and care for him. Sadly, Patch settled in Toronto months ago and never knew Phoenix lived here."

William realized it was probably better to refer to the men by their call signs as he added, "Blaze, Winds, and Patch barred me from approaching Phoenix when I arrived. Their expressions said they believed I would harm him. Hell, Winds put his hand on his weapon."

"He what?" Tom exclaimed as he stood and began to pace his office. "My God, what did you do?"

William leaned back in the chair. "Dressed them down and excused their behavior this time. Something serious is going on. Blaze thought I put Phoenix on blackout protocol. He said he's been searching for him—using his extensive network of resources for the past year. My brother said much the same thing to me. Why the hell couldn't they find him? We didn't have him on protocol. Someone is pulling strings. I feel like a marionette. This goes deep or wide. We're facing a significant problem."

He raked his hand through hair still damp from his shower. "Blaze asserted tonight they tried to see Phoenix during the review board period. They were told I ordered no visitors and refused entry, but their names were never entered into the log as people trying to visit him. I gave strict orders the only people allowed in were Blaze, Winds, Patch, and Mason and to record everyone who requested entry."

Tom sat heavily into his chair. "Shit, this is worse than we thought. What do you want me to do?"

William took a long drink. "I've given this some thought. Clearly, we have no idea who all is involved. It's going to require an investigation. Unfortunately, I think there may be people involved who we trust. Those damned photos have been coming to me ever since Phoenix applied to Special Forces.

"I'm thinking there might be something with Phoenix's service—things don't add up anymore. I've screwed up with him, but the level of hatred I viewed in the eyes of the unit as they barred me from him truly unnerved me. Something more than my hands-off attitude towards Phoenix must be driving their attitude. His records require a closer review, but I don't even trust my analysts anymore."

Tom responded, "We need someone not associated with SF to investigate. Bransworth might help. He's with Canadian Security Intelligence Service."

Staring out at the lights, William came to a conclusion. "I agree. But we need people we can trust. You trust Bransworth, and although he's with CSIS now, he was in SF previously."

"CSIS might be the right ones to engage here. Bransworth is one of the most trustworthy men I ever met. I'd stake my life he's clean in this ... whatever this is," Tom stated.

"No! I've already lost one child, and Pletcher tried to kill my other daughter. Apparently, he is still going after her with him ending up where we moved her. Although we don't know where he's getting his information, someone with access to us, must've shared her location. I won't risk Phoenix—not now that I might have a real chance of reconnecting with him. I need you to rush the clearances through on the TRF team."

Tom stood and began pacing again. "Not sure if that will fly. It'll be difficult making a case." He would allow William to think on this a while. His friend would come to the same conclusion he had—not knowing who to trust inside Special Forces now they needed outside help. Getting CSIS involved, Bransworth, in particular, would be the right option, especially since Pletcher had once been part of the Intelligence Branch of the Canadian Forces.

"Do what you can. If I have to, I'll call Jerrell," William stated.

Tom whistled. "You'd contact him over this?"

"Damned right, I would. This affects family, and I'm done being played with like some damned puppet. National security is at risk too. We've got a serious problem, and none of our usual people have found a goddamned thing. If someone can get to me through my family, imagine what they could do if they went after others."

William stood and gripped the balcony's rail so hard his knuckles turned white. Tom remained silent on the other end as both of them thought through what they faced. William released his hold. "I'm too tired to think clearly now. Do what you can to push through the clearances."

Then William conceded, "Perhaps if we have them coordinate with a CSIS liaison ... Bransworth, we can arrange enough clearance to help figure out what the hell is going on. This is important ... I can't lose my son now ... not when there's finally hope." He turned to the table and picked up his coffee cup before turning back to peer at the night sky.

"Okay, I'll do what I can. I'll contact Jerrell if necessary. Grab some rest and focus on the kid. I'll send you an update by zero six hundred Toronto." Tom sat down, swiveled his chair, and opened the drawer to pull out the folders he prepared when William requested security clearances for Dan's TRF team.

"Thanks," William said in a weary voice.

"No thanks are ever necessary. You would do the same and more for me if the tables were turned. Now, put the coffee down and get some sleep," Tom ordered sternly.

William chuckled and set the cup down. "I'll look for your update in a few hours." He hung up, turned off the jammers, and returned inside.

Grand Citadel Hotel – Dan's Room – 10:05 p.m.

Heather glanced behind her when General Broderick reentered the bedroom. She smiled as she pushed the sedative into Dan's IV port. The general appeared quite different in comfortable sweat pants and a loose t-shirt. No longer wearing his uniform, he seemed like any other ordinary man. Heather noted exhaustion in his care-worn features—a man like so many others she'd seen in her time as a nurse ... a father concerned for his son.

William gave the young woman a soft smile as she finished administering the medication per Patch's orders. "Thank you. I appreciate everything you are doing for my son."

Heather nodded slightly and smiled at the number of times she had been thanked so far. Turning to put the syringe away, Heather said, "Dantastic is worth the time and effort. If you don't mind, I'm gonna grab a coffee. I'll be back in a few minutes."

When he nodded, Heather hurried out to give the man a moment of privacy. As she left, the seriousness of this situation became clear to her. She stiffened, and a shiver coursed through her body as she observed the general placing a handgun on the nightstand.

After setting his Sig Sauer down, William gazed at Daniel. He wished Daniel was still a small boy so he could gather him in his arms and hold him while he slept. But his son was full-grown, so William would have to make do with being as close as the bed next to him. *At least there isn't one-way glass separating me from Danny tonight like in Kandahar.* He leaned down and kissed Daniel's forehead before he whispered, "Sleep well, my boy, I'll keep you safe."

Pardon Me, But What the Hell?

 *47*

Angus watched the monitors from the station set up in the main room. *Loki is dammed good, not a single blind spot. Impressive!* Everything remained clear as he checked in with Hal, Duncan, and Russ. Leaning back in the chair, Angus glanced at the vast amount of leftover food, contemplating grabbing himself an apple as Heather walked out of Blondie's room. "How is he?"

"Resting, fever is rising a bit, but I think it will peak soon and drop afterward." Heather helped herself to a bowl of grapes and poured a cup of coffee. "How's everything on the security front? Do you think any of your guys might want a snack? I can run one to them."

"No, they're okay. I wouldn't want them distracted. Something happens to Blondie on my watch I know eight guys and one feisty gal who will have my head on a platter," he chuckled but was deadly serious as he returned his gaze to the display screens.

The petite female TRF officer possessed a fierceness that scared him more than all the burly men put together. A tremor went down his spine as he recalled her threat. Angus hoped all remained quiet and uneventful the rest of the night because he didn't want to find out what Loki meant by functioning arms.

Grand Citadel Hotel – Gym – 5:00 a.m.

Jon ran at a steady pace on the hotel's treadmill as Bram entered the gym.

"Wow, thought I'd beat everyone," Bram said as he ambled over to the stationary bike. Being creatures of habit, Bram guessed the team would show up in the tiny gym this morning at the usual time. A workout would clear their heads and get their blood pumping.

Nick opened the door, smiled, and shook his head. "We gotta stop meeting like this." Nick chose the elliptical machine.

"Meeting like how?" piped in Loki as he and Ray entered. Ray went to the small selection of free weights. Loki plopped onto an exercise ball and enthusiastically bounced since there was no other equipment to use. "Wow, we need one of these, great workout," Loki said sarcastically, but secretly thought it would be fun to have one.

"He looks like an adult but acts like a kid. Can't take Loki anywhere," Jon baited. He smiled, waiting for Loki's retort.

Loki was about to respond when Lexa arrived. She smiled at Loki's antics on the ball. "Looks like I'm too late—no more toys. I see Loki's playing with the best one. You guys waitin' your turn?"

"Nah, Loki won't share. Make him share. He always hogs the bestest toys. Never lets me play with Lucille, either." Ray fake pouted.

They all chuckled. Today started out well with a sense of normalcy restored after a night's sleep, even if the situation itself was nowhere near normal. The team took turns on the equipment and maintained the usual banter though they all wondered what today would bring.

Two hours later, as they left the gym, Lexa pulled Boss to the side. "The commander called last night. I'm meeting with Agent Stevens at eight this morning. She offered to meet me here. So, I'm going to clean up and meet her in the lobby. I'll join you all after I'm done," Lexa said, her timbre subtly reflecting a burden.

"Understood," Nick replied. He picked up on the nuance of her tone and the glint in her eyes, so he ventured, "Lexa, you are aware you couldn't have prevented Garth from firing. It all happened so fast. Dan wouldn't want you to beat yourself up over this."

Nick noted the shift in her eyes, which conveyed to him he hit the mark. Aware she must work through the emotions herself, and nothing he said would change her mind, Nick smiled and wrapped a reassuring arm around her shoulders and tugged her forward. "Come on. I'll buy you a coffee."

Lexa grinned. The hotel had excellent *free* coffee.

Grand Citadel Hotel – Main Suite – 7:00 a.m.

William sat with his must-have coffee. He didn't sleep well as thoughts of the contents of the suicide note kept entering his head along with both Erik's and Blaze's assumption Daniel had been on blackout protocol.

West's note is the missing piece. If I knew then where Danny's mind came up with those words, would it have made a difference? Perhaps, but he was so traumatized, unreachable, and closed off after Sara died.

William wished to call Yvonne and talk with her about all he learned, but his wife's and daughter's safety was more important at this time. So, he must muddle through on his own, and pray he didn't screw up again. If Daniel realized he had not said those things to him, perhaps they could reestablish their connection.

But things remained so complicated, and he needed to sort out several issues. *Captain Blain appeared ready to hit me last night as I approached Daniel, and Winds went for his firearm like he believed I would harm my own son.*

Those thoughts brought back Daniel's words as he left his office in Kandahar after signing his discharge paperwork. *General, you failed, too. You failed to kill me. You tried for six fucking years, and you failed!*

His gut churned. *There is definitely something very wrong.* He had a sinking feeling his lack of oversight on Daniel's military career had insidious consequences. Particularly if his boy believed he wished him dead and accused him of attempted murder … coupled with the actions and behavior of Blain, Simons, and Shea yesterday.

William glanced at his wristwatch, noting he had two hours to prepare. Although uncomfortable, revealing his personal life to strangers would be necessary because he believed Major Plouffe sent those pictures. And albeit unsubstantiated, Plouffe might be behind more than William ever imagined.

Rising, he decided to spend time alone with his son before everyone arrived this morning—the proverbial calm before the storm.

Grand Citadel Hotel – Lobby – 8:00 a.m.

Promptly at eight o'clock, Lexa entered the lobby and found Agent Stevens waiting in one of the chairs. Stevens stood and said, "I arranged for a private room. If you would please follow me, we'll wrap this up as fast as possible since you have somewhere else you need to be."

Lexa started to follow, but halted when she overheard a conversation at the front desk.

A female said, "No, sir, I can't tell you that information."

The male replied, "But I must determine if General Broderick is staying here. It's important."

The remarks drew Lexa's attention, and turning she spotted an army officer.

"I'm sorry. I can neither confirm nor deny whether he's lodging with us."

Lexa couldn't see his face, but the man sounded quite agitated as he declared, "This is a matter of high security, I insist you answer my question."

Undaunted, the receptionist countered, "Sorry, sir, I cannot. Perhaps you should go through military channels to locate this general you're searching for. Is there anything *else* I can help you with, *Major*?"

Lexa's mind whirled. *Odd, someone is trying to find Dan's father. I assume the military would know how to reach him.* About to go speak with the major, Lexa turned back to the agent when Stevens asked, "Coming?" Lexa nodded and logged the encounter for later consideration.

Grand Citadel Hotel – Main Suite – 8:57 a.m.

NRB Agent Stevens executed an efficient interview and deemed Lexa's action an acceptable use of lethal force, so, Lexa ended up on her way to the general's suite before nine. She would be on time and wouldn't miss anything of importance.

Entering, Lexa noted everyone else assembled. She strode to the kitchen area, poured a cup of coffee and grabbed a cinnamon roll from the tray on the sideboard before joining several others at the table. *Wow, the general is making sure no one goes hungry. There is so much food again.*

Cognizant she should use her manners, she smiled and offered her appreciation. "Sir, thank you for all this."

"It's the least I can do," William replied, noticing the black circles under Constable McKenna's eyes abated a little. When Heather exited Daniel's room, he asked, "How is my son doing now?"

"His fever peaked and broke around eight. His color is better. Vitals are within acceptable ranges. I believe he is resting well, and his body is on the path to healing." Heather smiled at the soft sighs of relief emitted by various people around the dining table.

From his seat, Patch covertly observed Heather. *She is so gorgeous. I could gaze at her all day.* He shook himself from staring at her and turned to the general. "Blondie's doing better, but I believe it is in his best interest to keep him sedated today and wean him off tomorrow. Blondie's been put through the wringer, and he needs the rest."

"Agreed." William conceded for several reasons. First, his son did require rest. Second, the delay would allow Tom time to obtain the necessary security clearances and contact Bransworth. However, the main reason William approved is to stall. He still had not determined what to say or how to approach Daniel regarding Donner's note. Some people might find it amusing General Badass feared speaking with his own son, but so much rode on him doing things right this time, and he didn't want to screw up yet again.

More rested after several hours of sleep, Blaze took a sip of coffee before addressing the others. "Jon and I worked out the security teams and rotation schedule. We'll break into three teams of four. I'll lead team one with Loki, Nick, and Angus. Jon will take charge of team two with Lexa, Hal, and Duncan. Winds will run team three with Bram, Ray, and Russ.

"Mixing both TRF and SF on each team will keep us all apprised of any issues. We'll rotate on eight-hour shifts. My team is up first, then Jon's team, followed by Winds's team. The only exception is Angus will grab some shuteye now and join his team on our next shift. Jon graciously agreed to cover for Angus this shift."

Patch interrupted, "Whoa, where am I in all of this?"

"Always impatient, always. Patch, you and Heather are responsible for Blondie's health. You will be pulling twelve-hour shifts. Satisfied?" Blaze grinned aware Patch would do better being as close as possible to Blondie while the kid remained sedated. It always unnerved Patch when the kid was not able to defend himself. "Any questions?"

He received negative head shakes from all as the general's phone rang. Blaze listened the mostly one-sided cryptic call—a short conversation ending with an expression of relief on General Broderick's face.

When William disconnected, he scanned Daniel's teammates. Sutton came through without having to go through Jerrell. The TRF team now had temporary security clearance to assist in this investigation, working through a CSIS liaison and the unit men. William only hoped Bransworth turned out to be as trustworthy as Sutton believed.

Blaze refreshed his coffee before asking, "When are you planning to start the briefing, sir? I would like to take over security so my guys can sleep."

The front desk incident popped into Lexa's head at that moment, and she swallowed the last of her roll before she said, "Excuse the interruption, but I need to ask you a question, General."

William turned Lexa and allowed a ghost of a smile to land on his face. "Yes?"

"Besides those of us here, who is aware you're staying at this hotel?"

William instantly stiffened. "No one, why?"

Lexa took in the rigidity of his body, so like Dan's. "I observed something in the lobby and got a hinky sense things are a tad off." She recounted the exchange between the receptionist and the army major and noticed General Broderick's stoic demeanor locked right after something she couldn't read flashed in his sapphire eyes. "Sir, is that an issue?"

Forcefully relaxing his tense body, William asked, "Can you describe him?"

"Average height, brown hair, I didn't glimpse his face though. As I said, he sounded agitated," Lexa reported.

William stood, raked his hand through his hair, and paced as thoughts swirled. *Damn, sounds like Plouffe. Why is he trying to determine if I'm here? Sutton would've contacted me if something important arose. It must be Plouffe—but why is the major asking around about me?*

Blowing out a breath, William took several seconds to study those gathered as he altered his plans once again. "I hoped not to repeat the briefing. I would prefer Daniel heard everything at the same time. But yes, I think it might be important, and this briefing shouldn't wait until Daniel joins us. Therefore, I'll inform you all now and Daniel after he awakens."

Resuming his seat, he reached for his strong, black coffee and took a sip as he collected his thoughts. The only person not privileged to listen to the details would be the young nurse. Although Blaze trusted his unit, William couldn't risk Daniel's life. If his suspicions were leaked, they might never discover the information they required to nail the culprit or culprits.

William focused on Heather. "Young lady, I'm must ask you to leave the suite. Thank you for your care of Daniel last night. If you would be so kind as to head to your room now, it would be appreciated."

Heather smiled. The elder Broderick was so protective of his son. Her heart broke for him—she witnessed how restless his sleep had been. At every little sound, he became alert, ready to defend Dan. Each time he woke, the caring father would go to Dan and place a hand on his son's forehead, checking the fever, and he would inquire how his son fared.

She nodded. "Let me grab my book from Dan's room, and I'll be out of your hair." Heather turned to Jim. "I'm in room fifteen-o-seven. Call if you need me for anything."

Blaze noted Angus appeared dead on his feet, like the rest of his men. He returned his gaze to Broderick and suggested, "Sir, my men, need rest. If we watch the monitors from in here, that should be sufficient until they've gotten a few hours of sleep."

William recognized the benefit, both for the men as well as for the situation. He nodded. "I agree."

Loki sat at the monitors as soon as Angus rose. He appointed himself to the task and grinned when Ray sat beside him. "I'll keep an eye on half, and you can scan the others."

Waiting for the room to clear, William poured another coffee. Once Angus and Heather left, he said, "Please, take a seat, everyone. Captain, activate the jammers."

Blaze motioned to Winds, who sat near the large desk, to turn on the RF jammer, digital audio jammer, and white-noise generator as he strode to the opposite side of the room to switch on the other set of jammers Winds strategically placed there last night. He wasn't sure why, but it didn't bode well for what they were about to hear.

Patch rose from the dining table and dragged one of the chairs from the main area closer to Blondie's bedroom, which allowed him to listen and still keep tabs on his brother.

Once everyone settled, William peered at Blain and Simons. "You will understand what I'm about to tell the others." He turned to Shea and said, "So you are aware, this is the reason I had no choice but to reactivate you."

Patch's gut twisted as he nodded.

William assumed a calm facade as his tone imbued the gravity of his words. "Before I begin the briefing, I must inform you portions of what I'm about to share are considered highly-classified. You have all been granted temporary, level two security clearance. As such, you're bound by the Security of Information Act never to repeat anything you learn today to anyone outside of those in this room.

"If you do, you'll be in breach of trust under the Act. Any unauthorized communication of data presented is punishable by law. The default penalties fall into three categories. On summary conviction, you face detention for twelve months, a fine up to twenty-thousand dollars, or both. On indictment, you may be imprisoned for fourteen years. If the breach is found to involve foreign entities or terrorist organizations, you could be incarcerated for life.

"For those of you who are not clear on legal terms, let me clarify. You only have to be charged with the crime, not actually convicted to be put in prison per the definition of indictment."

The room went dead silent as everyone's expressions conveyed their shock, disbelief, and concern. Jon stared first at Nick, then shifted to Bram before settling back on Broderick. "Sir, pardon me, but what the hell?"

William noted the incredulity and nearly chuckled at Hardy's response. "When I learned I would be coming, Gambrill provided me all your names and personnel files. I rushed your clearances through the proper channels because I believed you might be involved at some point."

Nick inhaled, internalizing the potential implications. "Sir, we understand the ramifications. But my team must be given a chance to opt-out if they are not comfortable with this situation."

"I understand and concur," William responded.

As Nick's eyes roved over his team, receiving nods of agreement, he smiled. They would cover Dan's back no matter the entanglement.

Blaze grinned, his heart warmed, and gut settled witnessing Blondie's new team step up to the plate. *The kid's lucky. He found a new place to belong.*

Patch checked his watch. "Sir, can we hold a moment, I need to do a quick check on Blondie. It's about time for more sedative."

When General Broderick agreed, Patch hopped up from the chair. Everyone took the opportunity to grab more coffee, a donut, or piece of fruit and settled back into their seats, wondering what the heck the general needed to tell them that required clearance with such severe consequences.

Suspicions and Insights

48

Peering at Blondie, Patch's stomach tied in knots. Nils' suicide had been the straw that broke him and prompted his decision to leave the military. Now back under the command of a general, who demonstrated for years he didn't give a rat's ass for his only son, Patch was unsure how much more he could take. He hurt too much when his brothers suffered.

After pulling a chair close, he sat, checked Blondie's IV site, and sighed. "Damn, you never make things easy for me, do you?" He stood, grabbed his kit, returned, removed the infiltrated IV from Blondie, and began searching for another vein to use. "Small blessing, you're still out so you won't need to deal with a needle."

When he finished changing the IV location, Patch elevated Blondie's arm to reduce the swelling caused by infiltration. He administered another dose of sedative, pain meds, rechecked his vitals, and noted the antibiotic drip would have to be changed in a little while.

Standing in the bedroom doorway beside Blaze, Bram asked, "Is everything alright with Dan?"

Patch nodded. "Yeah, sorry. I had to restart his IV. The line became infiltrated. Happy I didn't have to start another one while he was awake."

"Why?" Bram took a step inside, his worry increasing.

Blaze patted Bram's shoulder. "Let's just say, the kid doesn't do well with needles."

Bram filed away the piece of trivia on Dan, but the way Blaze spoke made him think there might something more to it. He refrained from asking since General Broderick patiently waited to begin the briefing. The three men rejoined everybody else in the other room.

Grand Citadel Hotel – Main Suite – 9:45 a.m.

Patch kept Blondie's door open and repositioned his chair to keep an eye on the antibiotic drip before sitting and preparing to listen. Blaze and Bram resumed their seats, too.

William cleared his throat and got straight to the point without further ado. "After Richard Donner attacked Daniel, Walter called to inform me of what occurred. When Inspector Davis attempted to take crime scene photos of Daniel covered in blood, Walter promptly stopped him with an off-the-cuff excuse military security might be compromised if such pictures were ever taken and released."

"What?" and, "Picture?" emitted with confusion from several in the room.

"Gambrill didn't tell you about that?" William asked.

"No, we never received the full briefing from Gambrill. Davis showed up with the suicide note, and all hell broke loose," Jon responded.

Nick interjected, "Sir, the commander provided us some details on issues of a personal nature between yourself and Dan resulting from Sara's death. We also viewed a photo taken of young Dan at the accident scene." He rubbed a hand over his mouth as he composed himself when the memory flooded in.

"We'll respect your privacy. Those are matters for the two of you to address together. You only need to share things that are relevant to Dan's safety now," Nick concluded.

A bit relieved they knew the history, William believed it would be easier for them to understand having seen the heart-wrenching photo of his boy. *How to start? So many tentacles may or may not relate to one another—photos, Pletcher, Plouffe suspicions, pilfered mail, Daniel's words, and the unit's assumption of blackout protocol. How best to make everything make sense?*

All the details rolled around in his head as he sorted them and determined an approach. William began, "Walter is aware of the reasons behind my refusal to have my son photographed in distress. It stems from the snapshot taken the day Sara died. I decked the idiot photographer. In retaliation, he sold the photo to a tabloid paper, and they printed the image on the front page. I never understood why they would do something so despicable to a little boy."

William clenched his fist as he tightened his mask in place. *Now isn't the time to show emotion.* "Sorry, I digress. As you may have noticed, the picture captured my emotional reaction to Daniel's anguish and Sara's death. In my position, I am a target for many who will use almost anything to get to me.

"As a result, I've tried hard to protect those I care about from being pawns my enemies can use. That photo has been sent to me many times in the last decade. Until recently, I thought its purpose was simply to harass me. There was never any actual threat, only strange notes.

"However, I now believe there's a credible threat to my son's life, and it is connected to the photograph. And if my suspicions prove true, it will shake Special Forces to the foundations."

Blaze shared a glance with Winds and Patch. All three alert at the general's mention of shaking foundations. Blaze thought about Broderick's reluctance to allow Angus in here last night—odd because Angus was a member of a Guardian unit. As such, they were the most trusted members of the military, with the highest security clearances. He turned his full attention back to the general.

William took a sip of coffee. "I have no evidence to substantiate my beliefs, and I request you bear with me as I try to explain the various tangents and seemingly unrelated events. If something isn't clear, stop me and ask. I'll do my best to clarify, but there are items that still don't make sense to me. Elements neither my analysts nor me have deciphered.

"All I can say for sure is, after years of the same taunts, something changed after Daniel's last mission. As a result of that variation and other things that came to light in the past year, my gut instinct tells me the incidents I previously viewed as only harassment are much more sinister. If I'm right, recent events have placed Daniel in the crosshairs of a dangerous and unexpected enemy. I need your help to protect him and end the threat."

He paused and studied each of them. He had their undivided attention. "When Daniel was eighteen, and in boot camp, I received a copy of that photo anonymously. The words 'soft spot' scrawl across Daniel's chest in red marker unnerved me, but with no defined threat, there was nothing to do.

"I didn't receive another one until after Daniel joined Special Forces training a few years later. After that, they arrived on a fairly regular basis, mostly with some obscure letters and numbers on them, the meaning of which I still don't understand. However, some had clear taunts written on them." William stopped and took a small drink.

Hoping to profile the sender, Lexa asked, "What kind of taunts?"

William recalled every sickening word sent. "I received several, but three of the worst which hit me hardest are 'fly Danny fly,' 'Danny run,' and 'Toy soldier fallen?'—I still have them all. If you think they'll be useful, I can request my aide send copies of them."

Lexa witnessed the same emotionless mask Dan wore falling into place on his father. It struck her as one way they were alike—they both hid their emotions.

Still struggling to connect the pieces in that General Broderick shared, Nick responded, "Might be wise to review them if you think they're related to the current threat."

Lexa probed, "Sir, why did those messages make an impact on you?"

Blaze studied this new and bizarre general closely. He focused on Broderick's eyes mostly because he had learned to read the emotions reflected in the kid's expressive orbs. He wondered if the general possessed the same tell. He noted a slight shudder and glimpsed a momentary flash of sorrow in the sapphire shards before Broderick answered Lexa.

"Bec … ause—" William's voice stuttered uncharacteristically.

My God, did General Badass's voice crack? What the hell is going on? Where is the cold-hearted bastard? Patch gaped; slack-jawed as his own eyes rounded with surprise.

Halting and clearing his throat as he once again regained control over his emotions, William firmly stated, "I remember because each one arrived after Daniel was injured. Whoever sent them gained private details. JTF2 injury reports are not publicized due to the secrecy of missions. This led me to believe the sender is either in Special Forces or cultivated an inside contact. There's been an open investigation for years with no results."

The currents in Winds's mind began to swirl. *What would someone gain by sending photos to the general? How did 'soft spot' apply to Blondie since General Badass doesn't give a damn about the kid?*

William continued, "The messages never contained direct threats, only unsettling words about events involving Daniel. The analysts who examined them over the years found no leads and theorized the culprit only wanted to provoke an emotional reaction from me by twisting a virtual knife.

"I agreed with them until the last photo, but please hold your questions, I'll get there. As I said, the second photo came during Daniel's training. The message read fly Danny fly. It arrived a week after my son nearly died in a training exercise."

Loki gasped. "Sir, he almost died? How?"

"Leapt off a bluff to save a fellow recruit," William answered.

"Christ, he jumped off a cliff? I know Dano's reckless sometimes, but what the hell happened? Why'd he do it?" Jon asked aghast.

Although he didn't want to relive the experience, William decided to tell them anyway. "The major in charge of training contacted me directly after it happened because Daniel lost a lot of blood and things were touch and go by the time he arrived at the hospital.

"This incident occurred while the recruit cadre was in the first week of an eight-week language immersion phase. One of the training officers wanted to try a new exercise that was not part of our standard courses. They selected four men who excelled in languages to participate since doing so wouldn't put them behind the rest of the group. The lead instructor assigned Daniel to command the others in the drill.

"The intended goal of the exercise was to evaluate and develop leadership skills under pressure. The operation was conducted under open mics so the instructors would be able to listen and assess their abilities. Their mission task appeared simple—navigate up the mountain, rappel down the bluff, and return within a set time.

"However, unbeknownst to Daniel, the other three recruits had been instructed to be as obnoxious and difficult as possible. The real purpose was to determine if Daniel would be rattled or maintain composure and team cohesion. Due to safety concerns, the trainees were also told to cease the negative behavior during the rappelling phase.

"All the way up, they gave Daniel a hard time and tested his patience by questioning every order. Major White said Daniel made mistakes, as was to be expected. Daniel lost his cool at one point and called one recruit an asshat and told him with his bad attitude and lack of discipline he didn't belong in Special Forces. White also indicated Daniel handled himself well overall in the three hours it took them to trek to the top."

So that's where Dan learned to deal with people like Aaron. Lexa wondered how he maintained his equanimity in the face of Aaron's constant crap.

"When they reached the bluffs, Daniel directed his team to prepare for rappelling. As he secured his line, unfortunately, the men continued to hassle Daniel, forgetting they were supposed to stop at that point. Completely out of line, all three soldiers refused to comply with Daniel's repeated orders.

"White was about to intervene and remind the recruits of their instructions when Daniel firmly took command. My son reminded them their behavior put the entire unit at risk. He also stated he was in charge and if they didn't like it to take it up with a training officer later, but for now, he was giving them a direct order to fasten their lines.

"Two of them realized their error and swiftly prepped their ropes. However, the third man got in Daniel's face and yelled, 'Back off, Broderick. You're only here because Daddy pulled strings. You're the one who doesn't belong, asshole,' before shoving Daniel. Regrettably, the soldier lost his footing and fell backward off the cliff.

"Daniel hurled himself over the bluff in an attempt to grab the man. Incredibly, he managed to wrap his arms around the man's waist as they both fell. As Daniel's line reached its end, they slammed hard into the mountain several times. Daniel took the brunt of the impact because his body was between the recruit he saved and the mountainside."

William stood to pace, needing to move. "Somehow, Daniel maintained the presence of mind to attach his safety harness to the unconscious recruit before he too lost consciousness. The other recruits pulled them to safety, but if Daniel hadn't succeeded in catching him, the man would've fallen to his death.

"White said none of them could quite figure out how Daniel managed to clip the guy in and still hold onto him—let alone remain conscious long enough to do it, given Daniel's injuries. The collision with the rockface resulted in Daniel suffering five bruised ribs, a sprained wrist, a dislocated shoulder, a concussion, and a ruptured spleen.

"When I arrived at the hospital, my heart broke. Daniel lost so much blood he turned ghostly pale, and appeared so young and vulnerable. The surgeon stopped the internal bleeding by performing a laparoscopic partial splenectomy. I maintained a bedside vigil for two days—until he regained consciousness. His current bruised and battered state reminds of how he appeared back then."

William's eyes turned towards the bedroom, where Daniel currently rested. His boy constantly amazed him with what he endured physically and how fast he recovered. Daniel possessed an inner strength. His gaze shifted to Patch, the medic who went to impressive lengths to help his son over the years. "That is the first time Daniel amazed the doctors. Three days after waking, they discharged him, and he rejoined the cadre for the language courses, although he was excused from daily PT for six weeks.

"Worried about infections since he now only had a partial spleen, the doctor wanted to hold him out another eight weeks. However, Daniel wished to remain with his cadre. He worked hard to prove his physical fitness by the time the group moved into the parachuting and swim phase."

Patch glanced at Blondie. He was fully aware of the spleen issue and how his immune system didn't fight off infections as well as most people. One of the reasons Blondie became feverish so quickly. It was also the reason Blondie always complied with taking antibiotics when prescribed.

Blondie once told him he could deal with pain, so he avoided pain meds, but he wasn't about to die because of some damned infection. Speaking of which, Patch noticed that it was time to change out the antibiotic bag. He rose and headed into the room.

William spotted Patch rise and go into Daniel's room to check on his son. He leaned back into the chair, and his eyes clouded as he recalled when he first viewed Daniel in the ICU. He regretted giving Daniel the special dispensation to try out early—his son was too young, and he didn't want to lose him. Daniel would've died if they hadn't stopped the bleeding. He remained quiet, waiting as Patch replaced the bag of antibiotics.

The others were all shocked by the description of what Dan had done and his injuries. Lexa's and Loki's faces drained of all color. A few stood and shifted around the room, unable to sit still. Jon and Blaze paced slowly, both having similar thoughts along the lines of *'Damned crazy. He takes too many unacceptable risks for others.'*

When Patch returned to his seat, recognizing they needed to push forward, Nick prompted, "When did you receive the next one?"

William remained still for so long everyone began to wonder if he would respond. Gathering himself, refocusing on Blaze as he shared, "About four months after Daniel joined Blain's unit. This time the message said, 'run Danny run.' I received the package shortly after the building explosion, which injured Daniel and killed Gambit. I didn't understand the meaning until after I read the full after-action report."

Blaze witnessed something in Broderick's eyes he didn't expect—sadness.

Taking a small steadying breath, William kept his eyes locked on the captain. "I came to visit Daniel every night. I slipped in the second night when Mason nodded off. Daniel's face now reminds me of then. Thank you for watching over him. I hated to be so cold on the phone."

Flabbergasted by the general's words, Patch asked, "Why did you behave like such a cold-hearted bastard?"

William flinched as he shifted his gaze to the medic. "In one way or another, Daniel always paid the price for me being a general. The photo messages concerned me. I figured if I distanced myself from my son, made it appear as though I didn't care, then whoever kept sending those damned pictures would stop. I believe my actions would protect Daniel. I was wrong. The photographs kept coming, no matter how much distance I put between us."

Blaze gradually came to the realization he didn't know a damned thing about William Broderick. *Christ, he hides behind shields like Blondie. Who the hell is the real General Broderick, and does he genuinely wish to protect the kid?* He answered his question swiftly. *Yes, he does.*

Weighing what he observed of the general's characteristics before Blondie joined his unit, against his perceptions of his behavior after, he found a huge disconnect. Blaze's mind started to walk through Blondie's history with their unit, searching for whatever made his gut scream.

Nick glanced between Blaze and General Broderick, sensing the undercurrent. At this point, he recognized Dan's unit struggled to accept much of what Dan's father said, and believe a plethora of misconceptions abounded in his rookie's past.

"Can you tell us what happened to Dan at that time?" Bram asked.

Patch regained self-control and recounted an appropriately edited rendition of Blondie sprinting like the wind to save the unit from the rigged building and his swift recovery from his injuries.

Winds noticed Blaze appeared to be lost in what he referred to as *thinking mode*, so he told them how Blondie blamed himself for Gambit's death and got a slight chuckle from Jon and Ray when he shared the part about Blondie believing he could've dodged the bullet.

As Winds finished, Nick did a quick assessment of his team and the others in the room, noting they all need a little time to process all they had heard thus far. "We've learned a great deal so far. I suggest we take a short recess."

"I agree." William rose and headed straight for Daniel's room.

"Time for a security sweep." Winds stood, needing something productive to do as his mind swirled with skepticism, severe disconnects between past and present. He noted Blaze remained immobile in his chair—deep in thought.

"I'll join you." Jon rose as Bram said, "Me too," and all three men left the room together.

Lexa pushed out of her chair and followed Dan's father and Patch into Dan's room.

Rising, Nick stretched his back before ambling over to Loki and Ray. "How are you two holding up?"

Loki quietly said, "After hearing the first two accounts, I'm afraid to learn what 'toy soldier fallen?' refers to. That's a bizarre message."

Ray nodded in agreement.

Category Five

 49

July 17
Saint-Jean-sur-Richelieu, QC —
Canadian Forces Leadership and Recruit School — 1130 Hours

Major Mark Broderick made his way across the grounds of the basic training school as he searched for his son. Out in the field on maneuvers with his latest group of recruits, they had been unable to contact Jeff via phone. Mark grinned, as several platoons moved through drills.

Like most fathers, he held a sense of pride for what his offspring made of his life. Jeff grew into a fine man, who like his cousins Kyle and Daniel, opted for the enlisted route instead of attending university and joining the service as commissioned officers like his other male Broderick cousins.

Three of six boys chose the university route for various reasons. From an early age, Scott wanted to follow his dad's footsteps, so becoming an officer was his chosen path. Adam and Zach shared a love of flight, and their parents placed great value in higher education. Mark and the entire family recognized the effort his youngest brother Ryan and his wife Connie put forth to complete school despite their less than ideal start as a couple.

At only fifteen, Connie became pregnant with Adam. Ryan married Connie, and not only did they remain in school but raised their son in a loving home. Years later, Zach blessed their lives. Ryan and Connie encouraged their children to pursue knowledge and their dreams, so the boys both embarked on officer paths to achieve their goals of becoming military pilots.

Spotting his only son among the mass of men, Mark couldn't help grinning as he listened to him drill the new soldiers. Jeff also found his calling, and the military benefitted from Jeff's ability to turn soft civilians into disciplined, combat-ready soldiers. Mark stopped when he reached the area and waited for Jeff to finish or notice his presence.

Sergeant Jeffrey Broderick noticed his father long before he came to a halt. He continued with the exercise until he could hand it off to another instructor. Spotting his long-time friend Sergeant David Thompson heading his way, he hailed him. David agreed to take over while Jeff found out why his dad showed up unannounced. Jeff strode to his father, came to attention, raised his hand, and held his salute until receiving a return gesture from his superior.

After snapping a crisp salutation, Mark said, "Walk with me." They fell in step, their strides evenly matched as they headed away from the recruits.

Once reaching a distance offering more privacy, Jeff smiled. "Always happy to see you, Dad, but what brings you here?"

"Danny."

Noticing his dad's expression, Jeff tensed. "What's wrong with Runt?"

The nickname caused Mark to chuckle. "Runt? Seriously? Isn't Danny taller than you now?"

His father's laugh eased Jeff's worry. "Well, yeah, but he's still lower on the totem pole than me. He'll always be Runt—even if Zach and Kyle are younger than him. Dad, what's up? You wouldn't travel all the way to Quebec if it isn't important."

"You're right—as usual. Scott located Dan. He's been in Toronto this past year, working for Walter Gambrill as part of the Tactical Response Force."

"Really? Okay. How's he doing? Ready to reengage with the family?" Jeff asked with hope imbuing his tone.

Mark placed his hand on his son's shoulder. "Danny is injured, and the things I must share are going to make you angry at your uncle. But I need you to put that aside for now. I came in person because all the guys are planning to visit Danny soon. We need to give William a few days to sort some things out, but Danny's going to need our full support."

Jeff blinked. "What's Uncle Will done now? I swear if he's hurt Runt again. I'm gonna tear a strip off his hide this time—you won't be able to stop me. He's caused Danny too much hurt."

"Calm down, Jeff. William loves Danny. It's only …"

Jeff interrupted when his father trailed off, "What he did is wrong. No two ways about it, Dad."

"It's complicated. Now, I realize you must return to your recruits. How about we meet for dinner later? We can have a private conversation, and I will bring you up to speed."

Inhaling several times, Jeff allowed the anger he held for his uncle to ebb. "I'll ask David to cover my duties tonight. I have a feeling we're gonna be having a long conversation."

Mark blew out a breath. "Yes, it probably will be, Son."

"When and where do you want to eat dinner?"

"How about nineteen hundred at Restaurant Le Samuel. I'm in the mood for Mediterranean."

"I'll be there." Jeff saluted his dad again with a small grin before taking his leave. As he marched towards his recruits, Jeff wished Runt enjoyed a warm bond with Uncle Will as he did with his father. Those two missed out on so much with their strained father-son relationship.

Grand Citadel Hotel – Main Suite – 1:30 p.m.

The short break turned into a longer than expected interruption when a group of intoxicated men exited the elevator on their floor. The inebriated men refused to leave, insisting that they were on the correct level. Jon called in local patrol units to take the men to lock up after the drunks started throwing punches, and one man peed in a plant in the hallway.

By the time they resolved the situation, it was close to noon. General Broderick insisted they needed to refuel and ordered a selection of food for them. While waiting for the meal to arrive, Blaze woke his men. After they showed and ate, Blaze stationed Hal, Angus, Duncan, and Russ in the hall near both elevators in case other unwanted visitors attempted to access this part of the fifteenth floor.

As everyone settled into place, Loki said, "So we talked about the first two, fly Danny fly and run Danny run. What happened when you received, toy soldier fallen?"

Loki regretted his question when tears welled in Dan's father's eyes. Dumbfounded witnessing the reaction, Loki stared open-mouthed as the general pivoted away from the group and abruptly marched to the windows. His brows drew together with concern as he noted Broderick's erect posture slump and his head bow.

His eyes wide, and his mien conveying *I didn't mean to cause him pain*, Loki turned to Ray for support.

Ray patted Loki's shoulder as he murmured for his brother's ears only, "Not your fault." Although Ray's stomach dropped as Dan's scars came to mind and he realized when the message must've been delivered.

Stunned by General Broderick's reaction, everyone remained still and quiet. Tears sprouted in Blaze's eyes as three potential events popped into his mind. All three incidents wrenched his gut and almost claimed Blondie's life. This side of the general, one with unmistakable pain and guilt reflected in the elder Broderick's sapphire eyes, Blaze didn't think existed.

Blaze rose and joined his commander. With a soft voice, Blaze asked, "Sir, which event, Gleason, Washington, or Walker?"

William's gut clenched, recalling the three times he believed his son died, but only one event gutted him to the core because he failed so spectacularly and drove the wedge between him and Daniel so much deeper. "Gleason."

"When taken or after we rescued him?"

"Both, twice," William whispered.

"Would you like me to tell them?"

Unsure he trusted his voice, William only nodded.

Taking a steadying breath, Blaze turned back to the group. "Toy soldier fallen refers to when terrorists captured and tortured Blondie for three months. The general received one photo after they took him, and another when we found him." The loud intake of breath from several people and Lexa swiping at her watery eyes told Blaze he didn't need to explain further.

Undetected by the others, a storm brewed in Winds as he remained immobile. Hot and cold emotions roiled and clashed as a thundercloud formed, and a vortex began building speed.

"Whoever this person is, they're freaking despicable!" exploded Loki. "We gotta find him and stop this. Sending a message like that is just …" Loki trailed off, unable to put a strong enough word to something so contemptible without cussing.

William thought he had been prepared to examine this one with them—but he was not. He brushed away the welled tears and drew himself tall and taut. He pivoted and stated flatly, "I'm going to check on Daniel," before swiftly striding into the room and closing the door behind him.

After the door shut, Alpha Team started to discuss the meaning of the photos quietly but realized they required more information as several questions came to their minds. What is the goal behind sending the messages? The deliveries went on for years, so were they only sent to provoke emotions or something more sinister? If so, what?

As they began dispersing around the room, Loki pulled his laptop to him, wanting to uncover the vile character. Unsure what he should be searching for, he couldn't sit idle, so he tapped away, letting himself brainstorm.

Lexa, Ray, and Nick began discussing possible motivations endeavoring to build a profile of the subject.

Jon motioned for Bram, Blaze, and Patch to join him in the far corner. "Can you provide us any details about Dan's captivity, which might help determine who is behind these messages?"

Blaze told them the barest details. The kid was captured while on a recon mission with another unit, held and tortured for three months, and they found and rescue Blondie after an exhaustive search. He left out the plethora of classified details, including his unit went rogue to search for Blondie.

Bram shared with Patch and Blaze what Dan said in the bank and how he saved two of the three men by sharing his painful past. He halted when liquid welled in Patch's eyes, and the medic walked over to Dan's bedroom door, slid to the floor with his back against the wall, and buried his face in his knees.

Struggling with his own anguish, Blaze quietly said, "Patch kept Blondie alive when he should've died. That period was tough for Patch. The kid endured so much agony. We nearly lost Brody then, too."

Jon asked, "What do you mean? Was he taken too or injured in the rescue?"

Shaking his head, Blaze said, "No, but I've said too much as it is. Sorry, I can't answer any more questions. Some things I can't say and others aren't mine to share. I hope you understand."

Bram nodded, understanding completely.

Jon crossed his arms. He wished to know more. It might be essential to keeping Dan safe and perhaps getting him to take fewer risks. Although from what he learned so far—jumping off a friggin' cliff—retraining Dan would be difficult if not impossible, but he would damn-well try.

Winds continued staring at nothing—totally engulfed in the chaotic emotions warring within. A storm gathered strength, and not even Blaze was aware a category five gale was imminent.

Grand Citadel Hotel – Dan's Room – 1:35 p.m.

Slumping into the chair beside Daniel, William struggled with his thoughts. Exhibiting his emotions revealed his weaknesses … and foes used his vulnerabilities to harm him and the ones he loved. Someone used that damned photo for years against him … against his son.

I have failed Daniel too many times and destroyed our relationship. Daniel truly needed me after Sara died, and when eleven and sixteen, but I dropped the ball every damned time. So many things I wish I could change. I'm a piss poor protector of my son. Daniel always pays the price for my decisions.

Get control now, Broderick! Now isn't the time to try and sort this out. You're on the job. Put your emotions away in your fortress. Bar the gates and lock them down. They won't help Daniel now. You must maintain control!

William gained the upper hand and prepared to rejoin the group. He groaned as he realized how un-General Badass-like he'd been in front of his subordinates for the past day. *There will likely be repercussions for allowing my guard to drop so far, but with Daniel in the mix, it is getting harder to suppress my emotions. I'm so tired of concealing them. My boy seems to be hurt and in danger, regardless of whether I allow them out or not.*

Taking one last deep cleansing breath, he softly said aloud, "I'm not a coward. Time to face this, repercussions be damned."

William gazed at his son. "I promise to figure this out. You deserve better than I gave you. I'm sorry for messing this up so badly. I love you, Son. I hope one day you will come to realize I have always loved you."

Leaning down, he kissed his son's forehead, noting the fever abated. He stood and walked to the door. Self-control regained, William put a hand on the doorknob, locked his stoic mask, turned the handle, opened the portal, and strode out, exuding confidence once again.

Grand Citadel Hotel – Main Suite – 1:45 p.m.

William had seen the reactions of the group. They all cared for Daniel and possessed intelligence, which would be useful now. Although he tried with no success to resolve this puzzle for years and now held suspicions regarding a culprit, he needed hard evidence. Finding out about the blackmailer, whose name began with PL, put him on Plouffe's trail, but he couldn't charge the major of any crimes without proof.

And although Pletcher attempted to kill Becca and his surname started with those letters, his gut didn't think Pletcher was associated with the mail theft or the photos. Though he sought substantial proof, William also wanted to know why Plouffe would betray the brotherhood and go after him and Daniel.

Based on Walter's description of Alpha Team's skill set, William hoped the team would assist him in unearthing evidence of Plouffe's crimes. If what William suspected was correct, Daniel was in danger, and William needed help to end it once and for all. *Time to lay the rest of what I know and suspect on the table, and request their assistance.*

Coming to a halt, William asked, "Is everyone ready to continue?" After receiving nods all around, he said, "Although those three burned the hottest, I received many others over the years, most unrelated to Daniel's injuries.

"They would randomly arrive. Always the same photo. The messages on the ones not related to injuries always came with a slight variation. However, my analysts couldn't figure out what the cryptic code meant. The cipher made no sense to me, as well."

"What was the message, the variations?" Loki asked, hoping for something to research.

"HL and HB, both followed by a number. The letters remained constant; only the digits changed."

"FUCK!" Winds bellowed.

"SHIT!" Blaze roared.

"DAMMIT!" Patch shouted.

All eyes pinned to three irate men. Their anger and shock clearly visible.

Jon's stomach flipped, recognizing why the guys reacted. *What's going on?*

"Our code, our goddamned code," Blaze forcefully expelled before struggling to inhale, the words impacting like a gut-punch.

"Your code?" Alarmed, William's gut clenched.

A category five hurricane of words exploded from Winds, "NEARLY EVERY DAMNED TIME YOU SENT HIM OUT ON A MISSION WITH ANOTHER UNIT HE CAME BACK IN BAD SHAPE AND ON THE EDGE. THEY DIDN'T CARE ABOUT HIM!

"IT WAS OUR QUICK WAY TO MEASURE HIS PHYSICAL AND MENTAL STATE. HL, HOW LONG, HOW MANY DAYS DID HE SPEND ALONE WITH NO ONE COVERING HIS SIX. HB, HOW BAD, THE NUMBER OF TARGETS HE DISPATCHED TO HELL.

"YOU FUCKING COLD-HEARTED BASTARD, YOU NEARLY DESTROYED YOUR SON'S SOUL! YOU'RE HEARTLESS. THIS … ALL THIS CONCERN NOW … IT DOESN'T WIPE AWAY WHAT YOU DID TO HIM.

"BLONDIE NEVER GOT DOWNTIME. NEVER! WHAT THE HELL WERE YOU THINKING? YOU KEPT HIM IN THE FIELD FOR SIX STRAIGHT YEARS! THE ONLY BREAKS HE GOT WERE WHEN HE WAS INJURED—WHICH HAPPENED WAY TOO DAMNED OFTEN WHEN FORCED TO GO WITH OTHER UNITS.

"YOU NEVER PUNISHED THE ASSHOLES WHO LEFT HIM ALONE SIXTY KILOMETERS FROM BASE CAMP AFTER SEVEN DAYS IN HIS PERCH AND THIRTY-TWO KILLS.

"HE SAVED THEIR ASSES, AND THEY FORGOT HIM. THEY LEFT THE KID TO FEND FOR HIMSELF—UNARMED AND IN HOSTILE TERRITORY!

"BLONDIE ALMOST FELL OFF THE EDGE THAT TIME—TOO DAMNED CLOSE. TOO MANY TIMES, OUR BROTHER CAME TOO FUCKING CLOSE TO FALLING!

"HE WAS YOUR PERFECT SOLDIER—ALWAYS HIT HIS TARGET. YOU USED AND ABUSED HIM AT EVERY OPPORTUNITY. YOU HAVE NO IDEA HOW OFTEN I WANTED TO KILL YOU. YOU SHOWED NO CONCERN FOR HIM. HE SURVIVED DESPITE WHAT YOU DID TO HIM.

"BLONDIE COPED WITH OUR HELP. WITHOUT FAIL, HE DID HIS JOB. HE ALWAYS CAME BACK NO MATTER WHAT YOU THREW AT HIM—UNTIL HE FINALLY BROKE AFTER KILLING BRODY.

"I'M SO FUCKING HAPPY HE'S NO LONGER YOUR TOY SOLDIER. HE CAN LIVE A LIFE INSTEAD OF ONLY SURVIVING NOW THAT YOU CAN'T FUCK WITH HIM."

Slammed with a hurricane force of rage, William braced himself and assumed a steel-backed stance. His face hardened to stone, with an expression that would put fear in most men. He held his ground unmoved and met the diatribe spewing forth head-on.

When the gale blew out, William spoke in an icy and unyieldingly tone, "Corporal, you will stand down. These are not light accusations you make. Calm yourself or I will have you detained. When you can explain yourself calmly, I will listen." William set his jaw, becoming an immobile object as he locked eyes on Winds and waited.

Winds glared at the general as his body shook violently with fury and adrenaline, trying his damnedest not raise his fists and beat the shit out of Blondie's father.

Blaze stepped in to avert disaster before Winds lost the last ounce of control and cratered his career. "I'm taking him out. We'll be back." He placed a hand on his brother's shoulder. "Come with me now." The two left the room closely followed by Patch as the rest simply stared at each other unable to fathom what just happened.

Executing a crisp about-face, William strode stiffly to the window and stared out as fury thundered through him burning, searing, blistering, and shredding his heart. *This is worse than I ever imagined. The sick bastard was hurting my son all along, and I never suspected. How could Daniel be in the field for six years straight without me knowing? How? Why? Left alone, forgotten? Who? Why? When?*

The final photo and message make sense now. With the image of every message etched into his brain, William began adding up the HB numbers as hot, stinging, angry tears flowed down his cheeks unchecked—no longer caring if anyone saw.

He wanted to disembowel the bastard. If Plouffe stepped in the room now—he'd be dead.

Murder and Mayhem

 *50*

It took nearly an hour, Blaze, Patch, and a small amount of sedative to calm Winds enough to reenter the room. Winds flatly told Blaze he would never apologize for his outburst, even if it cost him what little remained of his career. He wanted to tell the general off for so long.

Blaze understood Winds compulsion to vent, though he remained relieved his best friend had not delivered the message physically. If Winds struck the general, his second-in-command would've faced severe disciplinary action and potential removal from JTF2.

While waiting for his men to return, William decided he must finish the briefing regardless of the animosity directed at him. They needed to be told the rest. Rebuilding relationships and righting wrongs must wait until he ensured this merciless bastard couldn't harm Daniel again.

Taking charge again as the men reentered the suite, General Broderick addressed the elephant in the room. "I've sorted through your words and accusations. Harsh as they are, as the highest-ranking Command Officer of JTF2, second only to the Chief of Defense Staff McFergus, it's ultimately my responsibility. I accept that fully. However, these actions were taken without my knowledge or my consent and are counter to all I value. I believe you've given me the means to finally bring to justice the sadistic bastard who has been pulling strings. There are, however, a few more things I need to share."

Directing his gaze at Winds, William asked, "Are you prepared to listen Corporal? Can you remain calm? I ask because what I'm going to tell you next will be painful for you—for everyone."

"Yes, sir. I will contain myself," Winds dully responded as he slumped further in the chair, an effect of the sedative.

After intently assessing each person in the room, William proceeded, "There is one more photograph ... the last one I received. It's the catalyst to where we are today. An envelope arrived soon after Daniel finalized his separation paperwork. However, this packet differed from its predecessors by containing not only a picture but also a short note.

"I believe it to be the work of a man who's long been a thorn in my side. However, if he is responsible for all this, he covered his tracks exceptionally well, and finding proof will be extremely difficult. And although my gut tells me he's the mastermind behind everything, others may be involved.

"In January, Inspector Austin Redmond, a detective in the Vancouver Police Department, contacted me about a murder. The victim lay slumped over what appeared to be an unfinished confession addressed to me about a crime perpetrated while in service. Details from the crime scene indicated the deceased suffered a single GSW to the head. The ballistic trauma and angle of bullet penetration indicate the trajectory originated in the trees outside his home, a sniper's kill-shot.

"The decedent, a former Corporal Sandeep Jheeta, worked in the mailrooms in both Ottawa and Kandahar. In his declaration, he admitted to intercepting mail to and from Daniel. The thefts occurred the entire time Daniel served in Special Forces.

"Regrettably, the bullet found its target just as Jheeta started to name the person who blackmailed him. He only managed to write the first two letters of a name, whether first or last, is uncertain, but my gut began to churn as one man's name popped to the forefront."

Jon interrupted. "Sir, I remember when Dan got a call from you. He believed you withheld his mail."

William nodded. "I'm sure he did. I chose my words unwisely, and ever since, Daniel's ignored every overture I made to clarify myself."

His brows drew together in confusion as Blaze murmured, "He stole Blondie's mail?"

"Yes. Initially, most appeared to be forwarded to the intended recipient, we presume, after the corporal's blackmailer read and returned the letters. But eventually, Mr. Jheeta received directions to burn all mail to and from my son. He complied for a while, but at some point, began saving the confiscated mail."

Patch's eyes widened as he recognized one falsehood they all believed for years. "His cousins never abandoned him, did they?"

William winced as he shook his head.

Nick spotted the fury in Dan's former unit and redirected by asking, "Did Inspector Redmond locate the blackmailer or the murderer, assuming they are not the same?"

"No. The investigation into Mr. Jheeta's murder and the reason behind the theft has been stalled for some time. Unfortunately, other recent incidents involving an attempt on my daughter's life confused things more and brought another potential culprit into play. I warned Daniel about him as well, when I called to tell him about his stolen correspondence.

"As I scrutinize all the knowns, the more I believe the threat to Daniel now is more related to the photos than his mail, but my instinct believes one man is behind both. If it's who I think, I can't figure out why he would do this—his motive eludes me completely."

Turning his gaze to Winds, William stated, "But now, thanks to your outburst, I fully understand the gist of the scrawled messages. Neither my analysts nor I ever deciphered their meaning.

"Gambrill is also now aware of the contents of the missive accompanying the final photo. One element recently changed. I firmly believe Aaron's death in the gang war now makes Daniel a direct target." William stopped and inhaled deeply to steady his nerves.

"Sir, what are the details?" Blaze asked as his gut raged.

Bracing himself mentally, William recited the words verbatim. "The note read, 'Nice long run with my toy soldier. He's innocent. Never hurt me. Fun watching you suffer. Couldn't knock him over. Always stood again. Wanted him to do it. Would hurt you most. Didn't work out the way I planned. Too bad toy soldier gone now.'

"The photograph used is one of Danny and Brody. Both are standing and grinning broadly with their arms around each other's shoulders. He wrote messages on both Daniel's and Brody's chests."

William's voice lost all its steel and audibly shook with emotion, "On Brody, it said, all-clear and the number one eighty-four. On Daniel," he sucked in a hitched breath, "Bite the bullet."

Silence enveloped the room for half a second.

Blaze seethed as he made the connection in his mind. Fury flared red hot as he exploded in a deafening roar, "I'LL KILL THE SOB NOW! RIGHT FUCKING NOW! MAJOR PLOUFFE IS A DEAD MAN!"

Pulled out of his lethargy, Winds focused on Patch. *Plouffe?* In the next instant, Winds rose to his feet, swiftly joined by Jon, Bram, and Patch as they endeavored to keep Blaze from leaving the suite.

Wholly enraged, Blaze stormed towards the exit with murderous intent. Determined to find and slay the blackguard, he would allow no one to stop him. Mayhem ensued as Bram, Winds, Patch, and Jon tried to restrain Blaze. All five ended up on the ground where Blaze struggled relentlessly to extract himself from their grip. Loki, Ray, and Nick placed themselves in front of the door as a last line of defense should the others fail.

So many voices yelled for him to calm down, but too engulfed in blind fury, Blaze never registered them and continued to fight. Grunts and groans sounded as several blows connected hard, but the exchange had no effect as Blaze fought them.

Patch, who stood, intending to grab his medkit, stopped when a flood of bitterly cold water doused Blaze's face—shocking his former CO into stillness as he sputtered for air.

Five men stared disbelievingly up at Lexa, who held a water pitcher in each hand as she glared at Blaze. The stern tone of Lexa's voice demanded immediate obedience. "Stop! Behave now or ..." Lexa tipped the second full decanter in a threatening manner—ready to let it flow.

"Christ, remind me never to piss her off," Patch breathed out.

Loki and Ray chuckled at all the surprised faces. With mirth in his tone, Loki explained, "She grew up with four older brothers. What'd ya expect?"

Lexa's glare persisted, and the pitcher remained poised to dump the contents. "Are you ready to behave properly?"

Regaining some semblance of his wits, Blaze nodded.

Jon, Bram, and Winds cautiously removed their holds on Blaze and stood— prepared to grab him again if this was a ploy to fake them out.

"Damn, Lexa, perfect way to put out his fire. I'll have to remember this," Winds said in awe.

Blaze lay quiet and still on the floor—gaping up at Lexa. Calmly, Blaze asked, "May I get up now, Ma'am?"

SPLASH

"What the hell?" Blaze sputtered out as he received a second faceful of ice-cold water.

"Wrong word. No one calls Lexa ma'am," Bram said, laughing almost too hard to get the words out as he grabbed a towel and tossed it to Blaze.

Lexa pivoted, marched to the table, set the pitchers down, and sat with a hint of a smile. "Got what he deserved. Just sayin'."

It took a long time for the room to settle, laughter ringing so loud the men guarding the elevator were probably wondering what occurred in the suite.

After everyone quieted, Nick said, "I assume from Blaze's reaction the man you suspect is Aaron Plouffe's uncle."

Jon's voice grated, "Aaron's uncle?"

Inwardly impressed by how Lexa defused the situation, William redirected his gaze from the petite TRF officer to Pastore. "Yes. Neither Walter nor I were aware of the familial connection until the day you delivered the death notification. According to Walter, you both met Major Plouffe on his way out of Aaron's parents' house."

William cleared his throat. "The note said Daniel was innocent, never harmed him. I believe the major will twist Daniel's presence with Aaron when he died as having hurt him now, which makes my son a target. I also think Plouffe is the man Lexa overheard in the lobby.

"I need your help. I must find solid evidence of his crimes against Daniel so he can be brought up on the appropriate charges. It may even point to treason if there's a connection to Jorge Pletcher—the man who attempted to kill my daughter and who I believe is still after her."

Confused, Ray asked, "Sir, I don't understand. What crimes?"

"Willful and malicious neglect of the welfare of a subordinate, for starters. With what I recently learned, I'm sure we'll find more." William raked a hand through his hair, sick to his stomach over the entire affair.

Recognizing Ray needed help connecting the dots, Blaze said solemnly, "I'm certain charges will stem from his involvement in the six straight years Blondie stayed in the field without a break."

Ray nodded in understanding as a sodden Blaze stood.

Continuing to wipe his face with the towel, Blaze added, "We should search for connections to abuses Blondie suffered while with the other units—like the ones who left him out alone. Other soldiers may require a huge serving of justice, too."

Patch, Winds, and William all nodded. The potential depth of this staggered all four soldiers, as the repercussions would indeed shake JTF2 to the core.

"I'm wondering if there's any connection to the training incident." When General Broderick appeared curious, Lexa added her reason. "You indicated they chose Dan to lead a non-standard exercise, so this deserves investigation since you received a photo afterward."

"Don't see the connection. Plouffe never participated in any training, but well, this whole damned thing boggles my mind, so perhaps it is possible," William admitted though he kept some thoughts to himself. *How could this happen right under my nose? I'm the general—I should've known.*

"We also need to find out how or why this all started. Assuming Major Plouffe is the culprit, what did he stand to gain? What is his motive? Sir, how long and how well do you know Plouffe?" Nick asked.

"Met him over thirty years ago, but we are not well acquainted personally. We move in different circles, so I've never socialized with him. Colonel Grasett promoted both of us to the rank of major at the same time."

Not willing to appear biased or betray his oath, William judiciously selected his words when divulging aspects of Plouffe's performance. "Never cared for the man professionally. His skills aren't up to the caliber I expect from my officers. I would've never promoted him to his current position, but while he's not an ideal soldier, I've never had cause to remove him.

"Colonel Sutton deals with him mostly. My interaction with him is minimal, except for an occasional planning session. Though a few times, I had to dress him down privately, and last year the need arose for a more public rebuke after a huge brawl. The fight injured several of the participants and did significant property damage."

Lexa's mind began generating a profile. "Perhaps he possesses a weak ego. He said he liked watching you hurt. Sounds like a passive-aggressive way to boost his self-worth and perhaps retaliate for some perceived wrong. What concerns me is with Dan no longer within his control, Plouffe may not be satisfied with only exacting emotional pain. He is likely to escalate and seek a way to inflict physical harm now."

Nick nodded. "Makes sense, but we need more to go on before we jump to conclusions. And there is also the other man to consider." He focused on the elder Broderick. "You called him Pletcher. Since you have no definitive proof, Plouffe is responsible, we should investigate both men. We're going to need information on both Plouffe and Pletcher from you, sir."

"I'll make the appropriate arrangements to grant you access to whatever you need," William stated with a hint of hope in his voice.

Patch went to check on Blondie as the group discussed what they required. Once they defined the essentials, William expedited access, sometimes using command prerogative for more immediate compliance with the order. He also contacted Corporal Merrill and requested his aide email the contents of the harassment file to Loki. By the time William finished making arrangements and facilitating a video call introduction between the TRF officers and Howard Bransworth, the CSIS liaison, dinner time approached, compelling them all to take a much-needed break.

While they ate the meal that General Broderick ordered from room service, Blaze and Jon revisited the security plan. With Blaze, Patch, and Winds now needed to access and review files above the team's security level, their original plan was no longer feasible.

Winds chatted with Lexa, asking her about growing up with all those brothers. Her clipped responses made it clear the subject was off-limits. So Winds redirected his questions to working in TRF. She gladly expounded on her answers, giving him an insight into Blondie's new life. He smiled, relieved the kid found another place to belong, and teammates who covered his six.

Loki, determined to find the information needed, focused all his concentration on the files, ignoring the spread of delicious food laid out for them. Aiding his friend's dynamism, Ray fixed a plate, grabbed an energy drink, and took both to him, but Loki didn't even notice. Leaving Loki to his work, Ray joined Jon and Blaze to assist with developing a new security strategy.

After dinner, William, Patch, Bram, and Nick sat in a far corner in quiet conversation. The topic involved when to wake Dan. Given all he would need to assimilate, they all were concerned about how Dan would cope with the past issues and the new threat.

Bram worried it would be too much for him to handle, and urged them to allow Dan to determine the pace. Nick agreed, thinking they should hold off on telling him about the current threat and let him deal with the other things first. William believed Dan possessed the capacity to sort through everything at once and come out stronger, especially given the training and experience gained during his time in Special Forces.

In the end, Patch supported Bram's advice, and William differed to the opinion of the man who kept his son alive for so many years. Nick also agreed with allowing Dan to be the one controlling his needs and pace.

As Blaze, Winds, and Jon rose to leave and temporarily replace the men guarding the hall so they could relieve themselves, relax, and eat, Lexa asked the general, "Sir. Assuming Plouffe sent the messages, what did he mean when he wrote, wanted him to do it, would hurt you most, didn't work out the way I planned?"

The meaning remained on the periphery Lexa's brain, but something barred her from grasping it—as if protecting her from its true meaning.

Naked emotion laced his words as William explained, "Again, I have no proof, but I'm fairly certain he is somehow involved in the friendly fire incident that ended Brody's life. I believe he thought Daniel would kill himself—eat a bullet—after discovering he fired the lethal shot. Daniel committing suicide would gut me to the core."

Lexa flinched. "What makes you think he set Dan up?"

Rage imbued Blaze's voice, "Because Major Plouffe is the one who gave the all-clear to fire order that I relayed to Blondie. I'm going to kill the bastard."

"Dan's stronger than Plouffe thinks," Bram quietly said. Recalling Dan's pain, he didn't share his private thought. *I wonder how close Dan came to pulling the trigger?*

Jon recalled the ivory-handled pistol he took from Dan and returned in a gun safe. He blew out a breath as his eyes locked with Nick's. *Dan's resilience is his métier. Without this strength of character, he might not have made it.* Both men grasped Dan had teetered on the edge of oblivion, and their interventions likely saved him. Thoughts they believed best left unsaid with raw emotions swirling around them. Everybody needed clear minds to resolve this situation.

Everyone turned and stared at Loki when he stated loudly with conviction, "Dantastic chose the beauty of life. He honored Brody by living." His eyes never left his laptop, almost done reviewing the photos which arrived while everyone else ate dinner.

"I understand the all-clear, but not one eighty-four. What's that?" Ray inquired.

Blaze and William locked gazes, conveying both understood the meaning, but remained unsure whether they should share. Before reaching a mutual decision, Loki broke the silence.

"Noooooo!" Loki wailed. Blanching, all color drained from his face as his chestnut brown eyes rounded with distress and grief before they welled with liquid.

"Loki, buddy, are you okay?" Bram called out as he and Ray rushed toward Loki, concerned by his outward appearance, worried he might pass out.

Loki couldn't respond—he had no words. His stomach clenched, and he fought the need to heave.

Barely above a whisper, Blaze shared, "Blondie's total kills. Brody being his one hundred eighty-fourth kill."

The information bomb annihilated all thoughts—sucked all the air from the room and threatened to asphyxiate the occupants. Ragged inhalations and exhalations were the only sounds for an extended period as each of them absorbed the number and reflected on what it would do to a man's soul to end the lives of so many.

Jon understood now how Dan seemed to be able to handle neutralizing subjects better than most—the rookie was no newcomer to ending a person's life. A deep ache dwelt in his heart for Dan—that many kills would have a profound impact on his soul. He recalled Dan's ragged breaths after each one of his lethal shots—death had become well-known to Dan, too damn familiar, though still not natural. A positive sign, an indication Dan maintained his humanity—doing his duty had not destroyed Dan's soul.

Nick rubbed his face as Dan's reasons for joining TRF rolled in his head. Dan wanted to make a difference by saving lives instead of taking them. Sadly, Nick fully appreciated Dan's motivation—his choice was not only about Brody. Dan took many lives to protect the world from terrorism—a heavy burden for Dan to carry. Nick believed Dan might be the one needing to be saved. *Our team can help him.*

Wordlessly, the group gradually returned to the tasks at hand. Although subdued, all appeared more determined than ever to find the proof needed to bring the responsible party or parties to justice.

Deeds Speak

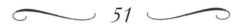

51

July 17
Grand Citadel Hotel — Room 666 — 10:00 p.m.

Major Plouffe contemplated his next move. Sheer luck gave him the detail he unsuccessfully demanded from the front desk. While in the bar, Nigel overheard two kitchen workers talking as they retrieved dirty glasses from behind the bar. They complained about the excessive full-body pat-downs and thorough search of the catering trays each time they delivered enough food to feed an army to a general on the fifteenth floor. One feared the intimidating glares of the soldiers and the assault rifles they carried.

Plouffe wondered if his toy soldier was here. It would make sense because he had not located the younger Broderick anywhere else. He checked his apartment today, and none of his neighbors had seen him in a few days. They assumed he was still in the hospital, given the news reports.

Nigel grinned as he thought about Aaron's blubbering fiancée. He found some people so easy to manipulate. Tammy believed he cared about her, and the other members of TRF lock, stock, and barrel. All it took were a few lies said with fake sincerity to convince her to supply him with the names of Broderick's teammates. Tammy met them all at the previous Christmas party, and she caved like a stone roof held up by toothpicks.

After obtaining names, with his resource, it took him no time to acquire their addresses. He executed a recon of their homes, searching for his plaything, but he was not at any of them. Him being here made the most sense. However, after learning of the security measures, General Broderick put into place, getting to either asshat here would be too risky and most likely unsuccessful.

Although he doubted the general would connect him to his past activities, Nigel needed a new plan. One of his moles warned him, Broderick rushed through security clearances for a group of TRF officers.

Tracing anything solid back him to would be near impossible since he took extreme care in all his dealings, but in case one of his spies screwed up, he realized he must rid the world of both Brodericks faster than originally planned. Though he wanted to draw out William's pain, it would be smarter and more in line with his ultimate goal of becoming general if he killed them soon.

Nigel's mind worked to come up with a solution, and he grinned as an idea formed. *Aaron's funeral might be the place to do it—would be fitting. The service is scheduled for two days from now at three o'clock. Most of TRF will be in attendance. If my toy soldier is well enough to be out of the hospital, his sense of duty will compel him to go.*

Plouffe laughed. Broderick's commitment to duty worked to his advantage for years. *The only problem will be General Asshat. The measures he is taking now are clear signs he suspects someone is gunning for his son.*

He will be like a mad dog protecting a bone, and getting close enough to knock over my plaything will be difficult. My plan must lure them away from any protection detail. If only Pletcher would take care of things, but I can't count on him to follow through in a timely manner.

Drifting to sleep, Nigel found a solution to his problem. A three-pronged approach wouldn't fail. His toy soldier would be dead by seventeen hundred on July nineteenth. *It will be so fun to observe William's pain as he helplessly watches his only son die.*

Grand Citadel Hotel – Main Suite – 11:05 p.m.

The entire group worked all evening diligently, endeavoring to find any shred of concrete evidence to connect Nigel Plouffe or Jorge Pletcher to the photos and stolen mail. A little after eleven, William pulled them together, wanting to review what the various avenues of exploration netted so far.

Lexa reported first. She and Blaze worked on investigating the training incident. She sat at the table across from the general as she shared, "We found out the training officer who suggested the new test had been a buddy of Major Plouffe. When Blaze and I spoke to Lieutenant Giles Tudor, he said his former friend developed the test and influenced him to try it. Apparently, the major convinced him you showed favoritism by allowing your son to join without meeting the age requirement.

"The lieutenant bought into the assumption the exercise would reveal if Dan possessed the maturity to be there. Tudor said they never repeated the drill because they believed the potential for grievous injury too great for recruits. Lieutenant Tudor regretted the outcome, and incensed by Plouffe's callousness when the major laughed about Dan's injuries, he ended his association with Plouffe.

"We also inquired what happened to the other soldier who fell. Tudor reported the recruit sustained only minor injuries—a slight concussion, and he passed and went on to join a unit in Special Forces. I asked for the soldier's name, and Tudor identified him as Corporal Murphy," Lexa finished.

"Blake Murphy?" Jon asked.

"Yes. Why?"

"The name sounds familiar, hang on a second." He rifled through some paperwork he and Winds reviewed. "Found it ... thought I recalled his name. You're not gonna like this," Jon said as he peered at Blaze. "Murphy was in the unit that left Dan sixty kilometers out."

Blaze nodded and banked the surge of fire in his gut. "Yes. I'm aware. Murphy's always been a thorn in Blondie's side. He truly doesn't belong in JTF2, but he's like Teflon. None of the shit he spews sticks to him. Plouffe seemed to favor him. Never figured out why?"

Bram asked, "From what the general said about the cliff incident, perhaps Murphy held a grudge against Dan. And maybe Murphy and Plouffe are in league. One hates the father and the other the son. Probably something we should investigate."

William rested his elbows on the table and lowered his face into his palms. *Why didn't I see any of this? Why didn't my analysts discover these things?* The weight of betrayal mounted with each detail the TRF team shared. *Someone, or perhaps several people I trust manipulated data and misled me.*

Loki reported, "Using the dates you received the HL/HB photos, we found corresponding unit reports and assignments. We've unearthed some potentially valuable evidence. The general's signature appears to have been forged on multiple documents, including several where Dan requested assignment to other units."

"My signature was forged?" William asked as he lifted his head.

"Blondie never requested to be reassigned," Winds stated.

Loki's eyes bounced between them and waited a moment.

Winds stared at his commander as confusion swirled in his mind. "Blondie always followed your orders. The last thing he wanted is to be sent out with units who didn't give a rat's ass about him."

"I didn't order him. I took a hands-off approach with his duties." William turned to Loki. "Can you prove the signatures are forgeries?"

Still unable to reconcile the two versions of General Broderick, Winds spoke before Loki answered. "I viewed the documents. You ordered him."

Blaze stepped in. "Plouffe must've been running two copies of orders. It's the only thing that makes sense. One he provided to Blondie, showing him his father signed the orders. And a second set he filed which indicated Blondie requested the temporary transfer."

William's voice came out soft, "If only I hadn't been so distant. I thought my son possessed ambitions like mine and requested the transfers I signed off on." His troubled eyes met Loki's. "How many docs are forged?"

A pang of sadness for Dan's father filled Loki. "Over half of them, sir. I'm sorry, but your signature is also bogus on the paperwork we found which classified time Dan spent recovering from injuries as downtime. We believe they were filed to avoid detection of his constant field deployment."

Loki flashed a slight smile before relaying, "Sir, we have what you might call a smoking gun. Blaze's speculation is correct. There are two sets of orders."

William stared at Loki, glimpsing the first ray of light being cast into this hellish black pit. "You found proof?"

Blushing, Loki confessed, "Did you know there's a program that secretly saves a copy of each order processed on a hidden server?"

William's expression reflected the same astonishment as everyone seated at the table. "Yes, I'm aware, though it is highly classified. How—"

Loki interrupted, "Please don't ask me," he said with a geeky smirk.

A rare lopsided grin broke out on William's face. *Damn, this man is excellent. CSIS could use someone with his skills—hell, I need someone with Baldovino's abilities.* He refrained from asking for details because William didn't want to be placed in a position to prosecute Daniel's teammate for hacking things he shouldn't. "So Plouffe isn't as smart as he thinks he is. He created both sets using the official software."

"Yep," Loki smiled as Patch hugged him.

"How did you recognize counterfeit signatures?" Bram asked.

Ray answered, "Easy to spot if you know what to look for." He smiled— the only positive thing to come out the time he spent with the Blooddrop Crew.

Incredulous again, William asked, "Will this hold up in court?"

"Yes, if you have a credible handwriting expert testify." Ray proceeded to show William two seemingly identical signatures, and explained the miniscule differences. "The question we still need to answer is who forged them?"

Nick said, "Sir, we may be able to discover the culprit if you provide us a list of the aides who handled the paperwork over the years."

"How?"

"To determine if there are links to Plouffe," Jon supplied. "For a cover-up of this length and complexity to happen, he would've needed accomplices or your staff changed with such frequency they didn't notice."

"Private Tina Jordan and Corporal Cody Merrill are the only aides to handle unit assignment documents in the past seven years. However, Private Jordan joined my staff only two years ago," William responded with a tinge of despondency, hoping neither were involved.

Corporal Merrill was always efficient and coolheaded, and William liked him. Merrill had been on his staff for over eight years and didn't strike him as someone who would be in cahoots with Plouffe, but at this time, no one was above suspicion. The potential magnitude of this betrayal hit William hard.

Squaring his shoulders, William stated, "If you're going to scrutinize them, I want you to delve into my entire staff. It could've been someone else even though they aren't assigned to handle those papers. I'll write out a complete list of the staff members I've had over the past ten years. It will be quite lengthy. Most staff rotate out after a year or two.

"However, there are five members who've been with me nearly the entire time Daniel served in Special Forces. Corporals Cody Merrill and Brittany Archer and Master Corporals Karla Weeks, Pierre Griggs, and Ian Forrest."

Perceiving the genera's dismay, Nick thought it might be a smart idea to wrap things for tonight. "We can begin again in the morning. Tomorrow will be soon enough for the list. We still have other paths to investigate related to the stolen mail, and to determine if Pletcher is connected in any way with Plouffe's treachery."

Weary, William stood. "Thank you all. You've made more progress in one day than others made in years." He peered at his soldiers and stated, "I'm sorry. I have many questions, and so must you. We'll talk tomorrow."

Blaze nodded. *Yes, we need to talk. He is right about this shaking the foundations of Special Forces, but this hits me at the core too. Why didn't I ever go directly to Broderick or Sutton with my concerns?* The guilt of everything he might've been able to stop settled heavily on Blaze. His failure to protect Blondie greater than he ever imagined.

Not burdened by the same weight as William and Blaze, Jon's thinking remained clear. "We need to locate Major Plouffe tomorrow and have someone keep tabs on his movements. Dan is in no condition to protect himself from this bastard, and we can't allow Plouffe anywhere near him."

Everyone agreed and began to prepare to head to their respective rooms as Patch ambled to Blondie's bedroom.

Grand Citadel Hotel – Dan's Room – 11:55 p.m.

Heather glanced up from her book and pulled out her earbuds when the door opened. Jim appeared quite weary. She stood when he arrived at Dan's bedside. "He's resting easy. No issues."

Patch checked Blondie before facing Heather. The kindhearted nurse refused any payment for her care. He appreciated Heather being here while he helped with the investigation. "Thanks, Heather. Can I bring you a coffee before I leave?"

"No, thanks. Should I give Dan his next dose of sedative or hold off?" Heather asked as she bravely laid her hand on Jim's arm, hoping he viewed it as a caring gesture and not her desire to touch this amazing man.

The gentle hand soothed Patch, and he wished it meant something more than a nurse's considerate action. "No, I want to stop the sedative tonight, so Blondie wakes naturally sometime in the morning. You have my cell number if he starts to rouse before I return. And contact me if he or you needs anything. I don't care what time of the night it is."

Heather smiled. "Dan means a lot to you."

Patch leaned over and squeezed Blondie's left bicep. Overwhelmed by all he learned tonight, he couldn't stop a sob from bubbling out. Patch dropped to his knees as his shoulders shook, and tears rained down.

Initially shocked, Heather acted without hesitancy, wrapping her arms around Jim, holding him as he released pent-up emotions. She sensed a deep pain in him, though she didn't understand the source. All she cared about at this moment was providing this kind and distraught man with comfort.

After several minutes, Patch began to regain control. Mortification flooded him as he realized Heather embraced him, and he totally broke down in front of her. He wiped his eyes and started to rise, and Heather surprised him as she handed him a tissue and spoke to him.

Heather settled on the floor beside and smiled at him. "Please, don't be embarrassed. Though I'm unaware of the details, it is clear to me you all are under enormous stress. I'm an excellent listener if you want to talk."

Patch blew his nose, shifted to his butt, and leaned back against the mattress. He gazed at Heather and only detected warmth in her concerned expression. With a voice a bit unsteady, he began, "He's my little brother. I patched him up for years and thought I did my best for him, but I failed him."

Heather placed her hand over his in his lap. "You did well. I've seen his scars and understand what it must've taken to keep him alive."

His brown eyes welled with hot tears again. "I didn't do well. I should've done more. I should've spoken up. I should've gone straight to his father and said my piece. Blondie suffered because I was too cowardly to tell off the general. If only I had ..."

William hadn't meant to eavesdrop. He came in to grab his things to go shower in the other bedroom. He squatted near Patch, and his firm voice was imbued with a hint of emotion, "This is not your fault. Without you, my son would've died several times. Please don't discount what you did for him.

"That man counted on everyone following protocol. We did, and the bastard got away with it for too damned long. But this is on me. I chose to distance myself from Daniel under the false assumption it would protect him."

William deeply inhaled and exhaled before he said, "As a result, you were all harmed. Thank you for always being there for Daniel. Your deeds speak volumes of the man you are, and I can never repay you what you deserve."

Patch saw the truth in his commander's eyes—struck again how they were so like Blondie's. Hard to accept, but he did now ... General Broderick truly cared about his son, and everything Blondie suffered broke him up as much if not more than him. Blondie's dad carried a weight Patch would never wish upon his worst enemy ... well, perhaps Plouffe and the terrorists who tortured his brother.

Giving Patch a pat on the shoulder, William rose and said, "Get some rest, soldier. You need it, and you've more than earned it." He grabbed his bag and strode out to go shower.

Heather whispered to Jim, "He's right."

After the general left, Patch peered at Heather before he stood. "Call me if you need to." He unhurriedly exited as his mind replayed Broderick's words, *Thank you for always being there for Daniel.* He never in his life expected to hear that phrase from General Badass, but they rang true in his heart.

Safe Harbor

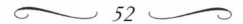 *52*

July 18
Grand Citadel Hotel – Dan's Room – 10:00 a.m.

Diligently scanning Blondie for the slightest sign of rousing, Patch readied a dose of sedative in case his brother woke unable to handle the onslaught of emotions. Patch set the needleless syringe off to the side, out of Blondie's line of sight, not wanting to add to his anxiety.

Cognizant of their desires and duties, Patch promised to inform them when he stirred. Each wished to be present in the room to support Blondie when he woke but realized they couldn't be in two places at once. Their need to continue compiling evidence against Major Plouffe compelled their absence.

He grasped they possessed an entirely different skill set, but the speed in which Blondie's team ferreted out information floored Patch. All of their minds drew connections so well, but Loki, the freaking amazing techie surpassed the general's minions in finding data faster than a terrier dug up a buried bone.

Spotting movement, Patch rushed to the door to alert the others. Within moments, everyone stood in a loose semi-circle near the bed's foot, attentively waiting for Dan's ascent to consciousness. Blaze warned them not to crowd close, and although Alpha wondered why, they complied without dissension.

Emotions on edge, William studied Daniel, hoping his son would accept the truth about Sara's death, and give him a chance to mend things.

Awareness seeped in around the edges of Dan's mind. Little by little, the fuzzy, aimless drifting dissipated. First, he recognized a pleasant warmth coalescing with comfort. His relaxed body lay on the plush bed, his mind numb, and experiencing no pain, Dan wanted to remain in this place of serenity.

As sounds filter in, he noted several familiar hushed voices, but they spoke too quietly for him to distinguish words. Ensconced and enjoying his peaceful, muted world, he wished to stay, but something urged him up and out.

Eyes fluttered open.

Unfocused, blurry images started to take form.

Lashes drifted down, returning to the warmth and security of his haven.

Multiple blinks and his eyelids lifted again.

Ten clear faces … *familiar faces.*

Tranquility beckoned him back as his lashes gently fell.

Gradually, his eyes opened again.

Anxiety, fear, pain, concern, grief, and guilt reflected on faces around him.

Brutal reality bombarded him with a vengeance.

Retreat … need sanctuary … his lids slammed shut to block it all out.

Someone called his name gently.

Dan ignored the summons.

Pain too real—like fire beneath his skin scorched him.

Wounds so deep, forever etched into his soul, threatened to destroy him.

Terror filled his mind … overwhelming him.

So tired of being alone … so alone … I can't face this alone.

Help … need a safe harbor.

Seek the one who can help … the only one who knows how to help.

Eyes cracked open a fraction … only enough to search.

Find the comforting one … the safe one … find Dad.

Found him.

Frightened, blue eyes opened wide … locked onto caring blue-green eyes.

Dan's voice sounded like a scared child, "Bram, help me."

Bram stepped forward at Dan's plea for help.

Nick whispered to the others, "We need to leave, now," as he started to shoo them out and exit himself. Everyone except William moved to comply. Nick tugged the general's upper arm and firmly pulled him from the room. Patch shut the door behind them.

"I'm here. You're safe," Bram crooned in the voice he used with his little girls when they became frightened. Unhurriedly, Bram lowered himself to the mattress as Dan's petrified, pleading eyes never lost contact with his.

Leaning down, Bram carefully gathered Dan close, nestling the young man's ear directly over his heart. Neither moved nor spoke while Bram held Dan, allowing Dan to draw in the compassion and strength flowing from Bram's steady heartbeat—his action reassuring Dan he would stay for as long as necessary. When Dan began trembling, concern for a more severe issue invaded Bram's thoughts until noticing dampness on his shirt. Grasping Dan cried silently, Bram murmured comforting words as he would with his daughters.

Time and the external world didn't exist for Dan. Terrified to be alone, painful emotions threatened to extinguish the last flicker of his light as he clutched the tail end of his rope.

Dan needed someone to clip him to a safety harness before he plummeted into the abyss. He came so close to falling into oblivion after Brody's death. Too many nights alone, always on his own, sitting with the ivory-gripped, cold, metal pressed against his heart—wishing to end his suffering. But he maintained a hold with all his strength and listened as Brody whispered to him to seek the beauty of life. It hurt too damned much to choose life sometimes, but each time he heeded the heartfelt plea.

But now, he couldn't hear his brother, and he possessed no more strength. Dan grasp on his lifeline faltered, and he started downward. In the nick of time, powerful arms encircled him and kept him from plunging into the void. A solid, steady heartbeat provided him solace, sheltering him in a safe harbor. No longer abandoned and isolated, years of unshed tears streamed down as Bram embraced him.

Bram had no idea how much time passed as Dan released his torment, but eventually, the anguished man stilled and quieted. Bram tilted his head to peer at Dan's face and found sleep claimed him. With his eyes closed, tear-streaked cheeks, and features lax, Dan appeared so young and vulnerable.

Drawing on his experience with his sweet daughters, Bram decided it would be best if he continued to hold him. His wife and four girls taught him so many lessons—but during the nights he rocked each one of his babies to sleep, Bram learned his arms offered them a sense of security in this big, bad, scary world. He would not abandon Dan in his time of need, no matter how anyone might interpret his actions.

About thirty minutes later, Bram recognized Dan began to stir as his breathing changed. Keeping his voice soft, he said, "I got you. You're safe. I'm here for you."

A sense of belonging, as if cloaked by one of Brody's hugs, Dan didn't give a damn another man embraced him, or he made a fool of himself by crying. *I'm not alone anymore.* Venturing to lift his gaze, meeting Bram's, he found what he needed … compassion and acceptance. "Thank you for catching me."

Bram allowed a smile to form. "Always." He hugged him lightly, cautious of his injured ribs, before carefully laying Dan down. "What do you need?"

"Time."

"I'll be here." Bram rose, pulled a chair to the bedside, and sat. He settled a hand on the mattress in case Dan required a lifeline. He did. Within a few seconds, Dan grasped his hand. He remained quiet, allowing Dan to lead.

Dan shut his eyes after reaching for Bram and began the agonizing process of sorting his emotions.

Sometime later, Dan's eyes reopened and pulled Bram from his inspection when Dan inquired, "Why?"

Seeking an answer to the broad question, Bram failed. There were too many whys, and he didn't understand which one Dan asked. "Talk to me, and I'll help if I can," Bram squeezed Dan's hand, encouraging him.

"I thought ... I believed ... but it wasn't ..." Dan faltered, eyes welling with hot, salty liquid. "I don't know how ... it hurts ... lost so much ... so confused. If he cares ...why? Why would he do what he did to me for years?"

Comprehending, especially after all they learned about Plouffe, Bram answered. "He didn't."

Dan's grip on Bram increased. "I was there ... he tried to kill me for six long years. If he loved me, he wouldn't have done—" Dan stopped before he revealed stuff he shouldn't, and legally couldn't.

"Someone else is responsible."

"Huh? What?" Dan's emotions swirled out of control. Bram's words made no sense.

Recognizing he would cause pain by sharing, but the knowledge would lead to healing, Bram explained everything they discovered regarding Dan's father and Major Plouffe. When Dan's tears flowed again, Bram sheltered him as the young man weathered another storm.

He released Dan when the gale ebbed, and they talked on and off for several hours. Dan remained silent most of the time, but he did open up and share several things from his childhood. Bram's heart ached for Dan's suffering and loss, yet he felt honored Dan trusted him enough to confide in him.

Grand Citadel Hotel – Main Suite – 1:00 p.m.

Everyone continued to work while Bram stayed with Dan, though their thoughts were somewhat distracted, and their eyes often strayed to the door of Dan's room. No one knew what to expect when Dan awoke, but the fear in his eyes and the way he pleaded for Bram's help shook them all to the core.

What they recently learned about Dan's past was dreadful—but he was definitely a survivor. Only three days ago, Dan smiled brightly, full of life as they worked out before that fateful shift. They chose to stay positive—Bram would help, and Dan would make it back again.

Lexa continued to glance at Dan's door and found herself also studying the general. He had not spoken in the past three hours—except to order lunch—which no one ate. He sat by himself, and they all gave him his space. His face remained unreadable—just like Dan's had been for so long.

Her assumption had been right. Dan's relationship with his father was way more complicated but no less painful than hers with her father. They were both alienated from their families, and the path back, if there was one, would be long and arduous. She hoped Dan could reconcile.

Part of her wished to offer Dan comfort, but she couldn't. *How will he handle the hurt and loss of nearly twenty years? I've endured four years of estrangement, and it is unbearable at times, I want to hide from the world. What would it be like to deal with the pain for twenty years—or as a child?*

Swiping away a lone tear, Lexa appreciated she at least she had wonderful childhood memories. But Dan—he didn't, having been estranged from his family at nine. Her ninth year had been so full of joy. Well, except for looking like a tomboy during the summer because she had to cut off all her hair. *Stupid Quinn and his honey and marshmallow cream.* But other than one minor blip, it was one of the happiest years she spent with her whole family.

Putting away her memories, Lexa refocused on her task. She wanted to nail Plouffe to the wall for what he did not only to her teammate but to everyone who cared about Dan. Lexa wondered if the team would truly ever know the full extent of the major's treachery because they were restricted from viewing many files. They must rely on the general and his men to evaluate documents, and they only shared relevant details within their clearance level.

This morning, before Dan woke, General Broderick told them yesterday they overheard some mission details which exceeded their level. He reiterated the consequences of divulging anything outside this room to anyone. The warning and the grave miens of the unit gave them insight into Dan. He didn't choose to be evasive by not talking about his time in Special Forces; he remained under a legal obligation not to reveal specifics.

Blaze, Winds, and Patch now sat together. Having seen Blondie on the edge before, they recognized he might fall completely, and hoped Bram would be able to tether him before their brother tumbled into the abyss.

Though surprised when Blondie called for Bram, since the kid always sought out Brody or him, Blaze's heart rejoiced because the man he claimed as a son found a place to belong and people who he trusted. Glancing at the elder Broderick, Blaze reassessed his commander. Now aware of the actualities, Blaze perceived the hurt and longing in his eyes. Perhaps with time, Blondie and his father would somehow salvage and rebuild a relationship.

His thoughts swirling as he stared at the wall with a heavy heart, William never wanted to view stark panic in his son's eyes ever again. Although grateful Bram responded without hesitation, William envied the man. He hoped Daniel would've realized he loved and would always be there for him no matter what, but recognized his choices and actions influenced his son's selection.

He failed his son too many times and had been blind to Plouffe's machination while his boy struggled to survive hell on earth. William shifted his gaze to his men sitting in the corner away from the others. He owed these three and Mason more than he could ever repay.

William stood and strode towards them. On his way, he grabbed a chair and pulled it close then sat facing them. He studied Patch first, glad he took the opportunity to thank him last night. Shifting his focus to Blaze and Winds, he tried to read their expressions and noted apprehension in Simons, but Blain's countenance appeared more open than he expected.

Maintaining a calm demeanor, not exposing his inner chaos, William said, "Gentlemen, I comprehend you are angry with me and rightly so. As a father, I failed my son. As a general, I failed you. Words cannot express my deep gratitude for everything you did for Daniel.

"I do not seek forgiveness. My actions and inactions are unforgivable. I vow to you here and now to make restitution in whatever manner is fit—up to and including resigning my commission. You deserve a better leader. Someone more aware, more engaged, and wouldn't allow these abuses to have occurred. I give you my word this matter will be investigated to the fullest, and we will locate and remove the rattlesnakes hiding within our ranks.

"Thank you for caring for and protecting my boy. I am aware you all went above and beyond for him so many times. Your efforts will not go unrewarded and unacknowledged."

"Sir, we need no reward, no acknowledgment," Blaze said, halting the general. "What we did for Blondie, we chose to do out of love for our brother, and doesn't require anything in return."

Striving to remain calm and speak respectfully, Winds said, "Sir, I won't lie, I'm still conflicted. The two versions of you are warring in my head. And even if the concerned father is the true you, I'm having trouble understanding how you never noticed what went on."

Struggling mightily to maintain his stoic mask, William listened to the brutally honest words.

Winds honed in on the general's sapphire eyes and glimpsed a flicker of hurt. "But, sir, you aren't the only one to blame. Every damned one of us, Blondie included, share the responsibility. If only one person approached you or Colonel Sutton with our concerns, this wouldn't have continued.

"There are so many who saw what went on. All the units knew Blondie remained in the field constantly, but not a damned soldier said anything. Some hated or envied Blondie because he is your son. Others were indifferent. And as we are aware, some actively targeted him. But no one—not a single person came to you and highlighted the abuse. We all failed Blondie."

Blaze stated, "Sir, if you believe you're not fit to command for your failure, then I contend none of us deserve to wear this uniform—especially the tan beret! Restitution comes in the form of ensuring this never happens again and by cleaning house of those who truly defile the honor of our uniform. And sir, to be clear, that doesn't include you.

"You're an honorable man who unfortunately made poor choices of a personal nature. Some of which appears to have been wholly out of your control. Blondie's a resilient and noble man. Give him a chance to forgive you. Given enough time and effort, you two may reestablish a relationship."

Left speechless for several minutes by the words of his men, William cleared his throat. "Good counsel. You are all exceptional men, and it is my honor to serve with you. We'll clean house as you say and put safeguards in place to prevent this from happening to another soldier. Deeds not words!"

Patch, Blaze, and Winds all repeated the Special Forces motto and tagged on the Guardian Unit axiom, "Deeds not words! Solidarity."

Grand Citadel Hotel – Dan's Room – 3:00 p.m.

Bram held Dan for a third time as he wept for the lost years, raw pain, and undeserved hatred he held for his father. When Dan quieted again, Bram gently laid him back on the pillows—both now emotionally exhausted.

Dan gazed at Bram, not believing he had been so open and cried in his arms three times. *I'm an emotional mess. Nothing is what I thought.* His voice ragged from crying, he said, "I need some time alone now."

Bram nodded. "You sure? If not, a whole bunch of people out there worried about you. I could send one of them in."

"No." Dan shook his head before he asked, "Is Patch here?"

"Yes. He's been taking care of you."

"Would you ask him if he has Beauty?"

"Sure," Bram agreed, wondering what beauty meant, but chalked it up to being another unit code.

When Dan winced as he shifted on the bed, Bram helped him move to a more comfortable position before striding to the door as he said, "I'll send Patch in. About time for pain meds, I think."

As Bram's hand reached for the handle, Dan said, "Bram."

Turning to face Dan, Bram answered, "Yeah?"

"Do you know De Haven means safe harbor?"

Bram smiled. "Yeah, I do. You'll always have a sheltered port in the storm with me."

"Thanks," Dan murmured as a few more tears slid down his cheeks.

"Anytime," Bram replied before opening the door and slipping out.

Strategies and Treachery

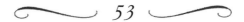

53

July 18
Grand Citadel Hotel – Main Suite – 3:05 p.m.

All heads turned as the portal to Dan's room opened. Bram slipped out and quietly closed the door and went straight to Patch. "Dan needs pain meds, but he also wondered if you have beauty with you."

A thousand-watt smile lit up Patch's face. "Gotta run and grab it, be right back." He sprinted from the suite.

The members of his team peered at Bram with questioning miens. Bram shrugged—he had no clue. They didn't have to wait long for Patch to return.

Lexa stopped Patch before he reached for Dan's door. "What's beauty?"

Patch held up a small, battered, blue MP3 player with straggly earbuds. The quizzical expressions made Patch smile again. "Brody put together several playlists. The music helps Blondie remember the beauty of life. Always helps. Out of habit, I always carry this with me fully charged. I'm ecstatic he asked for Beauty. Give him an hour or two, and he'll be ready to join us."

Blaze grinned broadly at the disbelieving guises. "He's not lying. Always a positive sign when Blondie requests Beauty. He'll make an appearance in two hours, tops." Blaze checked the time. "It's a little after fifteen hundred now. He'll be in here by seventeen hundred. Who's willing to bet?"

Grand Citadel Hotel – Dan's Room – 3:10 p.m.

Patch slipped into the room and found his brother's eyes closed. With quiet steps born from years of stealth movements, he tiptoed to the bed. Keeping his volume low, he said, "Hey, Blondie, lookie what I brought."

Dan opened his eyes and gazed at Patch. "Beauty. You still carry Beauty. I hoped, but …"

"Yeah, a habit I'm glad I never gave up. Fully charged, too." Patch handed the device to him. "Need to check your vitals and give ya some meds. Then you can take all the time you need. I'll make sure no one comes in."

Dan nodded and tried to put the earbuds in despite the soreness in his arms. The first attempt with his left hand failed, his wrist and fingers too swollen to manipulate the little plastic pieces into place. Shifting the plugs to his right hand, he managed to insert them.

After switching Beauty on and selecting a playlist, Dan closed his eyes as the gentle strains of classical music began. Relaxing despite Patch's intrusions, if asked, Dan would swear Brody murmured in his ear. *"Time to relax, Danny. Listen to the music, let the rhythms soothe your soul, and open your heart to the light within."*

Patch worked swiftly and completed his tasks in less than five minutes. After taking a moment to appreciate Blondie's calm expression, he whispered, "Say hi to Brody for me." He pivoted and left, content Brody through the use of Beauty would help.

Near Yellowknife, NWT — Safe House — 1:30 p.m. (3:30 Toronto)

Bored to tears and frustrated beyond belief with the tedium hijacking her life, Rebecca Broderick sat at the kitchen table absent-mindedly flipping through an outdated 'Elite Weapons' magazine while waiting for the water to boil. *Would've it killed them to procure at least one fashion periodical?*

Becca sighed, as the kettle's whistle penetrated her reverie. She stood, and after pouring water into the cups to make tea for herself and her mother, she picked up both mugs and headed for the covered porch.

Yvonne Broderick glanced up from her seat on the bench swing and smiled. "Ah, tea. Thanks, Becca," Yvonne said as she reached for the offered cup.

Distinguishing her daughter's brooding demeanor, Yvonne couldn't fault her negative thoughts. The last few months had been maddening for both of them, but especially Becca. Traveling like thieves in the night and being sequestered in the various safe houses ran their psyches ragged.

At least this one provided them beautiful surroundings and a lake to enjoy during their walks. They were freer here than in Vancouver, but Mother Nature's abundance still didn't make up for being cut off from everyone and everything part and parcel to their ordinary lives.

"Dear, how can I help?" Yvonne sipped her tea.

Becca lowered her svelte body onto the porch's railing and stared at the pine trees as a gentle, cool breeze caressed her cheeks and fluttered her long, straight golden hair from her shoulders. Though picturesque and tranquil, Becca would always be a city girl, preferring the hustle and bustle.

She turned to her mother. Concerned for her mother's health, Becca didn't want to stress her by adding to her worries, so she smiled. "I'm fine, Mom. How are you doing today? Up for a walk to the lake?"

Yvonne gazed at her golden-hearted girl who possessed eyes so like William's. "I'm up for it if you're willing. I realize being forced into seclusion like this is tough on you. Your father's doing all he can to resolve the situation."

Becca nodded, always in awe of her mom's quiet, gentle strength and ability to accept the constraints of being the wife of such a high-profile military man. Her mother had much greater capacity in that regard than she. Becca bucked at the restrictions but acknowledged the necessity. Jorge Pletcher wanted to kill her and almost succeeded in France.

"I'm aware Dad's doing everything possible. He always does. He will catch Pletcher, then we can go home. I only hope it's before September. I planned to attend fashion week in New York with Isabelle, Alphonse, and Jacqueline."

Yvonne rose and gracefully glided to Becca. She set her tea mug on the railing before cupping her lovely daughter's face with both hands. Soft, emerald eyes met sapphire eyes. "We always carry hope."

She kissed her daughter's cheek and linked her arm with Becca's. "Shall we stroll, Sweetheart? You can tell me all about the latest designs you've been sketching." Yvonne used a tried and true method to distract her youngest child from the reality of their confines for a little while.

Becca stood, a genuine smile lighting her eyes as the two ladies started down the steps to the path leading to the lake. As Becca enthusiastically described her newest designs, Mike, Drake, Jack, and Craig assumed their protective positions as unobtrusively as possible, scanning for threats and guarding the women their commander held most dear.

Grand Citadel Hotel – Main Suite – 4:15 p.m.

Bram shoved his cell phone in his pocket. Speaking with Kellie and his girls gave him the dose of love he required after everything today and reminded him to count his count his familial blessing. He enjoyed a loving and supportive rapport with his parents, especially his father. Though they moved to Antwerp ten years ago after his dad took over the Belgium branch for the company he worked for, Bram still spoke with them once a week. The girls loved video calls with their Opa and Oma and chatted their ears off every Saturday.

Kellie also grew up in a warm and caring family. They all benefited from her parents living close as the couple happily babysat their granddaughters whenever Kellie needed a break, or they went on a date night. Their girls also loved their Nana and Papa. His musing stopped when Dan's father sat near him, and Bram waited for the man to initiate the conversation.

In uncharted waters and unsure how to proceed, William studied the calm, burly man. Like Mason's brown eyes, Bram's blue-green orbs reflected sincere kindness, and he hoped to garner insight from the man who Daniel sought in his time of need. "May I speak with you?"

"Sure."

Releasing a breath, William said, "I understand you're privy to some of my contentious history with my son. I love Daniel, and I tried so many ways to restore our relationship, but something always goes horribly wrong. I've always sought experts when out of my depth, and this time is no different. Would you help me understand why Daniel reached out to you?"

Giving the issue some thought, Bram answered, "I'm no authority on the subject, and every relationship is unique, so I'm not sure what I can tell you. Two people connect, or they don't."

William nodded. "I appreciate your candor. I desire a better relationship with my boy, but I'm afraid I'll bungle things again. From Walter's updates, I grasped his entry to your team was rocky, and when discouraged by the lack of acceptance, he requested a transfer to another team. How did you go about fixing things with him? How did you connect with Daniel?"

Bram leaned back in the chair and considered his words. "By reciprocating the way I wished to be treated, which is with consideration, respect, and like I matter. I took the time to listen. I won't lie, waiting for Dan to turn the corner and accept my friendship tested my patience, but I recognized he needed to set the pace, not me. On Christmas Eve, my forbearance came to fruition."

Listening carefully, William asked, "How so?"

Smiling, Bram said, "He called me when he needed a friend. I answered without hesitation—a magical Christmas. My girls, especially Allie, fell in love with Dan while he stayed with us. Allie calls him Prince Charming."

Bram chuckled, leaned in close to William, and whispered, "You can't tell anyone on the team, but Dan plays tea party with my daughters. He lets them dress him in a prince cape and place a crown on his head—never seen anything so sweet. He is excellent with children, so caring and gentle. His eyes light up when he's around them."

"Daniel joined you for Christmas? Why?" William recalled how sad Yvonne had been this past Christmas. It broke his heart when she stared at the ornament on the tree. More guilt heaped on his shoulders as he realized his part in making her unhappy. *Daniel didn't choose to stay in the field all those Christmases. If only I had done something different.*

Bram shared how a distracted driver hit Dan on his way home from volunteering at Mayfield Soup Kitchen. As he revealed Dan's only plans had been to visit Brody's grave, Bram spied guilt reflected in the general's eyes.

The information pulverized William's heart. "Brody Hunter was an honorable man. He made Daniel happy. He died way too young. I wish I could turn back the hands of time and change so many things."

"Sir, you possess the magic key. Time. Don't rush Dan and be patient. Show him he matters, and you care about him through words and actions. He needs to accept he is loved and wanted," Bram suggested.

Perceiving the heavy guilt cloak weighing down the distraught father, Bram added, "We are all human, and even the best of us make mistakes. No one is perfect. Give Dan time to recognize your real feelings and to sort things out. He must relearn everything he believed to be true about your relationship. Time is the key and allowing him to determine the path and pace of his journey."

Internalizing the sage advice, William nodded. "Thank you for your guidance. I'm grateful you're in Daniel's life, and I appreciate you being here when my son needed a friend."

Grand Citadel Hotel – Room 666 – 4:20 p.m.

Receiver up to his ear, Plouffe used a soft, cajoling voice, "We're counting on you. It's important you speak to him alone."

A quiet, sorrowful voice asked, "Why alone? Why me? We've never met."

"Sweetie, this is for your peace of mind. We all want the truth of how he died—no one will tell us. I'm sure he'll talk to you. After all, he's an honorable man, and he wouldn't deny your simple request."

Tammy wept lightly. "My loss hurts so much. I can imagine how devastated he is … he saw Aaron die."

Plouffe grimaced speaking these lies, but kept his voice smooth, "Yes, Sweetie, he must be devastated too. They say he was in charge of Aaron at the time, and I'm aware of the emotional burden leadership carries when someone dies under your command. Sadly, death is never easy, but I can guarantee, speaking to you will help him."

Wiping the tears from her eyes and laying her hand on her belly, the phone slipped a little in her shaking hand. Lifting it to her ear, she said, "I don't want to cause him pain by asking him, but someday I want to tell Aaron's son of his father's courage. I'm afraid if I don't ask, we'll never learn what occurred."

Nigel took a drink of his rum and coke. "I agree. You're our best hope of finding out the real truth. You won't hurt him. Explain to him what you told me. This for Aaron's child."

When Tammy began sobbing again, Nigel smirked as his tone falsely exuded concern, "There, there, Sweetie, don't cry—it isn't good for the baby. You can do this. Everyone will be so proud of you for discovering the truth. Our family, my brother David especially, deserves the facts of Arron's death.

"David's a total wreck and won't be able to find the courage to approach him, let alone ask. And Aaron's mother, the poor dear is too distraught. You are strong and can do this. Just smile sweetly at him."

Tammy blew her nose, and in a sturdier voice, she answered, "I can do this. I will ask him."

"That's a girl. Now, remember, you must ensure he is alone since he's uncomfortable in crowds. You can put him at ease by taking him to the courtyard in back. He'll appreciate the kind gesture."

"Okay. I don't want him distressed."

Grinning, Nigel said, "Excellent. I'll see you tomorrow at the house. You can ride to the funeral with me if you want, Sweetie."

"That's so sweet of you to offer, but Aaron's father wants me to ride with them. You've been so kind to me these past few days. I understand why Aaron admired you. I think Aaron would've approved making you our son's godfather. Goodnight."

Nigel hung up the phone without acknowledging Tammy's last comment— no way in hell David would allow him to be designated the child's godfather, nor did he want to be. David hated him as much as Nigel hated his brother. The world would be better off without crappy weaklings like David.

Nigel laughed. *Tammy is so easy to manipulate. She is such a stupid twit. All it took is the right words, even if they are pure lies. He snorted. Broderick an honorable man—my ass.*

Aaron is the only one in the family worth a damn. Broderick should've been the one to die in the ravine. My toy soldier failed to fall, but tomorrow everything will change.

He laughed out loud again before slamming back the remainder of his rum and coke as his phone rang. He recognized the number and answered, "What?"

An irritated voice ground out, "I'm here. Is everything set up?"

"Yes, I made all the necessary arrangements. You need to be in place before the service starts."

"Does his blubbering fiancée realize what's going to happen?"

"No, she's clueless. Only a means to an end." Plouffe snickered.

Murphy groused, "And the promotion is a sure thing?"

Nigel bristled at Murphy's tone. "Yes, but this time you better not fail. He shouldn't have made it out alive."

"He wouldn't have, but his unit went rogue. I had no control over them," Murphy grumbled.

"I don't care what his unit did. You failed me multiple times. I had a hell of a time covering up your mistakes. The last time you were supposed to put a bullet in him and leave him in the desert—but you screwed that one up too."

Murphy clenched his jaw. *Not my fault, I couldn't pop Broderick. Damned Hunter showed up out of nowhere and blocked my shot. I couldn't make it appear to be a friendly fire accident with Hunter in my way.* Murphy pushed those thoughts away. "What if she's in the way tomorrow?"

"Shoot through her if necessary. I really don't care—she's expendable. You do what's required. I want him dead if he shows tomorrow." Plouffe hung up somewhat agitated.

He rolled thoughts around in his brain. *The idiot never follows through as expected—I better plan a contingency plan. The toy soldier will die if he is stupid enough to come to my nephew's funeral. He'll never see it coming.*

A new strategy started forming. *Yes, that will work perfectly ... better than perfect.* Plouffe fixed himself another rum and coke, sat, took a long drink, and began to plot the general's demise. It would be after the rest of the Broderick family met untimely ends. Nigel would revel in his nemesis's pain as every person William held dear bit the dust.

Healing the Rifts

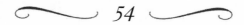

54

July 18
Grand Citadel Hotel — Main Suite — 4:50 p.m.

Dan's bedroom door opened, and he stood in the entryway on slightly shaky legs. He leaned on the jamb for support while his right hand clung to the rolling IV pole. With a casual smile, Dan said nonchalantly, "Hey, got anything to eat out here? I'm starving."

A stunned Alpha Team and William gaped at the visage of Dan in the doorway as he requested food.

Patch and Winds simply smiled with *told you so* expressions.

Yep, just under two hours. Beauty worked her magic again. Blondie will survive. Blaze recognized Blondie was not entirely out of the woods, and would still need time to come to terms with what he learned. But for now, the resilient kid processed enough to operate.

Closest to his brother, Winds trotted over to offer support, assisting Blondie to the nearest chair. "Damned glad you're up and about, Kid. Been a rough one, huh? How ya doing?"

Dan took a moment to scan everyone in the room. His gaze found Blaze, Winds, and Patch first, and a sense of calm settled in his heart. *My chosen brothers battled with me and fought for me when I couldn't fight for myself. They always keep me strong and helped me survive. I would willingly give my life to protect each one of theirs. Somehow they are still here for me ... even after Brody ... I still belong ... our bond of brotherhood isn't broken.*

His eyes roamed again and settled on Bram as he breathed in. When he exhaled, Dan shifted to Nick, Jon, Loki, and Ray, noting their surprised yet concerned expressions. *They're my new chosen family—dad, uncle, and brothers. They give me something I desperately need. They are a connection to a place I can begin to live again ... not only survive ... I belong here, too.*

Dan's eyes sought out and held Lexa's beautiful hazel eyes as her the golden flecks danced with the late afternoon light. *Sexy Lexie's eyes draw me— something is so right with her. Her eyes are the window to her soul. Is she my salvation … my beauty of life … my one and only?*

Pushing those questions to the end of a very long line of things he must to think about and sort out, Dan turned to view the general. Chaotic emotions flooded in. *The old doesn't apply anymore—everything is still too mixed up. Does my father truly want me and love me? Do I belong with my natural family?*

Everything too raw and not ready to deal with it all, Dan refocused on Winds and took a shallow, steadying breath. "I'm fine now, but I'll be okay soon." He still needed time to process the hurt and determine next steps, but for the moment, sufficiently sorted, he wanted to be surrounded by the warmth and security of his chosen families.

"Am I missing something, what do you mean?" Jon asked, confused by Dan's statement. *Okay and fine are the same. Aren't they?*

Not wanting to answer the question, Dan searched for a way to deflect. "What's a guy gotta do for food?" He flashed a lop-sided grin.

To all who observed him, they noted his smile didn't register in his eyes. They also recognized he might need a bit of normalcy while eating, so this would be enough for now.

Jon realized Dan's desire not to respond indicated the rookie possessed different definitions for fine and okay. Jon desired to learn the distinction but decided to drop the topic for now.

When William stood and went to the room's phone to order dinner, Lexa scanned the contents on the table, determining most of the available items would be difficult for Dan to chew given his injured jaw. Recalling the chocolate pudding she put in the fridge earlier, she rose and retrieved the cup along with a spoon, and a bottle of water.

She smiled as she approached Dan. "This should tide you over until the feast arrives." Lexa placed the items on an end table beside him before giving him a gentle hug, careful not to hurt his ribs.

Lexa straightened, glancing at his brace. His sprained wrist would make opening the bottle and removing the pudding lid challenging, so she unscrewed the top and pulled the foil off for him. Lexa's voice came out soft but firm, "You're not allowed to scare us like this ever again … understand?"

Taking the spoon Lexa held out for him, unsure if she meant his actions in the ravine, the briefing room, or both, Dan nodded at her rebuke. "Copy."

"Alright." Aware he would be embarrassed if she attempted to feed him, Lexa set the little plastic cup on Dan's left thigh so he could grip it with his left hand without moving. Dan would insist on doing this by himself, no matter how much his arms hurt. She stepped back an offered him a smile.

Dan sluggishly lifted a spoonful of the soft dessert to his lips; grateful for the pain meds Patch gave him a few hours ago—without them, feeding himself would be impossible. "Thanks, this is perfect." Mercifully, the smooth, cold pudding didn't require chewing and and didn't sting, but numbed the healing cuts inside his mouth as he swallowed.

As he ate, one by one, everyone came forward, and being careful not to jostle him, gave Dan a hug or a gentle pat. Each offered a variation of a well-wish and a normal quip or comment, creating a friendly, warm, inviting, and safe environment that restored a sense of balance for Dan.

William allowed the others to spend a moment with his son. He waited and watched, cheered by the depth of concern they all expressed for Daniel. With Bram's words fresh in his head, William guardedly approached his boy.

When his father came towards him, tension crept in, and Dan unconsciously shifted to an erect soldier-like seated position, back straight, shoulders squared, head up, feet flat on the floor, hands palm down on his thighs.

Everyone noticed the shift and tensed. Although worried General Broderick might cause Dan more distress, no one intervened.

William took a knee in front of Daniel, so their heads were level.

Shocked by the move, since in all prior experience the general always towered over him in a power position, Dan warily waited, unsure how to react.

Connecting with Danny's sapphire eyes, William allowed his orbs to reflect his love, sorrow, and hope as he spoke with a gentle tone, "Time, Daniel, we need time. We're human, and we make mistakes. I've made so many errors. I believe we can mend our relationship. I have hope, and I want to fix this. I understand the process won't be easy or quick, but we have time. You are the one with control. We will go at whatever pace you determine."

If those words had not knocked Dan off-kilter, his father gently embracing as he said, "I love you, Son. Someday I hope you realize I have always loved you so very much," him utterly shocked him.

Dan couldn't remember the last time the general hugged him or told him he loved him. His head spun with conflicting emotions as he received, but didn't reciprocate the hug—his body remained rigid, hands still on his thighs, and he said nothing in return.

William released Daniel after a brief embrace, stood, and walked to a quiet corner out of his son's sight to give Daniel a chance to absorb the change in his tactics. As he lowered himself into a chair, his insides cried out impotently, wondering if his son believed him. Daniel's automatic posture affirmed he drove his child too hard and too early. Behaviors William once thought would protect Daniel prevented his boy from accepting a father's comfort and love. *I wish Yvonne were here. She would be able to reach Danny.*

Dan's posture relaxed, and he sat quietly, catching bits and pieces of conversations around him, not paying much attention as he stared out the window. *My father hugged me. He said he loves me and wants to mend things, and put the ball in my court. What the hell? This is all so overwhelming.*

After approaching William, Bram kept his volume low as he spoke, "Though it may not seem like it from Dan's response, you did well."

William whispered, "Thank you for the words. I'll keep in mind what you told me, and I'll try to be patient, though I'm not by naturel. I do love my son. I'll do whatever it takes, so one day he will believe me. I have so much to atone for, and Daniel is important to me, so I'll do what is necessary in hopes he'll forgive me one day."

From all he learned recently, Bram nodded as he held hope William and Dan would mend their father-son relationship. *They only need time. Almost twenty years of history can't be undone in a day.*

Winds overheard the general as his internal conflict continued to roar. *I hope the loving father is the true version, and for Blondie's sake, they can reconcile. Every boy needs a father.* His eyes drifted to Blaze, and his struggle settled as he grinned. *The kid already has one though … Papa Bear loves Blondie as much as a brother and father.*

Thirty minutes later, after Jon and Blaze helped him move on unsteady and aching legs, Dan sat at the dining table with the others. As he surveyed all the food, Dan realized Lexa wasn't kidding. *Feast is an accurate description.* He noted a substantial selection of his favorite soft foods as Lexa filled a plate for him. He smiled at her and received one in return.

Dinner conversation consisted of fun and mundane topics, with a playful argument breaking out between Winds and Jon over which hockey team was the best. Dan appreciated the lengths everyone went to make this dinner seem normal in a completely abnormal setting.

Near the end of the meal, Loki asked Blaze, "So who won the bet?"

Everyone cringed, and Dan noted the unease. "What bet?"

Realizing his error, Loki made something up. "How much food would be left after we finished. The general here thinks he's feeding an entire army, so many leftovers you'd think this was an Italian's home."

Dan saw right through the lame attempt at deflection, but he let it drop, surmising he probably didn't want to know what the real bet entailed, especially with the *daggers* glare Lexa gave Loki.

Although every muscle in his body revolted at any movement, Dan managed to consume enough to slake his hunger. Though he believed Patch would likely say no with the stitches he sported in his face and arm, a warm shower would alleviate some of his aches, so Dan asked, "Any way you would approve me taking a quick shower? One would be nice before hitting the sack."

Patch assessed Blondie and registered the unspoken need. He should decline due to sutures, but he learned long ago from Brody and Blaze, showering would be beneficial for Blondie's emotional state. "Yeah, as long as it's short. I'll redress your wounds when you're done. Let's go, buddy." He rose and then helped Blondie make his way to the bedroom.

Blaze grinned. Blondie's desire for a shower was a positive sign, which meant the kid continued on the path of transitioning from fine to okay. He called out to Blondie, "Nick and Lexa went by your place, brought your personal kit, and clean clothes. If you need any help, holler. My hands are your hands if necessary."

Dan stopped, turned, and peered at Blaze. His words brought Mason to mind. Although fearful of the answer, he asked, "Does Mason hate me?"

Registering the fear in Blondie's eyes, Blaze bolted out of his seat and strode to him in a flash. Meeting his gaze head-on, Blaze smiled. "Ah, kid, don't you realize, Mason could never hate you. You're his little brother. I can't wait to contact him. He's finally going to forgive me for losing you."

Dan searched Blaze's eyes for the truth, and then shifted his focus to Winds who now stood beside Blaze.

Winds grinned, "Damn, Blondie. How could you ever think Mason would dislike you? I swear—I was as colorful as you when he found out how badly we failed you after Brody died."

Patch nodded and at Blondie's questioning mien. "I'll tell you all about the fracas while you're cleaning up."

As the two moved into Dan's room, Jon asked, "Who is Mason?"

Blaze grinned as his eyes moved from Jon to Bram. "Mason is Blondie's protective big brother—and I mean enormous brother." Exaggerating a little, Blaze added, "Mason makes Bram look like a munchkin."

Sobering as he absently rubbed his jaw where Mason belted him, Blaze said, "He's one man you never want to cross. Blondie sometimes called him a Highland heathen. His fists are deadly. I swear he could probably knock down a house with them if he wanted to."

Jon glanced at Bram. *Someone more massive than Bram? Now that would be impressive.*

Lexa asked Winds, "What did you mean you were as colorful as Dan? Do you bruise as easily?"

Winds chuckled and shook his head before sharing shared what occurred after Mason arrived at the base five minutes after Blondie's plane took off. He told them about the brawl and the aftermath and concluded with, "That's how I got busted down to private. I can't keep quiet around Major Puffy. When I found out no charges were filed against Murphy, I let loose on him."

Loki asked, "Aren't you a corporal now?"

"Yeah, for the fifth time. Plouffe demoted me so many times it isn't funny, but I earned back my rank over the past year. When the major's gone, I might attain Master Warrant Officer." He snickered, "That is if his replacement isn't a total jerk, and I can keep my trap shut."

General Broderick listened intently. When Winds finished, he said, "So that's what precipitated the mêlée. Everyone remained closed-mouthed when I inquired. Upset by the serious injuries sustained by many and the substantial property damage, I dressed the major down in public rather than privately for his lack of control over his men."

He focused on Winds as he stated, "I will investigate your service record and the demotions you received. I'll do what I can to restore you to your rightful rank and pay. Plouffe's befouled the uniform, and it appears as though there might be transgressions against a fair number of soldiers."

Stunned speechless, Winds stared at his commander as a bit more of his conflict ebbed away. *Blaze is right—General Badass is an honorable man.*

Conversation in the main suite returned to activities around the investigation. With everyone distracted earlier, progress had been slow today. Now that Dan appeared to be coping, they were reenergized and tackled their tasks with renewed zeal.

Jon left the room to check-in with Hal. After the first security plan had been shot to hell, they decided the Blaze's four men would split into two teams and rotate on twelve-hour shifts in the hall. With everybody else in the suite, Dan would be well protected.

Anything for A Brother

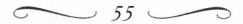 *55*

Though stiff and exceedingly sore, Dan conceded the hot shower released a bit of muscle tension. Standing naked at the sink and unhurriedly brushing his teeth, since the slightest motion still hurt, Dan took stock of his physical state in the mirror. *I'm a zombie-like mess. No wonder everyone stared.*

He noted the stitches over his eye, almost in the same place as his previous scar, a myriad of minor cuts and abrasions, and dark purple, blue, and red bruising all over his face. With each tiny movement, his right arm burned where he been shot, but at least he had the use of it.

His left wrist, hand, and knuckles had swollen painfully tight. Examining the abraded skin on his knuckles, he attempted to flex his fingers and grimaced. *Nope, using my dominant hand is out of the question for now. Damned glad I didn't bust them on Basto's rock-solid jaw.*

Dan recalled when his wrist bent weird when Basto fell on him. At the time, he thought for sure it had broken. *Luckily, my wrist is only sprained, though I hope I didn't tear any tendons or muscles.*

Leaning over to spit out toothpaste, Dan released a soft groan and hiss. *Shit, I hurt so much.* He tried to take a deeper breath, causing himself more pain. *Cracked ribs suck.* As he sluggishly straightened, he peered at deep purple bruising, which blackened the left shoulder. The discoloration, accompanied by a relentless, throbbing ache, suggested a fractured bone. *Wonder if I did? I can't stand slings, but maybe Patch will procure one for me.*

After rinsing his mouth, Dan smiled in the mirror, examining his teeth. On the plus side, no teeth had been knocked out. He dangled his boxers with his right hand, managed stepped into them, and to pull them up with tons of effort. Exhausted, Dan realized he required assistance to put his pants on.

Resting against the wall, waiting to regain some energy, Dan inspected the contusions littering his body, noting the marked degree of color change and intensity of the bruising. *Crap, how long have I been out? What is today?*

He grabbed his sweatpants and returned to the bedroom. Patch would help him put them on after attending to his injuries. *Damn glad Patch is here—I'm used to my brother helping me.*

Patch patiently waited as Blondie made his way to the bed at a snail's pace carrying the pants, somewhat surprised Blondie managed to pull on the boxers on by himself. He expected Blondie to request his help with the simple task. Though he surmised the intravenous painkillers he administered to Blondie before removing the IV must've made a difference

While Blondie showered, he placed a call to Dr. Fraser for oral medications, since Blondie hated being tethered and could now swallow pills. The doctor indicated antibiotics and a pain reliever would be delivered early tomorrow morning. He hoped the pain relief lasted through the night because he didn't want to restart Blondie's IV or give him a dose of meds via a syringe.

Dan lowered himself to the edge of the mattress before looking at Patch. "So, you left the military. Why?"

Taking the sweatpants and keeping his eyes on them, Patch squatted and held the garment as Blondie fractionally lifted his foot off the ground, allowing him to slip them on. As he repeated the motion on the other foot, Patch answered, "Several reasons."

The vague response prompted Dan to ask, "Like what?" as he stood while Patch pulled his pants up around his waist for him.

After finishing the task, Patch turned to grab the ace bandage and brace for Blondie's wrist as his former unit mate sat. Pulling a chair close, he settled and began wrapping the sprained wrist. "After Brody, and you ..." Patch trailed off still unable to meet his eyes. Everything still hurt too much.

Dan perceived Patch's avoidance, and remained quiet as he finished with his wrist before prodding, "Okay, so after that, what happened? What made you decide you were done?"

An extended silence told Dan more than words. His gut twisted. "Who? Who else died?"

Lifting his eyes to meet Blondie's, Patch's voice hitched. "Baboon."

Sucking in a sharp breath caused shooting pain in his chest—the pain not all related to his damage ribs—his heart ached at the loss. "How?"

Dropping his eyes to his lap, Patch clenched and unclenched his fists as tears welled in his eyes. "I didn't recognize the signs. None of us realized he teetered on the edge. When he requested a transfer after you left, we thought he needed to be away from us—from a constant reminder of how bad we all screwed up. He saved you, but we failed to save him."

Unbidden hot liquid slipped from the corner of Dan's eyes. His voice came out soft and filled with disbelief, "Baboon did it himself?"

Patch nodded.

Dan reeled. *Nils isn't the type of guy to take his own life. Baboon is … was so strong.* Sorrow filled his heart at the loss of another friend.

Anguish filled Patch's tone. "After that … everything became too personal. So many buddies I cared about died … I couldn't save them. I had to leave. If I didn't, I might've ended up like Baboon."

Witnessing his brother's agony, Dan wished he could take it away. Lifting his right hand, he lay it on Patch's shoulder—the only comfort he could offer at the moment. *Patch is always there for us—every single time. He gave of himself selflessly to keep us all alive. I never realized the burden he carried.*

Dan understood he didn't have to effuse words of thanks. The unit dispensed with them years ago. Each comprehended how much the others appreciated what they did for one another. No words were needed—usually.

Nevertheless, Dan believed it to be essential to convey his gratitude now and to recognize he wasn't the only one who needed to move on. "I never said thanks for everything you've done for me. All you taught me. I'm whole, strong, and alive because you care. Thank you from the bottom of my heart, Jim. I hope this change helps you heal too, brother."

Smiling, Dan added, "Can't believe we both ended up in Toronto. What are the odds? If you need anything, I'm here for you. Always."

Patch peered up at Blondie's use of his first name. He appreciated Dan taking the first small step to help him move beyond the military. "No thanks are needed, Dan. You're my brother, and always will be. Can you forgive me for hurting you?"

"Nothing to forgive. We were all grieving."

Blue and brown eyes locked and held one another, acknowledging both their souls must walk a path to healing. Their deep connection, born in the fires of hell, forged an unbreakable bond to last a lifetime. Without hesitation, the brothers would support each other on their journeys.

Patch nodded, pushed up out of the chair, and broke the maudlin tension. "Do you realize, you gained a reputation with the paramedics I work with? They say you're close to breaking Bram's record for getting hurt. Loki's nickname of Wile E. Coyote fits you. I also like Dantastic. So does Heather."

Dan laughed, winced, laughed, groaned, laughed, then sighed. "Don't make me laugh. This shit still hurts too much."

Patch grinned. "Well, laughter is the best medicine—releases endorphins that reduce pain. Let me rebandage the hole in your arm, then I'll help you put a shirt on." When Patch finished, he asked, "Better?"

"Much." Dan glanced at the carpet, and up at the ceiling as he debated whether to make his request. After putting on his shirt, his shoulder ached something fierce. Meeting Jim's gaze, Dan sighed. "Think my arm and shoulder might benefit from a sling. Can you get one for me?"

"Absolutely. I can ask Fraser to send one in the morning with the oral meds, unless you need it now, in which case, I'll run out and buy one."

"Tomorrow's soon enough."

"Alright. You want to go to bed or sit with everyone for a bit?"

Though tired, Dan needed to be close to his chosen family. "In the main suite … for a little while."

CFB Halifax – 2115 Hours (7:15 p.m. Toronto)

Lost in thought, Able Seaman Kyle Broderick scrubbed the last toilet on this deck. He spent the entire day cleaning every head on this ship. After his dad called him and told him about Dan, Kyle went to his commanding officer to request leave. He asked for a week's leave starting in two days. His CO denied him and set him to the task of cleaning all the latrines.

Kyle believed Chief Petty Officer Foccard was an SOB on a power-trip and who hated him because his last name happened to be Broderick. *No, that isn't right, Foccard hates everyone below his rank. Foccard is an equal opportunity prick who loves to make our lives miserable.* Shifting his focus to something more positive, Kyle began sorting through ways he might change Foccard's mind.

"BRODERICK, YOU'RE NOT DONE YET?" Foccard yelled. He wanted the peon to jump to attention. A Broderick coming attention to him—now that was a beautiful sight.

Dropping the scrub brush, Kyle scrambled to rise, inadvertently knocking a bottle of toilet bowl cleaner off the counter in the process. He watched in horror as the bottle bounced on the floor, and the contents, which contained bleach, splashed all over Foccard's dark pants. *Oh crap! I'm gonna pay for this one big time.*

Kyle came to rigid attention and swallowed hard. "I only have four more heads to clean."

Foccard recoiled as the liquid spattered his trousers. "BRODERICK, YOU'LL REGRET YOUR CLUMSINESS. YOU'LL BE CLEANING HEADS FOR THE NEXT MONTH. YOU'RE NOW ON MY OFFICIAL SHIT LIST."

Kyle nearly groaned. *Now for sure, I won't be able to swing leave. Dang, I wanted to be there for Dan.* He tuned out his CO's rant as his thoughts focused on his favorite cousin. *How severely is he hurt? I hope not too bad. Dad said there are things he can't tell me over the phone, but made certain I comprehended Dan didn't purposefully ignore us and Dan needs his family now.*

As Foccard's tirade tapered off, Kyle listened more intently.

"I came to tell you I approved your leave after consideration. But now, you'll be scrubbing down every inch of this ship while we are in port. YOU CAN KISS ANY LEAVE GOODBYE. When you finish here, report to the mess and begin a deep clean on the ovens." Foccard pivoted and briskly strode out without a backward glance after enjoying chewing out a Broderick.

Kyle relaxed after Foccard left. *Perhaps I should've gone the university route after all. Then I would be a higher rank than Foccard, and I would put him in his place for treating enlisted sailors like gum stuck on the bottom of his shoe.*

Though it remained one of the last things he desired, Kyle considered he might need to place a call to his father if he wanted to be there to help Dan. Relying on Dad to fight his battles didn't sit well with him, but he would do anything short of committing murder for his family, especially Dan. If his cousin needed him, he would be there come hell or high water.

Picking up the scrub brush and leaking bottle, Kyle set to work again. *Yeah, should've followed my brother's and father's paths to become an officer. Wonder if I can make a change.*

A Man of Duty and Honor

 *56*

July 18
Grand Citadel Hotel — Main Suite — 7:25 p.m.

Patch stayed close to Blondie as they reentered the common area in case Blondie faltered as his steps remained shaky. After his brother sat in a comfy chair, Jim placed a pillow in Dan's lap and carefully positioned Blondie's left wrist on it before going to grab him some water.

Dan smiled at Ray and Loki when they moved an ottoman close to him and lifted his legs on it. The heat of embarrassment flushed his cheeks, and he hoped his bruising hid his blush. He never liked being the center of attention, preferring to be more inconspicuous.

"Need anything else?" Loki asked.

"No. Thanks." He accepted the open bottle from Patch and took a sip before turning his gaze toward Nick. "Boss?"

"Yeah, Dan?" Nick glanced up from the file in his hand. He noted Dan's voice sounded more normal, but his appearance remained a wholly different story—he looked wiped out.

Dan inquired, "What's today's date?"

Nick closed the folded. "Today's the eighteenth." He paid close attention to the nuance in Dan's expression.

Wow, I lost three days. Another thought entered Dan's mind. "Boss, did I miss Aaron's funeral?"

His question grabbed the interest of everyone in the room, causing them to halt their activities and listen.

"No, it's tomorrow afternoon at three. But I don't think you should attend, given the threat against you. The major will be there," Nick stated firmly.

"I must go," Dan firmly replied as he met Pastore's gaze. *Sometimes there is no choice, and this is one of those times.*

Although against Dan going, Nick reminded himself he should try to comprehend Dan's thinking. He recalled all too well the price they all paid for not listening. "Why?"

"Because Aaron was under my command when he died. It would be a dishonor if I didn't go. He was a decent man." Dan noted disgust displayed on several faces. He narrowed in on Loki and Lexa, who sat close to each other. "What's that look for?"

Uncomfortable at being the ones called to account for their reactions, Lexa and Loki shared a glance before Lexa stated, "Because of Aaron's attitude and behavior toward you while searching section seven. His level of disrespect was uncalled for and unprofessional."

Loki added, "Aaron's been a first-rate jerk. You should've heard the things he said about you to Kirk and Frank before we all headed out." Wanting Dan to understand, Loki recounted everything they overheard.

Blaze, Winds, and Patch all bristled at how another constable, another Plouffe maligned their kid brother.

William sighed and closed his eyes. *Goddamned Plouffe's.*

Dan recalled Aaron's last words, ones no one else would ever hear. "Aaron didn't have to like me—not everyone likes everyone. Each person is entitled to their views. And even if he based his dislike on the crap his uncle spewed, his opinion of me doesn't discount the fact Aaron put his life on the line every day to protect the citizens of Toronto.

"I shouldn't say this because I haven't met with NRB yet, but in the end, Aaron covered my back. He did the right thing, no matter his personal opinion of me. Aaron came upon Basto and me when the gang leader leveled my gun at my head. Aaron caused a distraction, allowing me to go for my MP5. Without his action, I would be dead—shot with my own weapon."

Dan took a steadying breath. "Another subject appeared out of nowhere. Blood dripped into my eye, slowing my reaction time, and the unknown subject shot Aaron before I could neutralize the threat. Then Basto and I fired at each other at the same time. I hit Basto; he missed me."

Reliving the event and clearly shaken, Dan sat quietly for several moments. "So whatever Aaron said, whatever attitude he threw at me, whatever his bastard uncle did, Aaron deserves to be honored. He's an honorable man who served and made the ultimate sacrifice. I must pay my respects. Without him, I would be dead. He saved me." Dan added to himself ... *and I failed him.*

Everyone remained silent. They all wondered about the four shots and what occurred in the ravine. Each person speculated various scenarios, but no one placed Aaron in the role of saving Dan. Lexa and Loki both crossed their arms; neither quite prepared to forgive Aaron yet.

Nick sighed, he comprehended Dan's need, but also appreciated the danger. About to decline again, he halted when Dan pinned his gaze on Jon and, with conviction, said, "I *will* go—with or without your help. Do *not* doubt me for one second. Will you help me do it without taking unacceptable risks?"

Jon's eyes flashed to Nick's. *Damn, the rookie's learned something—points, shoots, scores a bulls-eye with his words.* Before he could reply, Dan's father intervened, though Jon noted Dan stiffened to attention when the general rested a hand on his shoulder.

William noted Daniel tensing at his touch and sighed. *Will this reaction ever abate? Probably not—it's too ingrained.* However, pushing his feelings aside, aware of how important this was to his son, William offered his backing. "I understand Daniel's sense of duty and his need to honor a fallen officer. I'll help him. Who else is willing to support Daniel?"

Shocked for the third time by the general's action tonight, Dan never expected his father to support him—let alone be the first one.

Jon acquiesced to the steel determination displayed by both father and son. "Dano, I'm only going along with this because the church will be full of constables. Plouffe would be crazy to go after you with so many witnesses."

Dan nodded.

A shiver coursed through Lexa as she reviewed Dan's words about Basto aiming Dan's handgun at him. Reluctantly, she uncrossed her arms, proud of her teammate for honoring Aaron despite the man's odious words and actions. "I'll agree. We've got your back if the major's dumb enough to try anything."

Her reward came with a lopsided grin, which sadly appeared somewhat pitiful due to the swelling of his face. Lexa fought the urge to kiss away his aches and pains. *Dang, he truly is under my skin. What the heck am I going to do?* Striving hard to push the desire to comfort him away, and needing a distraction, she stood and walked to the table to grab a water bottle.

Aware of the veracity of Blondie's threat about going with or without help, the kid quite adept at leaving even in his current condition, Blaze assumed his command persona. "Blondie, I'll agree but with conditions. Major Plouffe isn't to be given the slightest opportunity to come close to you. You'll wear a vest, my men and I will be armed, and we must devise a security plan. And finally, you're not to step more than five feet away from me. You got that, Kid?"

Jon grinned when Dan simply smiled and nodded at Blaze. He recognized Dan respected his former unit leader and would abide by his conditions. Relief for him and everyone else.

Winds focused on Sergeant Pastore as he said, "I don't like this one damned bit, but if Blondie's bound and determined to go, I'll be there to protect his six. However, I think your team should also carry weapons. The bastard played us for years. I wouldn't put anything past him."

Nick nodded. "I agree. We'll be equipped. We also need to alert the other teams to the potential risk. The more eyes watching, the safer Dan will be."

This isn't smart. I don't like this one darned bit, and I'm not ready to excuse Aaron's behavior yet, but Dan is family, and I'll do anything for him—even if I think this is the dumbest thing in the world to do. Loki rose, ambled over to Dan, and patted his shoulder in a show of solidarity.

Glad of all the support, but worn out, Dan had one more issue to address before going to bed. "Boss, one other thing. I want to do the NRB interviews tomorrow. With the funeral scheduled in the afternoon, can you arrange for me to complete them in the morning?"

"You sure you're up to that?" Bram asked. "You realize those can wait."

Dan shook his head. "Aaron's family can't be told anything until after the interviews. They deserve to know, and they shouldn't have to wait on me. I'll be fine—" Dan glanced at Blaze and changed the last word to, "okay."

Jon caught the gaze and word substitution. He now definitely concluded Dan attributed a special meaning and distinction between the two words. He determined to understand the difference because Dan used the word fine a lot when they asked him how he fared.

Nick conceded, "I'll make arrangements. For now, I think you need some more rest."

Slowly swinging his legs off the ottoman, Dan found Loki and Winds there helping him to stand. This was getting to be a bit too much coddling. He groused, "I can do it myself."

Winds stepped back, his gaze conveying to Loki he should do the same, as he quipped, "Okay, but don't complain to me if you ruin your pretty-boy face by falling over."

Dan chuckled. "Bit late for that, don't you think? I already look like a Zombie."

The sound of Dan's laughter and banter eased everyone's tension.

Moving at a snail's pace, Dan made his way to his bedroom. Stopping at the portal, Dan swiveled his head to view his chosen family. He flashed them all a smile, which lit his eyes before turning back and reaching for the door.

As Dan started to close the door, Bram called out, "Dan, if you need anything at all, I'll be right out here all night."

Dan nodded and shut his door, shuffled to the nightstand, and picked up Beauty. He managed to situate himself on the mattress in a semi-comfortable position, inserted the earbuds, and switched on Beauty. So drained he figured sleep would eventually come, but at the moment, his mind remained jumbled. First, he must sort out enough to deal with NRB and Aaron's funeral, then he would lock those memories in his safe place and focus on his future.

After Dan's door closed, Blaze asked Jon, "What's an NRB interview?"

Jon explained as an independent civilian authority the purpose of the Nonpartisan Review Board was to maintain police accountability in the use of force. He also described what the interview entailed. Jon experienced a twinge of guilt, recalling he failed to educate Dan on the process before he participated in one. He shuddered slightly. *Christ, his first one had been done by Donner. Who knew the man was so unbalanced?*

Blaze shook his head. "Wow, you mean you go through one of those each time you use lethal force? That's intense. I mean, I understand the reason why and all, but that's gotta hurt sometimes. I doubt I'd ever be TRF material, don't think I could handle doing that every time. And you say Blondie's got five of those tomorrow? I hope he's up to it."

He did wonder how Blondie would fare from an emotional standpoint. Blaze's gaze scanned the room. "Patch, do you have the charger for Beauty? Blondie might need Beauty tomorrow morning."

When Jon pinned him with questioning mien, Blaze smiled. "Just want to be prepared."

"I like being prepared, too," Jon responded with a grin.

William cleared his throat to garner everyone's attention, "How are we going to protect Daniel tomorrow? What's the plan?"

The group discussed the options and decided to enlist the help of the other teams would be the right course because although they were aware of Plouffe, Pletcher was still on the loose, and they had no idea if he posed a threat to Dan. However, due to the top-secret nature of the situation, they would have to be vague with details.

Blaze suggested, "Perhaps we show photos of Pletcher and Major Plouffe to the other officers, and provide a short explanation. Allude to a rocky history between Blondie and the major, and in his grief, we believe Plouffe might blame him for Aaron's death and seek retribution. Not a lie, but not the whole sickening truth."

When they agreed, Nick placed a call to the sergeants of Charlie, Delta, and Echo teams, asking them to join a planning session tonight. Bravo Team wouldn't be attending the funeral because they would be on shift covering for all the teams. About twenty minutes later, Charlie Team's Sergeant, Colton Harmon, and Tactical Leader Paul Miller arrived.

A few minutes later, Trevor McBride from Echo arrived. Trevor explained Sergeant Winter and their TL were unable to make it tonight, so he offered to come and would brief them in the morning. Frank Hudson, Delta's representative, arrived shortly after, explaining his team leaders were busy with arrangements for Aaron's parents for tomorrow.

Lexa asked, "Frank, how's the arm?"

Frank grinned. "Fine. It's great for getting sympathy from my whole family. I'll be back to active duty when my team returns to duty in a few weeks."

After grabbing beverages, everyone gathered around the large table and set to work developing a plan. Though they all sought perfection, too many possibilities existed with the open and exposed area, resulting in only an adequate strategy.

Heather entered the suite, noted the additional men and everyone in deep discussion, so she made her way to Dan's room after pouring herself a cup of coffee.

Patch disengaged from the planning session, and caught her before she went in. "Hey, Heather."

"Hi. How's our patient?"

"Unattached." Patch grinned.

New to flirting—never having felt the desire to do it before, Heather quipped, "Oh, I'm so glad he's single. He's quite handsome." She smiled as she caught a little flash of something in Jim's eyes.

Damn, Blondie gets all the girls. Patch forced a grin, "No, I mean no IV."

Heather laid her hand on his left arm, mimicking his manner with Dan on multiple occasions. "Only teasing. I figured you meant the IV. What if he needs pain meds?"

Patch's arm tingled, where Heather's hand remained. "He shouldn't need any before the oral meds arrive. There are two doses in syringe form, but if he needs any, you need to call me—I'll handle it."

Heather nodded. "Anything else?"

"I allowed him to take a shower tonight. Do me a favor and check his gunshot wound several times. With only a partial spleen, infections tend to take hold fast with him. Appeared fine to me when I wrapped it, but better to keep an eye on the wound." Patch opened the door for her.

As Heather went in she allowed herself to brush against Jim's body lightly as she whispered, "Dan's not the only handsome man—I prefer your looks." She blushed as their eyes met. *Oh lordy, I've never done this before either. What is it about Jim that makes me all gooey inside?*

Patch sucked in a breath. *Wowsers!* A dopey grin grew as he closed the door. *I'm gonna haveta give Heather a call when this is all said and done. Take her out on a date and get to know her better.* He strolled towards the table with a grin affixed to his face.

Blaze nudged Winds as he spotted Patch ambling back to the group.

Winds glanced from the blueprint he studied and at Blaze, who tilted his head towards Patch. He chuckled upon spying Patch's love-struck expression and whispered, "Me thinks Patch is besotted."

Blaze chuckled lightly. "Yeah. She seems nice. Hope she doesn't break his heart." He switched his focus back to the session, though happy Patch appeared to be moving forward, aware his former medic needed to heal. The past years had been difficult on them all, but especially on Patch. His brother was a true empath and absorbed all their pain.

After wrapping up, Blaze, Patch, and Winds approached Trevor, and as their spokesman, Blaze said, "Trevor, right?"

"Yes."

"I'm Blaze, and these two are Winds and Patch," he said, pointing at his buddies. "We are indebted to you and wanted to say thank you."

Confusion lit Trevor's face. "A debt? And thanks for what?"

"Do you remember the first time you met Blondie—Dan?" Blaze queried.

"You mean in the mess tent?"

"Yeah, actually outside it, but yes, in the tent, too. We owe you for that."

"For talking to him?" Trevor didn't understand why someone would be indebted to common courtesy.

Winds interceded. "What Blaze is muddling up is we are thanking you for saving Blondie. Your humanity kept him from falling over the edge before we arrived. He needed a show of kindness after a bad mission. So, thank you."

Recognition flared in Trevor's eyes. "That was you who came into the tent. That was intense. I don't see the guy who talked to him first. Is he here? After the shit Dan's been through, he sure could use a friend like that. The connection between them seemed quite strong … a forever bond.

"Dan appeared half-dead as he struggled to stand outside the tent. Hell, he looked like a zombie most the time. He was always there. Everyone else came and went, but he always stayed. Wondered about that. Is that some weird Special Forces thing? Don't you guys get the same downtime?" As he continued to speak, he noticed the demeanor of the men changing, and he sensed intense anger and pure hatred, so he halted.

Noting Trevor's confusion, Patch responded without answering Trevor's questions. "Sorry, our anger isn't directed at you. Only a response where Blondie's concerned … he's our little brother, and we protect him. Thanks for taking care of him. I think he ended up at TRF because of what you told him."

Blaze sighed. Trevor is right, even in death, Blondie's and Brody's bond cannot be severed. He softly answered one question for Trevor. "Brody died, but Blondie still has us. He'll be alright."

Unsure what to say, Trevor nodded. "Well, I'm glad I was there to help. Gotta go. See you tomorrow." Trevor waved bye to Alpha Team before exiting. As he walked down the hall to the elevator, Trevor exhaled heavily. *Well, that was almost as weird as the first time. Too bad Dan's friend died. When things settled down, I'll reintroduce myself to him … he might need a friend or two.*

Acceptance And Belonging

 *57*

Nick scanned the room and did his normal assessment of the team. They all appeared weary. In fact, Bram fell asleep on the couch over an hour ago. The past few days had been overwhelmingly emotional for them all and today, particularly draining for Bram.

He determined he must tell them to call it a day because if he didn't, they would continue working. They must be sharp for the NRB interviews and to protect Dan at the funeral tomorrow. So he had to force them to stop for the night. Strolling over to the desk where Loki and Ray worked, Nick lay a hand on Loki's shoulder. "Time to knock off."

Ray nodded and started to close the files he was reviewing and log off the computer. "Yeah, you're right. Read this document three times and I still don't recall what it said. I need a break."

Loki continued to tap away on his keyboard. Too concentrated on the search bot program he was writing, he didn't register the words or the Boss's hand on his shoulder. Loki had not delved into the darknet since right after graduating high school. He stumbled upon its existence when doing research for a school project.

Bransworth, his CSIS liaison, had been surprised to discover Loki knew it existed. Loki exchanged several emails with Bransworth as they discussed what searches might ferret out information on Plouffe, Pletcher, and anyone else involved. While Bransworth worked on program and Loki focused on another. Between them they hoped to unearth more evidence and connections.

"Loki, buddy," Ray said as his friend carried on to working. Still not getting a reaction, Ray put his hand over Loki's hands preventing him from typing.

"Hey!" Loki exclaimed as he knocked Ray's hands off his.

Nick said, "Loki, quitting time."

Loki glanced up at Boss and back to his monitor. "I gotta finish writing this program. It'll only take me thirty or so minutes. After I set it to run and grab some shuteye."

"I'll stay here and make sure he quits in thirty minutes," Lexa offered as she closed the file she had been reviewing.

Jon sauntered over. "Should I wake Bram and send him off to his room?"

Nick shook his head. "No, he said he would be here if Dan needed him tonight."

"I forgot. Alright, I'm heading out. What time is NRB scheduled?" Jon yawned as he stretched, ready for bed.

"Eight-thirty. Gambrill said we need to be here by quarter after eight. He wants to speak to us before the agent arrives," Nick shared.

Ray stood and caught Jon's yawn. "Loki, I'll expect you in forty mins … no longer, you need sleep." He turned to the others and said, "I'll see you all at eight-fifteen. I'm gonna skip workout."

Jon patted Ray's back. "Everyone should sleep in. No workout in the morning. Night." He started for the door with Ray when he noticed Nick didn't follow. "Nick, you coming?"

"I'll leave in a moment." Nick shifted his gaze to Lexa after Jon gave him a slight nod and exited. He noted how Lexa's attention kept going to Dan's bedroom. She appeared to be having trouble with all this and might still beating herself up for not being closer to Dan and Aaron in the ravine.

Nick strolled over and sat in the chair beside Lexa. Placing a hand casually on her knee, he drew her attention. "How are you holding up?"

"I'm fine. How about you?" Lexa's voice betrayed her true state, and she scrambled for a way to conceal her thoughts from Boss's uncanny insight, but came up blank.

Observing the play of emotions on Lexa's face, Nick offered her a warm smile. "It's been rough. Dan surely endured a painful past. There is lot for him to deal with, and he's gonna need support coming to terms with many things. Aaron's loss being one of them. He'll need a friend he can talk to."

She nodded and couldn't help glancing at Dan's door again.

"Lexa, what happened in the ravine isn't your fault. I'm aware of how your mind works because it's how we all tend to think. We take on guilt for things out of our control. Must be a prerequisite for becoming TRF."

His truism generated a snort of from Lexa. She latched on to Boss's train of thought and used it to cover up her more personal thoughts "Yeah, well, at least this is something else we're the best at. Logically, I hold no blame, that lies with the subjects. Emotionally, well, that'll take a little longer to accept. I only hope Dan doesn't blame himself for Aaron's death."

Boss usually read her with such ease, and sometimes it boggled her mind. Needing to escape Nick's all-seeing eyes and profound intuition, Lexa rose and turned towards Dan's room and blew out a breath.

Nick stood and came close to Lexa. The heart of the team might be able to assist Dan, and in doing so, it would also help her. "Why don't you go check on him? You and he developed a connection that is different from the one he shares with Bram. He is more open with you, and we've all benefitted from the conversations you've had with Dan while patrolling. He might need a trusted, gentle touch right about now."

Lexa turned to Nick in surprise but relaxed as she spotted the genuine warmth reflected in his hazel eyes and a fatherly smile. Though typically more aloof, she allowed him to pull her into a short hug, cherishing the relationship they shared.

After releasing Lexa, Nick said, "It would probably help you deal with this too. Be the friend Dan needs now."

She sighed as relief flooded in when she realized Boss missed the mark with her true conflict. "Yeah, I'll pop in and check if he's awake before making sure Loki goes to bed. Thanks, for always being here for me."

Nick's grin broadened, happy he helped the daughter of his heart. "Sleep well, Lexa." He turned and started for the exit with slow steps as the weight of everything in the past few days pressed on his shoulders. Nick sincerely hoped Lexa's brand of friendship would help Dan through this trying time.

Grand Citadel Hotel – Dan's Room – 10:05 p.m.

Lexa entered quietly and closed the door behind her. Heather sat in a chair in the corner, reading. The only light in the room came from a lamp near the nurse. As she peered at Dan, thoughts of the first night they slept together rushed in—it had been in this hotel.

Heather glanced up from her book and stood. She ambled to Lexa and whispered, "He's sleeping peacefully. If you don't mind sitting with him for a couple of minutes, I would like to pop out, stretch my legs a bit, and grab a cup of coffee."

Perfect. Lexa smiled. "Be happy to. Take your time. The general ordered up snacks about an hour ago. There's pie and ice cream in the fridge. Four different pies are left over."

Heather laughed softly. "Oh goodness, he sure orders an abundance."

Lexa nodded as Heather slipped out of the room, leaving her alone with Dan. Studying him as he slept, emotions rolled around in her head. Finally, she took a step towards him, then another, and shortly Lexa found herself standing right next to the right side of his bed.

Grand Citadel Hotel – Main Suite – 10:05 p.m.

Heather entered the common area and spied Bram sound asleep on the couch, and Loki still at work at the computer. The only other person in the room was Dan's father, who sat at the large table drinking coffee. She noted his exhaustion. Her heart broke for him. She didn't go out of her way to eavesdrop, but their voices drifted into Dan's room, and she overheard enough to determine the general must be devastated by all the events.

She asked, "Would you like a snack?"

Pulled from his thoughts, William focused on the kind nurse. "No, but thank you. Coffee's all I need."

Heather proceeded to serve herself vanilla ice cream and cherry pie. She picked up a bottle of water as she took her snack to the table. She set the dessert down before boldly swiping the general's cup and replacing it with the water. "Sir, you require sleep, not caffeine. Drink some water instead."

William stared at the plucky woman with an incredulous expression. *She took my coffee!* A court-martial-worthy offense most of his staff believed.

General Broderick's expression caused Heather to blush bright pink, but she held her ground. "Someone needs to take care of you, too."

A lopsided grin appeared on William's face. "Water it is then." He glanced at the pie, and his stomach roared. Although he ordered in loads of food, his appetite had until now been suppressed by all he learned.

Heather slid the plate to him. "Sounds like you need this more than me." She turned, went to the sink, and dumped out his coffee. She poured herself coffee and dished out another slice of pie. Returning to the dining table, Heather smiled when she noted he already consumed half the portion on his plate. She sat, and the two of them ate in companionable silence.

Grand Citadel Hotel – Dan's Room – 10:10 p.m.

Lexa stared at Dan for a long time, listening to his even, shallow breathing. Compelled to touch him again, Lexa lowered herself on the edge of the mattress, trying not to wake him.

Tentatively, she reached out and laid her hand on Dan's right hand. When he didn't stir, she absently moved her fingertips, lightly massaging the back of his hand as she allowed her mind to delve into the enjoyable memories of the two times they engaged in intimate relations.

Dan's mind too cluttered to sleep, he remained awake and in stealth mode. He overheard Heather speak to Lexa and leave. He waited patiently for Lexa to come near, and when her hand brushed his, sizzling electricity coursed through every neuron, transmitting white-hot fire to every cell, leaving only a heated sensation that begged for more.

He delighted in her touch for several minutes before opening his eyes. He found Lexa staring at him, and when she jerked away, he said, "Don't stop, feels wonderful."

Lexa put her hand back and continued the gentle massage, moving up a bit on his forearm. "I'm sorry I woke you."

Not wanting to give away he had been awake, Dan responded, "I'm not. What time is it?"

Glancing at the clock, Lexa answered, "About ten after ten. I only wanted to peek in and check if you needed anything before going heading to my room."

Relishing the sensation of Lexa's warm fingers on his skin, Dan quipped, "A full body massage would be great."

Lexa chuckled. "Yeah, I bet you could use one."

"You offering?" He flashed her a lopsided grin.

"Well, now … might be arranged … for a minor fee," she teased.

"I'll pay whatever the price." Dan winked at her and grinned.

"Hmm, now what should I charge? How about a burger and a beer? Once you're up to it, of course." Lexa reached up, and ran her fingers through his locks. She smiled when Dan lowered his lashes and made a sound of pleasure.

"Mmmmmmm … my mother used to comfort me like this." Dan's eyes flew open. He hadn't intended to say that out loud. *Where the hell did that thought come from?*

Registering his panic, Lexa sought to soothe him as she shared, "My mom did this to me too. I would lay my head in her lap on the sofa or next to her on her bed. It is one of the things I missed most after she died."

Dan relaxed, surprised Lexa disclosed something about her family. She didn't talk about them just like he never talked about his. A subject both learned to be off-limits or approached with caution. "When did she die?"

"A little after I turned thirteen. Things were never the same. My dad, well, he didn't cope well. My older brothers stepped up. They …" Lexa trailed off.

Noting the fleeting anguish in Lexa's eyes, Dan quickly said, "I'm sorry, I shouldn't have asked."

Lexa shook the hurtful thoughts of abandonment away. "No worries. It happened a long time ago."

"Doesn't hurt any less, though, does it?" Dan stated with true understanding as he wondered why he opened up so easily with Lexa.

Lexa continued to brush through Dan's hair and massage his scalp. "Time does dull the ache, but yes, I still miss her." She sighed and added, "Funny, but I've lived more years without her than I had with her. Though some days, I'll spot her reflection in a glass or mirror, and she is laughing and happy. Sometimes, although this might sound crazy, I swear she whispers to me."

"Not crazy." Dan kept to himself how he conversed with Brody, but reciprocated her openness with a bit of his own. "I only had seven years with Sara, but I miss my sister. She had the brightest smile and beautiful, emerald green eyes. Her laughter ..." he choked up as emotions overwhelmed him and liquid welled in his eyes.

"Shhh, I'm here. You're going to get through this. I'll help any way you need," Lexa whispered as she leaned in close and thumbed away the tears from Dan's cheeks as they flow.

As he struggled for composure, Lexa never stopped carding fingers through his hair. Her quiet presence and touch helped him pull himself together ... much like, yet different from how Brody aided him in the past. After several minutes, as he regained a modicum of control, he admitted, "I'm so confused."

"That is to be expected. Your entire life has been turned on its head. We all understand, and the whole team will be here to help you work through things. Just like we helped Loki when his stepfather divorced his ma." Lexa stopped before she revealed, *and when Boss and Bram helped me after my father turned his back on me.*

As Dan gazed at Lexa, a rush of newfound emotions surged forth. *She is someone special.* He needed a break from all the turmoil of his past and needed to focus on the future now. He smiled as he asked, "So ... have you thought any more on where we go from here ..."

Without expounding on his meaning, Lexa comprehended what he asked. *Can I take a risk like this? If I do and the team finds out, it might destroy us both. But, Dan is certainly like no other man I've ever met—he is definitely an outlier and intriguing.*

The halo on the little devil on her shoulder tilted to one side as she smiled. *"He's worth the risk."*

Lexa leaned down and tenderly kissed Dan's bruised and swollen lips before pulling back to murmurer, "Friends with benefits."

Ignoring the pain in his arms, Dan reached around Lexa and drew her to him. Their lips met again—the kisses soft and gentle due to Dan's battered condition, but also full of promise.

Dan's breath hitched with unexpected joy as a soothing sense of acceptance and belonging cascaded through him. *Lexa is willing to risk it all for me.*

Easing back from the kiss when Dan took in a ragged breath, Lexa whispered, "Breathe, just breathe ..."

Keep reading for a sneak peek
at Laura Acton's fourth novel
in the Beauty of Life series

OUTLIER
Blood, Brotherhood, and Beauty

July 18
Grand Citadel Hotel – Dan's Room – 10:30 p.m.

Lexa tenderly pressed her lips to Dan's again as his breathing steadied. She gently massaged his head to bring him a modicum of comfort. Her insides a jumbled mix of emotions, she decided not to resist the attraction to her teammate. Life was too fleeting not to take some risks—but this was a huge risk. If things went bad, this would destroy them both, but if this went well …

The thought abruptly stopped. Not ready to think beyond right here and right now she continued to kiss his bruised, full lips. Whatever this attraction was between them … they both need it … nothing else mattered.

At the light knock on the door and Heather calling out, she stopped kissing Dan and pulled back. His sapphire blue eyes, a tad unfocused, gazed up at her. She brightened registering the effect she had on him. "Dan, let go. Heather's coming in," she whispered when his arms remained around her.

Dan Broderick released Sexy Lexie, bereft at losing the warmth of her body and the touch of her soft lips on his. He missed the tingling sensation of her fingers on his scalp. A comforting touch which reminded him of long ago. The same comfort, yet different. Something deep inside him craved the sensation like he craved Alexandra McKenna.

Focused on her lovely golden flecked hazel eyes, he feared what might come—though he would never admit that to anyone. His fierce physical attraction to her drove him to be reckless and jeopardize all he'd gained in the past year. He wanted to care about her. She belonged in his arms, yet he needed to protect her. Fate always took those he loved away from him.

If he allowed himself to care for her, fate might screw with him and leave him alone and broken again. *Am I willing to risk everything for Lexa?* His nurse speaking to him interrupted his thoughts.

"Good to see you awake, but you really should be sleeping. How's your pain level?" Heather Barkley asked.

"I'm alright. Patch took care of me before my shower."

Heather glanced from Dan to Lexa, and by the expressions on their faces, she got a strange sense she'd interrupted an important discussion. "Well, if you need any relief, you let me know. Would you like anything to eat or drink?"

"No, thanks." He flicked his eyes to the bathroom door. "Gotta make a little trip, though." He pushed himself up, and he clenched his jaw as his muscles howled in protest at his movement. Stupid move—now the painful throbbing in his jaw increased.

After his one-on-one fight with Basto in the ravine, he hurt like hell. The former middleweight boxing champ gang leader had the advantage over him both in size and physical condition. His pre-existing injuries had made it difficult for him to fight Basto. Using Ripsaw's strategies saved his ass— Aaron's distraction also helped.

If not for Aaron Plouffe, he would be dead. Basto would've killed him— with his own gun no less. Another pain, not a physical one, sliced through Dan. Aaron died saving him, and he could do nothing to protect Aaron. Ironically, one Plouffe tried to kill him for years, and yet he lived today because of another Plouffe. A small groan slipped out as he used his right arm to push himself up.

At Dan's groan, Lexa and Heather both moved to assist him to stand. Refusing further assistance, he shuffled to the bathroom.

Once the bathroom door closed, Heather turned to Lexa. "I wouldn't believe it if I didn't see it with my own eyes. The fact he's up and walking with all his injuries … well, it boggles my mind."

"Dan isn't an average man," Lexa said.

"Yeah, I think you're right—he's Dantastic. I'm glad so many people care about him. Terrible what Donner did to him. My friend said Donner called Dan a murderer and accused him of putting you all at risk and putting blood on your hands. That disturbed man flung such horrible words at Dan. I hope he didn't take any of it to heart."

"We'll make sure he doesn't," Lexa vowed.

Yeah, Alpha Team is one of the rare ones, Heather thought.

Several minutes later, Dan exited the bathroom and found Lexa was still in the bedroom. He gave her a small smile. He hated to appear weak in front of her, yet he was glad she was still here. When he got to the bed, he tried to position himself with no help. He used his sprained left hand to scoot to the middle of the bed and clamped his jaw as a hiss escaped.

Due to the gunshot wound in his right arm, using it was out of the question. He cringed inside when Lexa and Heather came forward. Reluctantly he accepted their help to move into a comfortable position.

His little trip wore him out. Sleep beckoned him, and he found his eyelids heavy as he blinked trying to keep them open. Once he was lying propped up against a boatload of pillows, making breathing easier with his cracked ribs, he sighed and tried to relax. "Thanks."

Lexa smiled as she placed a pillow under Dan's left arm to elevate his sprained wrist. Then she sat on the bed and began to lightly brush through his golden blond hair once more. "Go to sleep now. You have a long day tomorrow with the Nonpartisan Review Board interviews and Aaron's funeral."

Dan lowered his eyelids in compliance. In no way did he look forward to either of those, but at least the NRB agent wouldn't be Donner. Dick was dead. He still had to sort out his feelings about the man who committed suicide in front of him. Richard Donner might be as much a victim of the events of Sara's death as he was.

Oh, crap! Today is the eighteenth. Which means tomorrow is the nineteenth. Dammit! I'm definitely not firing on all cylinders. Dan took a steadying breath. It was too late to change the NRB interviews. Now he must do it. Could he get through tomorrow without falling to pieces in front of everyone? Without crying in front of the general?

"Hey, are you okay?" Lexa asked seeing Dan's eyes squeeze tight, and his lips purse together so hard his split lip reopened—he was in pain. "Do you need meds? Should I call Patch?"

As he forced his eyes open, his tongue darted out to lick the blood off his split lip—it stung again. He outright lied. "Only a temporary pain. It's gone."

Lexa eyed Dan carefully. She believed none of the words out of his mouth—his eyes told a different story. Though it was clear, he didn't want to talk about it. She kept many of her own hurts private, so she didn't push ... if he wanted her to know, he would share.

"Alright. Close your eyes and let me help you relax." Lexa reached up to his head again and resumed her gentle massage. She watched as the tension slowly ebbed out of Dan's face and his breathing slowed.

Dan shelved his worries about getting through tomorrow, allowed himself to relax, and focused his mind on Lexa. He drifted off to sleep with the feeling of her fingers massaging his head and the memory of her lips on his.

Heather noted the small upturn of Dan's mouth when Lexa touched him. She went to sit down and left Lexa at the bedside. Heather picked up her book and took another glance at the bed thinking Alpha Team was extremely close. It made Heather happy but also caused her concern. She worried what would happen if one of them died in the line of duty—it would surely devastate the team. Heather heard Dan's soft regular breathing and assumed Lexa's massage had put him to sleep.

Once Dan fell asleep, Lexa stood. "Goodnight, Heather." Lexa headed for the door.

"Goodnight, Lexa." It was so sweet how Lexa helped Dan fall asleep—very touching. Heather opened her novel, "Secrets: Passions and Perils of Dating a Teammate" as a niggling thought crept into her head based on her observations tonight. A smile lit her face. *Could Lexa and Dan be dating? If so, that might be rather interesting.*

Grand Citadel Hotel - Main Suite - 10:40 p.m.

Lexa shut Dan's door behind her and scanned the main room of the hotel suite, ready to pull Loki away from the computer if she had to. If the team let him, Loki would work himself to the bone trying to find evidence proving Major Plouffe's crimes against Dan. Not finding Loki at the desk, she glanced about the room. A soft smile settled on her lips as she found him curled up on a couch near Bram. Loki's laptop was open on the table in front of him.

Turning, Lexa saw General Broderick coming out of the other bedroom connected to the large suite. Lexa was surprised yet again how much Dan took after his father. The general was muscular, had the same rugged good looks and golden blond hair as Dan, and their expressive eyes were the same shade of sapphire blue. Even though the general appeared more relaxed in his t-shirt and sweats, he was no less commanding than when he was in his uniform. Honestly, she admitted to herself, the general intimidated her—his moniker 'General Badass' fit him well.

General Broderick also appeared to be as complicated as Dan, and both father and son were so skilled at keeping their emotions hidden. Witnessing the tears in the general's eyes today had been difficult—there was so much sadness in them. Lexa recognized the general cared for Dan. She shouldn't judge the general—but she did anyway.

It angered Lexa a lot. Dan had suffered tremendously because the general had virtually abandoned him. His misguided way of protecting Dan caused Dan so much pain—much like her own father hurt her. Knowing she unfairly applied her feelings for her own father to Dan's dad didn't change they were similar. The general had ignored Dan in an attempt to protect him, but in doing so subjected him to greater harm.

Her father abandoned her because she wanted to be a cop. He wanted her to be safe and gave her an ultimatum—be a cop or be his daughter. He just didn't understand her desire to protect others and disregarded what made her happy. As a result, he caused her so much heartache when he cut her out of his and her four brother's lives. Lexa forcefully pushed away those thoughts—none of that helped.

"I don't think you ought to wake Loki. He looks comfortable, and he can sleep right there. There are blankets in the other room if you want to get one for Bram and Loki," William Broderick quietly informed Lexa.

"Yeah, I think I'll let him sleep here. He's exhausted." Lexa headed into the other bedroom and grabbed two blankets. She returned to the main suite and first covered Bram.

Dan calling out to Bram for help when he woke today was a good thing. It didn't surprise her it had been Bram. Dan had connected with him first, and Abraham De Haven had a fatherly vibe. It came from the fact he had four young daughters, and Bram openly showed his soft side. He was like a giant teddy bear. His blue-green eyes always reflected how much he cared.

She would always find shelter in Bram's arms—not that she allowed it often. Though on the rare occasion when things overwhelmed her, his hugs and soft-spoken words provided her the solace she needed.

Unfurling the second blanket, Lexa moved over to Loki and laid it over him. She noted Loki looked like a little boy in sleep—a baby brother. She liked having a little brother to watch over. She then realized Dan was one year younger than Loki. Goodness, they both appeared so vulnerable when they slept—all their defenses were lowered then.

The errant lock of black hair in Loki's face beckoned to be brushed back yet again. Perhaps the wayward lock wouldn't keep flopping down if he would cut his hair shorter. Then again, it was a part of Loki's boyish charm she wouldn't want him to lose. It also gave him something to do with his hands when he got nervous talking to Tia. Lexa let out a long sigh.

Tia and Loki seemed so right for each other. Perhaps one day Tia would give up her rule against dating cops and give Loki a chance. Ready to go to her room, Lexa straightened up. At least Tia and Loki wouldn't face the same hurdle as she and Dan did. Tia's was a TRF dispatcher, so the rule didn't apply to them the way it did for her and Dan. The Toronto Police Tactical Response Force protocol manual stated that no fraternization of a sexual nature was allowed between teammates.

Potential consequences for breaking the rule began with a verbal reprimand and reassignment to another TRF team up to the maximum penalty of being fired. Lexa knew she was taking a huge risk. Alpha Team was her family, and if she lost Boss, Jon, Bram, Loki, Ray, and Dan, then she would be all alone. And if she were fired, she would lose the only thing which gave her life purpose and meaning.

Lexa blew out a breath, put those thoughts in a box she crafted, ran a bead of liquid glue on the edges, slammed it closed, and nailed it shut ... *that will have to do for now.*

About the Author

Laura Acton, author of the *Beauty of Life* and *Strike Force Zulu* series, was born in Phoenix, Arizona, and raised with two older brothers by amazing parents. Her American father's poetry inspired her love of the written word, and her Canadian mother, provided her with a role model of a loving and courageous woman who always strove to find the beauty in adversity. After Laura's high school sweetheart returned from the Navy, they married and raised three sons.

Laura graduated summa cum laude from Western International University with dual degrees in Business and Information Technology. For thirty-five years, she worked as a Business Analyst for high-tech companies developing quality processes, documenting system requirements, and writing training materials.

From the time Laura was a teen delivering newspapers in the early mornings, she occupied herself by crafting stories in her mind but never had time to write them down. After her beloved husband passed and her sons no longer needed a Mom taxi, she had after work hours to fill. One quiet night with soft music playing, Laura discovered her passion for writing fiction.

Writing became an obsession, prompting Laura to retire early from the corporate world to become a full-time author. Now her dogs keep her company while she writes novels about valiant men and women who forge bonds through emotional and physical adversity. Laura enjoys creating brotherhood and family sagas filled with Special Forces and SWAT action, hurt, comfort, intrigue, romance, drama, angst, twists, turns, and connections.

Visit Laura's website for info on her latest novels and to sign up for Laura's email list: https://www.lauraactonauthor.com/

Made in the USA
Middletown, DE
15 June 2020